PRAISE FOR CAY RADEMACHER

'Rademacher understands how to draw a living picture of the post-war period. *The Wolf Children* allows its readers to embrace history without an instructive tone, wonderfully packaged in a thriller'
Hessische Allgemeine

'With his follow-up to *The Murderer in Ruins*, Rademacher has once again captured an intriguing view into a not-so-distant world in which everyone is fighting for survival' *Brigitte*

'Rademacher succeeds in describing history with tension'
Neue Presse

'Impressively, Rademacher describes life in 1947 with all its hardships and hopes. A piece of history comes alive and is immensely touching' *Hamburger Morgenpost*

'Once again, Rademacher combines an exciting crime story with a detailed description of Hamburg in the post-war period'
Aachener Nachrichten

'The name Cay Rademacher stands for historical competence. [...] In addition to its thrilling crime plot, *The Wolf Children* also provides a lively presentation of the oppressive black market conditions in the post-war years' *Geislinger Zeitung / Südwest Presse*

'The book sheds a light on a world out of joint. [...] A crime thriller with level and depth. Highly recommended' *Buch-Magazin*

'This is not just a vivid historical lesson, *The Wolf Children* is a nerve-racking hunt for a murderer and a great crime novel'
NDR Hörfunk

'Atmospheric, tight and gripping [...] A very successful mixture of crime and history' *Oberösterreichische Nachrichten*

'Exciting, authentic' Gerald Schaumburg, *Hessische Allgemeine*

THE WOLF CHILDREN

CAY RADEMACHER was born in 1965 and studied Anglo-American history, ancient history, and philosophy in Cologne and Washington. He has been an editor at *Geo* since 1999, and was instrumental in setting up renowned history magazine *Geo-Epoche*. *The Wolf Children* is the second novel in the Inspector Stave series, following *The Murderer in Ruins* (Arcadia Books, 2015). He now lives in France with his wife and children, where his new crime series is set.

PETER MILLAR is an award-winning British journalist, author and translator, and has been a correspondent for Reuters, *The Sunday Times* and *Sunday Telegraph*. He has written a number of books, including *All Gone to Look for America* and *1989: The Berlin Wall, My Part in Its Downfall*. He has also translated from German, Corinne Hofmann's best-selling *White Masai* series of memoirs, Martin Suter's *A Deal with the Devil* and Cay Rademacher's *The Murderer in Ruins*.

THE WOLF CHILDREN

CAY RADEMACHER

Translated from the German by Peter Millar

Arcadia Books Ltd
139 Highlever Road
London W10 6PH

www.arcadiabooks.co.uk

First published in the United Kingdom 2017
Originally published as *Der Schieber* by DuMont Buchverlag 2012
Copyright © Cay Rademacher 2012
English translation copyright © Peter Millar 2017

Cay Rademacher has asserted his moral right to be identified as the author of
this work in accordance with the Copyright, Designs and Patents Act, 1988.
All Rights Reserved. No part of this publication may be reproduced in any
form or by any means without the written permission of the publishers.

A catalogue record for this book is available from the British Library.

The translation of this work was supported by a grant from the
Goethe-Institut, which is funded by the German Ministry of Foreign Affairs.

ISBN 978-1-910050-98-9

Typeset in Garamond by MacGuru Ltd
Printed and bound by TJ International, Padstow PL28 8RW

ARCADIA BOOKS DISTRIBUTORS ARE AS FOLLOWS:

in the UK and elsewhere in Europe:
BookSource
50 Cambuslang Road
Cambuslang
Glasgow G32 8NB

in the USA and Canada:
Dufour Editions
PO Box 7
Chester Springs
PA, 19425

in Australia/New Zealand:
NewSouth Books
University of New South Wales
Sydney NSW 2052

The Boy and the Bomb

Friday, 30 May 1947

The dead boy's blood coated the five-hundred-pound British bomb like a red veil. Light coming through the shattered roof of the warehouse fell on the corpse and on the unexploded bomb, a thing the size of a man, like some monstrous fish that had buried itself in the concrete flooring. The rest of the warehouse was in darkness. It was as if the sunlight shining in on the boy and the bomb was some giant theatrical floodlight, Chief Inspector Frank Stave of Hamburg CID thought to himself.

Stave was in charge of a small team investigating the murder and had to prepare a report on the condition of the body and the presumed crime scene, take statements from witnesses, look for clues or traces of the killer. There was no question that the boy, aged about twelve, or fourteen at most, had suffered a violent death. But Stave was crouched down with a few other policemen behind the partially concealed steel frame of a broken crane, looking through a hole in the wall into the warehouse. There was just one man in the building, taking careful steps as he walked around the scrawny body of the boy and the fat bomb. He gave the corpse a brief glance before finally kneeling next to the bomb and gingerly setting down the big heavy leather bag he had been carrying in his right hand.

He was a bomb disposal expert, sent to defuse the thing. As long as the detonator was still active, it was far too dangerous for the investigation team to approach the body. I just hope he doesn't remove any traces the killer might have left, Stave thought to himself.

The chief inspector had been alerted to the incident by a phone call just as he was starting his shift. He had gathered together a few uniformed police and set off from the CID headquarters on Karl Muck Platz. Most of them were young, wet behind the ears, appointed by the British occupation forces. Stave spotted among them Heinrich Ruge, a captain who had helped on previous enquiries.

'The victim isn't going to run off on us,' Ruge had called out to him rather too snappily.

Stave had said nothing, just gave a sympathetic look at the lad who had beads of perspiration leaking out from under his helmet and running down his temples. Even at the best of times the uniformed police called their tall, uncomfortable headgear 'sweat boxes'. Today the temperature was nearly thirty degrees.

Stave though back with a shiver to the previous winter, a merciless six months when the thermometer regularly showed between minus ten and minus twenty – sometimes even lower. And now this spring was as warm as anyone could remember. It was as if the weather was going as mad as humanity had done all too recently.

The war's over, the chief inspector reassured himself. Ruge and another five uniforms were bent down next to him, shielded by the damaged crane, the sun right above their heads, no shade anywhere around them. He could smell their sweat evaporating. Was it just the heat? Or maybe it was fear that had them dripping with sweat?

A small, scraggy red-haired man whose freckled face was already glowing red from the sun crouched alongside them. Ansgar Kienle was a police photographer and at the moment, for lack of alternatives, Hamburg CID's sole crime scene specialist.

Only one person seemed to be suffering worse from the sun than Kienle – Dr Alfred Czrisini, the pathologist, whose bald head was going bright red. Czrisini just happened to have a British colleague visiting when Stave called him, and was able to borrow his Jeep to drive to meet them at the crime scene. Despite his sunburn, Czrisini looked pale as his shaking hands held a Woodbine to his lips.

'Do you think that's a good idea when there's a five-hundred-pound bomb being defused nearby?' Stave hissed between his teeth, even though he knew that nobody and nothing, not even a bomb, would stand between Czrisini and his cigarettes. The doctor gave him a brief smile and shook his head, a little pale blue wisp of smoke rising from his mouth over the sea of ruins. Stave had brought his men across the Elbe in a launch to Steinwerder. Blohm & Voss shipyard lay at the hammer-shaped end of a peninsula on the southern side of the Elbe. There were two huge docks parallel to the river, and a third jutting diagonally into the shore like a giant sword. Behind the two big docks there was a third basin. All along the riverbank stood long brick warehouses, cranes lined up in rows like soldiers standing to attention, and the tangle of rails for the puffing narrow-gauge railways that brought boilers, gun barrels and steel bulkheads down to the docks. Or rather used to.

It was only a few years ago that the battleship *Bismarck* had been built here by Blohm & Voss, and it was from here that nearly 50 per cent of the German U-boat fleet had first slid down the gangways into the sea. Stave could still see some fifteen almost-finished hulls, tubes of grey steel, some sixty or seventy metres long, with the closed torpedo door flaps in their hulls, rudders, gleaming propellor screws, a few of them so new they could almost set off immediately to patrol the seas, others already half-submerged beneath the waters of the basin, like stranded whales. Two or three of the wrecks looked as if they had been beaten to death by some giant right here in the shipyard. The British and Americans had bombed Blohm & Voss again and again.

Stave looked at the mountains of rubble, stretching hundreds of metres in every direction: toppled chimneys lying on the two- to three-hundred-metre docks, the walls of which had been blown in, heaps of molten metal produced in a matter of seconds in the ferocious heat. Bracken and sorrel bushes sprouted from the broken cobblestones. The old bulkheads with their shattered concrete now covered in verdigris. Beyond the last of the docks the Elbe flowed on, fast and grey. And beyond that again ruins upon ruins with only the tower of St Michael's rising in the heat haze like some giant tombstone.

Only a few years ago, even in the CID headquarters, they could hear the sound of the jackhammers echoing across the Elbe like a low humming, as continuous and unremarkable as the gurgling sound of a waterfall: after a while you simply didn't notice it any more.

Now it was almost totally silent. There were no ships in the docks, no sparks flying from welding machines or ice saws. The only noise came from a crane on rails at the far end of the dock, jerking and creaking as it pulled steel girders out of the ruins of a building and piled them on to a barge floating on the Elbe: material that could be melted down and recycled somewhere.

A fireman colleague of the specialist in the warehouse crawled over to the crouching police.

'How much longer is he going to take?' Stave asked him. He noticed that he was speaking softly, as if a word pronounced too loudly might set off the unexploded bomb.

The fireman spoke softly too, though: 'Hard to say. Depends on what type of detonator it is, and what state it's in. We've seen hundreds of bombs like that. Most of them have an ordinary detonator, one that should set the explosives off the minute it hits. Sometimes they get stuck, either because they hit a roof that was already damaged or because they were screwed in wrongly in the first place. Those we can deal with quickly enough. But some of these beasts have timed fuses set to go off hours or even days later.'

Stave nodded. He remembered how sometimes days after the horrific nights of the bombing raids, suddenly there would be an enormous boom and another building would collapse in ruins. The Americans and British had done it deliberately to make the job of clearing up the rubble more difficult – that was one of the reasons why the local *Gauleiter* Karl Kaufman had ordered prisoners from the Neugamme concentration camp into the ruins to do the clearing up. On two or three occasions he had been told to watch over them.

'Those types of detonators,' the fireman went on, 'sometimes don't work. When you look at them they can seem undamaged, but if you make the slightest mistake, even the tiniest vibration, the whole thing can explode in your face.'

'Would human footsteps be vibration enough?' the chief inspector asked him.

The fireman smiled. 'Sometimes, yes. But not in this case. My colleague has clearly already tested that.'

'Risk of the job, I suppose,' Stave muttered.

'We get extra ration cards for doing difficult work.'

'Sounds fair enough.' The CID man looked round and saw, about fifty metres way, a group of workers watching them morosely. Then he turned back to the figure crouching next to him.

'How long is he going to stay there leaning over the bomb?'

The fireman nodded at the part of the roof that had caved in. 'That's where the bomb hit,' he said. 'We call that a "wall hit", where the bomb hits the wall first, goes into a spin and eventually hits the ground at such an oblique angle that the detonator doesn't go off properly. It's complex. My colleague is going to be in there for an hour at least.'

'Wait here,' Stave ordered the uniformed policemen. They nodded, not exactly thrilled with the instruction. 'Dr Czrisini, come with me. You too, Kienle. Won't do any harm if we use the time to ask a few questions of the workers over there. They look like they're bursting to help us.'

'They look as if they think you're more likely to explode on them than the bomb,' replied the pathlogist. He pulled himself to his feet – no easy task given his weight – grunting with the effort, and followed the two CID men.

Five men in dark reefer jackets over collarless blue-and-white striped shirts, corduroy trousers, peaked caps and with hands like shovels shot hostile looks at Stave and his companions as they approached. The chief inspector introduced himself, whipped out his police badge and handed round English cigarettes: John Player, a sailor wearing a life belt round his neck on the packet.

The men looked surprised, then hesitated, before finally grabbing them, with sounds that might even be interpreted as thanks. Stave, who was a non-smoker, had been carrying a few spare cigarettes on him for a while now. At one time he had traded them with returning prisoners-of-war down at the station for any possible information on his missing son. But ever since he had found out that Karl was in a Soviet camp in Vorkuta, he no longer needed to do that. Now he used the cigarettes to make interrogations go a bit more smoothly.

Czrisini put a Woodbine between his lips. The men stood there silently for a few minutes, blue wisps of smoke twisting in the air between the cracked brick walls, the smell of sweet oriental tobacco oddly comforting against the background aroma of bricks and lubricating oil. There was a heat haze in the air, and a stench of rubbish and dead fish rose from the Elbe. Stave could have done with a glass of water.

The oldest worker present – Stave put him at sixty or more – cleared his throat and took a step forwards.

'Your name?'

'Wilhelm Speck.'

He was as skinny and hard packed as a smoked sausage. Stave didn't like to think how many times he must have heard jokes about his surname – 'bacon'.

'Was it you who called us?'

'No, that was the site manager.' He nodded towards a square red-brick building a few hundred metres away, which Stave guessed was the administration building.

'We found the bomb,' the man hesitated a moment before continuing, 'and the dead boy, just after we came on shift. We ran over to the office.'

'How long have you been working for Blohm & Voss?'

Speck gave him a surprised look. 'Forever.' He thought a moment and then added, 'Forty-four years. If you can call the past few years "work".'

His colleagues muttered in agreement. Even that sounded threatening.

'You don't exactly look as though it's been a holiday.'

'I'm part of the shit squad,' the old man announced proudly.

Stave stared at him in surprise.

'*Kettelklopper*,' Speck said, as if in explanation. Then he realised that the chief inspector still didn't get the message and repeated, in standard German rather than the thick Hamburg dialect: 'Kettle knocker: we climb inside the kettles – the hulls of ships laid up in the docks for refit – and knock on the walls to dislodge any dirt.'

'That sounds like hard work, harder than what you're doing now.'

'Work?' Speck said. 'Work is building ships or refitting them. Hammering, riveting. You start out with an empty dock and at the end a ship slides down the slipway into the Elbe. That's what work is.'

'And nowadays?' The chief inspector knew what Speck was getting at, but he wanted to hear it from the man's lips. It would make it easier for a man who wasn't used to speaking much to answer his other questions.

'Nowadays?' The man was getting worked up. 'Nowadays we're dismantling the yard. The English want us to destroy our own workplace. Or what's left of it after they bombed most of it to hell.'

It was true enough that the giant shipyard had been bombed to hell. Officially. Any machinery and tools had been sent off to other countries in reparation for the damage the Germans had done to them in the war. In Hamburg it was an open secret that the British wanted to close down once and for all what had been one of the best shipyards in the world. They wanted to eliminate a rival that had not just turned out warships and U-boats, but in peacetime had also built hundreds of ocean liners and freighters, orders that had more often than not been snatched from shipyards in Liverpool or Belfast.

Speck nodded towards a pile of machinery roasting in the sunshine some thirty metres away near one of the workshops: 'Lathes, welding machines, riveting machines, milling machines,' he said. 'Nine months ago they made us dismantle all that stuff and leave it over there. It's supposed to be delivered to the Soviet Union. They sent in English military police specially to keep an eye on us. And now it's all lying there rusting away. Comrade Stalin isn't interested in our machinery. The English just made us move it out there so it would fall apart.'

He had to be a communist, Stave reckoned. Since 1945, when the Brits allowed elections to take place again in Hamburg, one in every five shipyard workers had voted for the Communist Party of Germany. It wasn't hard to understand, he told himself, but out loud he said, 'You've been working here for two years, dismantling the shipyard, but nobody spotted an unexploded bomb lying around?'

Speck shook his head. 'Up until 1945, U-boat spare parts were stored in here. Ever since it's been lying empty. It was only by chance that we looked in this morning.' He hesitated for a moment, glanced round as if he was worried somebody was eavesdropping, and added in a quieter voice: 'All that machinery over there, we couldn't just leave it lying there. We wanted to move it in here to ...' he was looking for the right word, 'to keep it safe.' And then added hastily: 'Until the English come to take it away.'

'Absolutely,' Stave said in a sarcastic tone of voice. What the old man meant was that they wanted to keep their tools safe until the day when they could get Blohm & Voss back up and running again. But what business was that of his? 'And that's when you came across the bomb with the dead body lying on it?'

'We could hardly miss it,' Speck said, his chapped hands shaking slightly. 'We were shocked.'

'How close did you get? Did you touch anything?'

They all shook their heads. 'Touch an unexploded bomb? I'm not that tired of living yet,' Speck said. 'We're forever coming across them. The bomb disposal people could set up shop here, the number of times we've had to call them in.'

'So you didn't go past the entrance?' the chief inspector asked, glancing at the door lying open at the narrow end of the hangar, further away from the dead body than the hole in the wall they had been taking cover behind.

Speck nodded. 'Maybe a couple of paces, then we turned tail.'

'Did you recognise the boy?'

They all shook their heads again.

'Could he have been an apprentice? An errand boy?'

'No. We're not allowed to train any more apprentices. What would we be training them for anyway? And we've no need for errand boys.'

Speck dithered for a moment, until Stave gave him an encouraging nod and handed over another cigarette. Then he said, 'There are always lads running around here. Orphan kids. Refugees. Displaced persons, as they call them. Urchins with no homes and no parents to take them by the scruff of the neck. They steal anything they can get their hands on. You should know that, in the police.'

The chief inspector sighed. There were between ten and twelve thousand children living in the ruins of Hamburg. Kids of ten, twelve or fourteen years of age who had been the only ones in their families to survive the hail of bombs or the long trek west from homes they'd been expelled from. They stole coal from the freighters, pinched ration cards, worked as lookouts for black market traders or hung around the station selling themselves for sex in exchange for a couple of cigarettes and a bed for the night. Some of them had even gone so far as to kill.

'When the bomb disposal man has done his job, this man here,' Stave indicated Kienle, 'will take photos of the dead body. Afterwards he will pass them around the shipyard, and you need to ask all your workmates to take a look. It might be that somebody will recognise him, might have caught him up to something, chased him off. I need to know who he is, where he lived – or at least where he hung out if he was homeless. What he was doing here, in an empty shipyard hangar with a five-hundred-pound English bomb lying in it.'

After dismissing the workers with a nod, Stave and his colleagues tiptoed back to their cover next to the crane, where the uniformed police were still sitting motionlessly, dripping with sweat and scarcely daring to breathe.

'Why would the dead boy be lying on top of the bomb?' he asked Czrisini.

The pathologist coughed, causing the policemen to start with fright, and shrugged his shoulders. 'I'll need to take a closer look at the lad, that is, providing the bomb disposal man does his job well enough.'

'It looks as if the murderer deliberately deposited the body on a live bomb to make our investigation all the harder,' Stave muttered.

'Or wanted to send us a message,' Kienle replied.

The chief inspector turned to him in surprise, and the photographer gave an embarrassed smile. 'A dead boy lying on an English bomb – maybe the killer wanted to make a point? Tell us something? Or maybe it's a signature of some sort?'

'If that's his signature, then I'd appreciate it if he used a typewriter next time,' the chief inspector replied.

The bomb disposal man made a gesture towards his colleague who was taking cover alongside the police, then took from his pocket a longish object that looked like a steam hammer of some kind, reduced to the size of a man's forearm, and set it on the far end of the bomb, between the stabiliser fins.

'What's he doing now?' Stave asked, whispering unintentionally.

'It's got a timer fuse, housed at the end of the bomb,' the disposal team man replied. 'Shit things. The English dropped more than 100,000 bombs fitted with them, and one in seven didn't go off. My grandchildren will still live in fear of the things; that's if I live long enough to have grandchildren.'

He nodded in the direction of the odd piece of equipment his colleague had produced. 'That's what we call a "rocket clamp", the only thing that enables you to deal with a timer fuse. In a normal fuse there's a needle that strikes the charge and sets the whole thing off. But with a timer fuse the needle is held back by steel springs, like a bowstring. Between the needle and the charge there's a little celluloid plate. When the bomb hits, the impact releases acetone from a little glass ampule. The chemical gradually eats away the celluloid and as soon as it does, the needle is released – and BOOM!'

'The tricky bit about these things is that you can't see in. It may be that the acetone was never released and the celluloid plate is still intact, or on the other hand it may equally well be that the plate is long gone and the needle could strike at any moment, but has just got stuck somehow. Then one cough might well be enough to set it off. On top of all that the way the detonators are fitted means you can't just unscrew them. Try that and the answer's the same: BOOM!'

'Who on earth would think up something like that?' Stave mumbled.

'The same boffins who dreamed up the rocket clamp. It's a sort of specialist spanner that means you can get at the detonator and unscrew it. A lot faster at any rate than a human being could. But most importantly, faster than the detonator can react. Any minute now my colleague is going to set off a tiny explosive charge within the clamp and that will yank the detonator out in one go. The centrifugal force within the rotating detonator will squeeze all the mechanical components together for a fraction of a second, meaning that the released needle will be delayed that tiny bit so that it can no longer detonate the bomb, because by then the detonator will already be out. Most of the time, anyway.'

The chief inspector was staring at him disbelievingly: 'Sounds a bit like Russian Roulette to me.'

The bomb disposal man shrugged. 'There's always the possibility that the detonator got screwed in at an angle, in which case even a rocket clamp won't get it out quickly enough. Then there's always a chance that the explosive charge in the clamp doesn't go off properly and it's not fast enough. Nobody can be sure about that. When something like that happens, you can't exactly ask the disposal man what happened afterwards. This is the one occupation where there's no opportunity to learn from your colleague's mistakes or bad luck.'

The man in the hangar had by now carefully put the rocket clamp over the pointed tail of the bomb. He could be seen taking a deep breath. Then he made a brief movement, so fast the CID man barely noticed it. There was a short, sharp bang, like a gunshot.

Involuntarily Stave caught his breath, dropped to the ground and put his hands over his ears.

Nothing happened.

Ever so slowly, he breathed out, noticing that he was shaking and that there was sweat running into his eyes.

'Good,' said the bomb disposal man next to him. He was already on his feet, stretching his legs. He waved through the hole in the wall to his colleague inside. 'The detonator is out. The bomb is now just a big steel tube with a few chemicals inside. No longer a direct threat.' He glanced at Czrisini. 'But we'll have to ask you not to smoke when you're in there. It would be a pity if a spark were to drop through the detonator hole into the bomb.'

The pathologist looked bleakly into the hangar and seemed paler than ever under his suntan. Nonetheless he took long drags on his Woodbine until it was down to the tiniest of butts, and then carefully extinguished it.

Stave dusted himself down and said, 'Let's go and take a look at our corpse.'

The chief inspector massaged his left leg as if it had gone to sleep from all the crouching. That way his colleagues wouldn't think anything of him limping over to the bomb – he was ashamed of the injury he had suffered during the fire storm of 1943, even though he wasn't quite sure why.

He shook the hand of the bomb disposal man, who introduced himself as Walter Mai. He was a gaunt man of indeterminate age with glasses and receding hair. He might have been in his mid-thirties or just turned sixty.

'Your hands aren't even damp,' Stave remarked.

'I don't mind this heat,' Mai replied calmly, with a thin smile. 'I love this job, but the sight of a dead kid is distracting and I don't like being distracted.' Then he gave Stave a serious look and touched his fingers to his cap in farewell, adding: 'I'd be grateful if you could let me know who this lad was, and who did this to him.'

'I'll be in touch. But it'll take longer than it took you to disarm this bomb.'

'I can see it's likely to be a complex job too,' the disposal expert replied, without the slightest trace of irony in his voice. Then he nodded to his colleague and the pair disappeared into the building.

The team entered the hangar but took only a few paces, letting Kienle approach the body alone to take his photographs. Every time his flash went off it made Stave flinch nervously. Then Kienle spread white powder all over the area to look for fingerprints. But he shook his head. No such luck. To finish up he took a few more photographs of the dusty concrete floor all around, then called his colleagues over.

Kienle indicated the grey dust that lay like a carpet on the floor around the bomb. 'There hasn't been anyone here for ages. Those footsteps belong to the bomb disposal man,' he said, nodding at the tracks circling the bomb.

'I could have worked that out for myself,' Stave muttered.

Kienle gave him an indulgent smile. 'The boy and his killer came that way,' he said, pointing to the traces of footprints coming from a small door at the back of the hall that the CID man hadn't noticed, maybe an old emergency exit. 'Two sets of footprints.'

'Means just one killer,' Stave mused aloud. 'The other footsteps are noticeably smaller. We'll check, of course, but I'm pretty sure those belong to the boy.' He nodded at the boy's plimsolls, an old but well-preserved pair that would have been fashionable a decade earlier.

'Unfortunately the other footsteps have been messed about a lot. There's hardly anything much to be made out between the doorway and the bomb, and the bomb disposal man trampled all over most of them, and set his bag down on them.'

'He had other things on his mind.'

'It'll still be hard to get anything much from them.'

'But they are obviously larger.'

Kienle nodded. 'One man, I'd say. Doesn't look as if there are tracks of two people or more. There are lots of footprints in the dust around the walls of the hangar. Either the boy or his killer walked up and down over there or, of course, they could belong to the workers who spotted the body. Or somebody else altogether. In any case, it's hardly likely we'll be able to identify them.'

Stave looked at the ground. 'It seems as if the boy walked around the bomb. I can see his footsteps all round it, but his killer walked directly from that door to the bomb.'

'Coldblooded,' Ruge, the uniformed officer, mumbled.

'You find that about child-killers,' Stave said back to him, tetchily.

'But it's particularly true of our unknown perpetrator in this case,' the pathologist said. 'He's a lot more callous than your ordinary murdering thug.'

Stave looked down at the corpse and tried to force himself not to think of the deceased as a child. He was maybe fourteen years of age: thin, but not undernourished, wiry, deeply suntanned but with bad scratches on his arms. Brown eyes, long, brown, matted hair. Old canvas shoes, shorts, probably from an old Hitler Youth uniform, but dyed dark green, an improvised belt made from a bit of hemp rope. A collarless shirt, much too wide, the way the shipyard workers wore them, dirty, with a tear down the back.

The boy was lying with his back against the bomb, as if he were leaning on it, his open eyes staring up at the hold in the roof where the thing had crashed through. His backside was on the concrete floor, his legs stretched out in front of him. His arms were at an angle, the left resting on the stabiliser fin of the bomb, the other lying in his lap.

The chief inspector bent down closer to the victim: 'Index and middle finger yellow,' he muttered, pulling out his notebook and making a note.

'Traces of tobacco. He's young to be a chain smoker,' Crizisini added. 'Even I was older than that when I started.'

It was only now that Stave took a look at the wound: a big reddish-brown patch covered the boy's chest as far as his stomach, leaving a crust of dried blood on the bomb, too, and spatters on the ground.

'Looks like a stab wound,' the pathologist said, 'although I won't know for sure until I get his shirt off, but look at this.' He was pointing at parts of the shirt. 'There are little bubbles in the blood, bodily fluids, secretions: suggests that either his stomach or throat were injured.'

'There's a lot of blood in general. This is obviously where he was killed,' Stave noted.

Czirsini nodded agreement. 'That's what I mean by "particularly coldblooded": a murderer who can stab his victim to death on an unexploded bomb. It's a miracle a boy fighting for his life didn't accidentally set off the detonator.'

'Let's not come to hasty conclusions,' the chief inspector told him. 'It could have been that our killer was in such a panic that he couldn't care less about the risk. Or he hadn't originally planned to stab the boy. Maybe they only met up here, next to the bomb, got into an argument and he pulled the knife out without thinking.'

Czrisini pointed at the boy's hands. 'No sign of injury. No sign of a struggle. The boy looks like a vagabond. Strong, too. He would have fought back if he'd known that somebody was about to stab him. Suggests there wasn't a fight.'

'Anything else strike you?'

'It would appear the killer is left-handed.' The pathologist indicated the fan-shaped bloodstains on the bomb. 'You can still see the way the blood sprayed. If we assume that our killer was standing in front of his victim, then the blow with the knife or other sharp instrument would have come from the left.'

Stave pulled on thin black gloves and began to search the boy's trouser pockets and his shirt. No money, no papers, neither of which surprised him. Just a screwdriver with a wooden handle and sharpened point in the right-hand pocket of his shorts.

Stave whistled appreciatively looking at it. 'A weapon.'

'Unlikely to be the murder weapon. But we'll soon check that out,' Czrisini said, coughing. He looked in urgent need of a cigarette. He hands were shaking and he was glancing around impatiently

'He'll be all yours in a minute, doctor. We'll take the boy away and I'll hand in the paperwork for the autopsy to Public Prosecutor Ehrlich.' Stave bent down once more and pulled a packet of Lucky Strike from the boy's belt. Worth a fortune in times like these. The pathologist stared at them longingly.

'You're not putting one of these between your lips,' the chief inspector warned him off. 'They could be evidence.'

'I doubt very much some teacher gave him those for doing his homework well,' Czrisini said quietly.

'A weapon, cigarettes. I wonder what a lad like this was doing in a Blohm & Voss hangar?' Stave said.

'Especially one that's empty except for an unexploded bomb.'

'Empty now. But maybe there was something here that's gone now. A deserted part of an old shipyard would make a good place to hide something, especially when the English have declared it off-limits and only workers with special passes are allowed in, legally that is. And here we have an apparently empty hangar, of interest to nobody, with an unexploded bomb clearly visible so that anybody passing by would give it a wide berth. If I had something I wanted to hide this would not be a bad place.'

'Providing you were tired enough of living to risk going near an unexploded bomb.' The pathologist shook his head and pointed to the ground. 'Footprints but no sign of a box or anything else that might have been here.'

Stave replied by pointing at the walls. 'There are hooks and nails you could hang something from all over the place. Maybe that's why there are so many footprints over there. It might be connected.'

'So why did the kid end up in the middle? Well away from any of the walls?' Czrisini coughed again. 'I need a Woodbine. Let's go outside, and then I'll tell you what I think.'

Stave followed the pathologist. Outside the air shimmered in the heat and the tiles on the walls of the hangars glowed as if they had just come out of an oven. Stave's tongue felt furry and his throat hoarse. The uniformed police looked in a bad way.

'Kienle, take a look around,' the chief inspector ordered. The he posted Ruge and the other young officers around the barracks, where at least they would get a little bit of a breeze from the Elbe. 'The hearse will be here soon,' he said to cheer them up. 'Then we can all go home.' There was no sign of any of the workers.

The pathologist had by now taken a few deep drags on his cigarette and was a lot more relaxed.

'So, who's our killer?' Stave asked, half-jokingly.

'One of the workers,' said Czrisini without a shadow of a doubt in his voice. 'I would say the killer had to be a strong man, according to the marks on the body. He obviously knows the terrain – he managed to get into the hangar through a door that is so well concealed that even we didn't notice it at first. Nobody noticed him, or what he had done, so that means he can move around the docks without attracting attention. The only people allowed into the Blohm & Voss works are the workers. They're all strong, and they know their way around.'

'They all fancy themselves as hard men,' Stave said after a moment or two of silent reflection. 'Even in the trains they use to get here in the mornings you can see them punching and scuffling with one another. But to kill some teenaged kid? Why would anyone want to do something like that?'

'Maybe it's got something to do with breaking up the yard? The workers are furious. They're trying to conceal stuff from the English military police. The old guy told you straight out: they're hiding bits of machinery that they're supposed to be scrapping. Who knows what else they might be up to? Maybe the kid discovered them up to something they shouldn't have been doing? And somebody decided to shut his mouth for him.'

'In which case, why not simply throw the body into the Elbe? We'd probably never have found it. And even if we had, nobody would have made the link to Blohm & Voss. Instead of which we have the body laid out here as if on a presentation plate.' The CID man was thinking back to Kienle's suggestion that the killer was trying to make a statement of some sort.

Czrisini crushed the tiny butt of his cigarette between nicotine-stained fingertips. 'That's a puzzle for you to solve. I'm going to take the Jeep back to my British colleague and then tackle the corpse as soon as they get it to the lab. In this heat it's a good idea to get to work on a dead body while it's still in a good condition.'

Stave was thinking of the victims's matted hair, scratched arms, ragged clothing. 'That lad hadn't been in a good condition for some time,' he replied, and shook hands in farewell.

The chief inspector waited until the hearse arrived, trundling over the rough cobblestones. The undertakers arrived at the same time as a fire brigade team that had come to take away the defused bomb.

Good job the petrol rations have been increased, Stave thought to himself. Six months earlier they'd have had to use hand carts to transport both. He gave a last few instructions to his men and left the scene.

Between two damaged U-boats at one end of the Blohm & Voss basin a wooden pier jutted into the dirty water with a little barge tied up to it: a low motor boat with a little wheelhouse up front and a few rows of wooden benches on the deck behind it. Every morning and evening dozens of little barges like this would bob about on the waves taking tired argumentative workers back and forth between the public rail station and the docks on the other side of the Elbe. But it was midday by now and most of them were tied up by the riverbanks.

There was only one barge under steam, with little black clouds coming from its stumpy funnel. Four men in shabby suits with leather briefcases in their hands were sitting on the open deck. One of them had a knotted sweat-stained white handkerchief on his head to protect him from the sun, another was using a big brown envelope alternatively as a fan and to shield his bald head. The other two just sat there stoically on the hard benches, maybe because they were too tired to worry about the heat.

Stave and his men nodded silently to them, ignoring their inquisitive looks, and slumped down on the seats. A few seconds later the old steam engine below deck kicked in again, the iron hull creaked, water began gurgling behind them and the ageing vessel moved off.

The chief inspector stared back at the docks as they shrank into the distance. The words Blohm & Voss still stood out in big white letters, albeit somewhat washed out, on the wall of the big flotation dock. He took a few deep breaths. When the wind blew from the north-west it brought the tang of the sea and a taste of salt from the North Sea all the way to Hamburg. He glanced at the funnel, at the sooty clouds puffing out and gradually dissipating in the wind, a wind that was blowing from the south-east only, and stank of rotting fish and the acid scent of burning coal in the barge's engine room. The previous winter they hadn't had any coal because all the trains from the Ruhr had either been frozen in or their contents looted. Stave thought back on the icy conditions he had had to endure and swore he would never again complain about the stench of burning coal.

The further the little vessel moved out into the centre of the river, the higher the waves on either side. One minute the bow would be rising high on a wave, the next the barge was rolling from side to side, then the stern would be lifted up. At times the chief inspector had the impression all of that was happening at once. Even though the harbour was only a shadow of what it had been, there were once again more than enough ships passing along the Elbe and in and out of the basins to plough up the waves.

More than three quarters of the harbour had been destroyed by bombs. Stave couldn't think of a single shed that hadn't taken a hit. On some of the quays all the cranes were damaged. There were still wrecks lying in the river against the crumbled dock walls: ghost ships covered in white seagull shit, sometimes with only funnels, super-structure or just a bow or stern jutting from the water. By the end of the war the harbour had been blocked by more than 500 sunken ships.

On their other side, the *Leland Stanford* stood by one quay, the star-spangled banner flying from its stern. A so-called 'Liberty ship', with dockers hauling sacks out of its hold and on to their backs as none of the cranes were working. It might be sugar, maybe grain – who cares as long as it fills our stomachs, Stave thought. Coal was being unloaded from other freighters, on to small sailing barges, flat-bottomed boats that disappeared with their grey-black loads down the confusion of small canals or upriver inland.

In between the steam barges, sailing skips and freighters, tugboats puffed back and forth. The *Jan Molsen*, a wide-bodied ancient sight-seeing vessel was chuffing upriver. Three times a week it would make its way to Cuxhaven and back, often with thousands of people on its white-painted decks – not tourists these days, but the so-called *Hamsterfahrer*, scavengers who would take cigarettes and makeup to swap for potatoes or apples from the farmers of Holstein. People said the *Jan Molsen* was checked by the police a lot less frequently than the northbound trains. From its stern hung a red, white and blue striped flag, the international signal for the letter 'C', with a trian-gular cutout. The Allies had banned the use of the old swastika flag as well as all other national colours. They had to use this grotesque striped 'C', a flag of shame that didn't merit recognition from other ships. 'C' for 'Capitulation' probably, the chief inspector thought, and shrugged his shoulders. Serves us right.

Their barge passed by an old antique-looking ship with two tall funnels and an upright prow, the Soviet flag showing up bright red in the dirty grey monotone of the harbour, even if it hung limp from its flagpole.

Czrisini came up and pointed to the Cyrillic script on the stern. 'Up until 1945 that used to be the *Oceana*, one of the *Kraft durch Freude* leisure steamers for the Nazi trades unionists. One of my friends took a trip on it, back in '35 or '36, it must have been.'

'What about you?'

'I wasn't populist enough to be a *KdF* member.'

'Maybe you could go on it now. All you'd have to do is join the German Communist Party. Looks like it's a Soviet freighter nowadays.'

'Indeed. The name on the stern now is *Siberia*, not quite as poetic as the old name.'

'Hmm, Siberia,' Stave mumbled under his breath.

For the past two years his son Karl had been living in Siberia. He wondered what he looked like now. Before, he had been a sturdy, stubborn-minded kid who believed in Hitler and patriotism and had signed up to fight in a war that had already been lost – who had labelled his father, who wasn't even a member of the Party, a coward. For a long time Stave had heard nothing more of him. He was listed as 'missing'. Then, at long last, a letter had arrived via the Red Cross: a few scribbled lines in Karl's schoolboy handwriting. But then there had been nothing more, nothing for weeks now. Stave wondered if it was as warm as Hamburg up there in the far north? Or maybe there was still snow on the ground? And when might Karl get to come home?

Home. He thought of Anna, his lover. What a strange expression that was to use, not at all befitting an official in the CID. But for several months now they had been a couple, the happiest months Stave had known in years.

Anna von Veckinhausen had moved out of the grimy Nissen hut she had been living in since 1945 and three weeks ago had got permission to move into a basement apartment in the Altona district, 6 Röperstrasse: a damp cellar with a solitary window at ceiling height, damp tiled walls with peeling grey-white oil paint and the stench of Lysol disinfectant – but it was still one step up from the corrugated tin hut. And it had a bit of privacy. Every now and then she would spend the night with him at his apartment in Wandsbek, but more often he spent the night with her. The neighbours in her cellar apartment in Altona were less nosy.

It was impossible for her to move in with him, without a wedding certificate. Was that a possibility? Stave was a widower, but what about Anna? To this day he had no idea if she was unmarried, a widow or divorced – if there was a husband lurking like some ghost in her past. They were cautious in their conversation and referred to the years before 1945, if at all, only obliquely.

Stave dismissed the matter and simply stood there looking out at the river, enjoying the cool breeze, and thought tenderly about the woman he loved. It was nice to be able to look forward to the evenings, rather than fret over the long empty hours before it was time to go back to work.

By chance he caught sight of Kienle. The police photographer was standing a few paces away from him at the railings, with a very strange colour coming over his face: the green of seasickness overtaking the red of sunburn.

'When times are better, I'm going to ask for a transfer to Bavaria,' Kienle groaned when he spotted the chief inspector's worried look.

'Then you can puke your guts up in Lake Constance,' Stave replied in amusement. He nodded over the side of the ship: 'We're standing to windward,' he explained, 'the side the wind blows from. Anything that goes over the side here will come right back at you, if you get my meaning. You'd do better to find yourself a quiet spot on the leeward side.'

Kienle gave him a brave smile: 'There's only a few metres to the quayside,' he whispered, but nonetheless staggered over to the other side of the deck.

Stave looked after him with concern. Kienle was one of the few colleagues he actually liked. Stave had been an outsider back in the Nazis' day. He wasn't obviously suspicious to the Brownshirts in charge so they hadn't sacked him as they had the Social Democrats who were in the Hamburg police, but they'd left him in a backwater, doing an unimportant job: dealing with scams and swindlers. His career had taken a new turn after 1945 when he was considered to have no dirty laundry in his closet. A lot of the CID people had been fired by the English; some of those who had worked for the Gestapo were still awaiting prosecution. A few others had quickly rebranded themselves in front of the occupying army's suspicious eyes and were taken on, but now had to accept Stave, the former loser, on a par with them.

The CID chief himself – 'Cuddel' Breuer – had not only been a

Social Democrat but a concentration camp inmate which made him even more of an outsider than Stave, and had been responsible for landing him in charge of this case, this horrible murder of a young boy. Stave wondered if he was dealing with some madman who had a thing about leaving the bodies of boys on unexploded bombs. He wouldn't be able to sleep until he got to the bottom of this case. Maybe the killing did have something to do with the enforced dismantling of Blohm & Voss? In that case Stave would be dealing with a political hornet's nest, considering how much resentment there was in Hamburg over the matter. One way or the other, the chief inspector thought to himself, there was nothing much for him to win. But a lot to lose.

The barge pulled up to the quayside, the metal hull squeaking against the wooden piles. Kienle jumped ashore with a relieved smile on his face, ahead of even the office workers who stood next to the railings impatiently waiting for the sailors to put the gangplank down. Stave and the other followed him. At the end of the quay were the structures that had looked down on it for half a century like some fairy-tale vision of an ancient city wall, several hundred metres across with semicircular gateways in ochre stone, adorned with arches and romantic sculptures, topped with a tower that would have done credit to some medieval city. Beyond rose the dome of the Elbe Tunnel, based on the Pantheon in Rome, inside it a few shabby restaurants, ticket counters and offices.

Stave walked through one of the gateways: on the other side was a pre-war Mercedes-Benz, one of the police's duty vehicles, code-named Peter-2. The chief inspector insisted on driving himself. He enjoyed the feel of the big wooden steering wheel, the hoarse roar of the engine, the smell of petrol and hot oil. Kienle and the others packed in alongside and behind him – far more people than normally allowed in one vehicle, but who was going to stop them?

The old Mercedes rattled their bones as much as some ancient stagecoach would have done as they trundled along the cobbles of Helgoland Allee. On their right side was a small park with a hill on which a gigantic stone Bismarck stood staring sternly into infinity, completely unmarked despite the hail of bombs that had fallen around it. They passed Millerntor, where the Reeperbahn went off to the left, awash with black marketeers and idlers, everything looking just that bit shabbier than usual. Women in faded blouses with knotted handkerchiefs on their heads to protect them from the sun passed along tiles, bits of concrete and shards of wood from a bomb site until they made a neat pile on the pavement, and male workers, their naked torsos glistening with sweat, piled it on to an already dangerously overloaded lorry with worn tyres. Barefoot children in short lederhosen ran along the roadside. Men had their trouser legs rolled up and were stripped down to sweaty vests. Beyond the pavements lay a sea of bombed-out houses, perilously leaning walls, but also the bright yellow of buttercups growing on wasteland, brambles growing over piles of stone, even young chestnut trees and maples growing out of the bowels of burned-out houses. They drove down Holstenwall, past the Museum for Hamburg History with its brick walls showing shrapnel damage and scorch marks, before reaching the CID head office on Karl Muck Platz, where Stave let the heavy old Mercedes coast to a standstill, and the engine splutter to a stop. The chief inspector turned to the men in the back and called out, 'End of the road.'

'I hope that doesn't go for our investigation too,' Kienle retorted as he climbed out.

A Family in Mourning

When Stave entered the anteroom to his office on the sixth floor, his secretary looked up in shock. She had been reading the newspaper, its yellow sheets lying on her typewriter like a spread-out map.

'Chief Inspector, would it be too much to ask you to get some shoes with squeaky rubber soles?'

'Yes, but I'll tie a cowbell to my leg.' He smiled at Erna Berg. She was blond, eternally optimistic and a bit more rounded than she used to be. She was pregnant, four or five months, the CID man guessed, although he wasn't exactly an expert in such matters. It was nearly twenty years since his wife Margarethe had been pregnant with their only child. Between then and now Karl had become a ghost living in Siberia, and Margarethe's ashes were in Öjendorf Cemetery. The time when the two of them had been young and expecting a baby seemed to Stave as long ago as the heyday of the Roman empire.

'Have you got yourself a pass yet?' he asked, nodding at her baby bump. There was a curfew between midnight and 4.30 a.m. 'If you go into labour at night, you're going to need that scrap of paper so that the military police don't arrest you. It would be a pity if your baby were to be born in a British cell.'

She laughed. 'Application for special pass, apply at the City Hall, room number 306. I've done all my homework. But there's time yet.'

'Well, I'm afraid you're not going to get much chance to enjoy it over the next few days. Have you heard about our new case yet?' He was just being polite; obviously Erna Berg would have heard about it almost immediately through the office bush telegraph. There were times when he thought she knew more about what was going on than he did. Maybe I ought to hang around the office a bit more, have a cup of coffee and a slice of cake with the others, a chat in the washroom. Not keep rushing around to find out the latest news, just wait until it gets to me.'

'A dead boy found lying on a bomb. James rang to tell me.'

Lieutenant James C. MacDonald was a member of the occupying forces and also his secretary's lover and the father of her child. He would have been a pretty good catch for a secretary in the rubble that was Hamburg, if she weren't already married with a child, and the husband she had thought dead hadn't turned up suddenly on her doorstep a few months ago, after being released from a POW camp.

Ever since Stave had worked with MacDonald on the 'Ruins Murderer' case, he had been a reluctant witness to their complicated romance. MacDonald had got Erna Berg an apartment of her own. There would be a divorce, which would be nasty because she was, after all, an adulterer. If everything went as normal she would lose custody of her son.

Stave hadn't seen much of MacDonald recently, usually just when he came to pick up Erna Berg from the office in the evening, but he liked the self-confident Brit. Secretly he envied the man's casual sophistication. He and MacDonald both acted rather embarrassed in each other's company, as if they shared some guilty secret. As if they had shared the same lover, Stave thought to himself, though all they had really shared was success in catching an SS killer, hardly something they needed to be embarrassed about.

'Do the British find it a bit awkward that the body's lying on one of their bombs?' he asked Erna.

'Not in the slightest – as far as they're concerned, their bombs are our problem. They're just a bit nervous about the fact he was found at Blohm & Voss.'

Stave gave a wry smile. 'There's enough resentment at them having the works dismantled. I can imagine they're not exactly happy at what's being said about a murdered boy turning up there.'

'That's what James wants to talk to you about. He asked me to call and let him know when you got back.'

'Can't refuse a request from a member of the army of occupation,' Stave shot back, opening the door to his own office. He wasn't exactly pleased at the news. There could be problems if MacDonald turned up here at the office.

Half an hour later the lieutenant knocked on Stave's door and tiptoed in. 'It seems we're partners again, old boy,' he said, taking Stave's hand. He had long given up the habit of greeting him with a salute. Stave looked at his blond hair, pink cheeks, watery blue eyes.

'At least only half officially for the moment,' MacDonald added. 'I happened to be down at the Esplanade and got the nod from upstairs.'

The chief inspector nodded. Esplanade 6, he meant. Nice place, down on the west bank of the inner Alster Lake. That was where Vaughan Berry, the British civilian governor of Hamburg lived. He was a genial Labour politician who spoke excellent German, not a man to take rash decisions.

'Mr Berry would prefer if we didn't make a song and dance about my role in your investigation.'

'Are you telling me I shouldn't inform my superior officer that an English officer is involved in the investigation?'

'I'm glad we understand one another,' MacDonald replied with a smile. 'Things are complicated enough as it stands.'

Stave mumbled under his breath, if only to give himself time to think. As the representative of the occupying force Governor Vaughan Berry was the most powerful man in Hamburg. But the British had allowed elections to be held, and that meant that ever since 1946 the city had its first post-war mayor, Max Brauer, from the Social Democrats (SPD). Brauer ran City Hall in a coalition with the liberal Free Democrats (FDP) as well as four councillors from the Communist Party (KPD). That made carrying out an investigation at Blohm & Voss all the more complicated because it was the workers down there to whom the four communists owed their seats.

'Is the governor aware of your *special* aptitude for this case?'

Stave eventually managed to ask, a discreet reference to the fact that their previous collaboration had revealed MacDonald belonged to a branch of the British secret service. Stave didn't know all the details, but he knew enough to realise the young officer had more influence than most people thought.

'That's precisely why Mr Berry asked me to look into the matter. The dismantling of the shipyard is causing a lot of resentment towards us. Personally I think it would have been fairer to leave standing whatever our Royal Air Force comrades didn't take care of. But politics is politics. We are having the machinery dismantled and it's giving the communists the grounds they need to make life difficult for us.'

'I thought Stalin was your ally?' Stave replied, with just a hint of caustic irony in his voice.

'He *was* our ally, as long as Hitler was perpetrating his atrocities. These days we're not quite so matey with Uncle Joe over there in Moscow. The Russians have become the new Germans. And despite the fact that the day before yesterday we were bombing the hell out of the Germans, now we'd prefer to have you on our side rather than Moscow's.'

'We're supposed to be your new reserves, are we, like the Indians and the Africans?' Stave asked sceptically. 'We Germans have had our fill of war.'

'There's always a few types who can never get their fill of war,' MacDonald hit back. 'And maybe one of those types happens to be a communist who needs nothing more than the dead body of a boy found lying on a British bomb as an excuse to mount a campaign against Her Majesty's forces.'

'So that's why you're here?'

'Let's just say I'm here to prevent any fresh outbreak of hostilities.'

'Very discreet.'

'So discreet that when you solve the case, you will get all the glory. Officially I don't exist. I'm only here to help out if in the course of the investigation you come across something politically sensitive.'

'Such as?'

MacDonald shrugged. 'Let's wait and see. The only ones who know of my involvement are you and Mr Berry. And Erna, of course, but she knows well enough to keep quiet.'

'Well, I'm glad we can all rely on Frau Berg,' Stave chortled. He was beginning to enjoy this.

'So,' MacDonald began, 'what's your plan?'

'As an old French philosopher said,' Stave replied, 'if you want to give God a good laugh, start telling him about your plans.'

It was muggy in the office, even though Stave had opened the window wide. You could see dust particles hovering in the air, and the room stank of the contents of old box files. Kienle dropped in and set a few still-damp photos down on the chief inspector's desk, adding an extra fine aroma of developing fluid to the atmosphere.

'Pictures of the kid,' Stave said. 'I was waiting for these.'

'To give God a good laugh?'

'Indeed. Want to know what our plan is? First we find out who the kid is. Then we find whoever killed him.'

'Does that mean back down to the Search Office in Altona?'

Stave nodded. 'We have no name, no papers, no missing persons report. The boy was almost certainly a street kid. I've already rung the Search Office and registered the case. They didn't sound exactly overjoyed. They had some 40,000 registered orphans in Hamburg. Over the past two years they've managed to find parents or other relatives for nearly half of them somewhere in the zones of occupation.'

'That still leaves 20,000 unaccounted-for orphans.'

'Including some 600 who don't even know their own first names. The care staff just call them "love" or "poppet".'

MacDonald looked down at the police photographer's blown-up picture of the boy's face. 'Nobody called him "poppet". He knew his own name.'

'The question is whether or not he used it or whether he made up another name for himself.'

'If he was up to something illegal?'

'We found a sharpened screwdriver on him. And a packet of Lucky Strike cigarettes.'

'Black marketeer?'

'Maybe. A lot of the street kids do that. Arguments among black marketeers often end in a fight. But you don't get many down by the docks, and there's never been a case in the shipyard. What would black marketeers be doing down there anyway?'

'Nobody but the workers and military police should be down at Blohm & Voss.'

'I'm hoping that's going to make the investigation easier. The boy ought not to have been there. If we can find out why he was, that might give us a motive and maybe even a murderer. You don't get many people down there.'

'Don't you believe it. According to our military police they're busy every night with looters and scavengers who break into the docks looking for valuables. Smugglers who find all sorts of things from cigarettes to penicillin and even gold on board the ships and take them to sell on the black market. They steal from the Allied ships as well as German fishing boats. Once we had a gang who specialised in looting the American CARE* aid packets and therefore only raided American freight ships.'

'Sounds like people who know what they're doing. Shady characters but not idiots. Doesn't sound like the sort of people who willingly go near an unexploded bomb.'

'They might do, depending on how much profit there was to be made.'

'Or we could be dealing with a lunatic who just likes the idea of leaving a murder victim on a bomb. Or it has something to do with the Blohm & Voss dismantling.'

'I'd be more inclined to believe that if it had been one of your military police found lying on an unexploded bomb.'

---

* Cooperative for American Remittances to Europe.

Stave was wondering if MacDonald or his military police knew that the workers were deliberately sabotaging the dismantling process. 'Let's head down to the Search Office,' he said.

Just then there was a knock on the door and Erna Berg stuck her head round to say, 'There's a phone call from Police Station 31. They had a missing person reported a couple of hours ago: a boy from Barmbek, fourteen years old, last seen wearing Hitler Youth shorts – original colour – and a workman's shirt.'

'I think I can hear God laughing,' MacDonald said.

'Where's the local station,' the lieutenant asked as they climbed into his army Jeep outside the CID HQ.

'Barmbek South. Drive us as far as the Alster and I'll direct you from there.' Stave dropped thankfully on to the hard passenger seat. 'I'm relieved not to have to spend hours going through endless filing cards of nameless children.'

'Yes, you've done enough of that,' the British officer answered. After a brief pause he added, 'Heard anything more from your son?'

'He's still in Siberia,' was all the answer the chief inspector made. He was embarrassed talking to other people about Karl, reluctant to let them see just how relieved he was that the boy was still alive. Or how afraid he was that something might happen to him in the POW camp. Or about how the boy might react when he turned up back home to find his father with a new woman.

All of a sudden a dreadful thought struck him: 'If the Russians turn from being an ally of the British to an enemy, and we Germans are supposed to help the British, then Stalin might never release our captured soldiers?'

MacDonald was concentrating on seeing through the dirty windscreen, even though there was next to nobody on the streets.

'Uncle Joe isn't exactly the most generous of men,' he answered at last. 'Would you prefer it if I didn't take part in this investigation?'

Stave sighed. 'Whether I hunt down a child murderer on my own or in the company of a British lieutenant isn't going to make the slightest difference to those making the decisions in Moscow.'

'I enjoy the job,' MacDonald said, with the ghost of a smile. He put his foot down and the Jeep hurtled bumpily along the Jungfernstieg.

They were driving along the east bank of the Alster, the latter shining in the sun to their left. They could see two small yachts with slack sails, and Stave wondered if their helmsmen were occupation officers, or maybe local people again.

The big solid buildings along the Jungfernstieg and the Inner Alster looked a bit decrepit after years of neglect: there was plaster peeling off the walls, a few shell holes in the walls, although most were more or less intact. After that they passed the smart villas down Uhlenhorst, mid-nineteenth century, tasteful, subdued lighting, shady trees.

MacDonald glanced at him. 'You wouldn't think there'd been a war around here, would you?'

'Wait till you get to the next crossroads,' the chief inspector replied, nodding over to the right. 'Welcome to the wasteland.'

The lieutenant turned on to Mundsburger Damm. A sweating traffic policeman waved them through with a weary gesture. There were just three other cars, bumping their way over the cobbles. Lost in his own thoughts, Stave's eyes came to light on the number plate of an old, dented brown Opel Olympia trailing smoke from its exhaust: 'HG-8734' – Hamburg Government. We've become part of the British Empire, he thought to himself, like Calcutta or Hong Kong, but with bomb damage.

Where they were now it wasn't even possible to recognise what sort of buildings might ever have lined the streets. There were mountains of bricks on either side of the road, here and there a few walls that had remained standing, steel-reinforced rod meshes like giant spider's webs. And in between them the *Trümmerfrauen*, the women who worked tirelessly to clear the rubble, helped by teams of city workers, loading the debris on to carts. Dust hung in the shimmering air. The stench of petrol from the spluttering Opel mingled with the smell of mortar, sand, charred wood and open drains. Stave thought he could detect the sweet smell of corpses in the air, but told himself he had to be imagining it. That was how it had been during the great bombing raids when corpses lay decaying in the rubble for months on end. By now they were all dust and bones, though. At least he hoped so.

They continued along Oberaltenallee for a minute or two until, on Stave's instructions, MacDonald hit the brakes so hard that a cyclist riding alongside them nearly toppled and fell. The rider went red in the face and took a deep breath as if he were about to unleash a stream of invective, then recognised the Jeep and the British uniform. He muttered something under his breath and rode on.

'I guess he'll be voting Communist next time around,' MacDonald said, though he didn't look as if he'd care all that much.

Stave looked up at Police Station 31, a relic from the Kaiser's days when they still built them to look like little Renaissance palaces, from the outside at any rate. An architectural fantasy standing there intact amid a sea of rubble, looking at the same time much older than its fifty years and much younger, as if somebody had collected all the bricks from the ruins and built a brand new structure from them.

'I guess your bomber boys didn't get their aim right here,' Stave said.

'On the contrary, the boys knew there were Gestapo prisoners housed in cells above ground so they took care to drop their loads anywhere else.'

The chief inspector gave the lieutenant a quizzical look. Was he having a laugh at his expense? Or was this the secret service man talking, someone who knew more than most people? He shrugged his shoulders and pushed open the door.

Linoleum on the floor, wooden surfaces polished by countless hands. Somewhere in the distance the clatter of a typewriter. Stave could hear jazz coming from behind a closed door. The radio only broadcast classical music or pop during the day, so as not to have to deal with too many complaints about 'negro music'. Clearly one of the staff had a gramophone in the office. Maybe it made interrogations easier. Stave had hoped it would be cooler inside, but he was disappointed. It was hot and muggy.

He showed his ID to the duty sergeant and told him why he was there. He didn't bother to introduce MacDonald. One look at the lieutenant's uniform was enough for the man on the desk.

'Please follow me, Chief Inspector.'

He took them into an adjoining office, apparently an interrogation room with a table, three chairs, and a lamp with its shade turned up towards the ceiling. Stave thought back to MacDonald's comment about the Gestapo, then dismissed it. Right now there were more important matters.

A few minutes later he had a copy of the missing persons report in his hand: Adolf Winkelmann, born 2 April 1933. The chief inspector skimmed over the details. Father had been a clerk in a registry office, mother a housewife, no brothers or sisters. The parents lived in Horn, a district that had been popular with clerical workers, Stave recalled, before it was completely flattened by the bombing in 1943. Father and mother dead, since then. The missing persons report had been filed by the boy's only remaining relative, his aunt Greta Boesel, with whom he had lived, a widow in Barmbek.

Stave showed the paperwork to MacDonald, pointing to a few lines of italic type: 'Born 1933,' he noted. 'First name Adolf. I think we can guess how his parents voted.'

'Didn't do them much good,' MacDonald replied, ignoring the shocked look the desk sergeant gave him.

'But the boy survived all the bombing and even the winter of starvation that followed.'

'A lucky lad who ran out of luck.'

Stave flicked through the documentation. 'His aunt only reported him missing after he hadn't come home for a week. Seems like he often didn't spend the night there and she only began to get worried when she hadn't heard from him for a few days.'

'Is there a photograph?'

'No. Not even an ID card photo. The aunt said she didn't have any pictures of him.'

MacDonald just nodded silently.

'Adolf Winkelmann went to Hinschenfelde high school, but it seems they didn't notice him missing either. I guess he played truant a lot.'

'Do you reckon it is the boy found down at the docks? What would a boy from Barmbek be doing down there? It not exactly nearby.'

'It doesn't look as if he hung around Barmbek all that much,' Stave replied, tapping the paper. 'The clothes and the age fit. Time to go and see his aunt.'

Stave took the missing persons report with them. Greta Boesel, 594 Fuhlsbüttel Strasse. 'In the north of the city,' he told MacDonald, 'up near Ohlsdorf Cemetery. Abour four or five kilometres from here.'

'Good job you've got me and the Jeep,' the lieutenant laughed, and put his foot down.

They drove along Barmbeker Markt, snaking between heaps of rubble on streets that had still only been partially cleared, then down Fuhlsbüttel Strasse almost directly north. To their left and right stood the stumps of oak trees that had been burnt down or hacked to pieces for firewood, with here and there a tree that had somehow managed to survive all the attacks on it and had grown a crown providing welcome shade for people to sit in: men in linen suits with pork pie hats carrying briefcases, immediately recognisable as clerical workers in this sea of devastation; others in sweat-marked vests, tough-looking men, bleary from beer; women in blousy flowery dresses and headscarves, the colours faded, none of them wearing nylons, but that didn't stop MacDonald staring at them long enough for Stave to worry about them crashing into an oak.

They passed Barmbek Hospital, a collection of red-brown buildings in an expansive park. Requisitioned by the British. The entrance was fenced off, with 'Hospital 94' marked above it, and military police dozing in the sun. Stave's son had been born here. All of a sudden he had a vision of Karl as a baby, so incredibly small and light in his arms. His wife Margarethe pale, drenched in sweat, exhausted, but impossibly happy. Stave turned his eyes left, away from the hospital, away from MacDonald.

Ruins surrounded them on both sides, with just here and there almost obscenely well-preserved villas, façades plastered pale yellow, white or blue, some of them missing roof joists, as if somebody had taken a saw to them. Then a few hundred metres further on, three- or four-storey apartment blocks set back from the road by a patch of grass already gone yellow from the drought.

There were few house numbers to be seen. Stave looked out until he found one and then tried to work out how far they had to go, but it wasn't easy amid so much rubble. On the right there was a long row of three-storey apartment blocks with their roofs still intact, brick-built with balconies. They all had numbers.

'There are worse places to live in Hamburg,' Stave said, nodding for MacDonald to pull in to the kerb.

'Not enough to keep the boy here, though,' the lieutenant replied.

There were doorbells by the entrance, more than there used to be, which was normal these days, with strips of paper with names and dates of birth scribbled on them, signs of life from the survivors, those whose homes had been bombed and had managed to find themselves somewhere else. The chief inspector finally found a brass plaque that read 'Greta Boesel, 2nd Floor, Right.' Obviously she'd lived there before the bombing. Next to it was a piece of cardboard, ripped from a faded hanging file on which was scrawled 'Walter Kümmel, Adolf Winkelmann'.

'Walter Kümmel,' Stave muttered to himself. 'That name seems somehow familiar.'

'A customer of yours?'

Stave just shook his head.

They pressed the doorbell and waited. Nothing happened. They tried again, although Stave was fairly certain that the people upstairs had pulled the fuse out to save electricity. But they had to follow etiquette. The he grabbed the door handle and it creaked open.

He entered the building, slowly, getting slower with every step on the way upstairs. What was he going to say to the boy's aunt? It was always hard to tell someone that a relative had died. And then to have to ask them questions. He noticed the look the lieutenant was giving him. Maybe MacDonald had never had to do it. Neither of them said a word until they found themselves at a door painted a long time ago in pale eggshell white.

The chief inspector took a deep breath and knocked.

He could hear the muffled sound of music, a woman's voice, a sentimental song that had been popular even in the Brownshirt days. It had to be a radio – the new NorthWest German Radio station played old hits around this time of day. She obviously didn't need to cut back on that much electricity. Eventually they heard footsteps approaching the door, and then the noise of the handle turning. Nor was she someone who felt obliged to ask from behind a closed door who was calling, not someone to put a chain on the door. Either she was very self-confident, or she was expecting someone. Maybe the boy. That'd be just great.

He was greeted with a surprise. On hearing that she was a widowed aunt, Stave had automatically imagined a careworn old lady. But the woman who opened the door to him was a brunette of no more than forty, with long, wavy hair and doe eyes, whose curvacious shape was accentuated by a flimsy cream dress sewn from parachute silk. She had a small nose, lips painted red and a solid jaw line.

'Can I help you?' It was the husky voice of a long-term smoker.

'CID,' said Stave, because the sentence he had been rehearsing suddenly sounded absurd. He pulled out his ID. 'It's about the boy you reported missing.'

'Has Adolf nicked something?' Even as she replied Greta Boesel opened the door to let them in. It wouldn't do to let the neighbours hear.

The hallway had a few nails in the wall serving as coat hooks, the floorboards were badly scratched and one half of the narrow space was crammed full of wooden boxes, tea chests from India, Stave noticed. Whatever was in them didn't smell like tea.

She led them down the hallway and into the living room. There was an old, comfortable-looking sofa, a heavy table and cupboard, a glass cabinet and a big valve radio, maybe dating back to the last year before the war – as well as boxes everywhere and a few jute sacks.

Greta Boesel didn't seem to notice their looks of surprise. She turned the radio off and went over to the open balcony door, which looked out on to Fulsbüttel Strasse. Somebody had cobbled together a construction of old pipes and some yellow material to make a sort of sunshade. It looked like an old sail, the chief inspector thought, maybe come from down by the docks.

'It's not as muggy out here as it is inside,' Greta Boesel said, gesturing towards four wicker chairs.

Stave would have preferred to remain standing, but he couldn't think of a way to refuse. He didn't want to be any more brusque than he had to be. He took one of Kienle's police photographs out of his pocket and asked: 'Is that your nephew?'

He heard MacDonald catch his breath as though he was shocked at such a direct question. Stave ignored him. He would have preferred to lead in to the question a lot more subtly, but he hadn't been able to find the right words.

Greta Boesel took a look at the photo, which showed only the boy's head, not his bloodied body and certainly not the unexploded bomb he was lying on – but it didn't take an expert to see that those staring wide-open eyes were never going to close again.

'That's my Adolf,' she said at last. Her voice had all of a sudden lost its huskiness and sounded flat, empty. She flexed the muscles of her jaw, but when she handed the photo back to Stave he could see that her hands weren't even trembling.

'He's always out somewhere or other. I've known for ages now that he would come to a bad end,' she said.

'How did you know he came to a bad end?'

'Why else would you be here?'

'He might have had an accident.'

She shrugged her shoulders, went back inside, then came back out again with a lit cigarette.

'What happened to him?'

Stave thought of his son, of how much he had worried about him, tortured himself waiting for news, wondering if he would ever get another letter from the gulag, worried in case it was the wrong sort of letter, the sort that was written by some soulless bureaucrat: 'We regret to have to inform you that your son Karl Stave ...' Don't event think about it. He ought to be thankful to Greta Boesel for not making a scene. She was just the boy's aunt, not his mother. And she was a widow; she was used to bereavement. He suppressed the initial anger he had felt at the apparent cold-heartedness of this elegant woman, and told her as briefly and tactfully as possible the circumstances under which Adolf Winkelmann's body had been found.

'One of my colleagues will be along to take you to identify the boy's body down at the morgue. It's a formality, but an essential one, I'm afraid.'

'So there's a few days to plan a funeral.'

'When did you last see the boy?' Stave asked.

'A week ago. Adolf was always disappearing for a few days at a time, but never more than that. He got enough to eat here: a lad of fourteen puts away more than two full-grown men. At first I didn't think anything of his absence. It was only when I hadn't seen him for a week that I reported it to the police.'

'What did Adolf get up to when he wasn't here?'

She shrugged. 'He was very self-sufficient. He wouldn't tell me anything.'

'Where did he spend the nights?'

Greta Boesel exhaled a ribbon of blue smoke and made an 'o' shape with her red lips. Stave found it almost obscene and tried to avoid staring at her mouth.

'It might seem odd to you, Chief Inspector, but I was happy enough not to ask too many questions of Adolf. He let me get on in peace. It was a sort of private agreement between us. It can get crowded in here.'

'It looks like a warehouse,' Stave said.

'It is.' She sighed as if she'd already repeated what she was about to say a thousand times. 'I'm the chief executive of a company called "Boesel and Co", though you can ignore the "and Co", there's just me. My husband founded the company and built it up all through the difficult years after the crash of 1929, then through the Nazi period and even the war. But four months after the English arrived,' she gave MacDonald a glance that seemed warm rather than frosty, 'and the whole bloody mess was finally over, my husband got a lung infection and died. I had worked with him throughout all those long years, done the bookkeeping, dealt with the shipping papers and customs declarations. So I was able to keep the business going.'

Stave thought of how few cars there were available, how little rationed fuel was available, thought of the blocked streets and ruined factories. 'But how do you transport your goods? And what are they anyway?'

'I have three trucks, two pre-war models and one that came from the Wehrmacht. They keep breaking down. I send them out with drivers all over the western occupation zones. I buy up stuff you can get relatively easily from the English – tea, John Player's cigarettes – take it down to the Mosel and exchange it for wine, or down to the Americans in Frankfurt or Nuremberg and swap it for chocolate or corned beef. I only deal in expensive stuff, in order to cover the fuel costs, etc. If my driver has to spend the night in a farmhouse that costs me 100 Reichsmarks or a few packets of cigarettes.'

'How do you get hold of the fuel?'

She shrugged her shoulders and smiled. 'Is that question relevant to your investigation, Chief Inspector, or am I entitled to keep my business secrets to myself?'

Stave was pretty certain that at least half of Greta Boesel's business involved breaking the law: infringement of trading regulations, smuggling, bribery probably. On the other hand, how could she have kept the business going? He was reluctantly in awe of the woman.

'How did Adolf Winkelmann come to be living with you?' he asked.

'He's my sister's son. She and her husband died in the 1943 bombing.' She glanced at MacDonald again, hesitantly, cautiously this time. But the lieutenant just looked back at her politely. She continued: 'He came to us, there wasn't anybody else left in the family. I hadn't been particularly close to my sister, nor to her kid, but my husband said we should take him in, to succeed him in the business one day.'

'You have no children yourself?'

She blew a cloud of smoke into the air, stubbed out the cigarette in an ashtray, then lit up a new John Player's. A small fortune going up in smoke, literally, Stave reflected. The transport business had to be doing well.

'Adolf's a difficult boy, *was* a difficult boy,' she corrected herself. 'Hardly shone at school, lazy, cheeky. But he had something between his ears: good at arithmetic, gift of the gab – Goebbels could have learnt a trick or two from him.'

'Was he a Party member?'

She laughed: 'He'd been a *Pimpf,** and a member of the Hitler Youth, like they all were. My husband was a Party member, but only so he could keep the business going. We weren't so close to the Brownshirts, not like my sister and brother-in-law: they were 150 per cent on side.'

'What about after the war?'

'Things didn't exactly get better for him. When he was a Hitler Youth member he at least had to turn up regularly, for roll call, parades, physical exercise and stuff. That all ended in 1945. From then on the people he hung around with were even worse. One of

---

* The Nazi organisation for younger children aged 6–10.

the neighbours told me he'd seen Adolf hanging out with prostitutes at the station, kids who stole coal and a few Polish refugees. I can't comment, he never brought people like that here. But there's no doubt he'd become a street kid.'

'Did he work for your firm?' Stave was thinking of the packet of Lucky Strike they'd found on the body.

'Only very occasionally. Now and then he'd help load or unload a few things, But I could never rely on him turning up at a particular time and mucking in.'

'He was a bit more reliable in his work for me,' said a voice behind them. A man appeared in the doorway to the balcony: late forties, lean but with broad shoulders and the narrow angular facial appearance of a bird of prey, a long nose bent at the end as if from an old injury, like a hook, grey eyes, a crew cut, hard to say what colour, and a bright, light linen suit. 'Kümmel,' he said by means of introduction, holding out a scarred hand, 'Walter Kümmel.'

'My fiancé,' Greta Boesel added, looking embarrassed for the first time since Stave had arrived.

The chief inspector thought of his Anna. Would she introduce him to anyone as her 'fiancé'? It was a stupid old concept. A remnant of a more civilised age, perhaps. These days, when so many men and women had died, people were lucky to have anyone at all. And when those who did hardly bothered with documentation, what was the point of talking about someone as a 'fiancé'? He shook the man's hand. He had a strong grip. Greta Boesel was obviously relieved that he hadn't made a face. The CID man explained why he was there.

'What do you do for a living?'

'I'm in boxing. A promoter.'

'It was you who organised that fight between Walter Neusel and Hein ten Hoff!' MacDonald unexpectedly cried out, recognising the man and taking him by the hand. 'I was there.'

It suddenly dawned on Stave too. This wasn't one of the CID's old customers, this was a local celebrity, at least in the sporting world: Walter Kümmel had been an experienced jeweller, but changed occupation before the war. He had been an amateur boxer and realised it was more lucrative to get other people to do the fighting than climb into the ring himself.

He handed over a business card, hand-typed on a piece of uneven cardboard: 'Walter Kümmel, Hanseatic Boxing, Chile House, B, Hamburg.'

Not a bad address, Stave thought to himself. 'Boxing must pay well these days,' he said.

Kümmel laughed aloud, almost infectiously. It was the laugh of a self-confident man content with his lot in the world. 'I had "Hanseatic Boxing" registered as a business back in the autumn of 1945. The civil servants gave me a look as if I was trying to refound the Nazi Party. My first fight was in Kiel, a week later. Only one boxer turned up; the other one was stuck on a damn train somewhere.'

'You climbed into the ring yourself,' MacDonald interrupted. 'And won. It was a crazy story.'

'You do what you have to. But that was the last time I had to improvise. Since then I've organised more than forty bouts. I have four German champions on contract, and pretty soon I'm going to be sending the first of my boys over the pond. There's big money to be made in America.'

'And you employed a fourteen-year-old boy to run errands for you?' Stave asked.

Kümmel didn't seem bothered by the question. He took a packet of English Woodbines out of his jacket pocket and offered them round. Greta Boesel took one. Is she trying to kill herself, Stave wondered. He declined politely, as did MacDonald. Kümmel himself didn't light up, even though he had been the one to produce the packet.

'I was just being polite,' he said with a smile, noticing the expression of surprise on Stave's face. 'I like to keep fit, and cigarettes don't exactly help.'

As he put the packet back in his jacket pocket the chief inspector caught sight of a little glass tube of white tablets. Maybe cigarettes aren't enough any more, he thought. He remembered Kümmel's powerful handshake, looked at his broad shoulders and the fluid way he moved. None of that suggested he was on hard drugs. Maybe they were steroids of some sort, things to improve the muscle tone. Maybe Kümmel was giving his boxers a little help on the side. That might explain why he had so many champions on his books.

He put the thought to the back of his mind, concentrating instead on what the promoter was saying about the boy. 'Adolf could have trained with my boys. In fact he did on occasion: but he was too unreliable. He didn't turn up regularly at training. And when he did get into the ring, he'd end up getting hammered, even though he was big and strong enough for his age. He was somehow or other never quite there: more of a dreamer, a kid who was only ever working for himself. He needed a father's strong hand. I was just his aunt's fiancé – it wasn't up to me. And anyway I was too busy.'

'But he helped you out?'

'He did that. He put up posters advertising fights for me. Sometimes he would sell tickets at the door – though I was never too happy about him sitting behind the till, not without someone to watch him, at least.' He smiled and shrugged.

'Adolf wasn't exactly our little ray of sunshine,' Greta Boesel added with a sigh.

'So, who did it?' Walter Kümmel asked.

'We don't know,' Stave replied. 'Not yet at least. Can I take a look at the boy's things?'

Greta Boesel led him through her cluttered living room, down a poorly lit hallway, at the end of which a door opened into a tiny room, barely bigger than a decent wardrobe, with a little window the size of a handkerchief and a camp bed, neatly made-up, and a box on the floor. There was no bedside table, no picture on the wall.

'Didn't he have any photos of his parents?'

'They were all in their apartment and got burnt.'

'How was it that Adolf escaped?'

'He was at a Hitler Youth gathering that evening. Or at least that's what he told us afterwards. Maybe he was just off somewhere on his own. At any rate he wasn't in the building. Nobody who was survived the bombing.'

Stave glanced around the little room: no books, no toys, no radio, no stamp collection, no letters. 'May I?' he asked, bending town to examine the box on the floor. He opened it without waiting for an answer, and rifled through the contents: a pair of long trousers, a pair of swimming trunks, underwear, a worn-down pair of sandals – too small for him, Stave reckoned, holding them up – a couple of patched shirts, a scrappy winter coat. And right at the bottom, three packets of Lucky Strike. Unopened.

Greta Boesel gave the chief inspector a look of surprise. 'If only I'd known …' she said.

'If you'd known, you'd have smoked them,' Walter Kümmel added with a laugh. 'But I'd like to know what he did to earn that many cigarettes!'

'I'd like to know that too,' Stave muttered, closing the box, feeling like he was closing a coffin.

'Any of his personal belongings missing?' he asked, though he already knew the answer.

Greta Boesel and Walter Kümmel shook their heads. 'There's more in there than I would have imagined,' she said. 'How should I know if there's anything missing?'

'We'll take the box with us,' the chief inspector said. 'There might be something that could help us.' Not exactly correct protocol, he thought to himself, but he didn't feel like declaring the room off limits and hanging around until uniformed police arrived while he went off to get a warrant from a judge and prosecutor. It was getting stuffy in the apartment.

'Help yourself,' Greta Boesel said indifferently.

Stave and MacDonald lifted the box between them.

'It doesn't exactly weigh much,' MacDonald commented.

They put their package in the back seat of the Jeep. There was sweat running down Stave's forehead, though it wasn't as if he'd exerted himself.

'A family in mourning,' muttered MacDonald when they had driven a few metres down Fuhlsbüttel Strasse.

'I'd like to know what Boesel is carrying in those trucks of hers driving around the occupation zones,' Stave replied.

'She has to be picking up her cargoes down at the docks.'

'Well she certainly didn't pick up that sail hanging over the balcony down in the Alps.'

'Sounds as if we'll be paying another visit to Frau Boesel.'

The chief inspector gave him a grim nod. 'When we find out a bit more about exactly when the murder took place, we'll go back over her alibi. But, really, why on earth would an aunt murder her nephew in an out-of-bounds dockyard and leave his body on an unexploded bomb? I suppose he might have stolen her cigarettes. He has to have got his hands on those Lucky Strikes we found somehow or other. Maybe he did steal them from her and sent her into a blind rage, but what's that got to do with Blohm & Voss?' Stave nodded towards the ruins all round them and said: 'It's not as if there aren't enough places to murder someone without being seen.'

'And in any case the boy was big and strong. And if we are to take the word of her fiancé he'd also trained with professional boxers. Even if he wasn't very good, he would have been good enough to defend himself against a woman.'

'Kienle didn't find any cigarette butts in the Blohm & Voss yard. I can hardly imagine Greta Boesel going anywhere without leaving butts in her wake.' Stave took off his summer hat, ran his fingers through his hair, feeling the sweat drying on his skin. 'Even so, there are reasons enough to investigate her: her unusual transport business, the load of cigarettes the boy had … Something there stinks. And another strange thing: who were his friends? Adolf Winkelmann was essentially a street kid. But which streets? And who did he hang out with? Where did he spend his days when he didn't turn up at school? And where did he spend his nights when he didn't come home?'

'The girls who hang out at the station, the other street kids, Displaced Persons – none of them the sort of people you want behind your back.'

'Certainly not the sort of people a fourteen-year-old, however fly he might be, ought to be hanging out with.'

The stopped outside HQ.

'Are you coming into the office?' Stave asked. 'I can invite you for a glass of water. Sorry I have nothing better to offer, but in this heat it helps. And I can also promise to close the door to Frau Berg's office for at least five minutes.'

'Very kind of you. I'll come and spirit Erna away later, but right now I have a meeting with Governor Berry.'

'I imagine he'll be interested to hear your interim report.'

'He'll be disappointed to get an interim report at all, rather than hearing that we've cleared up the whole business and can close the file. Very disappointed indeed.'

Stave left the office that evening determined not to think about the dead boy for several hours at least. He went into a flower shop on a side street and bought ten red roses. Passing the Reichsmark notes over the counter, he felt as if he had got a bit of normality back into his life. The roses had bloomed early in the warm spring weather and you could get them anywhere without a ration card, without having to queue up or do a deal on the black market. When had he last bought something frivolous and useless?

He cradled the roses carefully, the way he'd cradle a small child, inhaling their perfume as he walked quickly down the street. Before long he was outside the Garrison Theatre next to the main station. It had previously been the Deutsches Schauspielhaus and when he could afford it he and Margarethe had bought tickets towards the rear. Nowadays British officers came here to listen to jazz and watch Noel Coward comedies performed by theatre companies from London with names that sounded like they'd been founded in the

Middle Ages. There were warning placards outside the main entrance proclaiming 'Out of Bounds for German Civilians'.

He had arranged to meet Anna here and just the thought of her brought a smile to his face. He would never refer to her as his fiancée, certainly not after the comedy he'd witnessed this afternoon. Would she one day be his wife? He still knew next to nothing about her. They had only been a couple for a few months. He knew she was originally from Königsberg, that she had family there, parents at least and maybe other relatives. But also that none of them had reached the west. Or even whether or not they were still alive? Maybe one day she would tell him about her family. And then maybe he would wish she hadn't.

Yesterday she had revealed, partly in passing, and with some embarrassment, that today, 30 May, was her birthday. I won't forget that, Stave had told himself: I'm good with dates. There was no sign of her as yet: he had got there too early.

And then he caught sight of her: slim, with long dark hair and almond-shaped eyes, wearing an old but elegant dress, and with a worn little leather case in one hand. She could easily have been taken for a passenger on her way to catch a train. But Stave smiled knowingly to himself and retreated a few steps into the shadow of the station entrance. He knew that brisk, sprightly gait wasn't a mark of self-confidence or the fact she was in a hurry: it was a reflection of her nervousness.

She was about to do a bit of small – but illegal – business.

Anna was right in front of the theatre now, her skirt brushing against the placard with the harsh English warning. An elderly, bespectacled British officer emerged from the theatre and took a few steps over to Anna. The pair exchanged a few words. She moved from one foot to the other and glanced around. She might as well have had a placard of her own around her neck declaring 'Illegal Business in Process,' Stave thought to himself. An old member of the East Prussian upper class doing black market business in Hamburg, it just didn't work. Stave was amazed that Anna hadn't been arrested more often by some of his colleagues. She looted the city's ruins for bits of jewellery, old paintings, antique books, bits of furniture, watches, and then restored them as best she could and sold them on to officers in the occupation forces. They paid her ludicrously low prices in Reichsmarks which they could get in thick wads in exchange for a few of their pound notes, or gave her cigarettes or chocolate they got rations for. But for Germans these were riches; Anna had been living on deals like this for a good two years now.

She opened her case and took out a little clock, the sort that might have stood on someone's mantelpiece, with a dark wooden and brass surround about the length of her forearm, and a large dial. The captain nodded and Anna put it back in the case and handed it to him. He took out a wad of Reichsmarks and handed them to her, before turning round and going back into the Garrison Theatre. Anna took a deep breath.

'Police, CID,' Stave said, just loud enough to hear as he emerged from the shadow.

She jumped, spun around and then smiled in relief when she saw him, a look of affection on her face.

Stave handed the roses to her: 'Happy Birthday.'

She hugged him, gave him a kiss, embarrassing him out here on the street. One of his colleagues might have seen them. She beamed and said, 'The first birthday present I've had in three years.'

Stave wondered who had given her the last one, back in 1944, but quickly dismissed the thought. He whispered in her ear, 'I have another one for you: the Schulzes downstairs have gone off to their allotment shed.'

'You mean you have no neighbours this evening?'

'No tonight.'

She took his arm. 'Seems it's my lucky day.'

'We might even get a bit of a breeze this evening. We could open the balcony door and cool down.'

'We might need to,' she replied, staring him in the eye.

Stave could feel himself blush. 'Good bit of business?' he asked, just to change the subject.

'Four hundred Reichsmarks.'

The chief inspector clicked his tongue: 'That'll buy two pounds of butter on the black market, more or less.'

'A good enough price for an old clock I only had to polish up a bit. The thing still worked perfectly. Amazing really! I found it in Rothenburgsort. A whole house had collapsed, four or five storeys it must have been. Looked as if it had burnt down. The snow, rain and heat of the past two years hadn't done too much damage. I cleared away a few bricks and found the clock in the middle of the rubble, as if somebody had deliberately left it there. Even the key to wind it up was on a hook in the casing. I put it in, turned it and the thing started ticking, just sitting there in the rubble. So loudly in fact, that I grabbed it and made off as quick as I could. But I'll go back and take another look around.'

'One of these days somebody's going to spot you and arrest you.'

She laughed: 'Oh, I have good contacts in the police!' Then she said, 'Let's not take the tram. We can walk to your place. I enjoy linking arms with you and feeling the sun on my face. It makes me glad to be still alive.'

With Anna on his arm, Stave felt as if the city was suddenly a brighter place. He became aware of the elder bushes by the side of the street and among the piles of rubble, white and pale yellow patches of blossom amid the grey and brown of the city, a note of fragrance, the noisy street urchins running past them, heading for a dip in one of the city's outdoor pools, or maybe just in the canals that flowed into the Alster, two girls sharing an ice cream, taking turns to have a lick, slowly, their eyes closed as they did. An old couple walking along, hand in hand like teenagers in love.

Stave felt he could shout aloud with happiness, but at the same time he choked up with sadness when he thought of all those who had not survived to see this spring. And then he corrected himself: it was not sadness, it was guilt. Guilt that he had made it through to see the joys of peace. What had he done to merit such happiness? He knew the answer to that one, had brooded on it time and again ever since a bomb dropped by a British aircraft had taken his wife while he had survived. He had done nothing to merit survival: it had been blind luck, an accident of fate, or maybe just a wicked joke by the angel of death that took the lives of tens of thousands only to let the odd individual escape.

At least make the best of it, he told himself. It wasn't just him: there was also his son, Karl, and the killer he was now hunting. There was more than enough for him to do, to atone for his luck: not least arresting a child-killer.

Stave had sworn to himself he would not bend his lover's ear on her birthday, of all days, with true crime stories, but suddenly it all came tumbling out. For an hour, as they strolled along together, he told her the story of Adolf Winkelmann, the unexploded bomb, Greta Boesel and her fiancé, cigarette packets hidden beneath underwear and bare walls without a single family photograph.

'It happens: people can lose it all,' Anna von Veckinhausen replied without meeting his eyes.

Stave was suddenly overcome by embarrassment, realising that he had never seen a photograph of any member of her family. 'I wasn't trying to make a point,' he stuttered.

She turned and smiled at him: 'Sometimes people can win too,' she said.

Eventually they reached the building on Ahrensburger Strasse where Stave had his apartment on the fourth floor. He had tried to do it up a bit since he had met Anna. He had scraped away patches of peeling wallpaper one Saturday, and gone off to the black market to get some oil paint, war material, probably stolen from one of the docks, from what was written on the tin. White, the colour they used to paint steamer ships. And bright yellow, probably for warning signs. He had mixed the two to give a pale yellow, which he used to paint the bare walls. He had ended up with a few blotches here and there and it wasn't exactly uniform in shade, but at least his apartment now felt brighter, and also felt nearly twice as large, particularly in the summer sunlight.

Anna had liked it. She had laughed when she first saw the flowers he had displayed in a jam jar on the window sill, and on her next visit brought him a white porcelain vase she had found on one of her looting expeditions.

This time she complimented him on what he had done on the balcony, then went into his tiny kitchen and fired up his little camp stove. He had got hold of some commercially produced sausages from the butcher's, not exactly delicatessen produce: they contained 10 per cent whale meat and 5 per cent bone meal, at least officially – there was probably more of each. He had also got some sausage broth, the water in which they had been cooked. That was cheap, even if there was a bit of fat floating in it. Add a couple of watery potatoes, a couple of leeks and some nettles for flavour, a couple of the semolina dumplings people called 'cement blocks', a bit of crumbly bread made with wheat, barley, corn and chalk dust, and to drink: water, albeit in a pair of champagne glasses Anna had found in the rubble.

It made Stave think back to what he would have eaten on a hot day like this when he was a child: chilled soup made from sour cherries with cinnamon, soup made from fresh berries with apple and bread dumplings. It would be a while before he could taste things like that again.

He took their scant dinner out on to the balcony. 'You're a miracle worker,' Anna exclaimed. It took him a minute or two to work out she wasn't being sarcastic.

They chatted about this and that, nothing in particular, toasted one another as if there really was champagne in their glasses, and made the most of every sip, every bite. The sun was setting on the horizon, casting a red glow over the houses, over the ruins, as if there was still one last incendiary bomb burning somewhere out there.

'I have one more little surprise,' Stave said, disappearing back into the kitchen. He came back with a bar of American chocolate.

Anna glanced back and forth at Stave and the chocolate bar, which he was holding out on a cushion as if it were a piece of valuable jewellery. 'Chief Inspector!' she gasped. 'I am shocked. This has to have been acquired illegally.'

'Not at all, the most legal source you can imagine: Dr Ehrlich, the public prosecutor has good contacts in England.'

'And you have a good contact in the public prosecutor,' she replied with a smile.

Later they lay together in bed, naked and exhausted from the exertions of their lovemaking. Anna sighed in her sleep. Stave took her gently in his arms, then turned his head to look out the open window. There was not a breath of air to be felt. Hamburg at night was still as dark as it had been during the blackout. But it was no longer as quiet as it used to be in those dark days. He could hear a woman laughing, music from a gramophone, a waltz, faint, a bit wobbly – the record must have got bent by heat. The cry of stray cats, in lust or anger, the squeaking of a rat, the bellowing of some drunk. Stave tried to make it out: it sounded a bit like the Nazi Horst Wessel anthem. Was it all coming from other people's open windows? Or were people no longer obeying the British curfew that forbade them going out on the streets after midnight?

He stroked Anna's shoulder softly. What would happen when his son came back from the POW camp in Russia? Or when another Veckinhausen family member from the east turned up? When things got back to what used to be normal? When they might once again have clean apartments to live in? When they would have cold berry soup again? Maybe this small moment of happiness was as good as it would ever get, the one moment in all the chaos when something that ought to be impossible was possible, and that at any time could be blown away?

Just be happy you're still alive, he told himself. Be happy Anna is lying next to you, and that Karl came through the war alive. Just be happy.

He kept staring out of the window, remembering the nightmares he used to have, in which he saw his wife Margarethe burning to death, horribly. He would wake up, soaked in sweat, sometimes screaming aloud. He had never told Anna about them, and didn't want to scare her by letting something like that happen again. Instead he forced himself to lie there with eyes wide open, listening to the sounds of the night until the ruins outside began to reflect the first grey light of dawn.

Home and Work

Saturday, 31 May 1947

They took breakfast together on the balcony. It all seemed incredibly normal, even if the coffee was bitter and made from chicory and they had just watery Quark yoghurt to spread on their bread.

'You look tired,' Anna said considerately.

'My face always looks like a rumpled overcoat first thing in the morning,' Stave replied off-handedly. 'That's not going to change until we get real coffee again.'

'I've heard they're going to increase our food rations.'

'Just rumours.'

'It's been two years since the war ended. I've got myself an apartment. Out of a Nissen hut and into a basement. Another two years and maybe I'll have an allotment garden shed!'

'Maybe you'll have your country estate back,' Stave ventured, immediately biting his tongue for being so nosy about her past.

Anna just looked out over the city. She's so pretty, Stave thought to himself. I just wish she'd turn and look back at me.

In the end she did, but there was no longer a smile on her face. 'The Russians are there now, and they're there to stay. They'll never let me go back. And even if they did, there's nothing left.'

Stave felt as if a huge weight had fallen from his shoulders, though he cursed himself for the fact that he was relieved to hear of all his lover had lost. But then he could not help thinking, 'nothing left' meant also 'nobody left'.

'Making a home on the Elbe isn't that bad.'

'"Home" to me sounds like something that's gone forever, like real coffee.' She smiled now. 'I don't want to go back anyway,' she said. 'I ended up in Hamburg by chance. For months I thought of nothing but just staying alive. Now I'm beginning once more to make plans for the future.'

'Do I figure in those plans?'

She kissed him. 'It's because of you I'm making plans again. But we need time to ...' he could see her looking for the right word, 'to open up to one another. And time is the one thing that, happily, nobody can bomb to nothing.'

It was almost midday by the time they finally had to come in from the balcony because of the heat.

'Do you have to work?' Stave asked.

'Don't worry. I give up being a rubble looter at weekends. Too many people strolling about. Somebody might call the police. Early mornings are better, and evenings best of all, just before the curfew cuts in. I'm going down to Hansaplatz to get some wood glue. There's a picture frame I need to repair. Then later I have a meeting with a gentleman from the British occupation administration who wants an antique brooch as a present for his wife.'

'And you have a meeting with me.'

'This evening outside the Kammerspiele theatre.' She kissed him before opening the door.

He watched her go. A wave of the hand, a blown kiss, but no exchange out in the stairwell where there might be a neighbour spending the day hanging about listening to folk. The way it used to be.

Stave stood in his kitchen, supping the remains of the Quark with a spoon. It was watery and tasteless. He had lost his appetite. But if he just left it, it would be gone off before the evening in this heat. And he wouldn't be back in the apartment until then; he had work to do.

Public Prosecutor Dr Albert Ehrlich was in his office seven days a week, at least when he wasn't dealing with an accused in court. He was a brilliant lawyer but had been thrown out of public service by the Brownshirts back in 1933 because he was Jewish. In the wake of the Reichskristallnacht pogrom he was sent to a concentration camp for a while until he managed to get hold of a visa for England. His wife on the other hand wasn't Jewish and couldn't leave: instead she took her own life in 1941, in despair at how she was treated for having a Jew as a husband. Ehrlich had come back home with the British Army of Occupation, and now spent every waking moment hunting down Nazis.

The chief inspector threw an old linen jacket that Margarethe had given him in the last summer before the war over his arm, put on a matching hat and went out into the blistering sunshine. He had left his service revolver hanging on a peg in his wardrobe, even though he had stuff to do today. He hoped it wouldn't require a weapon.

It took him an hour to walk to the impressive old building that housed the public prosecutor's office. He was sweating and thirsty. The door was opened by a bored, sleepy porter who'd been flicking through an old issue of *Die Welt*. The corridors were empty and quiet, save for the rattling of a typewriter. Stave smiled and pushed open the door of Ehrlich's office.

'Are you trying to put your secretary out of work, Dr Ehrlich? Have a bit of sympathy: there aren't many jobs out there.'

Ehrlich – late forties, small with big eyes behind dark horn-rimmed spectacles, with beads of sweat on his bald head – stopped and glanced up from his heavy Olympia typewriter.

'I didn't hear you coming in.'

'I could have driven past in a Sherman tank and you wouldn't have heard me. That thing is noisier than a machine gun.'

'No, it's not, believe me. I was a volunteer in the First World War, a machine gunner on the western front.' He sat up straight. 'It was only later that my eyes went on me: the result of reading too many legal texts.'

'It takes a public prosecutor to say something like that.'

Ehrlich smiled and offered him a glass of water and a chair. Stave sat down on the uncomfortable visitor's chair and found himself staring over the brim of his water glass at two skeletons dancing through a forest. Taken aback, he commented, 'That's new.'

'You may not have seen it before, but it's not new. It's twenty-three years old, a lithograph of a work by Ernst Barlach, from his "Dance of the Dead" series. It's Expressionist. From my old private collection,' Ehrlich explained in a low voice. 'I confiscated it from a former top Gestapo official. He had it hanging in his interrogation room. I think he intended it as a bad joke. A Gestapo man who liked "unworthy art" – funny thing, taste.'

'What happened to the rest of your collection?'

'Still missing. For now. But I'm working on it.' He waved a hand as if none of it really mattered. 'Is this about the dead boy? I've already authorised the autopsy. It would seem you get all the really nasty cases.'

'Somebody has to.'

'You're not the only one.' The public prosecutor leaned back in his chair. 'Go ahead, I'm all ears.'

'You got my first report. There's not much more.' The chief inspector briefly went over what he knew about the case, telling him in detail about his visit to Greta Boesel and her fiancé.

'I doubt very much if there's ever been any allegations about Frau Boesel,' the prosecutor said dismissively. 'Nor against her chum, even if his business is – how shall I put it – somewhat tasteless. Do you suspect the pair of them?'

Stave raised his hands. 'For now they're simply the boy's next of kin, and I went there to inform them. I've got no witnesses and certainly no suspects. The only thing that can be said is that Greta Boesel's transport business involves occasional trips down to the docks. And the fact that that is where the boy was murdered.'

'Yes, but in the shipyard, whereas you would expect a woman in the transport business to be down at the docks where the ships load and unload their cargo.'

'Well, that's where the links in my chain come to an end.'

'It's a pretty fragile chain. Are there no other suspects?'

'Unless we've got it all wrong, Adolf Winkelmann hardly spent any time at home. He wandered the streets. But where and with whom, I have no idea. But that'll change. We have to find out where he got hold of so many cigarettes. Did he steal them? Was it payment for some work he did? Did he get them in a swap for something else? He certainly didn't get them as a present from his aunt. She was far too surprised at seeing three packets of Lucky Strike in Adolf's box.'

'It sounds to me like an all too familiar tragic story of an orphan kid dealing on the black market. If it weren't for the fact that the scene of crime had to be Blohm & Voss of all places ... that's what's making our British friends so jumpy.'

Stave stared at the prosecutor's friendly face, damp with sweat, at his owl-like eyes, his gleaming bald pate. He looked so harmless. But somehow or other, Ehrlich already clearly knew about MacDonald's supposedly secret role in the investigation. Should he mention it outright? Or would that make him a loudmouth?

'I've already had experience of jumpy British,' he said. 'The only thing that calms them down is results.'

'So what will you do?'

'I'm going on a day trip out into the country. There's an orphanage called Home and Work on the southern side of the Elbe. The police take any orphan boys they find there. Girls are taken to a home in Feuerbergstrasse in Barmbek.'

'That's a long way apart.'

'Most of them run away after a few days. But as a few more get delivered on a daily basis there are always some there. I'm hoping one of them will know something about Adolf Winkelmann.'

Stave pushed himself to his feet. He had his hand on the door knob ready to leave when he nodded at the typewriter and said, 'So what's so important that you need to spend a sunny Saturday afternoon in the office?'

'There's a trial coming up with eighteen people in the dock. That takes some preparations.'

'Eighteen at once? Black marketeers or Nazis?'

Ehrlich gave a humourless laugh: 'Nazis. In March 1944 fifty English soldiers escaped from a POW camp, called Stalag Luft III near Sagan in Silesia. They were all rounded up, taken into the forest and shot.'

'Executing prisoners of war? Sounds like eighteen death sentences to me.'

The public prosecutor shook his head. 'That's what I thought too, but have you ever heard of a Dr Anna Marie Oehlert?'

Stave shook his head. 'A doctor of medicine.'

'I wish. She's a doctor of law, and one of just fifteen female advocates in Hamburg. She's young, slim, tall, dark eyes, long brown hair, clever, bewitching and unfortunately a lioness when it comes to fighting for her clients, and most unfortunately of all, she's representing two of the accused, number seventeen and eighteen. Seventeen is the man who drove the SS soldiers who committed the murder in 1944 into the forest. I can understand her defence in that instance maybe: the man was a driver, an accomplice – jail rather than the gallows. But number eighteen is one of those who was primarily responsible. How can an attractive and intelligent woman defend someone guilty of some fifty murders?'

'Beauty is a law unto itself,' said Stave, and nodded in farewell.

As he was walking down the long quiet corridors, he thought over Ehrlich's description: young, slim, tall, dark eyes, long brown hair, clever, bewitching. It sounded a bit like the public prosecutor might have fallen in love with the honourable counsel for the defence. And why not? After all, Ehrlich had been a widower for six years now. And given that he'd gone into exile in England in 1939 it was eight years now since he'd last held his wife in his arms. Even the greatest of loves fades with time. And there are odder places for love to blossom than a Hamburg courthouse.

It was only a short stroll to the CID head office. Stave had the floor to himself but even so closed the door of his muggy office. He could think better with the door closed. He took out his notebook and pencil and reached for the phone. Only a few people in Hamburg had a private line these days. One of them just happened to be his colleague in charge of Department S, responsible for policing the black market, who lived in the undamaged house that had belonged to his recently deceased parents who had got a telephone put in back in the thirties.

His bad luck, Stave thought to himself as the dialled. A few minutes later he had his colleague on the line. He sounded as if he'd just woken up from an afternoon nap.

'Has Greta Boesel ever been brought up for anything?'

'No.' He answered without the slightest hesitation. He might have been having a nap and in a bad mood but his memory for names was legendary. 'Never caught her trying to buy something on the black market. She's neither a racketeer nor a smuggler.'

'What about Walter Kümmel?'

'The boxer boy? He hardly needs to buy stuff on the black market. He earns more than enough. Why the questions about those two?'

'Enjoy the rest of the weekend,' Stave replied and put down the receiver.

Then he lifted it up again. He had just had another thought. Mac-Donald. Not even every British officer had a phone of their own, but one who worked for the secret service as well definitely did. He listened to the rustling, whispering noises on the line, feeling like some researcher listening into the ether, hearing ghosts, the voices of the dead, humming in the phone wires.

Get a grip, he told himself, and was about to put the phone down when he heard MacDonald's voice.

'It's me,' said Stave.

'Hello, old boy. Want a word with your secretary? Need to give Erna some dictation?'

Stave knew she spent most of her time with her lover. But he was still so surprised at MacDonald's nonchalance that for a moment he was lost for words.

'No, I've nothing to dictate. Not at the moment at least. I'm just looking for a bit of information before I head out on a trip to try to fill in a few gaps in my knowledge. Did you ask around among your colleagues? Does Boesel have any history with the Brits? Or her fiancé for that matter?'

'That's a gap in your knowledge I could have dealt with on Monday. The bloke, nothing. But Greta Boesel was stopped at a roadblock in Lower Saxony once. She was driving the truck herself. It was just routine. The MPs checked her documents. There was nothing wrong with them. Nor with her load either. She has a commercial licence. Clean. Neither of them have ever been caught out after curfew either, nor have they been up in front of one of our magistrates.' He paused for a second, then said, 'Where are you headed for on this trip of yours?'

'An orphanage south of Hamburg. An hour's drive away at least. Maybe one of the boys there will turn out to have known our victim. It's a bit of a long shot. Want to come along?'

Stave smiled to himself. You're a hunter, my friend, he thought. You're nosy, but on the other hand it's a Saturday and you're probably in bed with your lover.

'You can tell me all about it on Monday.' MacDonald finally replied. 'Have a nice trip.'

Stave hung up, not sure whether he was annoyed at being rebuffed, or pleased that he would be able to carry out the investigation the way he preferred: on his own.

He picked up an old Mercedes from the car pool, opened the petrol cap, sniffed, then tried to shine a torch in. The police mechanic who'd been watching him came over.

'Are you going far, Chief Inspector? Have you got clearance from the Tommies?'

'I don't need it,' Stave said. Journeys by Germans of more than 80 kilometres required permission from the Occupation Authorities. He reckoned it was about 50 kilometres to the orphanage, as long as the main roads were passable again as far as the other side of the Elbe. He did need to keep an official log of his journey, though; every German did. He entered his name, the date, time and purpose of the journey.

'Do you reckon I've enough fuel?' he asked the mechanic without turning to look at him.

'There's enough in there for about 100 kilometres.'

'In that case it'll be empty when I bring it back this evening.'

'The chief needs the car first thing in the morning. He won't exactly be pleased. We won't get any more fuel delivered until Monday at the earliest. An American tanker hit a mine in the North Sea, but I heard another one had arrived in port. Maybe there'll be more than usual on board. But that's not much help on a Sunday morning.'

'Cuddel Breuer has more than his fair share of sources in this city. That includes fuel sources. He'll know somewhere he can fill up.'

'He's still not going to be happy. He'll look in the log book to see who's taken it out and he'll see your name.'

'He already knows it.'

Stave roared out of the garage leaving the mechanic in a cloud of blue exhaust smoke. He rolled down the windows of the big old car and let the refreshing breeze wash over him.

In the centre of town all the roads had been cleared of rubble, tank treads and wrecked car. There were lots of pedestrians out for a stroll, as well as a few cyclists, some of whom had got their hands on bicycle tyres again, while others just rode along on the rims. A British Jeep passed him and the driver gave him a suspicious look but didn't pull him over. In theory Germans were not allowed to drive between 6.00 p.m. Saturday and 6.00 a.m. Monday, because fuel stocks were so low. But there were exceptions for doctors on call and for police. The Brit must have recognised the old Mercedes, Stave thought to himself. After all, there weren't that many of them on the road.

The car rattled over the Rathaus Platz, passed the empty plinth where a statue of the poet Heinrich Heine had stood. The Nazis had melted it down. He'd been Jewish. He negotiated his way carefully through the warren of streets beyond the city hall. In the old days he could have driven around Hamburg with his eyes closed, but these days he had to tack this way and that. Every so often a street he would have liked to take was blocked by the collapsed façade of a building, while others might be buried under a mountain of bricks, and then there were some that were clear but the heat of the Blitz had been so intense that the tarmac had melted, swollen up and then cooled down into a solid greyish black soup of strange bumps and ridges that the old car's steering couldn't cope with.

Nonetheless he found his way as far as the bridges over the Elbe, turned on to Bremen Chaussee and then a bit later, turned left again. He passed the 'Undaunted' barracks, which had been a base for the German army, then the British army and was now Hamburg's dumping ground for the hopeless: the place where doctors and police brought the terminally ill and the permanently bed-bound, to make space in the few hospitals that were still in one piece for those there was at least a hope of curing.

Finally he was clear of the heaps of rubble and the stink of dirt and smoke from the steamers in the harbour. He was among fields where the wheat was already half-grown and shone yellow in the sunlight. There were a few fruit trees, copses of woodland, poppies by the side of the narrow cobbled country roads, as red as drops of blood on a skirt. There were blue flowering thistles, and a smell of dusty dry earth. Stave put his foot down and felt like singing out loud, except that he would have been embarrassed to do so.

Eventually he had to make a U-turn after taking a wrong turn on a street with no signposts, so it was late afternoon before he reached Sodersdorf. There wasn't a lot to it: a tiny station, a junk shop, so locked up he couldn't tell if it was just closed for now or closed down forever, cobbled streets, a narrow bridge over the River Luhe which ran through the centre of the hamlet. Apart from that there were about a dozen farmhouses, undamaged, shimmering red in the setting sun, a couple of dogs that ran barking behind the growling Mercedes, until eventually they gave in and stood there panting with their tongues hanging out. In a field three cows were lying on the grass chewing the cud, along with an old, shaggy brown horse. Stave brought the Mercedes to a halt and sat there staring at them. When had he last seen live animals? Even most dogs had ended up in the cooking pot during that last winter of starvation.

There was nobody on the street, nobody in the shade of the trees, not a cyclist in sight. But curtains twitched behind windows; Stave had the feeling he was being watched.

He steered the heavy old Mercedes carefully over the bridge. The water was nothing more than a dirty trickle, the meadow on the other side dried up and yellow. At the crossroads there was a wooden signpost with the sort of arrow-shaped board that engineer units in every army in the world put up: '*Heim und Werk*' it said: home and work, and pointed to a rutted street that led up a hill. In the distance Stave could see some huts near a little wood. It looked a bit like an old army barracks.

He turned out to be right. As he drove up the hill he passed an old gatehouse with a barrier, and though it was raised he could make out a few numbers scrawled on the wall and a few words in English. The Tommies must have been here.

The chief inspector parked on a patch of roughly raked gravel outside one of the barracks. Before he could even get out of the car, a door opened and a man appeared, mid-sixties, a round face, broad-shouldered, grey-haired, grey-faced.

'You bringing me another boy?'

Nice way to say hello, Stave thought to himself as he closed the car door. The man had recognised him as police straight away.

He introduced himself and showed the man his ID.

'Gustav Bartsch,' the man said in return, shaking his hand, gripping it hard. 'I'm in charge of the hostel. If you've haven't come to bring me a boy, are you here to take one away? One of them done something wrong?'

'Any of them not done something wrong?' Stave retorted with a smile. 'I'm just looking for some information.' He gave the man a brief outline of the case.

The man led him into the barracks, into a sparsely furnished office with just a few pale violet flowers in a jam jar to give it a hint of colour. The heat was oppressive despite the windows being wide open.

'Typical army barracks,' Bartsch said. 'Come in here in summer and you wish it was winter, in winter you freeze and dream of the summer. That's one of the reasons the lads who end up here don't stick it for long, not the main one though.'

'How many are here at the moment?'

'Exactly two dozen. At least that's how many turned up for morning roll call today. A few of them may have done a runner since then.' He shrugged and held up his hands: fat fingers, hard with callouses. 'I'm a master locksmith not a prison guard. Used to be at the Phoenix Works in Hamburg, until the autumn of '45. Then I retired.'

Bartsch gave a bitter laugh. 'If that little Austrian corporal had won his war, I suppose I'd be getting more money. But I'm an old Leftie. I was in the Social Democratic Party until 1933, and I rejoined in 1945. Things could have been worse for me, a lot worse.' He shook his head silently. 'The English asked me if I'd take charge of this place. I agreed because in the first place I needed the money, but also because it means I get the chance to help a few lads out; I've no children of my own, but I used to give a few lessons to the apprentices at work. I enjoy it.'

'But a lot of them run away.'

'I don't really understand why in one way, but then again, in another I do.'

Stave gave him a quizzical look.

'You should see these kids when they're brought here, Chief Inspector. They're starving, lice-ridden, filthy, stinking clothes, often no shoes or underwear, with scratches and scrapes, sometimes even festering wounds. And you wouldn't believe the language they've got used to speaking, straight from a public house, or worse. Here they get cleaned up and get something to eat. Most of them get extra rations to build them up. Some of them can only manage soup at first, they're so starved they can't keep anything solid down. We give them new clothing, stuff made out of dyed old army kit. As soon as they get a bit of steam up, so to speak, we send them off to work, usually with the farmers out in the fields, sometimes to chop wood in the forest. Honest jobs with honest wages, fresh air, decent food, no rubble all around – that's the bit I don't understand: why abandon all that to go back to a city where you starved and got covered in lice.'

'Why indeed?'

Bartsch lifted one of his hands as if he were about to slam it down on the metal table, but instead lowered it to the surface with a remarkable air of calm. 'They aren't children any more. Legally they are, or else they wouldn't get brought here: they're underage and have no parent or guardian. But in reality all the lads who end up here all worked either in the anti-aircraft batteries, or got sent as fighters to the Russian front, and ended up as refugees, thieves, black marketeers, fences for stolen goods. They've been through too much to be children the way we were. Why should a seventeen-year-old whose education was learning how to fire a *Panzerfaust* grenade at a tank, who made his money by dealing cigarettes on the black market, suddenly develop a love for chopping wood in the forest? Why should some kid who's spent years living in bunkers and whose main source of nourishment has been moonshine liquor and Senior Service cigarettes, decide to spend his days dozing peacefully in a barracks on the banks of the Luhe? Most of them clear off as soon as they get back on their feet.'

'And you don't stop them?'

'There's only me here, and I'm just pleased if none of them puts a bullet through my skull. In any case there are no fences here, no locked doors. I talk to the lads and try to convince them to try another way of life. Sometimes it works. A couple of them have found decent jobs down at the port, three of them have even taken to going to school. One of them married a girl from the village and now looks after his father-in-law's farm. If you saw him today, you'd never believe that just two years ago he was taking out T-34 tanks. That's what I work to achieve. Things like that are little victories, but mostly it just ends in defeat.' He shrugged his shoulders.

'I need to talk to the boys. One at a time.'

Bartsch nodded and thought for a moment. 'A real defeat for me is when one really goes off the rails,' he said at last. 'I don't recall ever having an Adolf Winkelmann here but I know that the life out on the streets is dangerous for these kids. I hope you catch whoever killed him. But I don't want to create problems. If I call the lads together and tell them a man from the CID is here and wants to talk to them, they'll be out the door before you can count to three.'

'So what do you suggest?'

'I'll go down to the woods and bring one of the boys back. You can ask him your questions while I go back and fetch one of the others. The first one will stay here while you question the second so he can't go back and warn the rest. That way we'll end up with all of them here, and hopefully none will run off.'

Stave smiled. 'As you like.'

'Consider my office your police station,' Bartsch said, nodding as he left.

A few minutes later the hostel manager came back with a skinny lad with short brown hair, a gaunt face but suntanned skin, wearing khaki shorts, a collarless shirt and sandals.

Bartsch introduced him as 'Friedel Bertram, fifteen years old, been with us two weeks now'. He sounded proud as if merely having the lad still there after two weeks was something of an achievement.

'You from the cops?' Friedel burst out as soon as Bartsch had closed the door and left them alone.

'CID, Chief Inspector Stave.' He nodded towards a chair.

'I'm clean,' the boy replied, ignoring the gesture.

Stave looked at the boy's skinny legs. There were strange scars on his legs as if from shrapnel or shotgun pellets, barely healed.

Friedel noticed his look and blushed. 'I had a rash,' he stammered.

'All over but it was worse on my legs. The doctor gave me cream for it and now it's mostly gone but he said I'd be left with scars on my legs.'

'Girls have a thing for boys with scars,' Stave said, though it hardly sounded convincing. 'I'm not here for you. I'm hoping one of you will be able to give me some information that could help me with a case. A murder case.'

'Wow!' said Friedel, and sat down after all, obviously interested.

I wouldn't mind knowing what he's been up to, thought Stave to himself, given how obviously relieved he is. Then he told him everything worth telling about the murder of Adolf Winkelmann.

'I know Adolf,' the boy said. 'Knew him, I mean,' before quickly adding: 'Not well though.'

'From school?'

Friedel burst out laughing so loudly Stave was quite taken aback. 'Nobody's taking me back to school.'

'From where then?'

Friedel hesitated a minute.

'It's better if you tell me the truth.'

'The black market,' the boy blurted out. 'On the Hansaplatz. I keep a lookout. Used to, I mean. I'm clean these days.'

'Of course you are.'

'Adolf turned up there once or twice. He wasn't a professional, or at least didn't act like one when he was at Hansaplatz.'

'Was he dealing in cigarettes?'

Friedel shook his head. 'He was an amateur. One of those who turn up from time to time with something or other to flog.'

'But you remember him.'

'I do, because I remember what it was he would flog – boxing tickets,' he said with a broad smile.

'Boxing match tickets?'

'If it hadn't been for Adolf, I'd never have seen Hein ten Hoff's last fight without climbing up some tree to try to see into the HSV Stadium. He got me in. Front row seat even. At least until one of the security staff spotted me.'

'Adolf Winkelmann was selling tickets for fights on the black market?' Stave could hardly believe it. Buying and selling boxing tickets was legal, so why go to the effort of selling them on the black market and risk being caught up in a police raid and put up in front of a judge in one of the British summary trials.'

'Adolf had a stepfather or something, who organised the fights. He stole a few tickets from him, exchanged them on the black market for cigarettes. Way too cheap. A real amateur.'

'How do you know this?'

'When he turned up at the Hansaplatz the second time I bought the ten Hoff tickets off him. I told them he was selling them too cheap and he ought to watch out for cop snitches. No offence meant, Kommissar.'

'It's Chief Inspector, actually. So he told you all about himself.'

'Just what I've just told you. I didn't even know where he lived.'

'Anything else?'

'When I was telling him to look out for the spies and snitches, he started to get really worried. He said his stepfather would go mad if he found out he'd been stealing from him. He'd have beaten him. He's have to be careful.'

'And was he?'

Friedel shrugged.

'We agreed he should turn up again. If he had tickets to sell. Or even just so. I showed him a few tricks of the trade.' Then the boy realised what he had said and went red.

'I'm deaf in that ear,' said Stave. 'I won't pass anything on to my colleagues who work on the Hansaplatz.'

Friedel smiled. 'Cigarettes were our business. Adolf really went for those Yankee ciggies. But I never saw him again.'

'When did he sell you the tickets?'

The boy thought to himself, counting off the days on his fingers. 'Must have been about four weeks ago when I last spoke to him. March or April: just when it had begun to get a bit warmer.'

Could that have any connection to the murder, Stave wondered.

But that would have been at least a month beforehand. 'You've been very helpful,' he said. 'And remember to let the village girls see your scars.'

Gustav Bartsch brought a line of boys up to the barracks until the sun outside began to change from bright yellow to a gentle pink. Stave was sweating. He could have done with a glass of water, but couldn't find any.

The conversations that followed Friedel's were brief. The oldest boy was seventeen, the youngest just twelve, skinny, suntanned, in clothes far too big for them, some of them with horrendous scars, probably war wounds, or shrapnel from the bombing, or maybe just fights on the black market. Did my son look like that at their age, Stave wondered? Maybe he still does.

None of them had seen or heard anything from Adolf Winkelmann – at most they had heard the name – or at least that's what they said. The chief inspector had the impression one or two of them might have been lying. None of them liked talking to a policeman. He decided not to go too hard on any of them. He'd get the information he needed sooner or later if he didn't hassle them too much.

Eventually Bartsch opened the door again and said, 'Your last customer is here.'

Stave looked down at his notebook. 'This is number 16. You told me there were two dozen.'

Bartsch shrugged. 'Done a runner, I suspect. There's nobody else down in the forest. It's Saturday, lots of them go missing at the weekend.'

'I suppose there's fewer police and fewer Tommies out on the roads.'

'Indeed, they've got a better chance of getting back to Hamburg.'

'Show the lad in.'

Arne Thodden, sixteen. He was so thin his shoulders and the bones of his legs were visible through his skin, almost as if he were reduced to a skeleton. He was wearing an old shirt, torn workmen's trousers and homemade wooden clogs. His face was gaunt, wan, his eyes sunken and red below hair shaved almost to the skull. He'll have been lice-ridden, the chief inspector thought. The boy's head looked like a dead man's skull. He told him what he needed to know about the murder.

'Did you know Adolf Winkelmann?'

'Got any cigarettes?'

'Why, because your hands are shaking?'

'I don't smoke. I just want to be paid.'

'Don't you do anything without being paid?'

'I'm a businessman.'

'Dealing in cigarettes?'

'Cigarettes are money. Better than those Reichsmarks rubbish if you ask me. I do good business.'

Stave leant back in his chair. Was this kid making fun of him? The skeletal face looked back at him, expressionless, unless there was a hint of irony in those eyes. Stave looked at the hands of the boy facing him. They seemed unnaturally big for the rest of his body, with calluses and torn fingernails. To hell with it, he thought, I need to get out of this sweathole. Let's get it over with. He put his hand in his pocket and conjured up a single John Player's.

Arne Thodden made a grab for it, but the chief inspector pulled the cigarette back.

'Cash on delivery,' he said.

'OK,' the boy said, with a thin smile. 'I would see Adolf on the Damm tracks from time to time.'

'Damm tracks?'

'The railway lines down by Dammtor Station,' Arne explained with a bored sigh. 'We'd go down there to take coal from the freight cars.'

A coal thief, Stave realised. The kids who would climb on to the open freight cars and unload coal in bags to take away and sell. He looked back at the boy's hands. No wonder you've got those big paws, he thought.

'Was Adolf Winkelmann a coal thief?' he asked out loud. It would fit: he could hardly sell boxing tickets all the time.

Arne shook his head. 'Not usually. Just every now and again, but he did it more for a laugh. I didn't know him very well. He didn't fit in ...' he searched for the right words, '... with my business partners,' he finally managed to say, with a broad grin. 'Adolf had other friends. The wrong sort.'

'Such as who?' For the first time, Stave felt he might be on to something important.

'Wolf children.'

Wolf children was what people called the boys and girls from the east. Orphans who had lost their parents in the fighting in Silesia and East Prussia or afterwards on the flight westwards. Fathers shot, mothers raped to death, houses burnt down. Children who survived in the woods and on the moors, like wild animals, begging, stealing, eating whatever they could get hold of. Many of them didn't even know their own names. They would make a home in burnt-out barns or the ruins of houses, and somehow or other managed to reach the western occupation zones. There were supposed to be a few hundred of them living in the ruins of Hamburg.

'What did someone like Adolf Winkelmann have to do with wolf children?'

A shrug. 'The wolf children set up gangs. You steer clear of them if you know what's good for you. But somehow or other Adolf got into one of the gangs. Maybe he had a girl rather than a widow.'

'A widow?'

Another weary sigh. 'You're supposed to be in the CID. You must see widows all the time, given the number of dead we've had.'

Stave had to suppress a wave of anger. 'We're not in German lessons here, you don't have to explain the meaning of the word to me.'

Arne raised his hands apologetically. 'Widows around here are like sand on the seaside. Young ones and some not so young ones. Pretty ones and some not so pretty ones. Ones you would and ones you wouldn't. You can take your pick.' He gave a short cruel laugh. 'Their men are either buried under the earth somewhere or squatting on the ground in one of Ivan's camps freezing off their wedding tackle. The women are very grateful if somebody's a bit kind to them, gives them a cigarette or a sack of potatoes.'

'Or a sack of coal.'

'If you have coal, you're the king of the widows. There's always one willing to share her bed for the night. Makes it harder for your colleagues to get their hands on the likes of us. And it's pleasant too.' He gave the same mirthless laugh. 'You just have to watch out in case Ivan's let the hubby out and he turns up at the door.'

'My colleagues got their hands on you.'

'I was a bit careless down at the Damm tracks. Just bad luck.'

'So why haven't you done a runner, back to your widow?'

Arne shook his head, in earnest. 'I was threatened with being taken before one of those English kangaroo courts. It was better to be sent here. Keep my head down until the air clears, know what I mean? A couple more days and the Tommies will have forgotten all about me. You were lucky to find me here, Chief Inspector.'

'What's the name of the wolf children Adolf Winkelmann was hanging around with?'

Arne laughed. 'They don't even know their own names.'

'Where do they live?'

'Somewhere in the rubble. Like I said, I preferred to have nothing to do with them.'

'When did you last see Adolf Winkelmann?'

'I've been here for six days. Before that I saw him down by the Damm tracks, but not on the day your lot picked me up. So the last time I saw him was maybe ten or eleven days ago.'

'Did anything about him strike you? Was he different in any way?'

Arne thought for a minute, then shook his head.

'OK, you can go.'

'What about my cigarette?'

Stave pushed the John Player's across the table to him and watched the boy get to his feet, his knees and elbows swollen. Probably got water in them, Stave thought. He wondered if Arne Thodden would ever get better. What would he be doing in ten years' time? He'd probably end up as one of their 'regular customers', he told himself. Then he had an idea.

'Have you ever been down at the Blohm & Voss shipyard?' he called out as the boy reached the doorway.

'That'd be another Player's.'

Stave threw a cigarette to him impatiently.

'No, never,' Arne said with a laugh. 'Now I've done better business than you, Chief Inspector.

On the way back Stave drove slowly along the country roads. He needed to think. And he also wanted to save fuel. From time to time he listened to the noises coming from the engine. A breakdown was the last thing he needed: to be stuck somewhere south of the Elbe with the car the boss needed – and he had arranged to see Anna that evening.

Just before he reached the Elbe, he ran into a British roadblock. A sweaty, bad-tempered sergeant waved him over. Stave handed him his police ID card and watched the man study it carefully. Stave was in a hurry, but he was wise enough not to let the man notice. It would not be nice if the sergeant ordered him out of the car as he and the two soldiers searched it. Eventually he was let go, and drove on down the street alone, alone with his thoughts.

Wolf children. The chief inspector had heard of them, but rarely ever seen one, never interrogated one. Could it be true that Adolf Winkelmann had a girlfriend among them? Or that he was doing business with them? What sort of business? Stave could hardly imagine wolf children being very interested in tickets for boxing matches. But then maybe there were other goods: stolen from his aunt or her 'fiancé'. Or maybe coal. It seemed the late victim had had a wide range of business interests. Time to go wolf hunting, Stave told himself. But what could these orphans or coal stealers have had to do with Blohm & Voss, that was what he couldn't imagine. He was being nagged by the uncomfortable feeling that there was something he had overlooked.

Eventually he made it to the police garage and delivered the Mercedes back to the mechanic. The man knocked on the tank and clicked his tongue: 'I'm glad I'm not on the early shift tomorrow when the boss gets in.'

Stave glanced at his watch. He had no time to go back to his apartment to change before heading to the Kammerspiele theatre. But if he went straight there he would be early. So he walked upstairs to his office. There was nobody in the corridors or in the anteroom. He flopped down on the seat, then glanced in annoyance at something lying on his desk.

Then he saw it was a letter from the Red Cross.

He stared at it long and hard. Swiss postage stamp. The address typed out: Frank Stave, Ahrensburger Strasse 91, Hamburg, British Occupation Zone, Germany. Number 91 – his old address, bombed out. A postal mistake. Stave sat there, still staring at the envelope without touching it. Lots of stamp marks all over it. It had gone back to Switzerland, then come back to Hamburg. Somebody somewhere had at some time put a line through the address in pencil and then, in a barely legible scribble, had written the address of the CID headquarters. How long ago had the letter been sent? He bent down over the envelope and made out the first date stamp: some four weeks ago.

Eventually he touched it carefully, stroked it with his fingers. Then he took a deep breath and ripped it open, snatching out the sheet of paper inside. He closed his eyes, then opened them and read: 'Dear Herr Stave, this is to inform you that …' It wasn't a death report.

He moved closer to the window, into the last rays of sunshine, with the letter in hands that were no longer shaking. Just a few lines in official bureaucratic German. Stave had to read them twice before he could cope with their meaning; Karl was being released.

All of a sudden the office was too small for him. He leapt to his feet, ran through the anteroom out into the hallway and began walking up and down, for once ignoring his limp.

Karl was being released.

Joy, confusion, excitement. Happiness at the thought he might soon see his son again. Worry about his state of health. Would he recognise him again? All at once the chief inspector worried that he wouldn't, and hoped that he would. Before his son had signed up as a volunteer in 1945, he had denigrated his father as 'un-German'. He was a through-and-through Nazi by the age of just seventeen. Would he now be as cynical and brutalised as the boys in the home? Would he be as starved and sickly?

So many thoughts were flowing through Stave's brain that it took more than a few minutes for him to realise the importance of one simple thing: the letter was already four weeks old.

He scanned the last few lines again: 'In approximately one month your son will be delivered to a reception and release centre in the Soviet Occupation Zone, from which he will be sent back to his home.' One month! Stave suddenly had a vision of Karl standing outside the locked door of his apartment at this very minute. That was if Karl even knew where he lived. After the night of bombing in which his wife Margarethe had been killed, Karl had been taken in by a colleague in the Hitler Youth. Then he had signed up as a volunteer. Clearly nobody in the Red Cross had known that, not that that meant anything. They were hardly going to go around Siberia asking every POW about to be released where he lived. They would use the address given in the Wehrmacht records. And up until 1945 Stave had still officially been registered at the old address. Partly because he couldn't bring himself to break what he felt was the last link to Margarethe, partly because he didn't want to know who had lived in his new apartment.

I need to go home, he told himself. Then he remembered: Anna was waiting for him.

Think rationally: Karl was only going to be released in a month's time. Then he would be sent to a reception centre before being set on his way home. It was going to be five weeks at least. Maybe six weeks, seven, eight before he got back here. The letter was four weeks old at most. Don't be stupid. There's no way Karl could be here yet. But soon …

What was he going to tell Anna? Should he tell her anything at all? Stave was afraid Anna would not take it well. He remembered the old saying: 'Don't count your chickens.' Don't go around telling people your son is coming home before he gets here. Anything could happen in his last days in the camp or in his final weeks in Siberia.

The chief inspector carefully folded the letter until it was very small, tucked it into the inside pocket of his summer jacket, carefully closed the door to his office and left the CID headquarters. The doorman was dozing and hardly noticed as Stave went past him and muttered the usual word of greeting.

Stave glanced at his watch; thirty minutes until the performance in the Kammerspiele theatre. He would make it. He hurried past the Planten en Bomen park and turned into Rothenbaum Chaussee, with its villas, many of them requisitioned by the British. Even the road surface here was undamaged, the pavements had been swept. There were people strolling up and down, some of them elegantly dressed, heading in the same direction as him. He passed the HSV Stadium where Walter Kümmel had staged some of his most popular boxing matches. Stave was too excited and emotional even to think about the murder case. Tomorrow would do. Tomorrow he would get back to normal and get things sorted out for his son's return. But what was there to do. He was systematic, he would make a list, little notes of things to do. He had to get everything right. Tomorrow.

Fifteen minutes later he turned into Hartungstrasse, a narrow street, still cobbled, with four- and five-storey buildings from the mid-to-late nineteenth century. A few metres on he spotted the Kammerspiele, with a crowd of people outside, their voices and laughter rising into the pale blue sky, the sound of people anticipating a good time. The Kammerspiele was only a couple of years old, set up in an old cinema with an elegant façade that fitted in well with the grand buildings nearby, even if it was only a mere three storeys high. Stave wondered how Ida Ehre – the founder, manager, star actress and soul of the theatre – had managed to persuade the English to give her permission to open a venue here in the finest, least damaged part of the city. It would have made a grand officers' club.

'May I bring charges?'

Stave flinched involuntarily. Anna was standing behind him, having moved away from the crowd. Stave hadn't seen her, hadn't even been paying attention. He pulled himself together and managed a slight bow.

'Against whom do you wish to bring charges?'

'My lover. Because he's not making advances towards me.'

Stave felt himself blush. In the 'brown years' it had been frowned upon to show affection in public. And after the death of Margarethe it had been years since he had been close to another woman; he enjoyed the feeling of togetherness.

'Consider it done,' he said and kissed her.

Anna took his arm and guided him slowly towards the entrance, where the theatre attendants opened the glass doors to the foyer for them.

'I'm sorry about that, I was lost in thought. And I'm afraid I'm not exactly dressed for the occasion. I feel a bit shabby among all these finely dressed people.'

'You're not embarrassing me,' she said with a laugh, then turned serious and asked: 'Long day at the office?'

Stave just nodded.

'Successful?'

'I've got a few more potential leads,' he said, vaguely. His mind, of course, was not on the murder case but Karl's release, but he didn't want to mention that.

The two of them made their way silently to the cloakroom where they had to queue for minutes on end. Then, without speaking, they found their seats. Still silent they leafed through the programme brochure. Stave couldn't help noticing that every now and again Anna would shoot questioning glances his way. He was glad when the lights went down.

The play was *The Skin of our Teeth*, by Thornton Wilder. Stave could still remember the headline reviews it had had in March: 'Glittering First Night! Modern, Elegance and Drama!' A breath of fresh air from the big, wide world after all the dullness of the 'brown years'. Stave had been very proud to have laid hands on tickets for Anna and himself. Tickets that should have been far too expensive for a CID official.

But now he found himself hardly paying any attention. It wouldn't have mattered to him if they'd been speaking Chinese rather than German. Only the title kept going round and round in his brain – the skin of our teeth – that was how close it had been, for both him and Karl. Karl, Karl, Karl.

Afterwards, he and Anna walked hand-in-hand through the streets, still without saying anything. The chief inspector was aware of the awkward silence and wanted to break it, but he was afraid even to discuss the play, in case he ended up admitting he had hardly been listening. Should he try to talk about something else? But what? He had lost the power of having normal conversation.

'What is the matter with you?' Anna asked.

Stave didn't know how to reply. 'The truth is always the easiest,' that was what he was used to telling suspects he was interrogating. But he was afraid to tell her about Karl's release. He was afraid it might alienate her. He knew too little about her to have any idea how she would react to someone returning from the war and maybe coming between them. 'I'm just tired,' was all he could think of to say. It wasn't a lie.

It took them an hour to reach Altona. Eventually they began to speed up because both of them were by now in a hurry to reach the door of her apartment, to make an end to the evening.

Röperstrasse 6 lay in darkness, with moonlight falling on to the cobbles between the tall, simple apartment buildings. The door leant at a bit of an angle and next to it were pieces of cardboard with the names of the inhabitants of the ten apartments. To the right was the basement window, at street level.

A few hours earlier Stave would have been longing for this moment, the excited meeting of eyes as he and his lover crept into the building. They would have left the lights off, smiled at one another conspiratorially, kissed in the darkness, and then ...

Now he gave Anna a quick kiss on the street, shyly. 'One of these days,' she whispered to him, 'tell me what happened today. You're not yourself.'

Stave nodded, partly sad, partly relieved to be alone. 'You'll find out soon enough. I just have to ...' he searched for the right words, 'sort out a few things. Don't worry.'

She stroked his face gently and said, 'Life would be boring if we had nothing to worry about.'

He waited until he saw the glow of her 15-watt bulb in the cellar window, for maybe a quarter of an hour or so. Then all was dark again.

'Sleep well,' he whispered to the window, turned and started out on his long way home through the city.

The Wolf Child

Stave caught up on the sleep he had missed the night before, and regretted it. He woke up out of a coma-like sleep, but instead of getting up, he had just turned over and nodded off again. That was when the old nightmare came back to haunt him: the flames raging through the burning house, black smoke in the apartment, not the one where he and Margarethe had lived, but in his new home. In the dream his wife was still there with him, but strangely her body wasn't on fire, it was shrinking to nothing until he could no longer see her. He screamed out her name until his lungs were bursting, and then he woke up with a burning in his throat. He probably really had screamed aloud. Good thing Anna hadn't been there.

Anna. It had hardly been the perfect evening the night before. Did she suspect something? He would have to make it up to her – and tell her the truth. At some stage. He had arranged to meet her that very afternoon in a café. They would talk, although he wasn't sure what about.

Stave sprang up, got washed and dressed and swallowed a couple of slices of bread washed down with a glass of water. The water was still only trickling out of the taps because the pressure was so low since the start of the heat wave that was currently plaguing Hamburg. The water that came out was lukewarm, reddish-tinged and tasted metallic. If only I had some coffee, he thought to himself.

Stave turned on the old radio and waited for the valves to warm up. Classical music, the typical comforting sound of a Sunday morning, nothing too exciting, too modern. Mozart, he suspected. He turned the radio as loud as he could without causing the neighbours to complain. He found himself fussing about the room, moving a chair here, straightening something or other. In a little room that he had done out as his son's room, though Karl had never slept there, he made up the bed with the only spare clean sheets he had, and laid a woollen blanket on the end. It was, of course, stiflingly hot, but maybe Karl would be cold after endless months in Siberia?

He looked at the bare walls. Maybe he should hang up some pictures – Karl's childhood drawings, their family photos had been burned. All he had of Margarethe and Karl was their passport photographs, creased, slightly blurred, both of them staring into the camera with the same surprised, suspicious look on their faces. He carried them in his wallet. If the day ever came when film and developing fluid became available again, he would get copies of them made.

Maybe he should ask Anna for one of the pictures she had salvaged out of the ruins. Something pretty, a landscape, or a seascape. But maybe Karl would refuse to have it on the wall when he found out where it had come from. Stave left the room as it was, but didn't close the door. For the first time in years, he left the door open.

But he was still a chief inspector and had an investigation on. He had left the apartment and was already in the stairwell when he stopped, turned around, went back in, found a 1946 calendar in a drawer under the kitchen table, pulled out a blank page and wrote on it: 'Dear Karl, I'm out at work. Please wait for me, Dad.'

It wasn't exactly poetry but he couldn't think of anything better. He found a tack and attached the note to the front door. Then he hesitated again. The neighbours: they would all see it. They would all find out that Stave was expecting his son. Sooner or later someone would accost him in the stairwell with nosy questions: well, is your boy back yet? Not yet? What can he have done for the Ivans to hold him so long? Or maybe he's become a communist?

The chief inspector took the note down and then put it back again, this time with the written-on side to the door. That only meant some busybody had to lift it up and read what was on the other side. But would somebody dare do that? On a CID officer's door? Stave hurried down the stairs and out on to the street before he had any further doubts and took the note down altogether.

Three quarters of an hour later Stave was at the central station, looking around the white steel concourse, tinged grey with smoke from the locomotives. The leaden air tasted bitter from the burning coal. Stave felt dirty. Bright rays of sunlight coming from the broken glass in the roof cut through the air like long knife blades. The whole building echoed with screeching brakes, hissing engine boilers, wheels scraping along the rails, incomprehensible loud-speaker announcements, guards' whistles. It was as if he had been drugged.

He felt like a hunter at the edge of a jungle, staring into the thicket, eyeing out the lie of the land before entering. He checked out the platforms. Platform 4 had a train filling up with the 'potato people', those Hamburg folk who went out to Lüneberg with sacks, boxes or cases to head off into the countryside on foot and hand over their family heirlooms to farmers in exchange for anything edible. The British had ordered that the harvest be turned over to the German food distribution organisation so that it could be released to the public via their ration cards. Every now and then they would raid the station and search everybody coming back from the surrounding countryside. Even so, particularly on Sundays rather than weekdays, hundreds of them would charge down from the upper gallery where Stave was standing to storm the 'potato train'. Housewives, school-children, clerical workers, people who once upon a time would never have dreamed of breaking the law. The old steam locomotive had a train of standing-only coaches behind it, carriages where all the seating had been ripped out to fit more people inside.

The chief inspector turned away. He wasn't going to find who he was looking for among the 'potato people'. A few tracks away there were trains on either side of the platform. Stave read the destinations on the boards: one with just open goods wagons attached was headed to Dortmund via Uelzen. The other, also with pre-war carriages, was headed for Munich. The journey cost seventy Reichsmarks, one-way. There were only a few people waiting, but they were extremely well dressed, smoking and chatting to one another. Where on earth did they get that sort of money? That was the platform Stave wanted.

These were long-distance passengers, people with luggage, money, cigarettes. That's where he would find the strays, the orphans, the drifters, the pickpockets, the black marketeers, the street girls. The chief inspector didn't have a plan, he just hoped to come across a few orphans at the station, wanted to listen to the gossip, ask a few questions, show around the photo of Adolf Winkelmann that Kienle had given him.

He went down to the platform and mingled with the passengers, feeling a bit out of place in his 1938 summer suit, the original white linen of which had taken on a yellowish tint. He stood at the back right next to one of the carriages, half in the shade, for five, maybe ten minutes or so, watching the passers-by. He had time.

He spotted a skinny girl with strawberry-blond hair, woven into a plait, with green eyes, wearing a skirt, white knee socks and a ruched blouse that made her look like a ten-year-old although Stave reckoned she was at least fourteen. She gave off conflicting signals: the girlie eyes, the bright red mouth far too thick with lipstick, like a red light in the darkness. She was a station hooker.

I've seen her somewhere before, the chief inspector thought. Then he remembered. The previous winter she had come on to him in the station, he had given her two cigarettes out of sympathy. She had had a Berlin accent.

Slowly he wandered along in the shadow of the carriages until he was standing near the girl. She was looking as if she was just bored, but in reality she was checking out the people around her. She'd already noticed him. Her feline eyes dwelled on him a second longer than a casual glance would have done. She took in his shabby suit and then turned her eyes away to search out a better bet. But nobody was paying any attention to her.

'On your own? The train won't leave for another hour, at least.'

It was a little girl's voice, but with the same Berlin accent. He hadn't got it wrong.

Stave was standing right next to her now. He shook her hand as if greeting a friend. She gave him a look of irritation, unused to that sort of thing. But Stave didn't let her hand go. Instead he put his other hand into his jacket pocket and pulled out his police ID. She tried to pull her hand away, but Stave held it tight. It was only a little hand.

'Don't try to make a run for it. I only want to ask you a few questions, and nothing to do with the business you're in,' he added to reassure her. 'I'm not from the vice squad.'

'I get it, you're just a nice uncle from the church community.' She kept trying to wrench her right hand out of his grip.

'Murder squad, actually.'

She stopped resisting. Suddenly the girl began shaking. Stave let her go and gave her a handkerchief.

'Wipe that lipstick off,' the chief inspector didn't want to be taken for a punter, standing there asking a young prostitute questions. He nodded to one of the carriages. 'Let's sit in that carriage. If you were telling the truth about the train, then nobody will bother us.'

He let her go first, opened the door of an empty compartment, pushed her over to the window on the other side and sat himself down next to the door. That way she couldn't make a run for it. If they'd stayed standing on the station platform sooner or later she would have noticed his limp and made a dash for it. He felt slightly disappointed that she didn't remember him or the conversation they had had and that he had given her a present in return.

'What's your name?'

'Inge Schmidt.'

'The longer you keep lying to me, the longer we'll keep sitting here.'

'Hildegard Hüllmann.'

'Age?'

She looked him up and down, shrugged and said, 'No point trying to fool you. Fourteen.'

'Date of birth?'

'15 March 1933.'

'Where?'

'Are you from the census office?'

'Where.'

'Köslin.'

'Never heard of it.'

'East Prussia.'

'You have a Berlin accent.'

'Practised it, with a girlfriend. Blokes prefer it. Before I used to get called a "Polak whore" because of my accent, and they refused to pay me. Afterwards.'

'And before this?'

'I've been in Hamburg for a year,' She sighed. 'What is it you want anyway? You can check it all out with the vice squad. I'm sure they've got me on their books.'

Stave took the police photo of Adolf Winkelmann out of his pocket. 'Have you ever seen this boy?'

Hildegard Hüllmann gave him a contemptuous look and took a disinterested glance at the picture, then suddenly put her hand over her mouth.

Stave sprang to his feet and threw open the compartment door.

'It's OK,' she choked out. 'I'm not going to throw up over the upholstery.'

The chief inspector waited until she was breathing normally again.

'Have you got a smoke?' the young prostitute blurted out.

Stave handed her a Player's and lit a match. Her hands were shaking so badly that Stave nearly had his fingers burnt before she managed to light the cigarette.

'Where do you know him from?' he asked, after she'd taken a few long draws.

'I don't know the lad. I'm just not used to people sticking photos of the dead below my nose.'

The CID man gave her a long, hard look. 'If you keep on like this, we'll take this train all the way to Munich.'

'It's the truth. Even if you beat me up.'

'I'm not going to hit you.' Stave realised there was no point in threatening the girl. He had to try another way.

'If you stick to your story, you can go. But,' he added in a gentle voice, 'if you do, I may never find out who killed him.'

The young prostitute hesitated.

'I haven't seen Adolf for ten days or so,' she whispered eventually. 'It wasn't like him, just to disappear like that, without saying a word.'

The chief inspector leant back in his seat. He felt sympathetic towards Hildegard Hüllmann, who right now, despite the cigarette, did indeed look like a ten-year-old: small, fragile, innocent. But he knew that he had to take advantage of her weakness and confusion to get as much information as possible out of her – information he might otherwise lose forever.

'Did you know him long?'

'What happened to him? You said you were from the murder squad. That means somebody must have killed him.'

'You tell me your story first, then I'll tell you mine.'

'I got to know Adolf a few weeks ago. Here, at the station.'

'A customer of yours?' Stave asked in surprise.

'No, no,' she gave him an angry glance, then looked down at her feet on the dirty floor of the compartment. 'I was waiting for the long-distance train from Ostende,' she said softly. 'For a punter. You often get punters on the long-distance trains. They're in a strange city, a long way from mummy.' She gave a harsh laugh. 'Adolf was waiting for a customer too, after a fashion. Even though I didn't know it at the time. He took a suitcase from some man and was about to leave.'

'What did this man look like?'

She shrugged. 'Just a man.'

'Tall? Short? Fat? Thin? Hair colour? Old? Young?'

She interrupted him with an impatient wave of her cigarette.

'I don't look at men, do I? The less you take in, the quicker you forget them. He could have been my father and I wouldn't have noticed.'

'Your father lives in Hamburg?'

'No.' She gave another harsh, humourless laugh. 'He died in the war. 1943. Stalingrad. Just so you know.'

'OK, go on.'

'Adolf crashed into me carrying his suitcase, it was so heavy. We just collided. He went red and apologised. I found that funny and somehow or other ...' She was looking for the right expression, but couldn't find it. 'Anyhow, nobody had apologised to me for anything in years. So we got talking. Then the next day I saw him again at the station and eventually the penny dropped.'

'What penny?'

Hildegard Hüllmann gave him an impatient look. 'Adolf was a smuggler. He picked up the stuff at the station and delivered it to the black marketeers on the Hansaplatz. And took stuff back from them to the long-distance trains heading over the border, to Belgium and the Netherlands in particular.'

'What stuff?'

She shrugged her shoulders. 'He didn't talk about it much. Sometimes it seemed the suitcases were very heavy. Sometimes they were light, maybe even empty. Once or twice he opened a suitcase for me to have a look. He often had cigarettes and was generous with them. Sometimes some sort of pills, on one occasion it was three watches. One time he had an entire suitcase full of Nazi medals. I'd like to know who buys that stuff these days.'

'Didn't he talk about his customers?'

'Do you have another cigarette?'

'It's my last.'

She blew the sweet-smelling smoke towards the open window.

'Adolf didn't talk that much. I don't even know his surname. I imagine he'd lost his parents.'

'Why?'

'Just a feeling. He never spoke about them, never complained about his "old man".'

'Same as you?'

'Don't give me false sympathy.'

'I ask the questions, you give the answers.'

'You want to hear my story? My parents had a tailor's shop in Köslin. In 1945 my father was already dead by the time the Russians arrived. My mother didn't want to leave our house, we didn't run away. It wasn't exactly her best idea.'

'No?'

'Do I need to go on? I'm sure you can imagine the rest of the story.'

'I'd still like to hear it.'

'An Ivan came in and raped my mother,' she said in a voice devoid of emotion. 'Then he smashed up everything he could find, fired his gun all around the place and threw us out of our house. It was freezing cold. We just set off, vaguely towards the west. After a few days my little brother Siegfried died of starvation. My mother put his body in a cardboard box and buried him next to the wall of a house. He was three months old. He wasn't my father's child, but that's another story. My other brother, Hagen, was four years old. One evening he just leant against me and died. Just like that. I covered him with snow as a sort of burial. I couldn't bury him properly because the ground was frozen solid. And in any case I was too weak. Then my mother died, of fever. Then some more Russians came. I have no idea where we were by then. This time they took me, there wasn't another woman around. Afterwards I hid in a forest where I came across some other children.'

'Wolf children.'

'Yes. We stuck together. During the day we would stay hidden. At night we would sleep in ruins, or crawl into the barn of some Polish or Lithuanian farmer. We stole stuff, or ate what we could find in the forest. All the time heading westwards, as far as possible from the Ivans. One of our group was already sixteen and had served in the

Wehrmacht. He knew what he was doing. I didn't even know in which direction to go. We crossed rivers on tree trunks or rafts we cobbled together. Once we even managed several kilometres on the back of a Russian goods truck, but we were nearly caught. Eventually we ended up in Hamburg. Can't say life here is much better than it was in East Prussia. But at least the Tommies aren't as bad as the Ivans.'

'Where do you live here?'

'Here and there.'

'That's not exactly the answer to give to a policeman.'

'We wolf children are clever. When it's warm we sleep in cellars or knock up a shelter in the ruins. All we need is a few planks, some stones and a bit of cardboard. When it was cold sometimes we'd find shelter in one of the anti-aircraft bunkers. But after you've been in one of them for a few days, your clothes begin to stink of disinfectant, even your skin and hair begin to smell as if you'd used Lysol for perfume. Not exactly ideal if you're in the business I'm in. So sometimes I spend a few days hanging around a client's apartment, but never more than a few days.'

'Are they violent towards you?'

'I can cope. It's apartments I can't cope with. Those closed doors. Are you sure you don't have another cigarette?'

Stave shook his head. 'How am I to see your relationship with Adolf? You were never at his place. You move around a lot. Where did the two of you meet?'

'At the station. On the Hansaplatz. Mostly there. We would talk. Sometimes I would find a customer there, somebody who'd done a bit of business on the black market and had so many Reichsmarks they were burning a hole in his pocket and he had to get rid of them. Adolf would now and then take a break from ferrying stuff to the station and back and would stop and chat with me before disappearing into a hotel or café to collect or deliver a suitcase. A couple of times we met in the Planten en Bomen park. He knew it well because sometimes he had stolen coal from the railway lines nearby. But we just went for walks there.'

Stave was astonished to see Hildegard Hüllmann blushing. She quickly turned and looked out the window. 'Nothing more, Chief Inspector. I hadn't known Adolf that long. And in any case he knew what I did for a living.'

Stave tried to muster his thoughts. 'Adolf Winkelmann, orphan, smuggler, ticket salesman, coal thief. Someone who hung around with wolf children like Hildegard, but never got close enough to them to tell them his surname or where he lived.

'Now it's your turn to tell me a story,' Hildegard interrupted his thoughts.

Hildegard Hüllmann said she could cope, and Stave believed her. So he told her all he knew of Adolf Winkelmann – including how and where his body had been found. All the time he was speaking, the young prostitute sat and stared out of the window.

'Did Adolf ever mention Blohm & Voss? Or say he had something to do down by the harbour?'

She shook her head.

'Did he have other friends? Or do you know the men he did business with?'

'I never saw them. He used to talk occasionally with other boys on the Hansaplatz. He also spoke to some boy down at Planten un Blomen, somebody he knew from stealing coal. It wasn't exactly friendly.'

'Did it feel threatening?'

'No. More like a conversation between two people who can't stand each other. A bit of teasing, a bit of needling. But Adolf didn't take it seriously. He just laughed about it as we walked on. He never introduced me to any of the other boys. I think he liked being with me.' Yet again her cheeks burned bright red for a few seconds. 'Not that it matters now,' she said.

'It does to me. I want to find his killer.'

'Have you got any suspects?'

'I'm casting my net wide. I'll see who swims into it. Boys from the Damm tracks? From the Hansaplatz? Smugglers, black marketeers? Dock workers? Or maybe … wolf children?'

'Should I listen out for you?'

Stave took a crumpled card out of his pocket and handed it to her. 'My telephone number. You can call me any time anything occurs to you. Or if you hear something. But don't start any investigations of your own, right? That's my job.'

She nodded and took the card, 'You are the first policeman to give me his telephone number,' she replied, trying to accompany it with a cheeky grin that didn't quite come off.

'As an officer of the law, I'm afraid I can't just let you out on to the station platform. Underage prostitution is a crime.'

'I thought I wouldn't get off that lightly.'

'We're going to go on a little trip together: to Barmbek.'

'To the children's home for girls. Spare yourself the effort, Chief Inspector, I'll do a runner straight away.'

'I'm afraid it's part of my job to do things I know aren't worth the effort. But I still have to do them.'

'Sounds a bit like my job,' she replied brazenly, and stood up.

A quarter of an hour later they were sitting next to one another on the tram. Stave was relieved that Hildegard Hüllmann hadn't tried to get away from him.

'You could go back to school again,' he said, just to break the silence between them

'That's the most stupid idea I've heard since my mother decided she wasn't leaving our house.'

'It's the only way to get out of the shit you're in,' he said, unfazed by her cheekiness.

'I went to school up to fourth grade back in Köslin,' she said. 'It made sense back then. I'm happy enough to be able to read and write a bit. But what school would take me?'

'Lots of them.'

'And what would I learn?' Hildegard Hüllmann pointed at the ruins the tram was rumbling through on its antiquated rails heading slowly north. The air between the ruins was filled with clouds of yellow dust floating above piles of rubble. 'I don't need to know my times tables out there. I've learnt everything I need to know. I'll do OK.'

They got out near Ohlsdorf Cemetery and went the rest of the way on foot. At this time of day Feuerbergstrasse was quiet. They walked past a few detached family homes built of brick, then a row of allotment sheds, small, old, crooked, like witches' hats.

The girls' home lay at the end of a cul-de-sac between two railway cuttings. It was built to resemble a castle, like the old grammar schools from the days of the Kaisers: built of brick with a double staircase curving in from either side below white windows. It was impressive, and intimidating.

Stave called at the porter's lodge near the entrance and waited until somebody turned up. A young woman with a fresh face and sprightly gait hurried up the internal staircase. Smiling.

The chief inspector didn't explain how he had come across Hildegard Hüllmann. He just produced his ID, murmured something about how he had come across this orphan at the station. His young prostitute charge said nothing, just stared into the distance somewhere between the two of them.

'We'll look after her,' the young woman said, taking Hildegard Hüllmann gently by the arm. Then she led her away. Neither of them looked back at Stave.

It took a couple of stations on the tram, then a long walk before the chief inspector finally reached Harvesthude where he had agreed to meet Anna. They had arranged to meet only later in the afternoon, but he was not keen on just sitting in his empty apartment in the meantime. Part of him was actually afraid to be there – in case Karl suddenly knocked on the door. You're being ridiculous, Stave told himself: you're looking forward to seeing your son.

All the same he needed to keep MacDonald up to speed, so why not do it now? As a result he found himself outside the requisitioned villa in Innocentia Strasse that was currently occupied by three young British officers. There was American jazz music coming from the room that would once have been the lounge. The lieutenant was at home and took him upstairs to his rooms, which Stave was surprised to discover had previously been two children's bedrooms. The wallpaper was white and pale pink. There were thin dark lines under nails hammered into it, and ghostly shapes of oval frames that must once have hung there. White curtains let enough of the sunlight through to create playful patterns.

'I'll need to get used to the décor, according to Erna.' MacDonald had noticed Stave's reaction. 'She means it's going to be a girl.'

Stave thought back to Hildegard Hüllmann who would never see a room like this. 'Speaking of girls,' he replied, 'I've just been talking to someone who might have a lead for us.'

He gave a full account of his conversation with the young prostitute.

'You think she is one of the wolf children,' the lieutenant asked when he had finished. 'I hope not. Their gangs are worse than the partisans. If our killer is one of them, he'll just vanish for good.'

'Thanks for referring to him as *our* rather than just *your*, Lieutenant. At least that way we'll share blame for the failure to find him.'

'Yes, but it we do fail, there's only one of us going to end up in Palestine or India.'

For the first time, Stave noticed how young the Scot seemed. Worn out. 'A divorce is always horrible. But it's not a reason to go to the other side of the world.'

'I wouldn't go willingly,' MacDonald said, making a fist. Then he smiled. 'No offence, old boy, you seem to be the only person in the empire who doesn't object to me having fallen in love with Erna Berg. Despite the fact that you'll be the worse off for it: she is after all your secretary.'

'I'll certainly miss her.'

The lieutenant rubbed his temples and went over to a child's desk and opened the top drawer. 'Whisky,' he suggested, taking out a bottle and two glasses.

Stave took one look at the amber liquid and was thirsty. But after the night before the last thing he wanted was to meet up with Anna smelling of alcohol. 'Sorry, not on duty,' he said.

MacDonald shrugged and poured himself a two-finger measure. 'A few of my colleagues have married German girls. Every soldier needs special permission from the governor to do so. So far, so good. But sometimes there are problems. I know one officer who married a Hamburg girl with all the papers and permission required. He'd thought of everything, except his own family. They were so furious at the thought of him bringing a German home with him that they threw him out of the house. Now he has a brand new wife, but no parents and no brothers or sisters any more. Not one member of his family will speak to him. I envy him.'

'Why?'

'More people than I'd like want to talk to me. It's not my family that are the problem, it's the army. Marrying a German girl is all well and good. But getting a married woman pregnant is a different matter altogether, not so good, even though it can be sorted out. A painful divorce? That's something else again. And when the husband was a soldier who lost a leg fighting the Russians, who could well be our next enemy? To steal the wife of a war veteran and cripple? Not exactly the conduct of a gentleman, and for an officer in the occupation forces, absolutely beyond the pale.'

'So being sent to Palestine or India is a real possibility?'

'One of the disadvantages of having a global empire. The men upstairs can always find a hot spot far away. The Jews and Arabs in Palestine. The Muslims and Hindus in India. Oh yes, they'll be glad to see me.'

'What if we solve our case?'

'Then I have one more bargaining chip with the gentlemen involved to persuade them that I'm more use here in Hamburg, divorce or no divorce.'

'So far I have two half-leads. Maybe Adolf Winkelmann got into a fight with the smugglers who do their dirty business between the Hansaplatz and the station, and which ended in his death. Or maybe he had a murderous enemy among the coal thieves. Both were just possibilities the young prostitute had hinted at. But it was clear that Adolf Winkelmann was one of the gang who robbed the coal trains coming into the Dammtor Station. That was a dangerous business, but a profitable one. In the past winter people had been murdered for a sack of coal.'

'But you still refer to them as 'half' leads.'

Stave raised his hands in apology. 'What has either of these hypotheses got to do with the shipyard? Why was the boy hanging around Blohm & Voss?'

'And that,' MacDonald said with a wry smile, 'is precisely the thing we need to find out.'

Stave was exhausted by the time he finally sat down opposite Anna. They were in the Grimm Quell, not far from St Katherine's church. It had been an old corner bar; all that had survived was the remnants of the four walls. But where the ground floor had been there was now a small square, which was still paved with the tiles from the stairwell and living quarters, and a few wonky tables and chairs. The kitchen was in the cellar of the damaged house next door, while what was the old upright stump of the former heating stove stood in the middle of the square. A few red roses had been arranged in pots at the foot of the walls and the name of the establishment had been painted in overly large black letters on a whitewashed background. It was hardly romantic, Stave thought to himself, but it was possibly the right place to tell Anna about his son.

He threw his jacket over the bare wooden back of the chair. A sign that reminded Stave of the ones put up by the Wehrmacht on route marches announced 'Fresh daily: chicken broth and cold buffet'. Instead he ordered ersatz coffee and biscuits with ersatz marmalade for both of them.

Stave didn't know where to start and just made small talk for a while, realising how phoney it all sounded.

'Is this a comedy?' Anna interrupted him to ask.

'Give me time,' Stave replied. 'I've got a lot on my plate at the moment. Too much. But it'll get better.' It didn't sound much more convincing. He wished this tacky little café at least had sunshades. The air between the brick walls was like an oven, only one that stank of cement and stone dust and brackish water from the old drains.

'Would you mind if I joined you for a few moments?'

Stave, still lost in his thoughts, jumped at the voice of Public Prosecutor Ehrlich.

He sprang to his feet, pulled up a third seat, and called the waiter over. Awkwardly he introduced Anna von Veckinhausen. On the one hand he would have preferred to be left alone with his lover, on the other he was relieved that he wouldn't be able to raise the question of Karl.

Ehrlich was suffering in the heat, beads of sweat on his bald head and dark patches below the armpits of his summer shirt. That didn't stop him rubbing his hands together, eager to discuss business.

'How's the case going?' he asked the chief inspector. 'Have you demanded the death penalty?'

Anna shot him a shocked glance, but the prosecutor shook his head almost jovially: 'This sorry business is going to take up a few days in court.' Then he told Anna about the case. Stave was unhappy to see how keen an interest Anna took, and how well the public prosecutor could tell a story – far better than he could ever explain his cases.

'So how are things going, Chief Inspector?' Ehrlich finally got round to asking. He sipped at his nettle tea, causing his glasses to mist up. But the gaze of those bright eyes behind them was as alert as ever.

Stave shifted back and forth on his seat in embarrassment. Was he to tell the whole story here and now in Anna's presence, including him approaching a fourteen-year-old prostitute at the station? A hooker he was already acquainted with? Instead he talked in vague terms about a street urchin as he recounted Hildegard Hüllmann's story. His own words seemed stale and almost phoney to himself, even though he was completely accurate in his account, save for that one small detail.

As he came to an end, Anna said, 'When I was making my way westwards, children among the trekkers would vanish every day. Some of them ran off at night. Others were there one minute, then gone without trace the next. I used to think they had succumbed to hunger and cold or maybe the wolves.'

Ehrlich shook his head: 'A lot of the children ended up here, or in Berlin, Dresden or another of the big cities.'

'The little ghosts of 1945,' Stave mumbled. For a moment the other two gave him a look of irritation.

'Little ghosts indeed,' the public prosecutor admitted. 'It'll take us years to get them reunited with their families. That's if any of their family are still alive. I'm afraid many of them will remain estranged from society, maybe from civilised life altogether.'

'What will happen to them?' Anna asked.

'They will keep Stave and me in work until we're pensioned off.'

Stave was silent, thinking about his son and whether someone who at the age of just seventeen had already survived life in the Wehrmacht and Vorkuta gulag would be as lost as one of the wolf children. He was so sunk in his own thoughts that he hardly noticed when and how the other two changed the subject. He suddenly found himself left out of a conversation about art. Ehrlich was talking about his collection of Expressionist masters and their work. Anna's taste was more conservative, something she didn't conceal, but she still managed to add little items of interest that even Ehrlich didn't know. The pair of them were chatting enthusiastically, laughing and arguing about well-known artists and obscure pieces of art, about *entartete Kunst* – 'unworthy art' – the modernist works the Nazis had banned, and lost treasures from galleries that had been destroyed. Stave had nothing to say about any of it. He felt unnecessary and ignored.

He would have preferred to stand up, take Anna by the arm and stroll off down the Alster, inhaling her perfume and finally telling her all about Karl and his worries for the future. But he didn't want to seem impolite so he just sat there, silently, with a forced smile that began to make the corners of his mouth ache. I've made a real pig's ear of this, he thought to himself.

The evening sun was sinking slowly over the ruins as they finally left the café. Ehrlich made his farewells politely and walked off, a contented, sweaty little figure. Anna watched him go, then finally turned to Stave with a disappointed look on her face. Stave tried to muttered some vague apologies but couldn't find the right words.

'I'm tired,' Anna said at last. 'I'm going home.' She gave Stave a brief kiss on the lips without asking him if he wanted to come with her.

Homecoming

Monday, 2 June 1947

Shortly before 8.00 a.m. Stave found himself at the gate of the school on Graudenzer Weg in Barmbek. He'd known of it for ages, from the newspapers. This was where in the summer of 1945, Hamburg's schools first reopened in peacetime with British occupation officers in dress uniform, a few German politicians with clean records, and masses of children. The school had been chosen because it was large and modern, built during the Weimar Republic. It also helped that it was one of the few educational establishments that had not been hit by bombs.

The chief inspector looked at the interlocking brickwork on the main body of the building, the white-framed rows of windows that looked almost like they belonged to a military base, the tall towers of the stairwells. To him, having grown up with the nineteenth-century Kaiser Wilhelm schools with their curved staircase entrances, imposing pillars, allegorical statues over the doors, this institution looked more like a factory. But I suppose a bit of sobriety can do no harm, he told himself.

All around him children were rushing to their classrooms, all boys: the girls were taught in separate premises a few metres down the street. They were thin kids in short trousers, tanned, tousled hair. The chief inspector noticed two fifth-graders wearing hand-sewn shoes. Most of the others wore sandals with soles made from the rubber of truck tyres. A few of them were barefoot. Those were the ones who dodged school in bad weather because it was too cold to go that far with nothing on their feet. He pushed the heavy handle of the gate and entered the building.

He had to ask directions before he found himself in the rector's office.

'Doctor Bruno Kitt,' the rector introduced himself. He was a lean fifty-something wearing round glasses with curved rims, and had a goatee beard and ears that stuck out.

Stave explained to him as gently as he could that one of his pupils had been murdered. The rector ripped his glasses off and wiped his eyes.

'That's the third boy we've lost under frightful circumstances,' he said quietly. 'I tell the boys a thousand times that there's nothing good to come of the black market. Two others played with unexploded bombs, one of them still in hospital, the other in Öjendorf Cemetery. These are hardly the best years to be a child.'

'When is a good time?' Stave returned. 'Did you know Adolf Winkelmann?'

'The name rings a bell. I think he got told off not so long ago for skipping classes so often. But the fact that he did is probably why I can't put a face to the name. He was probably hardly even here. I'll look in the class rolls, he would most likely have been in the eight grade.'

'How many children do you have per class?'

'Fifty, maybe sixty, when they're all here. Which is almost never the case.'

The chief inspector cursed under his breath. How long was it going to take to interview all of Adolf's classmates?

'Here we have him. He was in 8a. You're in luck, they've just started their morning week.'

'Morning week?'

'As long as the other schools in the neighbourhood remain in ruins we have so many pupils that each classroom has to be used twice. One group has lessons there in the morning, the other in the afternoons. We swap over weekly, so that they all have to deal with getting up early. Today's the beginning of 8a's week. They'll all be tired. I'll take you down there.'

The rector led him down high-ceilinged corridors until they came to a door that was painted partly grey, partly orangey-beige. Stave thought of Karl. He had been a star at school. He had gone to the Matthias-Claudius grammar school and done so well that he had skipped a year. But what was it all for in the end? To get an emergency leaving certificate to be sent to the front line and spend the best days of his youth sitting in a gulag.

But I'm lucky, Stave persuaded himself. It could have been a lot worse. Dead in action. And even if he had stayed at school? Karl had been a brilliant scholar, but an out and out Nazi. He would have gone straight from grammar school to the Nazi Police Academy and then into the SS. And today? He'd be standing in front of Public Prosecutor Ehrlich listening to him demand the death penalty. He drove the thought from his mind.

'I'll wait in the hallway,' Stave said. 'We don't need the whole class to know all at once what's going on. I'd be grateful if you'd ask their teacher to step out.'

'I hope,' Kitt hesitated, 'you'll be ... tactful.'

'It's not the first time I've done this sort of thing.'

The rector nodded, and disappeared through the door. A few minutes later a young man, as skinny as his pupils, with black hair, rather too long, and dark eyes, came out. Failed artist, Stave thought. The rector remained in the classroom, which was totally silent.

'Dr Kitt tells me there's been an unfortunate incident.'

'You might call it that,' the chief inspector replied and repeated once again the story of the murdered boy. 'Your name, please?' he asked, taking out his notebook.

'Johannes Thiele. I'm their form master: German and history.'

'Have you known Adolf Winkelmann since the first year?'

'No, I only came here in 1945. I wanted to go to university, but the English insisted I come here. There are a lot of vacancies.'

'When did you last see Adolf Winkelmann?'

'Fourteen days ago. At the end of last week I went to see the rector about his repeated failure to turn up. He gave him detention. Not that that would have particularly worried him. If he were still alive, that is.' The teacher blushed and turned to look out the window.

'Did he often not turn up?'

'Most of the time, actually.'

'Did that not worry you?'

Thiele sighed and looked at the chief inspector as if he were a particularly dim child. Stave had to make an effort to remain polite. 'Do you know why most of these kids turn up to school? It's for the school dinners the English provide: hot soup every day, soya meal and meat extract or semolina with sugar. That's three hundred calories, three hundred good reasons not to miss school. Of my fifty, barely half of them have any interest in the subject. Not that I can make it any easier for them. The English have banned most textbooks from the Nazi era: too much propaganda. But there aren't any new books. What am I to do? Well, I use the old German textbook and the old history textbook, but keep them under the desk, you might say. Always afraid that one of the lads will squeal on me to the Tommies.'

'Was Adolf Winkelmann one of the types who might have squealed on you?'

'He never bothered with books. Despite the fact that he was bright. I mean, if he had realised, as a few of them here have, that the only way to get out of this mess is with hard work, then he might have gone on from the 9th grade to a technical school or grammar school. Adolf was smart, but he had no ambition. Or to be more precise he had no ambition for what you learn in school.'

'But for things you learn outside school?'

'He was a good businessman. Coal, for example. During the last winter all the pupils were obliged to bring in coal, wood or briquettes to heat the school just a little. For some of them that was difficult because it was so bitterly cold, even at home. Not for Adolf, if he turned up. Twice he came in with an entire sackful of coal. He was very generous with it. And not stupid. It got him off detention or any other punishment. Who's going to reprimand a boy who brings so much coal? He was clever enough.'

'And well-to-do, in a manner of speaking? It seems the school dinners didn't matter much to him.'

'Indeed. He's got it good.'

'Had. Until last week,' the chief inspector added.

Stave spent a seemingly endless morning questioning the pupils, who had to come out one by one to talk to him in the corridor. In most cases the interrogation lasted only a few minutes. At the end the chief inspector knew that Adolf Winkelmann had no friends among his classmates. He was a loner. Someone the others were impressed by and afraid of. Impressed by the cigarettes he had and his worldly ways. Afraid of because of his shady contacts in the world of the black marketeers they'd all heard of, but knew little about. He hadn't been in any punch-ups on the few days he turned up at school, no threats, none of the classmates or teachers who could be classed as his enemy. Nothing at all about his school life apart from the lessons.

By the time Stave finally left the school he felt as if he was reversing out of a cul-de-sac. He had found no one new who might have been friendly with Adolf, no new leads. Only his activities as a coal thief.

On his desk back at headquarters there was a note: 'My report is ready. The boy died approximately twelve hours before the body was found. If you need more, see me. Czrisini.' The night of Thursday to Friday, that meant, Stave calculated. Right now that wasn't much more help than anything he'd heard at the school. It looks like the investigation is running into the sand. I'm going to have to start again from the beginning in case there's something I've overlooked. It can't do any harm to have another chat with his aunt.

An hour later he was ringing the bell of the apartment at Fuhlsbüttel Strasse 594. As Greta Boesel opened the door a trail of cigarette smoke came after her.

'Go out on to the balcony,' she said, hardly looking at him. 'I'll be with you in a second.' Then she disappeared into another room, leaving the chief inspector alone. Taken aback and somewhat embarrassed he went out into the open air and sat under the sunshade. He could hear Boesel talking, but to whom? It was some time before Stave realised there wasn't actually anyone else with her in the room.

'You have a telephone?' he asked in amazement when eventually she joined him. 'In a private apartment?'

'In my office. I'm a businesswoman with a telephone. Is that so extraordinary? Times are changing. Cigarette, this time?' She went back into the living room.

Stave declined. Before he got a chance to ask his questions he heard the sound of a key in the outside door and Walter Kümmel strode in, made straight for Greta Boesel and gave her a passionate kiss. A look of surprise and embarrassment crossed his face even as he was kissing her.

'Don't let me disturb you,' said Stave. He was thinking of Anna and how long it had been since he had last kissed her like that.

'Should I be jealous,' the boxing promoter asked, nonetheless shaking his hand. 'Any news about our Adolf? When will we be able to bury him?'

'The boy's body is still in the morgue. But I think the doctors will soon release him. I have a meeting there later today. That's not why I'm here however, it's to ask you a few questions about the night of Thursday, the twenty-ninth of May, to Friday the thirtieth.'

They both exchanged a brief look.

'That's when Adolf died,' the boy's aunt said, 'and now you want to confirm our alibis?'

'Where were you on that night?'

'Here, in this apartment,' Greta Boesel replied. 'First of all I listened to music, the NDR channel, then I went to bed.'

'Perhaps you remember what it was you were listening to?' Stave took out his notebook. He could check whatever she said later with the radio station. So he was disappointed when she shook her head. 'I never pay that much attention. I just have the radio on for company.'

'Is there anyone who could confirm you were here in the apartment?'

Kümmel cleared his throat: 'I can confirm it for the second half of the evening. I was working late at the office, but I came back about two in the morning and was here the rest of the night.' Greta Boesel blushed slightly and nodded.

'At two in the morning? That's after the curfew. How could you get here from the Chile House? Have you got a permit?'

'I know my way around,' Kümmel smiled. 'I didn't want to sleep at the office and made my way to Greta via the back way: paths between the ruins, streets that haven't been cleared of rubble yet and are therefore impassible for Jeeps. The Tommies didn't come across me. I hope you will forgive me, Chief Inspector.'

Stave thought over what he had just heard. Neither Greta Boesel nor Walter Kümmel had an alibi for the time between dusk and 2.00 a.m., and after that their only support for their alibis was each other. There were no independent witnesses and their alibis were unconvincing, but not even such that he could test them out.

'Can we talk about coal?' he said, changing the topic.

'Not our business,' the transport manageress said.

'But maybe it was Adolf's? I've been asking around. It seems the boy often,' Stave swallowed the word he had been about to use, and said, 'was involved in organising it.'

Silence. The chief inspector could see the pair of them weighing up what they should say in reply.

'There's nothing to be ashamed of, but it could be a lead for me.'

Greta Boesel sighed. 'Every now and then Adolf would bring home a sack of coal.'

'We had a cellar full,' her fiancé added, rather proudly.

'Did it never occur to you to ask how a fourteen-year-old got hold of coal? In a winter where other people were freezing to death in their homes?'

'He obviously stole it,' the boy's aunt replied. 'Like all good boys. What else was there to do? I never asked him about it, I didn't want to know his business. But at least that way he was paying his share of the cost of living.'

'We all had to muddle our way through. Adolf was bright enough to realise that.'

'Not bright enough to realise that going to school would have been more important. He hardly ever turned up.'

'Last winter good schoolboys ended up dead schoolboys, frozen solid,' Greta Boesel hit back. 'No sentimentality. New times, new ways, Chief Inspector, and that doesn't refer simply to the telephone. Half the world is lying in ruins and will remain that way for a good while yet. What's the use to a boy of declensions and quadratic equations? Better to get a good grip on life's realities.'

'Did you ever hear the names of any of your nephew's friends? He was a bit of a loner, an outsider in the classroom, but apparently not on the Hansaplatz.'

Shrugs.

'No,' Walter Kümmel said. 'Not that I can recall.'

'Hildegard Hüllmann?'

'Who's that supposed to be?'

'A friend of Adolf's. An acquaintance at any rate.'

Greta Boesel laughed. 'Boys that age tend to keep things about girls to themselves. Even good boys. Have you got children, Chief Inspector?'

Stave wasn't about to go into that. 'Did your nephew ever talk about the main station?'

'Was he on a train?'

'He took things there and collected things.'

Kümmel looked up and said in a voice more of recognition than surprise: 'That would explain a few things.'

'Did you know Adolf was also peddling tickets for your boxing matches on the black market?'

'I had a suspicion, nothing more. Like we said, the boy knew how to help himself. But I wasn't born yesterday either and I cut off his source. Mind you, it was after that that he stopped bringing home bags of coal. But then winter was over by then.'

'Did he ever mention getting into a fight with coal thieves?' The chief inspector could also imagine why the supplies dried up.

'One time he turned up at home in a bit of a bad way. It was a long time ago,' Kümmel replied.

'Bit of a bad way?'

'He had a nice big bruise.'

'Why? Who gave it to him?'

'He didn't say, and I didn't ask. It's better if boys sort those things out between themselves.'

Stave closed his eyes and thought to himself: Adolf Winkelmann worked as a courier for smugglers down at the Hansaplatz, ferrying hot goods to the station and back. He sold off tickets and maybe other things on the black market. He hung out with wolf children. He stole coal now and again, probably from freight trains. Somewhere at sometime he had a fight with somebody. His aunt and her fiancé didn't know the details, but knew enough to have a rough idea of what the boy was up to. They tolerated it, even encouraged it, because at the end of the day they profited from it. Just an everyday story of family life these days.

'I'll keep you up to date,' said Stave, getting up out of his chair.

If it hadn't been situated next to Dammtor Station, Neue Rabenstrasse would have been idyllic. As it was, the dirty steam from the locomotives hung in the trees that lined it on both sides, while the screeching of wheels on rails and the hissing of the engine boilers was everywhere. The chief inspector strolled up to house number I, a villa that had had a bit of a bad time in the war years: there were scorch marks on the once gaily plastered façade, shell holes in the walls, windows boarded up. A bit of noise and dirt was something that most of its inhabitants these days could put up with, Stave thought to himself. This was in any case where Dr Czrisini and his colleagues from the pathology department sliced open the bodies brought to them.

He met the pathologist in his small, smoky office. Official notices and typed reports lay on a desk covered with a dirty tablecloth. Shelves lined the walls to the ceiling filled, according to some incomprehensible system, partly with ring binders, partly with bottles storing shrivelled organs swimming in formaldehyde. The grime on the windows was so thick that even the blaring sunlight looked milky and pale as it pushed its way into the claustrophobic little room.

'Your corpses have more room on the autopsy table than you have in here,' the chief inspector said as he moved a load of ring binders off a seat, looked around for somewhere to put them and finally opted for the linoleum-covered floor.

'There's no point in tidying up,' the doctor quipped, 'I have to move out soon.'

'You're being moved?'

'We're being moved,' Czrisini laughed. 'The whole institute. We bought this villa from the Catholic Church in 1938, legally as far as I know. But now my lords, bishops and prelates are demanding their house back, saying they were forced to sell. I'm fascinated to know what the church wants to do with a place that's been used to carve up hundreds of bodies over the last ten years.'

'Maybe they'll turn it into a school,' Stave mumbled.

'Is that a coded reference to the Adolf Winkelmann case?'

'I got your report.'

'Do you want the details or just the conclusion?'

'I can get the details from the file. Right now I just want the abridged version.'

'Fine by me,' Czrisini said, but in a tone that reflected his irritation with the fact that his work wasn't taken more seriously. 'Time of death: Thursday night. Cause of death: violent attack, a dagger wound, straight to the heart. Massive damage to said organ. More than two litres of blood in the chest cavity. Stabbed with extreme force: the murder instrument cut clean through a rib.'

'A knife?'

'Probably, but probably not a kitchen knife. Their blades tend to bend or deflect when they come into contact with bone. My bet would be a big strong blade of the type used by soldiers, or maybe fishermen.'

'Or seamen in general?'

'Could be. No obvious signs that the victim tried to defend himself. No cuts to the hands as there might have been if the boy had tried to grab hold of the knife. No obvious signs of passive defence either, on the underarms for example, as you might expect if he had used his arms to shield his body. Looks more like the attacker took him by surprise.'

'He wasn't expecting the attack, and almost certainly hadn't seen the weapon in his attacker's hand.'

'Or he did see it, but didn't reckon the killer was about to attack. Maybe the killer had been using the knife to open something, a parcel maybe. In which case it would have been normal for him to have a knife in his hand. Then one quick movement and – hey presto, a life gone.'

'Anything else unusual?'

'The contents of his stomach. Lots of edible grain, bread, fat, probably butter too. The boy might have been thin, but he was hardly undernourished. He was a lot better fed than the average child of his age in Hamburg today.'

'Any traces of coal?'

Czrisini stared at the chief inspector in puzzlement.

'Sorry,' Stave said. 'That might explain the boy's affluence. He used to steal coal. I was wondering if there were any traces on the body. Under his fingernails for example, or in his hair?'

The pathologist scratched his bald head then leafed through his report which he pulled out from the pile along with five others. 'Nothing at all. In that respect at least, the boy was clean.' He began coughing.

Stave waited until the attack passed. Czrisini looked pale, beads of sweat on his forehead. 'You really need a bit of fresh air in here,' the chief inspector said, as he took his leave.

Over the next few days Stave asked his colleagues from Department S, which dealt with the black market, to ask around among their informers. They told Stave about gangs of children who broke into shops and canteens and even English barracks to steal chocolate they could sell on the black market. The juvenile courts had dealt with more than 50,000 such cases in the past year alone, ten times more than had been the case in the 1920s. But it appeared that Adolf Winkelmann was either a very small fish in the pond, or wasn't involved at all. He was never caught in a raid, never arrrested, never up before the juvenile court, no informer had ever mentioned his name to the police. He was a blank page.

One morning Stave visited the University Clinic Eppendorf, the biggest hospital in the city; if he was going to get any information about sick or wounded children, that was the place to be.

The main building on Martinistrasse, opposite Eppendorf Park, looked partly like an army headquarters, partly like a castle. This grandiose appearance was, however, marred by the presence of a cuboid concrete bunker sprouting from the ground next to it. Stave pressed down the handle of the gateway above which, in heavy gold lettering, the name University Clinic Eppendorf glistened.

The chief inspector had an appointment with Professor Rudolf Degkwitz. Stave had his eyes on the swaying rear end of the nurse who led him to his office. He remembered that Karl had called nurses 'Stukas' – the last time his father had seen him. By then he was already in the Wehrmacht, having been given a rushed school diploma in order that he might be sent to the final battle for Berlin. One evening, which until then had been spent in silence, he started talking about a military hospital the young recruits had been taken to visit. Why they'd been taken there he didn't say, any more than what they'd seen there. He talked of only one thing: crude jokes about the nurses whose swaying rears were compared to the turned-up wings of the diver bombers. 'You've never even seen a Stuka,' his father said. They'd all been shot down by then. He hadn't gone so far as to add that point but his son had got the message. Another argument. That was the last conversation they'd had, father and son.

'The professor is expecting you.'

Stave came back to earth and realised he was standing at a desk. He nodded to the nurse, grateful if slightly confused. She gave him the encouraging smile of a woman who was used to seeing more confusion than that on a daily basis.

Degkwitz was an average-sized man of about fifty with brown hair sharply parted on one side. He shook Stave's hand and said, 'Cigarette?'

The chief inspector declined but encouraged the professor to go ahead and light up his own Lucky Strike. 'What do you know about wolf children?' he asked.

'If you hadn't already used that term to me over the telephone, I'd have to tell you I'd never heard it. Why have you come to see me?'

'These children must get treated somewhere. Logic dictates that most cases would end up in the largest hospital.

Degkwitz leaned back in his seat. 'I'm a TB specialist. Over the past two years my experience in the field has improved dramatically. Unfortunately my capacity to treat cases has over the same time decreased dramatically. We get hundreds of cases of TB in all its stages here. Obviously that includes children. My colleagues here see children with severe starvation, with serious skin and genital problems, as well as wounds of every sort. The babies born here are sometimes so undernourished they look like little worms. Whether these kids are gutter vagabonds or nice children from good homes in Blankenese is a matter of the most complete indifference to me.'

'But don't you get concerned when a child is brought in who has no parents or relations?'

'Not any more. If our little patients have no relatives, we inform the authorities. Usually sooner or later somebody comes and takes them to an orphanage. Sometimes the girls or boys run off before they can be collected.'

The CID man had hoped the hospital might be able to put him in touch with some friend of the murder victim. But Stave now realised that no matter how badly wounded they might be, wolf children didn't get noticed in the hospital. They were simply treated until they were on their feet again, and then they ran away. Obviously he would be able to go through the records here, and get details of the types of wounds common in conditions of war and strife, even attempted murder. But what help would that be, if he had no idea whether or not the victim was a wolf child?

'I'd like to ask if you could find out whether an Adolf Winkelmann was ever treated here,' he said, tired and already half-resigned to the answer.

The professor shook his head sympathetically. 'We have already gone through all the archives for the past few years, including before 1945. I'm glad to say we still have those records. No Adolf Winkelmann. Not to say that means he was never treated here. Boys who end up in here give us whatever name they like. How are we to check it out if they have no ID card, or no registered address? In any case, that's not our business. I'm fairly certain that the sort of children you're looking for are exactly the sort who make up names for themselves. We have dozens of Peter Müllers and Heinrich Schmidts in our records, and that goes for the older patients too. There are more than enough adults around who don't want to hear their real names mentioned again.'

On the long way back from the hospital to CID headquarters Stave kept an eye out for children on the street. And discovered they were everywhere. He hadn't noticed before. Boys in short trousers chasing a ball made of rags. Girls in skirts their mothers had made out of bedsheets. Kids trundling tyres along the streets. Playing in the ruins as if it were the most natural thing in the world, as if they were woods and forests – particularly the two older boys Stave passed who were building medieval castles out of broken bricks on the remnants of a Panzer's tank tracks, glittering in the hot sunlight.

This isn't my world, he thought to himself and all of a sudden felt a sorrow descend upon him like a yoke around his neck. Children, games, adventures. When had he last enjoyed any of that with Karl? The boy spent all his time with the Hitler Youth. Don't feel sorry for yourself, it was your fault too. Who else would Karl have shared adventures with? With his father, who spent all his time at the police station? He had done overtime as well as his normal duty so as not to come to attention for political reasons, so that despite not being a Party member he could hang on to his job and his pension and that little taste of power and self-worth that even a policeman who'd been knocked off the promotion chain still possessed.

I'll do better this time, when Karl gets back from Vorkuta, he thought, straightened himself up and began to walk faster. But there was still that nagging doubt: would he make a hash of everything again? Things hadn't got any better with Anna either: they hadn't spoken properly to one another in days.

Nor was he getting any further with the case. Sure, he had leads. But none of them led anywhere. Coal thieves? Smugglers? Family? School? Somewhere out there a secret was buried – a secret that would explain the brutal murder down at the shipyard. It was up to him to unearth it.

Under the giant pillars that held up the front entrance to the CID headquarters he nodded in passing to the bronze elephant the lads in the office had nicknamed 'Anton' – the thing was a relic from the days when the eleven-storey building had been the headquarters of an insurance company. And the days when people had the money and enthusiasm to waste on such frippery. In the anteroom to his office Erna Berg looked up when he came in. She waved a newspaper printed on cheap yellowing paper at him: 'Here, this will interest you.'

'Sounds dangerous,' he said, taking the newspaper from her. *Die Zeit*, four pages in small print – there was still a shortage of paper in the British zone. His secretary had folded it so that his attention fell on a single column story on page three: an article about young people stealing coal.

Stave rustled the paper and said, 'I owe you twenty *pfennigs* for this. I'll read it in my office. Keep this up and we'll soon be changing places.'

'Men think about things, women feel them,' she replied good-naturedly. 'I already owe you for one favour or another. Most of your colleagues would have suggested I be fired in my situation, or would if they knew who the father of my baby was.'

'Times change,' said Stave, closing his office door behind him. He read the article through quickly, then a second time, more carefully. It was nothing particularly new. An estimate of how many tonnes of coal were stolen from the railway tracks in Hamburg, how many children were involved, where they emptied the freight cars and who benefited most from it.

'Somebody here knows what they're talking about, though,' Stave whispered aloud. The author was an old acquaintance, Ludwig Kleensch, who'd written a report on the murderer in the ruins. Stave flicked though one of his old notebooks, which he kept, organised chronologically, in a drawer of his desk. It didn't take long to find the journalist's number at the paper's editorial department.

When he heard Stave's name at the other end of the line, Kleensch said nothing for a few seconds while he tried to place him. When he spoke he sounded curious.

'I don't speak often to the CID on the phone. What can I do for you?'

'I need information.'

'You don't say! What about?'

'Coal thieves.'

'Ah, a reader! Congratulations. And what precisely do you want to know about the kids?'

'Everything.'

There was a long silence on the line. Then he could hear Kleensch taking a deep breath. 'Not on the telephone, Chief Inspector. The line's so bad, I'd be hoarse from shouting by the time I'd finished, and my colleagues would all have gone deaf listening to me. Let's meet up at my apartment, at say five o'clock in the afternoon. Curienstrasse 1. Sixth floor. Right next door to the *Zeit* offices.'

'That's handy,' Stave replied.

Curienstrasse 1 was an eight-storey slab erected behind the Nazi-built 'House of the Press' which *Zeit* now inhabited. Stave's eyes lit on a relief in brown stone on the right above the entrance: a *Kogge*, the traditional Hanseatic trading vessel, in full sail and as large as two delivery trucks. On the leading sail was a motif, a round circle like a medallion, suspiciously empty, as was the rest of the relief.

'There used to be a swastika there,' Kleensch explained when Stave mentioned it at the door of his flat. 'The building manager had it quickly removed in 1945, before one of the Tommies could get a closer look.'

The journalist led him into a small room, with small windows, a hard couch for sleeping on and a piano that looked as if it had had to be squeezed in, and above it, a faded reproduction of a painting of an elderly grandmother.

'*The Madonna of Cologne*, by Stefan Lochner. To remind me of home,' Kleensch said.

'You're a Rhinelander?'

'And Berliner, and Hamburger, and Russian nomad. Originally I was trained as a classical conductor, but then I became a reporter for the *Vossische Zeitung*, in Berlin.'

'Were you in the Party?'

He laughed and made a dismissive gesture.

'The good old "Auntie Voss", was the only rag in the brown country where there was still a bit of freedom. Not that it was a big bit. Following my articles, it was suggested rather pointedly to me at the outbreak of war that I would do well to sign up. Which I did. I became a Stuka pilot. Flew 250 missions over enemy territory in the east. Shot down twice.'

'But never a prisoner of war,' Stave muttered, ever so slightly enviously.

'Lucky boy. To make it from the eastern front here to Hamburg and *Die Zeit*. and now here I am with a real "commissar" in my little place. Life is full of surprises.'

The chief inspector gave Kleensch a quick once-over. Over thirty years of age, trim, freshly shaved, youthful-looking, hair an indeterminate colour somewhere between blond and brown. Could have been almost anyone anywhere. In the old days he wouldn't have paid the slightest attention to someone like him, so friendly, harmless, run of the mill. Yet this man had flown 250 missions on the eastern front. What must it have been like to be shot down? Did he have to make a crash landing? Did he parachute out? The fire, the smoke, the stench of burning oil, wounds, pain. Did Kleensch still have nightmares about it?

'Let's talk about the coal thieves,' he said. 'Where did you get all your information?'

The journalist shrugged. 'About the amount of missing coal? From the administration and the British. But I suspect you're not as interested in the coal as in those who took it. I spoke to a few of the lads, but it wasn't easy.'

The chief inspector explained his case. 'The one thing that is certain is that from time to time he was involved in stealing coal. And it would appear that at least once he got into a fight with another of the gang. That's not much of a lead to go on, but at least it is a lead.'

'Most of them are perfectly normal kids. For the younger ones it's almost a game, even if a very dangerous one. It can always happen that you try to jump on to a cart and end up under its wheels instead. Then they find an arm lying on the tracks, often a little arm.'

'Do you know Adolf Winkelmann?' Stave asked, showing him the photo.

'Never seen him before.'

'Did you hear anything about a big fight among the kids?'

'There are fights all the time. Like I said, most of them are perfectly normal, but there are also the kids with no roots.'

'Wolf children.'

'Yes, that's what they call themselves. Kids from the east. Others link up with travelling artists or have run away from parents who beat them or from hard jobs cutting peat in Lower Saxony or forced labour in the uranium mines in the Sudetenland. Many of them are as crazy as grunts sent to the eastern front. And even more brutal. Then the fists fly. None of the vagabonds have ration cards. If they didn't have coal to steal, they'd starve. So if anybody interferes they tend to take things into their own hands.'

'For example somebody who dabbles in smuggling, sells boxing tickets on the black market, lives in the nice cosy home of his aunt and has no need to steal coal for himself,' Stave replied softly, thinking it through. 'Do you have any names?'

Kleensch laughed. 'I didn't exactly get that close to them. In any case our editorial would have vetoed it.'

'Afraid, are they?'

'They're afraid for their display windows. One of our photographers just happened to be on hand when two policemen arrested a particularly well-known black marketeer. They'd reacted fast and it made a good photograph. We printed it in the next edition. That was put up in the display case outside the building, and guess what: all of a sudden a few guys turn up in the editorial office and suggest rather strongly that we might like to change the display if we wanted to stay on good terms with the gentleman concerned. It's hard to get hold of glass these days, Chief Inspector, and we can't afford to keep a guard looking after the display cases. So they changed the window and everything was OK. And I got a quiet word not to be quite so enthusiastic over the next few weeks. No names in the paper, no photos of that type. The big players on the market at least send out their tough guys to make their opinion known in advance. The vagabonds down at Bahndamm aren't quite so polite.'

'And the former Stuka pilot is content to hunker down at his desk?'

Kleensch stared at him, then laughed and said, 'Are you trying to provoke me? Aren't you afraid you might get bad press? Whatever would the mayor say?'

'I'm trying to find the killer of a fourteen-year-old boy.'

The journalist turned serious again, nodded and thought for a bit. 'OK, I have an idea – an idea it might be better our editorial bosses heard nothing about. I'll take you to the coal thieves. You can talk to them yourself, and risk your own neck. Meet me at Planten un Blomen, down where the park meets the railway tracks near Dammtor Station, Saturday, six in the morning. Saturday is a day off school for most of the kids, which means there'll be more of them than on other days. We need to be there early because they're only at it before the day really gets going when there aren't many people about.'

'I'm an early riser,' said Stave, picking up his summer hat.

He set off down the staircase with a spring in his step. At last a lead. A chance to take things a step further. One of the coal thieves is bound to have known Adolf Winkelmann. One of them would talk.

He felt brave enough now to put the rest of his life in order. He missed Anna. Why not drop by and see her? They talked too rarely these days. Maybe Saturday will give him something to celebrate? He'd go down to the Bahndamm tomorrow and lie in wait for the kids. Maybe by the evening he'd have the case solved. He would invite her for dinner on Saturday evening. Back at his place. After that she'd be bound to stay the night. He could have whistled a little tune, if he didn't think that would make him look silly.

Röperstrasse led down towards the Elbe from elegant Palmaille, a cobbled cul-de-sac barely a hundred metres long. It could have been mistaken for an entrance to somewhere else because the only access to Röperstrasse was a big, U-shaped gate in a long rental apartment building on Palmaille. The four-storey rental blocks behind it were dilapidated but unmarked by bomb damage. Even the doors were pre-war: painted green with white wrought-iron depictions of seagulls. The street ended in a slope of grass, bushes and rubble that led down to the Elbe. Beckoning to foreign lands. Then Stave remembered that in her flight to the west Anna had nearly drowned on board the *Wilhelm Gustloff*. He wondered if seeing ships the moment she walked out of her door still frightened her. He would have to ask her some day.

He knocked on the door to the basement apartment, but there was no answer. It was late afternoon; Anna would have left long ago to look for antiques amid the ruins. Stave tried not to be disappointed. He pulled a page out of his notebook and scribbled on it: 'Dinner at my place Saturday evening? I'm cooking for two if you don't tell me otherwise. F.' Minimalist stuff. He couldn't bring himself to add anything more. He pushed the note into the gap between door and frame, then thought a moment, pulled it out and changed the 'F' to 'Frank'.

Saturday morning. It was still too early for the heat to have risen and Stave enjoyed the cool breeze on his skin. There was a haze in the air, milky light that made the rubble on either side of the street look like it had been rendered in pastel. The chief inspector was awake and up by 5.00 to be sure of getting to the meeting place on time.

He reached the entrance to the park nearest to Dammtor Station. Before the war there had been a thatched park-keeper's house there, and a lecture hall for the university nearby. Now the chief inspector found himself carefully stepping over black charred remains of both buildings. Beyond was the botanical garden with its exotic plants in straight rows, like soldiers on a permanently stationary parade. A few beautiful ancient trees emerged from the haze, their leaves silvery-damp. There was a smell of pine needles in the air. There was nothing left of the once great expanse of lawns ever since the city had allowed the people to plant potatoes in the park. Steam rose from the upturned earth, while the pathways in between were littered with the droppings of the oxen and carthorses that people had somehow got hold of to pull their makeshift ploughs. Throughout the park fearless black crows hopped here and there. Stave thought there were more of them than there used to be, a lot more. I'd rather not think about what they live on, he thought to himself.

As he reached the rose garden on the other side of Dammtor Station he began to be more cautious, making his way through the shrubbery or in the shadow of big trees. The rose garden itself was round with a Turkish metal pavilion in the middle. The roses were red, yellow, pink and white, knee-high or on occasion twice the height of a man: bushes, climbers, arches, releasing a perfume that could have been that of a seductive woman.

A small shadow appeared from within the pavilion: Kleensch.

'Let's hide in the bushes,' he whispered. There were bramble bushes behind the rose garden. Stave hoped the thorns wouldn't tear his trousers. They were his second-to-last pair. The last thing he wanted to be forced into was paying a fortune on the black market for a new pair of trousers.

The journalist swore under his breath, holding up his left thumb where a drop of blood was pooling. 'Glad I was in the Luftwaffe,' he whispered, 'the comrades in the infantry had to endure that every day here. But we're almost there.' He pushed a twig to one side and nodded forwards.

At the end of the park, between the zoo and the main road, the tracks curved towards Dammtor Station. On the main road there was a row of late nineteenth-century residential buildings, prestigious apartments: brick with white or pale yellow plasterwork. One corner building had even survived in a sort of orange colour with white Greek pillars supporting balconies, like antique temples, which seemed absurdly frivolous against the wasteland all around. Stave glanced up at the balconies and windows, looking for a sign that anybody was awake so early. There would be a good view of the park from up there. But there was nobody to be seen.

There were four tracks in the railway bed, which lay some two metres below street level, like a stream of gravel and steel. He could just make out – vaguely in the morning mist – figures on the embankment: ten maybe twenty boys hunched down, kneeling or just lying there, with sacks in their hands. And big sticks.

'It would be better if they don't see us,' Kleensch said.

'I would never have thought that,' Stave mumbled.

'Take your time.'

Five minutes passed, ten. Gradually the sun drove the mist away. Just a few seconds more and any one of those kids who glances up here will spot us, the chief inspector thought to himself. The palms of his hands were damp. The he heard a short, sharp whistle. One of the lads on the far left of the embankment sprang to his feet and waved.

'The spotter,' Kleensch said, his own voice sounding tense. 'A train's coming.'

Just a few minutes later Stave indeed heard the panting of a steam locomotive just before it came puffing into sight. It was an old engine, dented with a slanted boiler, pulling behind it a dozen open coal wagons, its wares glistening in the morning sun. In the long curve leading into Dammtor Station the driver had to slow down. At that point the embankment was steep, making it the ideal site for an ambush.

The boys had ducked down, clinging to the embankment like feral cats, let the locomotive and the first, then the second wagon pass – and then they jumped to their feet, nimble, scrawny figures, running, running, running, sacks in their little hands. Stave didn't hear a spoken word; all he could hear was the screeching of iron wheels on the rails, the rattling of the wagons, the puffing from the funnel. A sudden leap and the first one of them clung to a wagon, somehow held tight, then climbed up and up until he reached the surface of the open load. Then a second, then a third. Once up top they began shovelling coal into their sacks with their bare hands. Skinny kids with dusty hair and soot-smeared naked arms.

'Some of them imagine themselves as Apaches from a novel by Karl May.* The older ones are just professional cat burglars.'

Stave stared at the train, watching how in just a few minutes most of the boys had grabbed their fill of booty and cast it off the train on to the embankment with a dull thud. Its owner followed, clambering

---

* A famed early twentieth-century writer of cowboy stories.

down the side of the freight car until near the iron wheels themselves, then sprang off, rolled along and eventually staggered to his feet and seized his sack, so heavy that he could hardly heave it over his shoulder but had to drag it along behind him. Then the next lad was down, then the next. One of them collapsed near the train under the weight of his load, a skinny little kid who Stave guessed could be no more than ten years old. He'd filled his bag with too much coal and now could hardly shift it. Nobody made a move to help him.

The last wagon passed. The squeal of the wheels and the drone of the engine faded.

'Careful,' Kleensch whispered. 'They'll all run into the bushes now in case the police show. They'll spot us and won't be at all happy. We really ought to go.'

Stave was watching one boy, the one who'd been first to jump on to the train and pack his sack. 'I'm going to stay,' he said, and nodded towards him: 'I'm going to have a talk to that one.'

'He's the leader of the gang.'

'Let's see if he remembers me,' Stave said, releasing the safety catch on his pistol.

The chief inspector crawled through the shrubbery, then ran the last few metres to the Bahndamm and said, 'Good morning, Jim.'

The boy jumped, let his sack of coal fall to the ground and a rusty Wehrmacht knife pulled from his belt suddenly appeared in his right hand.

'Wouldn't be the first time, would it?' Stave said accusingly. His own right hand had disappeared into his trouser pocket and was now clutching the grip of the F-22. He hoped he wouldn't have to fire on the boy.

Three, four others approached, obviously the older members of the group, the younger ones having vanished into the bushes. They were holding builders' tools or heavy rocks.

'What's all this about, Kommissar?' their leader, who had pulled himself together by now, spoke up.

'It's Chief Inspector these days.'

'Since when was a few missing sacks of coal a matter for CID?'

'I'm not remotely interested in what you've just done and whatever might be in those sacks. I'm interested in something else altogether.'

'You're not arresting me, then?'

'Certainly not for this messing about on the train. On the other hand, it depends on the answers you give me to a few questions I have.'

'Sounds like a deal I can't refuse,' he said, sticking the knife back in his belt. He winked to the others and said, 'This guy's OK. He and I are old acquaintances.'

'You can go,' Stave said, reassuringly. Otherwise things were likely to get out of hand. There was in any case no way he was going to be able to interrogate them all in one morning. Better to concentrate on one of them without the others interfering.

'I'll catch you up,' the group's leader shouted after them with a skewed smile. Then he turned towards the chief inspector with curiosity rather than fear written all over his face. 'This is about another murder, isn't it?'

'You can join our ranks when you get a bit older,' Stave quipped back. Wilhelm 'Jim' Meinke, fourteen years old, unkempt brown hair, front tooth missing on left side. The chief inspector remembered him as he was then. He had been a witness in the ruins murderer case. On that occasion he'd been picked up near the site where one of the bodies had been found: down by Billekanal, at the end of the harbour. Stave recalled that Meinke's parents had both died in the bombing. His father had worked at Blohm & Voss. The boy had said under interrogation that he had often gone with his father and knew his way well around the shipyard.

Stave showed him the photo of Adolf Winkelmann. 'Familiar face?' he asked. Meinke whistled through the gap in his teeth. 'Somebody really did a job there.'

'I take it that means the answer is yes?'

'Does that make me a suspect?'

'Yes.'

'Always a troublemaker, Adolf, even when he's dead, it seems.'

'You sound grief-stricken.'

'He's not exactly a great loss to Hamburg, or the rest of the world.'

'You're a fine one to pass a judgement like that.'

'Sounds like it to me. I knew Adolf better than you.'

'Then bring me up to speed. Let's start with you. I thought you hung about round Billekanal and gathered coal here. What are you doing here?'

'It was pure chance you picked me up that time down at Bille-kanal. I do as much business in coal as Erik Blumenfeld.'

Blumenfeld was Hamburg's biggest coal merchant and also happened to be a citizens' representative in the Christian Democratic Party. Kids like Jim Meinke could have ruined either or both businesses for him. If Stave arrested him, he'd have a powerful ally. If he let him go he'd do better not to mention it to his colleagues. 'So this is where you get most of your supply?'

The boy shrugged. 'So, so. When the coppers clamp down here, it's better to hang around the harbour. There's also the advantage that with a coal cargo ship there's no danger of falling under the wheels.'

'Worst that can happen is a bath in the Elbe.'

'It's better than a sawn-off leg.'

'So where did you get to know Adolf Winkelmann?'

'On the train tracks.'

The chief inspector was surprised. 'Not down at the harbour? At Blohm & Voss?'

'No.'

'Are you sure?'

'What is this? A Gestapo interrogation? My territory down at the harbour is the Billekanal and round about. That's where the coal boats come in. Inland waterway traffic. I've never been further upriver. Not my thing, far too dangerous. Lots of Tommies on guard too. If Adolf was hanging out up there, I know nothing about it.'

'But your father did work at Blohm & Voss?'

A nod.

'And you often went down there?'

'When my old man was still alive, he used to take me with him sometimes. It was supposed to be forbidden, but the old boy was OK and didn't worry about stuff like that. Since he's been gone, I haven't been back. What would there be for me down there?'

Stave stared at the fourteen-year-old. In the old days, even hardened criminals wouldn't have answered him so self-confidently. 'OK then, the railway tracks. When did you first see Adolf Winkelmann?'

'Not the foggiest. All of a sudden he was just there.'

'Can't you be a bit more precise? Last month? Last year?'

'When it was so cold. More and more people kept turning up, old people too, and girls.'

'November or December 1946?'

'I don't possess a calendar.'

The chief inspector thought it over. The beginning of the winter of starvation. Most trains had stopped running because of the lack of coal. Boxing matches and other entertainments were cancelled. Not exactly good times for a smuggler with a sideline in selling boxing tickets. And what was it his aunt had said? That sometimes he brought coal back home. That all made sense.

'Did he turn up often?'

'Only now and again. He was an amateur. Not even. Adolf was mainly down by the railway tracks because in winter there were other children there, children who had no business being there.'

'Wolf children?'

'Polak packs. They should have stayed back east with the Ivans. What did they think they were doing here in Hamburg?'

'Surviving, maybe. Names?' Stave produced his notebook for the first time.

Meinke shook his head. 'If I'd known I would have the opportunity to grass one of them up to the cops, I'd have asked for a visiting card. But I have no idea what they were called. They were a nuisance. And when they came to be too much of a nuisance we picked up a few builders' tools and explained things to them. I think they ply their trade somewhere else these days, but they aren't here any more.'

'But Adolf Winkelmann wasn't exactly a wolf child.'

'Everybody knew that. He always acted the big man with his black market stuff. A ciggie here, a ciggie there. If he was such a good businessman, what was he doing hanging around here? We steal coal, but that's a thousand times more honest than going down to the Hansa-platz to smuggle butter in shoe polish boxes or sell old alcoholics industrial alcohol and call it schnapps, until they go blind. Maybe that's why Adolf hung out with the wolf kids, they were the only ones who would be doing with him. I guess he paid them, they can be paid to do anything, if you know what I mean.'

'I get the picture. Did Adolf Winkelmann get beaten up when you drove the wolf kids away from the railway tracks?'

The boy was silent for a while. 'You're not trying to pin something on me, are you, Kommissar?'

'Did you beat him up or not? I'm going to keep asking until I get an answer. If I have to I'll order up a few hundred police in uniform and close down these tracks until you've used up your last lump of coal.'

Jim Meinke stared up at the sky, then sighed theatrically and spread out his arms. 'I would have loved to give him a kicking, but I didn't. Nor did anybody else here. We weren't fast enough.'

'Fast enough for what?'

The boy made a dismissive gesture. 'You'll find out soon enough. Adolf was an amateur. He only rarely jumped the trains. It's not that easy to do. From the sidelines trains seem big and slow, but get close up and try to jump on to one with a sack in your belt or in your hand. You have to catch the stepping plate and then try to get a handhold. Not easy to do in the summer. A lot harder in the winter, when everything's frozen hard and your hands are as stiff and unfeeling as those of on old schoolteacher. And, in winter, the lumps of coal on the open wagons are frozen together. You can't exactly fill your sack in a few minutes. You have to pull the lumps apart with your bare hands. And the wind's blowing up there. And then the frozen coal is slippery …' His voice faded away.

'Go on.'

'One morning, Uwe Oldenburg, one of my lads, lost his balance on one of the wagons. He cried out, then fell off, backwards, not to the side. He fell between the tracks and the next wagon. There wasn't much of him left by the time the train had passed. The funny thing was that Uwe had been a good climber, never lost his balance before. Just this one stupid day. A day when it so happened there was another boy on the same wagon with him.'

'Adolf Winklemann?'

'Good guess. At first we tried to do the best we could for our pal, but there wasn't much to be done. Then I looked around to try to talk to Winkelmann. But he'd vanished, hadn't he? He must have done a runner while we were all down on the tracks with Uwe. That was the last time I saw him. Believe you me, I wouldn't have minded bumping into this Adolf Winkelmann again.'

'You think he pushed your friend off the train?'

A shrug. 'Pushed? Nobody saw him do that. Maybe it was just because he was an amateur. Lost his balance himself, or was bashing away too hard at the frozen coal, and somehow or other bumped into Uwe, and hey ho, end of the show.'

'Might it not just be that Adolf Winkelmann didn't touch the other boy at all. But when he fell off he knew he'd get the blame. And you'd make him pay for it.'

'One way or the other, he did a runner. That's all I know.'

'When was this?'

'Towards the end of the winter.'

'February? March?'

'Herr Kommissar, I'm pleased enough that I know how old I am. You're asking me about months and days? It's just not important.'

'It is to me, and it could be to you.'

'So I am a suspect. You're keeping an eye on me? Well, you won't be able to hang this on me.'

'Revenge is a good motive.'

Meinke took a step backwards. 'No way, I'm no killer. I might have beaten Adolf up, but I didn't do that.'

'Nobody's saying it was you,' the chief inspector stressed. 'But every one of your gang had a motive. Maybe one of them met up with Adolf Winkelmann … and settled his account.'

'No, none of us would do something like that.'

'That's the second most frequent thing policemen hear. Comes just after "I swear I'm innocent". You can't speak for each and every member of your gang.'

Meinke shook his head. 'If it had been one of my gang, he would have talked. He wouldn't just have done away with Adolf Winkelmann like that and not mentioned it to anyone. He'd have mentioned it, if only to get the praise for it. That's not the way it was. And in any case we've all forgotten the incident by now. If you hadn't shown me the photograph, and asked all these questions, I'd never have thought about it. It's not that I'm heartless, just that that wasn't the only accident. You get used to it and just carry on as before the next day. Put it like this: these things aren't that important at the end of the day.'

Stave didn't know whether to believe Meinke or not. When a suspect was lying, he always tried to portray himself as the best character in some made-up story – not exactly what this boy had just done. On the other hand it might just be a particularly devious lie. Paint a bad picture of yourself so that the cops will believe you, but not bad enough for them to pin the crime on you.

'Where are you living?'

'Still in the basement in Rothenburgsort.' Meinke gave him the address. The chief inspector wrote it down, the name of a street that was so reduced to rubble and as yet uncleared that you could hardly say it existed any more. He doubted very much if he could ever find Meinke there if he tried to. But he knew about the railway tracks and the inner harbour around Billekanal. Even vagabonds had to live somewhere: he would be able to find him in one place or the other.'

'Thanks for the information,' he said, adding: 'You can go now.'

'You let him go?' Kleensch asked when they met up again in the rose garden. The sun was now high in the sky, dust shimmered in the air, dried leaves, blood-red, lay strewn on the path. The first few couples had invaded the park, some walking hand in hand, others keeping an eye out for convenient shrubbery or undergrowth, where they might enjoy a few fumbled passionate moments in private. Stave stopped himself thinking of Anna.

'None of the coal thieves would have come willingly. Remember the huge fights we had last winter when 800 looters set on a few police with sticks and stones.'

'That was in a winter when people were starving. These days there are only a few kids hanging out on the tracks. I assume you're armed.'

The chief inspector gave him a wry smile. 'You'd have a good story if I'd drawn on him. "Policeman Threatens Hamburg Children." All those good law-abiding families of this city would freeze without these adventurous children.'

'You really think that badly of me?'

'You do your job, just like I do mine.'

'Did you get anywhere?'

'Further than in the last couple of days. I have grounds for suspicion.'

'It doesn't sound as if you're going to tell me any more.'

The chief inspector laughed. 'It's too early for that.'

'Nothing's ever too early for a news desk,' Kleensch sighed. 'OK, no news story for now, but when you do have something you let me know before the others. That's the price for me crawling out of bed so early on a Saturday morning.'

'You'll get your story.'

He said goodbye to Kleensch and strolled back to the CID headquarters. The heat was suffocating, but on the other hand it was a relief in that the pain in his left foot wasn't so bad.

On the way he thought over what he had learned about the coal thieves. Revenge for the death of a friend was a good motive. All at once he had a dozen or two potential suspects. First and foremost had to be Jim Meinke, who was strong, had a Wehrmacht knife and was leader of the gang – the one the others all expected to deal with stuff. He also knew his way around the harbour. Even though he denied it, he might well have been down at Blohm & Voss; he certainly knew the lie of the land. It was a plausible story, maybe even good enough to convince Public Prosecutor Ehrlich to issue a warrant for his arrest. If it weren't for one little detail: when the chief inspector had startled Meinke he had pulled his knife as quick as lightning, in his right hand. And according to Dr Czrisini, Adolf Winkelmann's killer had used his left.

Stave wondered if a kid like Meinke might be ambidextrous. He tried to remember how the boy had climbed on to the coal wagon. He'd been strong, agile, but when he got up there he had held the sack open with his left hand and shovelled the coal in with his right. Typical right-handed behaviour. In any case, it would have been too simple, the CID man told himself. Also he didn't think the boy capable of such a cold-blooded murder.

The air in his office was stale with the smell of old paper: files, files and more files. And now he was about to add a few more. He would write a report on Meinke's interrogation and put it in the narrow green filing cabinet. He enjoyed doing reports on a Saturday because nobody interrupted him. Erna Berg was off, most of the other offices were empty, only from the far end of the corridor came the click of a typewriter: evidently one of his colleagues felt the same.

As he walked over to his desk, it occurred to him that the 'Adolf Winkemann Murder' file was going to be thicker than they had thought. On top of it was a note in MacDonald's careless handwriting.

Old boy,
I've been trying to get hold of you for hours so I hope you get this
note. I've been asking around among our people and I've found out
a few things about Blohm & Voss. Our comrades in the Royal Air
Force flew thirty-eight raids on the shipyard but even so it continued
production right up until the end of the war. Even in February

1945, there were still 16,339 men employed. Now this is where it gets interesting. Most of them were forced workers. Some 600 prisoners from the Neuengamme concentration camp did shifts there; in fact they erected a subsidiary camp. Most of the rest were forced workers brought in from all over Europe, although mostly from the east. They were housed in twenty-six camps scattered all around the shipyard and out at Blohm & Voss's aircraft factory at Finkenwerder.

Unfortunately there are a lot of gaps in the documentation. I've read through it all and not been able to find any link to the Winkelmann family and as far as I can tell no member of the Winkelmann family ever worked for Blohm & Voss. But, about half of the concentration camp inmates who worked there survived, and, as we noted, several thousand of the forced workers were still there at the end of the war. It is quite possible, though I have not been able to ascertain this yet, that a good number of them are still in Hamburg. Displaced Persons who don't want to be repatriated to Eastern Europe. You know that a lot of DPs are now active as smugglers or black marketeers. They know the harbour area a lot better than you or I. And wasn't Adolf Winkelmann in contact with smugglers? And black marketeers? Maybe that is a lead? He could have been doing business with DPs who used to work at Blohm & Voss, and then something went wrong – and his body ended up lying on that bomb.

Enough questions to think about there on a fine Saturday afternoon. (Erna says you're bound to be in the office.)

MacDonald

Stave rubbed his eyes. If he had to interrogate all the coal thieves and now all the DPs in Hamburg he was going to be working most weekends. He wasn't keen on the lieutenant's theory but he could find nothing to say against it. So now he had two leads.

He worded his report carefully, bashed out on the typewriter with his unskilled fingers, struggling with a loose ribbon and the cheap yellow paper. He had almost forgotten the time. The sunlight coming through his office window was no longer bright yellow but red and gold. He leapt to his feet. Anna!

He took the tram, then walked the rest of the long way home. She hadn't turned him down. He would tell her all his problems. He would tell her about his son, who was going to show up one of these days. No secrets, no gaps in his life from now on. They would sort it all out. Together. They would eat out on the balcony: at sunset even ruins could look romantic. And then, the night together.

The stairwell was already as dark as the grave; the small window at the top hadn't been cleaned for years and the glass was covered with layers of grease and dirt and pigeon droppings. Stave ran up the four floors, exhilarated now. Then he stopped. There was a shadow on the floor above, right outside the door to his apartment. He held his breath. His heart was pounding. He fumbled with his right hand beneath his jacket to reach for his FN22.

Then a voice came from just above: 'Are you going to shoot your own son?'

Stave thundered up the stairs. He hadn't heard that voice for so many years. *You mustn't crack up.* With shaking hands he reached for a match, lit it and held up the flame.

'Karl …'

'You've got a few grey hairs.'

Stave climbed the last few stairs with uncertain steps. He wanted to embrace his son but didn't dare. He fumbled clumsily with his keys in the lock, scarcely daring to glance at his son.

'Come in,' he whispered. 'Have you been here long? How did you find me?'

Sunlight flooded the apartment. Now Stave could see the hard lines in his son's face, his grey skin, the bags under his eyes. Karl was a head taller, he had always been thin but now he looked wasted, the skin on his cheeks pulled so tight you could see the bones. He was wearing a dirty blue dyed Wehrmacht greatcoat, draped over his body, and underneath trousers of an indeterminate colour, a ripped shirt, cloth shoes with holes in them, not the ones Stave had bought for him on the black market and sent to Vorkuta. The swine!

Karl had the same pale blond hair as he did, but Margarethe's deep dark blue eyes. But they were no longer the eyes of a boy, not even of one of the little snot-dripping fanatics of the Hitler Youth – just tired, suspicious, hard. Nineteen years old, Stave thought to himself, and the war has turned him into a man, a damaged man. Stave blinked to hide his tears. He hadn't cried since he was a child. This is no time for me to start howling. Who knows what Karl would think?

'Still working away, Father? Even Saturdays, just like the old days?'

'Were you waiting long?' Stave's voice sounded awkward.

'If there's one thing I've learnt to do, it's wait.' Karl looked around the room. 'Nothing from our old apartment here?'

'It was all destroyed.'

Stave closed his eyes. Please don't let us start arguing again, he prayed. Where were you when the bombs hit our house? Why weren't you with Mother? Karl himself had been on a camping trip with the Hitler Youth that night. It had saved his life. I suspect he feels guilty himself, Stave surmised.

To his great relief his son said no more on the subject. He smelled of dirty clothes, sweat and disinfectant. He had no bag, no suitcase, Stave only just realised.

'At long last, no barracks, no camp, no huts.' His son wiped his eyes with one hand. 'I sat for weeks in a cattle car going through Russia. I thought I'd be on the thing forever. Then eventually we reached Camp 96.'

'Camp 96?'

'Release facility, where they set free those POWs who've made it that far. In Gronenfelde, near Frankfurt on the Main. Because I'm from Hamburg, they put me on a train. This morning at the release facility by the Kunsthalle here, I got my discharge note. I've been debriefed. God, but I'm tired. And hungry.'

Stave leapt to his feet. 'I'll surprise you.'

He hurried into the kitchen, filled the little stove with kindling, little chopped bits of wood he'd found in the rubble days ago. He took the round ex-Wehrmacht pot and set it on the coal oven in the kitchen from which he'd removed the hot plate. That way the smoke would go down into the ceramic tiled stove that heated the apartment and through its chimney out into the open air, rather than filling the room. It worked as long as he remembered to clean the pipes once a week. Otherwise the damp dirty wood filled it with a thick layer of greasy soot.

Stave put a pot on the stove, carefully in case his wobbly construction tipped over. 'Bahndamm soup with blocks of cement,' he called to his son, trying his best to be light-hearted. 'Vegetables like you find by the railway tracks, nettles, yarrow, semolina dumplings as hard as cement, accompanied by sausage made with whale meat and bonemeal.'

'Smells good,' his son replied in a tired voice. 'For the past few years all I've had has been mouldy bread with *kapusta*.'

'*Kapusta*?'

'Russian cabbage.'

Stave was about to reply when suddenly he saw a figure at the door of the apartment, which he'd forgotten to close.

Anna. She was wearing a cream-coloured summer dress he hadn't seen before, her long hair plaited. In her right hand was a little package, wrapped up. A surprise for him, he guessed. She was going to be the one surprised. She glanced swiftly from him to Karl. She had understood straight away.

'Anna,' Stave said. He couldn't think of anything more sensible to say.

She gave a forced smile. 'Maybe it's better if I leave you alone?' she managed to say.

'Karl, may I introduce you. Anna von Veckinhausen. Anna, this is my son Karl.' Stave felt ridiculous even as he said it.

His son said nothing, just stared silently at the table.

Anna was already back in the stairwell. 'Wait!' Stave called out, rushing after her. He didn't know how to explain. 'Won't you stay?'

For a moment he thought his lover was going to say something. But then she just brought her right arm up to her chest, as she always did when she felt under stress. 'You need to spend the evening with your son. On your own.'

'I had no idea he would be back today. I mean, obviously I'm pleased he's here,' he stammered.

'I'm pleased for you.' She brushed her fingers briefly over his cheek. Tenderly, with no doubt that it was a parting gesture. He stood there a few minutes on the stairs, not knowing what to do, then he went back into the apartment.

'A replacement for Mama? Nobility too, and you a secret Social Democrat all those years?' His son hadn't stirred from where he sat.

Stave closed his eyes. 'It's complicated. Too complicated for this evening. I'll tell you everything.' Already he was avoiding the truth, and his son had barely been home ten minutes. Not a great start. He was relieved when he heard a bubbling sound from the kitchen and ran to see to it, happy and sad all at once, confused and helpless. He was beginning to dread the evening ahead.

While he stirred the soup and added salt, he surreptitiously watched his son. He's going to fall asleep before he gets anything in his stomach. I have to get a move on. 'Just a few minutes more on this old stove,' he called out.

'Have you a cigarette?'

Stave looked at him in surprise, but didn't ask any questions. He put his hand in the pocket of his jacket hanging on a hook and tossed him a pack of John Player's. 'You smoke too these days?' Karl asked in surprise, taking a smoke from the crumpled packet and lighting up.

'No, that's my substitute wallet. You get better value on the black market with cigarettes than you do with Reischsmark notes.'

'Same thing in the POW camp.'

'No mouldy bread or cabbage at least today.'

'Nettle soup and whale sausage instead. The Russians won the war and we lost but in the end it hasn't made much difference either way.'

'Wait until you meet the British, then you'll see the difference between winning and losing.'

'That bad, is it?'

Stave thought of MacDonald. 'We're lucky the Red Army didn't get as far as Hamburg. When you think of what we did to the British, they treat us really rather fairly.'

'You said "we". You used to be proud of not being a Nazi.'

'Which made you very angry,' Stave could have bitten his tongue. It just came out. Talking to his son, thinking of MacDonald. There were minefields everywhere, and if he wasn't careful everything would get blown to smithereens.

Karl looked him in the eye again for the first time in minutes. 'I've had it with the Nazis,' he said wearily. 'With politics in general, Nazis, Communists, Tommies, Amis, you're welcome to them all. Liars all.'

Stave said nothing. At least that's something, he thought to himself. The war had chased the brown fleas out of his head. He wondered to himself what his son had been through in the war. His head spun. Concentrate on the meal, he told himself.

The soup was steaming. Along with it he had a few carrots and a little head of lettuce, bought on the black market from an allotment gardener. Karl took a bite of the vegetables, chewing the carrots carefully. 'My teeth are loose,' he explained and managed an awkward grin. Then he took a spoon and began gulping down the soup. Stave watched him: bent over the bowl, not looking up, short quick movements, one spoonful after the other, slurping greedily, like some half-starved animal. The he stopped and stared.

'What happened to your finger?' he asked. His son was missing the end of his right index finger.

'One of the Ivans shot it off,' Karl mumbled between bites, continuing to wolf down the soup. 'I've got used to it.'

The chief inspector couldn't drag his eyes away from the red, scarred stump. It broke his heart. Did it happen at the front? Or in the camp? Did it still hurt? Could he still grip things, write? Stave didn't dare ask.

'Have you got another bowl?'

'Of course.'

Stave had cooked for two, but his son could have a double portion if he wanted. He needed it more.

'Was it bad out in Vorkuta?' he asked cautiously, putting the second bowl of soup down on the table.

'First the Russians let go all our comrades from Austria. All of a sudden they weren't German any more. We were jealous. Then they took all the SS men away, even those who had managed to find a Wehrmacht uniform before the Ivans captured them. They were led off, and we never saw any of them again. But I don't think they were sent home like the Austrians. They got what they deserved from the Russians.' He gave a short laugh, then bent down over his soup again.

Stave was confused. What had he expected? An epic description of life in a camp on the icy steppes? He would have to figure it out from the few brief sentences his son said. It would take time. I will really listen to him, not like in the old days. He'll tell me everything, sooner or later.

He had kept two slices of crumbly bread and some reddish ersatz jam. With a cup of coffee, real Mocha, it had cost a fortune on the black market. Anna would have been delighted. It didn't matter now.

'Can you get this every day here?' Karl asked in surprise. Before his father could answer, he nodded and his expression darkened a little. 'The upper class lady? Did I spoil a romantic evening?'

'You didn't spoil anything,' Stave replied, louder than he had intended. 'But I can't afford this every day, so eat up and enjoy.'

'Sir, yessir, Herr … what rank are you now? Did the Tommies promote you?'

Stave felt himself blush. Don't get provoked, he told himself.

'Police Chief Inspector, it's a new rank the British introduced. That's what they call their people back in Scotland Yard, I'm told. But I'm still doing the same work as ever: murder squad.'

'Fine,' mumbled Karl, clearly a bit embarrassed by his own words. 'Don't mind me. I'm just tired.'

Silence. His son chewed slowly on the bread and jam. The expression on his face was almost blissful. He supped ever so slowly at his coffee. Stave couldn't think of anything to say. Gradually, darkness began to creep over them. Stave fumbled around in a drawer until he found a stub of candle that gave a flickering light.

'In Vorkuta we had one candle for each hut,' Karl said without being asked. 'In winter it was all the light we had.' Then he struggled to his feet, reeling. 'I need to go to bed.'

The chief inspector led him into the room he had prepared for him. At last, Karl was there! He had to hold on to the wall to keep himself upright. His son didn't notice his joy, just crawled on to the bed. 'A mattress, and a sheet. I'm a civilian again.' At last he took off his coat, shirt and trousers. He had no vest, underpants with holes in them, ribs sticking out below tight-stretched skin. He lay down on the bed and within five seconds was fast asleep.

Stave looked down at him. In his sleep his features relaxed and he looked like a boy again, he thought to himself. But he had not forgotten that Karl had been a soldier. He didn't dare to touch him, in case he woke up in fright and started lashing out. Who knows what he had been through? Stave just stood there next to the bed, looking down at the thin body, the haggard face, his maimed right hand. Even though it was still warm and there was no draught from the open window, he spread the woollen blanket carefully over his son. Gently he picked up the rags from the floor. He would put them all in the bin. He laid one of his shirts and a pair of trousers over the back of a chair. The trousers would be too short for Karl but they would have to do until he found some on the black market.

He stood there in the door for a long time, the candle in his hand, not wanting to leave the room. Leave him to rest, he told himself in the end. Don't get too sentimental. Karl has been through a lot. You have to take care of him.

Stave went into his own room, but turned away from the bed and went out on to the balcony. The city was dark with just a few red candle lights glowing within the ruins, and just here and there a brightly lit window where they had electricity again. The headlights of a British Jeep, its growling engine. I hope the patrols don't wake my boy. He waited with bated breath until the vehicle passed the length of Ahrensburger Strasse, listened out to hear if there was any noise from the other side of the closed door. Nothing. Karl was asleep.

He pulled up a wooden chair and sat down on it on the balcony, thinking about Karl, about Anna, about how life would be from now on. There was no chance of him going to sleep.

Off His Own Bat

Monday, 9 June 1947

Heat. The stench of faeces rising from a stretch of wasteland because the pipes leading to the drains had collapsed. Stave wasn't looking at the ruins of the city; he was trying to breathe as shallowly as possible so as not to inhale any more than he had to of the suffocating haze. He headed slowly towards the office. Monday at last, a relief after a torturously quiet Sunday. His son had slept soundly, so soundly that the chief inspector eventually ventured into his room, afraid that the boy might have died during the night. By the time he finally got up, the room was bright with noonday sun, too hot to sit out on the balcony. Breakfast was laid out on the wobbly kitchen table: bread, Quark, tap water, which still only trickled out.

'We'll be sitting here with nothing to drink if this goes on,' Stave had said jokingly. He couldn't think of anything more to say to his silent son. What will you do now? That would sound like a demand. The boy had to get back on his feet first. In any case Stave wouldn't have known what advice to give him. Study at the bombed-out university? Should he train as an engineer, even though the Allies had forbidden any new German industry? No ships, no aircraft, no cars. A teacher – in one of the ruined schools full of criminal kids? Maybe even the police?

Should he take Karl on a tour around Hamburg and show him what was destroyed in the final years of the war? How miserable a life they would be leading from now on? A boy who just two years ago considered himself part of the ruling class of a new elite. And now would have to work like a coolie in a rice field just to live from day to day. You've first of all got to bond with him, Stave told himself.

But how? Go to the cinema? Karl and he hadn't gone to see a movie together since the boy was twelve years old. Stave had hated the news magazines, the weekly droning of Hitler and Goebbels. But at the same time he had been ever so slightly afraid of his son in his *Pimpf* uniform, watching his face for the slightest sign of weakness or mistrust of the Führer. Karl had understood why his father wouldn't take him to the cinemas any more. But Stave had never said anything: he had known he would never manage to get Karl out of the clutches of the Nazis. At first he hadn't taken the *Pimpf* uniform and all the parroted repetition of propaganda seriously. He'd grow out of it. It was only when it was too late that he realised he'd lost Karl to Hitler and Goebbels. And after the death of Margarethe, he simply hadn't the strength left to fight against the undertow sweeping his son away from him.

And so they had spent Sunday talking occasionally about trivia, Stave carefully, helplessly, Karl in monosyllables, still exhausted. But at least they had talked.

No word from Anna, but how could there be. If only we had telephones, Stave thought to himself. I wouldn't mind the expense just to exchange a few words with her, to explain things and arrange another meeting.

So he had crept out of the apartment without breakfast, leaving his ration on the kitchen table for Karl, who was still asleep. Stave was hungry and thirsty but relieved. He had taken his son's documents with him to go down to the housing department and register permission for him to move in, get him ration cards and a normal ID card. It would take time, but Stave was determined to get everything in order. He felt he wouldn't be at so much risk of him slipping away if he had signed and stamped official documents, something that still seemed like a dream.

He came back to the apartment and set down the papers, forms and new documentation on the kitchen table next to the bread. Not a sound from the room next door. At least Karl didn't have night-mares that woke him up screaming. He would have to tell him about those.

As a result it was nearly noon before the chief inspector turned up at CID headquarters. As he trudged up the stairs it suddenly occurred to him that none of his colleagues knew about Karl. They all knew the story about his missing son, of course, but should he now tell them that the boy was back home again? What would the others think, those whose boys hadn't come back from the front? Stave wasn't particularly popular as it was, and that would hardly win him any new friends.

He only made his decision when he opened the door of the anteroom to his office. Erna Berg, heavy and round now, crouched behind her typewriter as if it was a defensive barrier. She looked tired and unhappy. It was her divorce, Stave reckoned, her lover MacDon-ald, her husband who'd come back from the war with only one leg, the courts, her worries that she wouldn't be able to retain custody of her elder son. This was hardly the right moment to tell her about Karl. So he just gave her a nod, forced a smile and disappeared into his office. Sort out this case, he told himself, and then you can deal with the rest when your mind is clear.

His best witness was still the young prostitute. It might be worth having another word with Hildegard Hüllmann, he reckoned. The girl was one of the wolf children. She had been in Planten un Blomen with the victim. Maybe she'd got wind of more about Adolf's prob-lems with the coal thieves than she'd let on at their last meeting. Maybe she knew which of the Bahndamm gang disliked him most.

'I'm off down to the station, investigating,' he called to Erna Berg, as he grabbed his hat. There was no point in going down to the girls' orphanage in Feuerbergstrasse. She'd have got out of there ages ago.

First of all the chief inspector went past the station to the Hansa-platz, an almost exactly rectilinear square which had once been a model of middle-class propriety. It was cobbled and lined with five- or six-storied apartment buildings from the late mid-nineteenth century with white stucco fronts, now black in places or just blown out, with pillars or railings in front of tall wooden doors. The rows on the north and east sides had gaps where the bombs had found their targets. In the middle was a 17-metre high golden fountain with a female figure meant to represent the Hansa, the medieval trading organisation, with a gold crown on her head. In her left hand was a trident while the right pointed into the distance. Pathos from the days of the Kaisers, a queen presiding over a sea of rubble. Stave asked himself, as he had done so many times before, why so many hospitals and schools had been reduced to ruins, yet something like that remained standing. Was it chance? Or was it that, as MacDonald sometimes joked, those in the Royal Air Force who aimed the bombs were extremely accurate? Did one of them, flying high over Hamburg in a night sky alight with raging fire and searchlights, decide in a moment of cynical omnipotence to destroy the populace's morale by wiping out everything but the most useless monuments?

Stave went into the Lenx bar on Brenner Strasse, which led off the Hansaplatz, to get the lie of the land, and to fill his stomach. A potato salad, a glass of water and an ersatz coffee all for a few Reichsmarks. A customer was complaining loudly to the tired manager. There was jazz on the radio, but the customer wanted old German songs.

'I'll turn the radio down,' the manager said to appease him and fiddled around with a knob under the counter. Stave thought the jazz was as loud as ever, but the customer seemed satisfied and ordered another coffee – a real coffee, the chief inspector recognised from the smell. Damn black marketeer, he thought, you make a fortune out of selling American cigarettes, then complain about their music.

A bit later Stave wanted to head back to the Hansaplatz again. It was afternoon and the black marketeers would be out. He might see if he could find anything for Karl. It would be awkward though if his colleagues from Department S picked him up. He kept a look out from his table by the window for any of their grasses he might recognise. For half an hour he sat there, then an hour, playing with his potato salad. He didn't spot any of them. There won't be a raid today, he told himself.

The air on the glass station concourse was still. Stave could taste coal dust in his dry mouth. At this time of day the platforms were empty. There were only a few long-distance trains leaving. The suburban lines were quiet. But even so he didn't have to go looking for the young prostitute; she found him. All of a sudden she was standing next to him, plucking at his sleeve.

'I can tell you aren't a punter, that's for sure. Those lads have their eyes on you; you walked straight past me.'

'What makes you think I'm looking for you?'

'Going on a journey, are you? With no suitcase? Going foraging, without a sack or a basket? You still haven't found Adolf's murderer, that's why you're here.'

'Word gets around.'

'I've been asking questions of my own.'

Stave looked at her. So thin. Her braided hair glowing strawberry blond, even though it almost certainly hadn't been washed for days. He tried to imagine Hildegard Hüllmann as a schoolgirl, but somehow he couldn't picture it in his head. He led her down to a bench at one end of the platform.

'You're investigating off your own bat?'

'It's not illegal, is it? As long as I don't break any laws.'

'Have you broken any?'

She smiled, happily rather than cheekily. Stave was astonished to realise she liked him. 'The boys down at the tracks were pretty annoyed, I hear, to find you spying on them on Saturday.'

'Have you spoken to any of them?'

'I've been keeping my ears open. Can't exactly say they're friends of mine. They weren't Adolf's best mates either.'

'I believe there was some trouble.'

'Whatever that Jim Meinke boy said, Adolf wasn't responsible. He never pushed anybody off a freight train, not even by accident.'

'Meinke doesn't agree.'

She snorted angrily. 'They didn't like him because he was cleverer than they were. All they could do was steal a sack of coal. Any ten-year-old can do that. But Adolf, he had a bigger view. He had built himself a business. He only went down to the tracks to have fun with his friends.'

'The wolf children?'

'Anyone who's found their way here from the east isn't stupid, Chief Inspector. We're a lot smarter than these mummy's boys from Hamburg.'

'Meinke is no mummy's boy. His parents are dead too,' Stave said, a little more sharply than he had intended.

'Don't make me cry.'

'You mean Adolf was doing other business besides coal?'

'On the Hansaplatz.'

'Black market?'

'And smuggling.'

'Cigarettes? Jewellery?'

'Sometimes, but Adolf really was one step ahead of the others. Tapes.'

'What was the point of that,' the chief inspector asked, puzzled. 'Nobody has a tape recorder any more. And in any case there's no electricity for it.'

She shrugged her shoulders. 'Like I said, I've been asking around. There's a kid on the Hansaplatz who acts as a lookout, he told me about it. Adolf was dealing in tapes.' She gave a shy smile. 'Off his own bat, so he said.'

Stave took out a handkerchief to wipe the sweat from his brow. Why would Adolf Winkelmann be smuggling tapes? Who would he sell them to? Big players on the black market who had too much money? Farmers from Holland who had made enough from selling potatoes to buy themselves a tape recorder and now wanted to record music?' Absurd.

'Who bought these tapes?'

'I don't know but I'll find out.'

Stave thought back to where the body had been found and what MacDonald had said about Blohm & Voss in the war. 'Was Adolf doing business with DPs? Former forced workers? Russians? Poles?'

'If he'd been doing anything with the Russians, I wouldn't have had anything to do with him,' Hildegard Hüllmann said with conviction.

But maybe that's why he didn't tell you anything about it, the chief inspector thought to himself. Nothing new about the coal thieves. He wondered if this young prostitute was holding out the tapes story in front of his nose as bait to distract him from the real story. Or if that really was all she knew. She had only met the boy a few times, after all. Or so she said.

'Be careful,' he said to her and got up from the bench. 'Keep away from Meinke.'

'He's nowhere near as dangerous as the aunt.'

Stave stopped. 'Greta Boesel?'

'If that's her name, it'll do. Adolf told me more than once that his aunt was an iron-eater.'

It wasn't a term the chief inspector had ever heard before. He raised an eyebrow.

'It's a boxing expression. Hard-headed. She was raking money in. Adolf said she was into really big business. He was afraid of her.'

Stave found himself trying to imagine Greta Boesel stabbing her big nephew on top of an unexploded bomb down at the shipyard. Clearly the aunt and her nephew had their secrets from one another, and clearly both of them were playing a game on either side of the law. But murder?

'Did he feel threatened by his aunt?'

'No, no,' Hildegard Hüllmann conceded. 'He was just wary of her. From all I knew of him, she was the only person he really respected.'

Which in turn meant that Adolf Winkelmann was hardly in awe of Meinke and the coal thieves and he had probably let them know, the chief inspector thought. That might have been his mistake.

'Can I go now?' she asked politely. 'No little excursion down to Feuerbergstrasse? Don't forget. I approached you. I could have avoided you.'

He smiled and shook his head. 'It might look a bit suspicious if the same policeman kept bringing you back.'

She blew him a coquettish kiss and strutted off. He watched her go, then turned around, towards the Hansaplatz. Slowly he limped along the platform, almost alone. There was only one female passenger waiting, just a few metres ahead of him. Stave was thinking about what he had heard, and what he would buy for Karl. He had nearly walked past the woman when he finally recognised her.

Anna.

'I tried to invite you to lunch. Your secretary told me I'd find you here,' she said in a cool voice. 'But I didn't want to interrupt.' She nodded with her chin towards the skinny little figure of Hildegard Hüllmann, running up the stairs at the other end of the platform.

'I'm in the middle of an investigation,' the chief inspector stammered.

'Do all your suspects blow you a kiss when they say goodbye?'

Stave wanted to take her arm, at least stroke her arm with his fingers. But he didn't dare take the two steps that separated them. 'It's about the murder of a boy down at the shipyard. I told you about it. She knew him.'

'Maybe. I don't seem to know you any more.'

The air in the station tasted like a damp sooty soup. 'You don't think ... that girl and I ...'

'I don't know what I'm supposed to think.' Anna's face was pale. 'Nor do I.'

She gave him a sad smile. 'I know. I'm the one who didn't answer any questions. I thought we could take our time. We could get to know one another slowly. But neither of us was coming from nowhere. We both were carrying the burdens of our past. The days before all this.'

'My son has only been back two days,' he whispered.

'And you mustn't send him away,' she interrupted quickly. 'You told me about Karl. I knew that I would have to meet him sooner or later. But only when you yourself had got back together with him. When you yourself knew how things would work out with him. Do you know that yet?'

Stave held up his hands, then dropped them helplessly to his side. 'I can't think more than a few hours ahead,' he admitted. 'I'm going to the black market to buy a few things. As long as none of my colleagues spot me there. Then I'm going to go home. That's as far as my plans go right now.'

'Karl is angry. Angry about the years he's lost. About the life he missed. Angry at you. And at me, because I'm here instead of his mother.'

'Please don't leave me,' Stave said, choking.

'I can hardly stay. Imagine it. I come round to your place in the evening, sit down at the table next to your silent son, who looks at me the same way he might have looked at a Russian soldier. Then we go to bed, and he's in the room next door and we both imagine he's listening. Or you come round to my place? You tell him he has to spend the evening on his own, next door to your old family house, where his mother died? And you're spending the night with me?'

'We can start all over again,' he whispered. 'We can't all sit here forever, vegetating amid the rubble of the past.'

'Listen, we grabbed hold of one another, like two people drowning. But we're not drowning any longer. We're swimming now.'

'Please don't go.'

'You have to get your life back on the rails, you and your son. And I have to work out for myself how I might fit into that life.' She took the two steps between them, stroked his cheek briefly with her right hand. 'I'm not going away forever,' she whispered. Then she turned on her heel and went down the stairs to the platform.

Stave watched her go, her lean body, her dark hair tied back tightly, her white summer dress tossed by a rare breath of wind. So frail, he thought to himself. And wondered if her last sentence had been anything more than an empty promise.

It took him nearly half an hour to get to the Hansaplatz, even though it was only a few hundred metres away from the station. Stave felt dejected, his ankle ached, he was so distracted that he didn't even sweat. He had a headache, as if there was a tumour in his brain, as if every movement he made caused something to irritate the inside of his skull. His life was a void. He thought back to that night four years ago, when the fires made the night as bright as day and he pulled Margarethe's corpse out of the ruins of their home. At first he had felt no pain, just the impression of being trapped in a dream, from which he would soon wake. Was he now going to find his new love slipping away from him, after a few gently spoken sentences on a station platform? Once again he felt he was caught up in a dreadful dream.

Pull yourself together, he told himself. You need to be here for Karl now. Look around: see any grasses? Any uniformed police? He limped along the little streets around the Hansaplatz: Ellmenreich-strasse, Bremer Reihe, Stralsunder Strasse. There were people out for a walk, children, one or two tired prostitutes, a few drunks – and lots of men and women with briefcases, shopping bags, old rucksacks, heading for the Hansaplatz. It was getting towards closing time, the square would be full.

Eventually Stave dared to go out on to the square itself. He saw the figures in doorways, next to the fountain, all apparently wandering aimlessly over the cobbles. Whispers here and there, bundles of Reichsmarks, carefully counted cigarettes. Here and there young men dressed perfectly, with Swiss watches on their arms, the kings of the black market. Stave looked around again, wandered about. Even if he was here on business for his son, he couldn't help thinking about what Hildegard Hüllmann had told him: recording tape. He spent more time on the Hansaplatz than he needed to, increasing his risk of being picked up, but he didn't spot a tape recorder anywhere. Concentrate on Karl, he told himself.

He had taken everything there was from his emergency supplies in the bottom drawer of his desk. 'Men's trousers,' he went around whispering, 'shirt, shoes ...'

Half an hour later he had paid out a small fortune in cigarettes. In exchange he now had a pair of light linen trousers, a crooked tear in the right leg sewn up with black thread. A shirt dyed to an indeterminate brownish-green colour, obviously a former uniform shirt. 'Luftwaffe,' the elderly lady who sold it to him had whispered, but Stave suspected it had probably been a Party uniform. It would have been golden brown until 1945. Shoes with tatty leather uppers and soles almost as thin as paper. He would have to pad them with newspaper, and they were almost certainly at least one size too big for Karl. And then a briefcase made of black leather, with a broken lock, so that he could carry his purchases home without it being too obvious.

Stave left the square with a sigh of relief. At least there hadn't been a raid. He could taste iron in his moth. When he reached Steindamm he took a long deep breath. What else? He felt around in his trouser pocket. He still had a bundle of leathery Reichsmarks. A hundred metres away there was a chemist's. The large owner, sweating heavily, was standing by the door struggling to fit a hook into a wooden shutter to pull it down over her empty shop window.

Stave ran up to her. 'Have you got skin powder?' he asked. His voice was croaking. It was hardly an impressive way to introduce himself. The woman didn't even turn to look at him; she'd finally managed to get the hook into the loop on the shutter.

'We're closed,' she snorted. 'In any case there's nothing left. And we're not expecting more any time soon.'

The chief inspector was thinking about Karl's dried and damaged skin. 'I'll pay UT,' he whispered, even though he didn't know the shop owner. He held his breath until at last she thought him worth even looking at. UT – under the table – a small, secret deal. Totally illegal. Against all the trade regulations set by the occupation forces. An English summary judge would give him on the spot a week in jail, maybe a month. I hope she doesn't recognise that I'm a policeman, Stave prayed.

'Let's see,' she said at last. She pulled down the shutter and squeezed through the shop door. With a sigh of relief Stave followed her into the dimly lit interior.

'Children's skin powder, ointment.' She fished a tin and a bottle out of a cupboard beneath the counter. 'The real stuff. The Diaderma brand.'

'How much?'

'Sixty cigarettes.'

Stave made a face. He felt like a punter arguing with a prostitute over her price. 'I've just used them all. All I have left is money.' A single John Player's cost seven Reichsmarks: he put 420 on the counter, hesitated for a moment, then added another tenner. Half a year's salary, but then what was money worth these days?

The fat woman grabbed the cash surprisingly quickly and shoved it under her apron, not into the cash till, Stave noticed. You're not on duty, he reminded himself, as he threw the ointment and powder into his briefcase, said goodbye and left.

It was silent in his apartment. The bread, Quark and last few bits of sausage had gone. Karl must be asleep again, the chief inspector told himself for a second, but he already knew that couldn't be the case. He could feel it: the apartment was too quiet. He couldn't hear a breath. He dashed into the little bedroom in horror: it was empty.

Stave set the briefcase down, his heart racing. He was at least relieved not have found Karl lying dead on the bed. Where could he be? He looked on the kitchen table and in the living room for a note, but there was nothing. The boy's just gone out to stretch his legs, he told himself.

He laid out the items of clothing on the bed, noticing that his hands were shaking. He was glad nobody could see him. He turned the tap in the kitchen. Water gurgled out, reddish and tasting as metallic as blood. He drank some nonetheless, and wondered if he should stick his head under the tap. He would welcome the coolness but it might make him even dirtier than he was. In the end the heat won: he bent his head under the tap, and stood there for a while with his eyes closed, letting the water run over his skull, trying to think of nothing.

The cloth he used to dry his head turned rust-red, but at any rate he felt freshened up. He went out again, this time with his ration book in his hand. Time to hit the shops before they closed. He had already used so many he wouldn't have enough for the rest of the month, but Karl would get his own ration book soon.

When he came back again, the apartment was still empty. Stave sat down on a kitchen chair, dumbstruck, staying there for an hour or so. How quiet the apartment could be. He had never noticed before, nor how shabby it was. He wondered where his son could be. Maybe he was out looking for a job? It wasn't the first of the month, but it was a Monday. Maybe somebody might hire him for the week? Don't fool yourself. Nothing happens that fast. Maybe he was meeting some friends? But they had all been in the Hitler Youth. Would they still be alive? And was that a good circle for him to get back into if they were? Unrepentant Nazis? Or those young ex-soldiers with the grim, hardened faces you saw on the black market? There was no end of things to worry about.

Eventually he could take it no longer, he had to get away from the mugginess of the room, the endless silence. He ran down the stairs.

Aimlessly he wandered the streets. Golden sunlight, floating dust particles. The piles of rubble had stored up the heat of the day like little volcanoes. Days after the bombing raids of 1943 the heaps of rubble still glowed. It was like wandering through an oven. Margarethe. What would his wife have done now? She would probably have spoken quite differently to their son. She would surely have thrown her arms around him long ago. Stave closed his eyes and walked on, across Ahrensburger Strasse, and shortly after came to the Wandse, a stream with parkland on either side, a green kilometre-long strip between collapsed houses and grey apartment blocks. It was like a meadow along its banks. New growth coming up where bushes had been hacked down. Grass. Dandelions. The black earth thrown up by moles in heaps between the sunbathers lying there.

Couples lying out on torn sheets, children, families. One young woman was even wearing sunglasses. Stave stared at her until he realised how rude it was. The only sunglasses he had seen in years were those on the faces of occupation officers. Eventually the chief inspector ended up by the Outer Alster. There were four dinghies out on Hamburg's inland sea, their sails limp. The water was as grey and smooth as a sheet of polished lead. One oarsman in a single skull was cutting a neat ripple across the otherwise perfect surface on either side, like a giant line of stitching across the water. The villas on the bank and the green willow branches shimmered, the white slab of the Atlantic Hotel on the left, the spires of churches and the city hall in the distance. He thought of Anna, and the two of them walking along the banks here at the end of that terrible winter. Their first kiss. It wasn't even that long ago. He turned left, limping along the bank. At some stage he found himself on the western side, turned right and wandered down Rotenbaumstrasse. How had he ended up here? Stave realised he had fooled himself, that he hadn't been wandering as aimlessly as he imagined. He was only a few hundred metres from Dammtor Station and the line the coal thieves stole from was just on the other side. This case is consuming you, he thought. Tear yourself away from it, just for one evening. So he turned right, down the next side street, away from the main avenue. Hartungstrasse, he realised. He had been here with Anna a few days earlier.

Stave came to a sudden stop, astonished to see his way blocked by elegantly dressed men and women. Ladies in high heels picking their way cautiously over the cobbles, gentlemen in dinner jackets, British officers in immaculately ironed dress uniforms. There had to be a première in the Kammerspiel theatre, Stave realised. He was about to turn away when he heard someone call out his name.

An officer emerged from the crowd on the other side of the long shadows cast by the rows of houses. MacDonald. The lieutenant shook his hand. Not that long ago, such a thing had been forbidden: fraternisation with the enemy.

'I didn't know you were a theatregoer,' Stave said.

MacDonald laughed. 'There's so much acting in the army, you soon get to be an expert.'

'What's on?'

'The stage version of a radio play. *Draussen vor der Tür,* by Wolfgang Borchert.'

'That author is hardly likely to be there,' Stave muttered. He vaguely remembered hearing that Borchert had died during the last winter, from some horrible fever he had probably brought back from Russia, where he had served in a penal battalion on the eastern front. NWDR radio had broadcast *Draussen vor der Tür.* He had sat down by the radio to listen to it, but had fallen asleep – or maybe the electricity had cut out. One way or another he had no idea what it was about.

'Do you know something, old boy. I'll invite you.'

Stave blinked at the young lieutenant in astonishment. 'You've got two tickets?' He felt terribly shabby in his patched jacket, totally out of place among such elegant company. He looked for an excuse to turn down the invitation.

'I had hoped to surprise Erna,' MacDonald said. His voice sounded carefree, but the smile on his face had frozen.

'She wasn't feeling up to it, in her condition?' the chief inspector suggested.

'Let's say that was the official excuse. The reality is she didn't feel she should be seen here.' He wiped his hand across his eyes. 'And she's probably right. Too many of my comrades here. They already chitchat enough about me and my little pregnant German girlfriend. If she'd come one or another of my senior officers might have thought I was taking the mickey.'

'No scandal.'

'No scandal, but I feel like some of the houses over there: all façade but nothing behind it.'

'I accept your invitation.'

MacDonald slapped him on the back. 'A bit of culture never did anybody any harm, not even a chief inspector in the CID. Don't worry, I won't introduce you to anybody.'

Twenty minutes later Stave was sitting next to the lieutenant in a middle row. Somewhat embarrassedly, he flicked through the programme. Hans Quest as Sergeant Beckmann, Erwin Geschonneck as the cabaret director, Käte Pontow as the soldier's wife. Directed by Wolfgang Liebeneiner. None of it meant anything to him. MacDonald is right: I really am a philistine, he thought. There are other things of interest in life beyond murders and killings. This is something I could tell my son about. Or Anna. If either of them ever turned up again.

The lights went out and the chief inspector was transported into another world: Sergeant Beckmann, wearing a pair of glasses made out of a gas mask coming back from war. His wife with another man. His parents already 'denazified', if only by gassing themselves in their apartment. Just as he was about to throw himself into the Elbe even the river rejected him, and he found himself back in his miserable life.

When the curtain came down, it was initially quiet in the auditorium. Only after a minute or so did the applause begin, slowly at first, then louder and louder. Stave clapped too, but didn't dare glance at his neighbour. A good job Erna Berg hadn't come along.

Eventually MacDonald got to his feet. 'Good actors,' he said casually. 'But the play was very German.'

The chief inspector had no idea how to reply.

'Should I drive you home? My Jeep's parked on Rothenbaum Chaussee.'

Stave suddenly realised how exhausted he was. 'Bit of a one-sided evening. You give me a free ticket, then you act as my chauffeur. I feel I've not paid my share.'

'Think of it as a business engagement,' MacDonald said, smiling for the first time in two hours.

Outside it was as hot as ever. Hot enough that the lieutenant folded down the windscreen so that at least they got the full benefit of the breeze while they were driving. The off-road vehicle bounced over the holes in the road, the officer driving more slowly than he needed to. But then he was probably in no hurry to get back to his villa. He wondered where Erna Berg was spending the evening.

In order to distract MacDonald from his thoughts and end the awkward silence, Stave thanked him for the note he'd left the previous weekend. He virtually had to shout aloud to be heard over the roar of the twelve-cylinder engine.

'Doesn't sound as if you think too much of my lead,' MacDonald replied.

The chief inspector felt as if he'd been caught out. MacDonald must have noticed his lack of enthusiasm. 'Adolf Winkelmann hung around with wolf children,' he said as if to justify himself. 'Coal thieves, vagabonds. The older and brighter ones were possibly already big players on the black market. But none of them had anything to do with the shipyard.'

'DPs and concentration camp prisoners from the east worked down at Blohm & Voss. The wolf children fled from the east. Maybe there's a connection of some sort?'

'The forced labourers were Polish, Russian and Ukrainians. The wolf children are German. Not exactly the best basis for a friendship.' The chief inspector remembered the expression of disgust Hildegard Hüllmann had given, even though prostitutes couldn't exactly afford to be choosy.

'In the world that boy inhabited,' MacDonald replied, 'nobody has friends. They don't need them. Maybe Adolf Winkelmann found a business partner among them.'

'If he did, it was pretty low-level business.'

For a while they drove silently through the empty streets. Stave wondered if he should tell MacDonald that his son Karl had come home. But then family stories probably weren't what he wanted to hear at the moment. On the other hand, the lieutenant himself was going to be a father soon. And so, he used the reference to the 'east' as a link and mentioned, as casually as he could, Karl's return from Vorkuta. To his surprise MacDonald clapped him on the shoulder, genuinely pleased for him.

'You only mention this now. And here am I dragging you to the theatre, when you'd far rather have spent the evening at home with your son.'

'We need to get to know each other again,' Stave replied, embarrassed at having revealed so much personal detail.

'I understand,' MacDonald said, staring straight ahead.

'Sometimes I wonder if normal family life will ever be possible again after this war,' Stave said wearily.

'As long as there are lawyers and bureaucrats, my answer is always going to be: forget about it,' the lieutenant added grimly.

'Your divorce case?'

'I would rather sign up for the next war than go into that courtroom. Not least because I am there as a powerless witness. Erna has to sort it out herself.'

It would have been a hopeless case under normal circumstances: there was no way Erna Berg would have been granted custody. But MacDonald was her ticket to a better life, and the only one she was likely to get.

'Is there anything I can do?' asked Stave.

MacDonald smiled, briefly, thankfully, but also somehow triumphantly. 'To be honest I had hoped you would ask me that question, old boy. I wouldn't have dared to ask.'

'For what?'

'To call you into court. As a character witness. Say what you can about Erna. How hard she works. A chief inspector of police in the witness stand might give the judge cause to consider.'

And it would become the talking point of the office, Stave thought to himself. He wished he'd never offered. But he had fallen into a trap of his own making and there was no way out. 'I'll do that,' he promised.

When they reached 93 Ahrensburger Strasse, Stave expected Mac-Donald to let him out and speed off. But the lieutenant switched off the engine. It was uncannily quiet. Somewhere they could hear baby rats squealing. The moon was like a thin sickle in a black sky. The ruins and the façades stood there like scenery in an Expressionist stage play. Stave felt as if he were an actor who had stumbled on to the stage without knowing which role he was supposed to play.

'I'd invite you up for a glass, if I had anything decent to offer you,' he said embarrassedly.

MacDonald smiled and reached behind the driver's seat. In the pale yellow light the chief inspector recognised a bottle of Dujardin Imperial brandy. 'Time for the British and Germans to share their spoils of war,' MacDonald said.

On his first evening back Karl had come across Anna, without any prior warning, Stave was thinking as he dragged his feet up the staircase. Now here I am, bringing a British officer home. The boy is going to have to get used to changed times. But as he opened the door he realised that his son had not come back yet.'

'Karl isn't home,' he said unnecessarily.

'That means more brandy for us,' MacDonald said, acting as if he wasn't surprised.

Over the next few hours they sank into a cosy warm mist. Stave hadn't drunk alcohol for years. The sharp, amber liquid inflamed his throat, burned in his stomach and brought tears to his eyes. It took time to get used to it again. He and the lieutenant sat by the kitchen table, with two old water glasses on a wooden tray. They got drunk systematically and in silence. They finished the bottle in less than two hours. Eventually MacDonald staggered up from his chair, like an old man.

'Do you want to lie down on the sofa?' Stave asked, struggling not to slur his words.

'My Jeep knows the way home,' the lieutenant replied, taking two turns to grab hold of his cap.

Later Stave lay in bed with a heavy head, the shabby walls of his room dancing before his eyes, but if he closed them he just felt dizzier. All it needs now is for you to throw up all over the place, he told himself.

At some stage, when he had halfway drifted off, he was suddenly awakened by the scraping noise of a key in the lock. A squeak, creaking floorboards. Then a bumping noise and a barely suppressed curse. Stave must have forgotten to move the kitchen chair out of the way. He sighed with relief. Karl was home again. He was tempted to jump up and ask him where he'd been all this time, just to see him again. But when he tried to sit up he got dizzy again. Should he really stagger out of his room in this state, stinking of brandy?

He fell back on the pillow. Next door in the little room he could hear the clunking of the chest of drawers: the top one always stuck. Then the gentle creaking of the bed. Stave closed his eyes, happy at least that he could hear Karl back home.

At the Grave

Tuesday, 10 June 1947

Stave and his son sat together silently opposite one another over breakfast. Stave idly stirred his grey ersatz coffee, his stomach turning even at the smell of the roasted acorns, his head aching as if his brain was being punctured by a thousand needles. Karl didn't look much better. The CID man wondered what he had been up to the night before but repressed the urge to ask. Silence, blistering heat, bright sunlight that stung the retinas. The only sound the tinkling of the lead spoon in Karl's coffee cup as he stirred it in endless circles.

Eventually Stave couldn't take it any longer. For the sake of something to say, he came out with 'Should we go and visit Mama?'

'Still living next door, is she?' Faked surprise, his old ironic wit. Stave was almost relieved that at least the war hadn't blunted it. 'Go and visit her grave, I meant,' he said.

'Is she still out at Öjendorf Cemetery?'

The chief inspector gave him a puzzled look: 'Where else would Mama be?'

He shrugged. 'People might have used it to plant potatoes like on the lawn in front of the university.'

'You were at the university?' A sudden spark of hope, suddenly he was wide awake. Don't push him, he warned himself.

Karl didn't bother to answer. 'This afternoon,' he said instead. 'We could go do the grave this afternoon, if you can get the time off.'

Stave would have liked to talk about the university and Karl's plans for the future. A new start in life. Who knew, maybe in that case he too could fulfil his own dreams. Anna. But better to be patient. 'Yes,' he said. 'Will you wait in the apartment for me?'

'I'll be here.'

When he reached his outer office the chief inspector was annoyed to find it empty. Was Erna Berg not feeling well? Was it that time yet? Or was she absent because of the impending court case?

One of his colleagues knocked on the door. 'We all need to go down to the landing stages in the harbour.'

'All of us?'

'It's an order from Cuddel Breuer. We're to take weapons along.'

All I needed, thought Stave. On the way he asked around among his colleagues: British Engineer Corps had marched into Blohm & Voss that morning. They were going to blow up the cranes and gantries. News had got about town and now more and more people had gathered down by the banks of the Elbe, staring across the river.

Cuddel Breuer assigned a group of men to Stave when they got there and told him to mingle with the crowds on the Baumwall elevated railway station. The station was rammed and the chief inspector thought the steel beams that supported it might buckle under their weight.

Men, women, children. The station was more than ten metres above the harbour promenade and had an open view over the Elbe and the huge dockyard belonging to Blohm & Voss. Nobody said a word. There were no protest placards, no clubs being wielded, nobody making provocative speeches. Nonetheless Stave could feel the tension: everywhere there were bitter faces, angry whispers. You could almost hear the suppressed anger crackling in the air.

The view across the river was still remarkable. The cranes and gantries stood like giant spiders hanging above the dockyard, gaps in their rows, of course, because some had fallen victim to the bombing raids. Tiny figures could be seen along the docks through the haze hanging over the Elbe but nobody could make out if they were workers or in British uniforms. A British patrol boat was coasting slowly up and down the river, the Union Jack hanging limply from its mast. Stave noticed there were none of the usual cross-Elbe ferries on the water, that there were not the usual waves dancing in the sun. The water was as grey and smooth as a tablecloth. They must have closed the river, he guessed.

An hour they waited. He was hot. Salt had formed a crust along the cardboard stiffener inside his hat. His shoulder ached from the weight of carrying a gun while remaining relaxed. Ever more people were pushing their way up the stairs to the station. Should he pull out his police ID card and order people back? He tried to glance questioningly at his colleagues, but he could only see two of them and they were as hemmed in as he was. One of them ignored him, the other merely shook his head ever so slightly. Not a good idea to reveal ourselves to be police right now.

All of a sudden there was a huge collective groan, as if thousands of people had taken a deep breath at the same time and held it, a sigh like a giant wave. On the other side of the Elbe, for a tiny surreal splinter of a second, a cloud of black smoke hung over the docks. Then the sound followed it. The loud boom of explosions and then a strange squealing noise. Steel, Stave thought to himself, steel cranes. The mighty constructions shook, wobbled and began to fall, slowly at first, then ever faster, to one side, finally crashing down and vanishing in grey and brown clouds, dust and dirt and a new thunder. When at last the pall had faded, the cranes and gantries were no longer to be seen.

'They collapsed on to that brand new U-boat,' one man in working clothes cried out. 'They got rid of two birds with one stone.'

'They ought to be ashamed of themselves,' one woman replied. 'The war's over, isn't it.'

Stave looked around. Everywhere he saw angry faces, lots of men shaking their fists. If this gets any worse there is going to be a mob looking for a target to exact their vengeance on. The only question was what that might be. Then he spotted Cuddel Breuer, shaking his head, but unflappable as always, ploughing his way through the crowd and down the steps. An honest citizen, horrified, but going home now. Two or three figures followed him at first, then a few more. Stave nodded to his colleague discreetly. The man tipped his hat back and also headed for the exit. A few more followed him. There were murmurs of protest, curses, widespread disgust, but nobody was staying put. Within ten minutes the platform was empty. Within half an hour there was nobody on the riverbank but casual strollers. Only above Blohm & Voss was there still a big angry cloud of dust.

Cuddel Breuer gathered his men together at the landing stages and said, 'Good work, men, we got the crowd to break up without anyone even noticing we were there.'

'It went well this time,' one officer interjected.

Breuer brushed his hand across his head. 'There's something brewing over at Blohm & Voss. We're going to be holding our breath for a while yet. Right now we can go back to our normal jobs,' he said, rubbing his hand. When he turned around Stave noticed that his boss's shirt was soaked with sweat from his shoulder to his waist.

An hour later the chief inspector was sitting at his desk with the files from his murder case spread out across it. The photos of the dead boy, the photos from the autopsy report, his own notes. Which was the best lead? The forced labourers at Blohm & Voss? Seemed unlikely. There was nothing pointing in that direction except for MacDonald's note. The smugglers and dealers on the black market? He had no suspects, no motive, and no link to the scene of the crime. The coal thieves? He had a motive and a suspect, but still no connection to Blohm & Voss. But it was the best he had. It went against the grain in him to arrest a suspect who was little more than a child. But then the victim too had been little more than a child. In the end he decided to ask Public Prosecutor Ehrlich to issue an arrest warrant for Wilhelm Meinke.

Maybe it wasn't him. Stave had his doubts, but with the kid behind bars it might jerk his memory and get more out of him. Also I've got something to show if Cuddel Breuer asks. Or one of the

British. And the sooner I can pull down the curtain on this case, the more time I have for Karl and Anna, an inner voice whispered, even though he knew how dangerous such a temptation could be.

'The public prosecutor has gone out for a walk,' he was told a few minutes later by a grey-faced clerk who clearly found the news irritating to pass on. Stave too was amazed not to find Ehrlich in his office. 'Not much work then?'

The clerk turned a shade paler. 'On the contrary, we have lots of cases. The trial tomorrow …'

'I was only joking,' Stave interrupted him. 'Did Herr Ehrlich say in which direction he was heading?'

The young man was almost mortified with shame: 'Planten un Blomen,' he managed to blurt out.

'Not exactly a brothel,' Stave muttered and nodded goodbye. It was only a few hundred metres from the prosecutor's office to the park. It had to be a coincidence that Ehrlich would take time off today of all days, and of all places choose Planten un Blomen for his walk. It just might be that the Herr Public Prosecutor is following my footsteps on one or another of my leads, Stave considered. Doing his own investigation into the coal stealers? But why would he? Doesn't he trust me?

He paid the thirty *pfennig* entrance fee – in coins that were effectively worthless – and wandered down the pathways. Visitors sitting in the shade of the trees, women in colourful dresses that had somehow survived the nights of bombing, men in linen suits, children working hard at getting paper kites to fly although in the motionless air they kept falling to earth like dead birds. There was a smell of dried earth from the lawns that had been used to grow potatoes, where the pale green plant tops were wilting in the heat. It's not exactly going to be a remarkable harvest, Stave suspected. For a brief second he wondered how the uniformed police protected farmers' fields in autumn. They must have to deploy hundreds of men, just for a few spuds.

He had to go as far as the rose garden before he came across Ehrlich. The public prosecutor was wandering between the rose bushes, stopping from time to time, to pick a leaf or inhale the scent of a red or yellow bloom. He was in the middle of an animated conversation, more enthusiastic than Stave had ever seen him before. No wonder, given the beautiful woman at his side – Anna.

Quickly, Stave moved behind a bush, a thousand questions running through his mind. It was just a harmless stroll in the park, after all. But both of them were talking quietly, seriously, making gestures with their hands. The conversation couldn't have made him more jealous if Anna had kissed the man. Don't make a fool of yourself, he thought. This is the hypercorrect public prosecutor out with Anna, who makes a living by sneaking through the ruins stealing lost artworks. On the other hand, was it any less absurd than her hanging out with a chief inspector of police?

Stave couldn't just sit there behind a bush like some moral watchdog. He moved away, taking care to choose pathways where he was unlikely to be spotted from a distance. When he got back to the entrance he took a deep breath. What on earth was Anna doing with Ehrlich? Or had the public prosecutor asked her to come and see him?

He waited for half an hour, hidden in the ruins of the park-keeper's cottage, until he saw Anna and Ehrlich shake hands, very formally, and say goodbye. Nonetheless, the CID man waited until the public prosecutor was out of sight. It would be absurd now to go to him to request an arrest warrant as if nothing had happened. He wasn't a good enough actor to carry it off without giving himself away. Should he just let Anna go too? He came out of hiding and walked after her. She didn't notice him until he was almost alongside her.

Anna breathed in sharply as if someone had struck her in the face. 'Have you been spying on me?' she asked, speeding up her pace.

She looked immensely cross, Stave thought to himself, and immensely beautiful. 'I had to speak to Ehrlich,' he said, more brusquely than he had intended. 'But apparently there was a queue.'

She stopped dead and stared at him. 'I will talk to whoever I want to, whenever I want to and wherever I want to. You have your life, I have mine.'

'What were you talking about?'

'You just can't give up, can you, Chief Inspector?'

'It's an addiction that goes with the job.'

'And you're always doing your job, aren't you? At least we have that in common.'

'You were talking to Ehrlich about art?' Stave asked suspiciously.

'I got to know him in the restaurant,' she reminded him. 'The three of us were talking about art.'

'The two of you, you mean.'

'It would appear that subsequently the public prosecutor made some …' she looked for the right word, then shrugged and said, 'enquiries. About me.'

'Enquiries?' The chief inspector was concerned that Ehrlich might know how things stood between him and Anna.

'To be more precise, about how I earn a living.'

'Did he threaten to have you arrested?'

Anna laughed in surprise and shook her head. 'Ehrlich is a most charming man.'

'A charming man who's sent more men to the executioner than any other public prosecutor in the British zone.'

'Men who deserved it, I feel certain.'

'Nice.'

'Don't be so sarcastic. We were just talking about art, his mostly. He wanted my help.'

'He wants you to find artworks for him?'

'He wants his own back. At least the masterpieces from his collection.'

Gradually the chief inspector began to see the light. 'He wants you to be an informer, in case some of his pieces turn up on the black market for stolen art?'

'Art that in the brown years was stolen from the Jews who had owned it. Ehrlich's own collection was plundered.'

'I saw a picture from it,' Stave said.

'Since 1945 we don't call it "unworthy art" any more. The museums are bringing back pieces they hid, galleries are putting on exhibitions.'

'Like the Junge Galerie, where they had that exhibition by some British major a few weeks ago?'

'William Gear, an Expressionist. I was at the preview. Ehrlich wasn't there, he had a trial to prepare for. But he came along later. He noticed how many people were pouring in, and the prices on the frames. That's when he realised that what had been stolen from him could be sold today. For a lot of money.'

'But not legally, because legally they still belong to him.'

'And who would dare try to sell off art belonging to Hamburg's most dreaded public prosecutor? It would have to be under the counter.'

'The black market, smugglers, British officers.'

'That was why Ehrlich wanted to talk to me. He's given me a list of his missing artworks. A very impressive list. I'm to keep an eye out for him, to see if any of them turn up. Anywhere, in anybody's possession. He's sure his pieces are still in Germany, maybe still here in Hamburg.'

'And what do you get in return?'

She glared at him. 'It's always good to have a public prosecutor as a friend. You of all people should know that,' she whispered, turning sharply on her heel.

The chief inspector walked off as if in a stupor. There was no way he could go to Ehrlich now, to persuade him to issue an arrest warrant for young Meinke. Would Anna tell the public prosecutor that he had been watching the two of them? That wouldn't make working with Ehrlich any easier, let alone his own private life. That was if he still had anything worth calling a private life after the conversation he'd just had.

When he finally got back to Ahrensburger Strasse he found a long line of men, women and children with tin cans, buckets, glass bottles and battered Wehrmacht canteens in their hands queuing up at a water pump in the street. They were inhabitants of the upper-story apartments where there was already no more water to be had from the taps. Calcium deposits, somebody had told him, had blocked up the filters in the main water works. Who would have thought that the good people of Hamburg would one day be longing for rain, he thought to himself sympathetically as he passed the long line of people standing there apathetically in the hot sun, too exhausted even for the usual chitchat. Three teenagers were hanging around the pump offering to wield the heavy pump handle for them. More than a few in the queue were indeed sufficiently exhausted to throw the kids a few coins for doing them the service. Clever lads, thought Stave. He made a note of their faces; he didn't doubt he'd come across them more often down Ahrensburger Strasse.

It was only when he turned the key in the lock of his apartment that he realised he hadn't got any flowers.

'You're on time,' said Karl. He sounded surprised.

Stave was about to make a sarcastic remark of his own in return, but just managed to stop himself in time. He was tired from the long walk, and exhausted from the stress of his conversation with Anna. He would have liked nothing more than to lie down for a quarter of an hour, massage his damn ankle and think things over. Instead, rather too loudly, he said, 'It's a long walk to the cemetery. We shouldn't hang about.'

'Haven't had a good walk in ages,' his son replied, yet more sarcasm in his voice. Stave couldn't avoid noticing Karl glancing at his crippled leg, just briefly. He couldn't tell if it was a look of scorn or sympathy.

It took them an hour to get to Öjendorf Cemetery. At times they walked down clear streets, at others they had to take paths through heaped rubble so narrow that they had to walk in single file. Stave didn't mind; it made the silence between them less oppressive. He watched Karl, walking ahead of him, and noticed that the boy unconsciously rubbed at the stump of his right index finger, as if he could somehow encourage it to grow again.

'I didn't know you knew all these short cuts through the ruins,' Stave said, for the sake of saying something.

'I used to go to the cemetery sometimes,' Karl replied without looking round.

Stave was so surprised that he nearly tripped over a sharp-edged broken piece of concrete. After the funeral he and his son had never gone out to Öjendorf together. He had assumed Karl had never visited his mother's grave.

'How often were you there?' he asked, cautiously.

'I didn't count. The dead don't keep a visitors' book.'

Some of the ruins resembled ancient garden walls, waist-high stone walls as if they'd been deliberately erected on either side of the path. Behind them lay heaps of rubble, often as high as the houses they had once been. The bricks radiated heat, and a column of dust lingered in the air in the canyons between them, making Stave's eyes go red. All I need now is to burst into tears, he thought to himself, using his handkerchief to mop the sweat from his brow. Whatever might have happened to Karl in Vorkuta, he hadn't lost any of his strength. Quite the opposite in fact. Stave would have slowed down a long while back if he hadn't feared being left behind.

Suddenly Karl turned off the path and climbed up a pile of rubble twice his height. 'Have you lost your orientation?' Stave asked. 'We're almost there.'

'That's the point.'

'What were you looking for?'

'Something for mother, a little gift.' He stood up. In his right hand were three blue and three silver thistles that had been growing in the cracks between lumps of rubble. 'Tough things,' he said. 'No wonder Mother always liked thistles so much, despite the prickles. Not exactly a mourning wreath though.'

'She'll like them,' Stave managed to get out. He was deeply moved by his son's gesture. At least he hasn't lost his soul altogether, he reflected hopefully.

Öjendorf Cemetery is Hamburg's City of the Dead, out to the

east, criss-crossed by road. Before the war even buses had gone through it, dropping off thousands of mourners at stops on the way through.

'We're almost there,' Stave said again.

'Sooner or later we're all there,' Karl replied, 'but hopefully not right now. When the time comes, do you want to be buried next to Mother?'

The chief inspector stopped in his tracks. 'Why do you ask?'

'Because of the other woman.'

'The "other woman" is called Anna von Veckinhausen, and I have no idea whether or not I'll ever even live with her, let alone die and be buried near her. I'll let you do what you like with my ashes.'

'I'll deal with them,' Karl replied, leaving Stave uncertain as to whether he was being sarcastic or deadly earnest.

They entered the grove set aside for burial urns, a few hundred metres beyond the main entrance. A rose bush, a lavender bush, the flower heads still green and unopened, giving off only a little scent, evergreen bushes, a ring of cypress trees and willows spared the woodcutters' axes in the last winter. In the middle an empty plinth, where a half life-size statue of a weeping woman had stood until somebody stole it. In a semi-circle around it dozens of urns were buried in the summer of '43, when nobody had the time or energy to lay out row after row after row of individual graves.

Stave didn't look at the spot where Margarethe's ashes were buried. Instead he fixed his gaze on the empty plinth, unable to get any words out. Don't hold it against yourself, this is something different: shame. You're ashamed because now you love another woman. Ashamed that you didn't manage to get Karl, the visible legacy of the deceased, on to the straight and narrow. At least not in the Nazi years, and maybe not now either, if you don't know what to do or say.

His son laid the thistles on the ground where the urns were buried. Then he made an awkward gesture; for a moment Stave thought he was going to put his hands together as if to pray but in the end he put them behind his back.

They stood there, silently, stiffly, as if they didn't know why they were there. Stave tried to address Margarethe's ghost, to tell her about his new life. But he felt foolish. A prayer? The last prayer he had uttered was at his confirmation and that had been a cascade of words he'd learnt by heart with no meaning to him. Should he put his hand on his son's shoulder? It seemed a phoney gesture. And so he just stood there, three paces from the empty plinth, three paces from his silent son.

'At least Mother's at home,' Karl said, out of nowhere. The he turned and began heading back towards the main gate with that same, long, powerful stride he had used to navigate his way through the maze of ruins. He didn't look back.

Stave could feel the sweat running down from his crown over his neck into the collar of his shirt. Only when Karl had reached the main gate did he start out after him.

Somewhere amid the ruins he caught up with his son. Karl had waited for him. 'I'm going to move out,' Karl announced casually, staring over the top of an indoor heating stove that had remained standing like some pillar from antiquity while the house around it had burned to the ground.

'Where to? Accommodation is hard to find.' Stave tried to sound relaxed, even though his heart was breaking.

'Into an allotment colony towards Berne. Little shed with water on tap, a camping toilet and a heating stove. Not as if I'm going to need that over the next few months.'

'An allotment garden?' Stave choked out. Previously he had ignored the existence of such things, considered the world of allot-ment gardeners who lived there at the weekends boring. Since 1945 those with allotments and sheds had become little kings and queens, growing potatoes, lettuce and even tobacco on their jealously defended little patches. Anyone who had one could make a fortune on the black market in a good year. 'Who's going to let you move into his allotment shed?'

'A war comrade. He was in Vorkuta too and came back a few weeks ahead of me. His parents had an allotment and shed. They died in 1943. Some other people had taken over their patch.'

'Some other people?'

Karl shrugged his shoulders. 'Somebody had just moved in and was squatting there. My friend threw them out.'

'They left voluntarily?'

'My friend had better arguments, ones he'd learnt in the Wehrmacht.'

This isn't good, Stave thought to himself. Karl hadn't mentioned his friend's name, and he didn't ask. But he feared that the boy was getting in with the wrong sort of people. 'When do you plan to move out?'

'Straight away. I've already packed. Wasn't as if there was very much.'

Stave pretended to stumble, to conceal the effect on him. He reached out a hand to support himself against a brick wall. 'So soon?'

'I'm not leaving Hamburg.'

'What will you do?'

'At first I'll cut tobacco leaves and dry them.'

'They're looking for people to do repair work: builders, plumbers, installation people.'

Karl looked at the ruins around him and gave a bitter laugh. 'I can imagine.'

'The British are looking for car mechanics, even shipbuilders.'

His son gave him a sympathetic look. 'I asked around yesterday how things were. One of my comrades is the doorman at a hotel for the British. He used to be an officer on board a steam ship. Another looks after the tracks on a stretch of railway line. A third makes ships in a bottle and sells them on the black market. I'm going to grow tobacco. You do whatever you can find.'

You stayed at school to take the final leaving certificate just to go and grow tobacco, Stave wanted to yell at him. But he checked himself. Maybe the younger ones would come to terms with the new times better than we oldies who made such a hash of everything. They walked the rest of the way home in silence, Stave walking more slowly, not just because he was already exhausted but in order to spend more time with Karl. He wracked his brain in vain searching for something he could talk to him about, without causing any difficulties. This can't be happening, he said to himself, that he should turn up as if from the dead outside my door just a couple of days ago, and already we have nothing more to say to one another.

Back at the apartment, he watched as Karl gathered together his few items of clothing and packed them into an old leather school satchel he must have got hold of somewhere or other. He had to fiddle about quite a long time with his crippled hand at the ties that held the flap down. Stave had to fight the impulse to rush over and help him.

'Will you stay for supper?'

Karl shook his head. 'Down by the allotments they've got potato soup and then a special garden pipe to smoke. I won't be a burden on you any more.'

'You're not a burden to me.'

For the first time Karl looked at him considerately. 'I'm grown up,' he said slowly, almost tenderly. 'A lot more grown up than you can imagine. I've been a soldier on the front line, and a prisoner in a gulag. I go crazy if somebody else is in the same room with me for any length of time. I'm going to look after the allotment for my friend. He isn't there most of the time. He's already done a good bit of business and got himself an apartment. I'll be able to relax. And so will you, if you want to get together with that woman again.'

Stave closed his eyes. 'Anna isn't throwing you out. She doesn't want to do that. Nor do I.' And she may in any case never set foot in here again, he added to himself.

'Even so, it's better if I go.'

'Will you at least look in from time to time?'

'I'll be in touch.'

Karl nodded, an awkward gesture from a teenage boy become a

man far too early. Stave listened at the door to his footsteps descending the stairwell. Then suddenly the apartment was uncannily still.

For a long time Stave sat and stared at the closed door. Grief and a feeling of failure weighed on him like a ton of bricks. Then he got up and ripped open the windows and the door to the balcony, feeling as if he was going to suffocate – not that it helped, the air was like liquid lead. He grabbed all the bottles, pots and non-recyclable glassware he could find in the kitchen cupboards and filled them all with the rust-tinged water from the taps. Better to fill as much as he could now while the water was still running. He filled the bath too even though he knew that if it sat there a long time it would leave horrible rings on the enamel that would take hours to scrub clean. Eventually he went out on to the balcony and sat down, chewed on the dry bread and washed it down with water tasting of iron. He watched a truck rumbling down Ahrensburger Strasse. Maybe one of Greta Boesel's deliveries, he thought briefly, hoping that the case might distract him. A haze fell over the street, and in the distance he could hear children playing and laughing.

That's all I need, he told himself, to sit here like some old-age pensioner listening to the noises of the street. One of his younger colleagues had a few days ago lent him one of the new American novels that had been banned in the brown years but was now available in a German translation. It was a thin volume more like a compact magazine, printed on cheap paper, a picture scrawled on the cover of human figures on a coast somewhere, and beneath that the price – fifty *pfennigs* – and the title *In Another Country*. I can understand that, Stave thought to himself – I feel as if Hamburg is another country.

He began reading but within half an hour he realised that he couldn't remember a single sentence of what he'd read. Angrily he closed the book. Outside the setting sun had turned the ruins a fiery red. He wondered if Karl was still roaming the streets or if he had already arrived at the allotment. He tortured himself with the thought that he might have wasted the one chance to put things to rights between himself and his son.

He was almost relieved when there was a cautious knock on the door.

Constable Ruge was standing in the stairwell, his young face tanned from the sun. He was about to speak when the chief inspector interrupted him. 'You are the Angel of Death,' he growled at him. 'Come in and tell me what's happened.'

'We've had another murder.'

'And I'm supposed to take it on, on top of the Winkelmann case?'

Ruge's already red face took on an even deeper shade. 'On the contrary. Cuddel Breuer has put Chief Inspector Dönnecke on this case.'

'So why are you here?'

'Because I think there's something you need to know. The body was found near the railway tracks down at Dammtor. It's one of the coal thieves.'

'Wilhelm Meinke!' Stave announced, grabbing his hat and shoulder holster.

'I knew you would be interested,' Ruge said proudly, trotting down the staircase after the chief inspector.

'Did Dönnecke send you to me?' he asked in amazement as he clambered into the Mercedes, trying to roll down the stuck passenger window to let in a bit of air.

The young officer stared straight ahead, screwing up his eyes against the low evening sunshine. 'No' was his short reply.

'You came off your own bat?'

'Nobody thought there was any need to tell you. So I decided I would.'

I'm amazed, Stave realised, both delighted and almost embarrassingly touched at the same time. This boy has been following my case and as soon as he thinks that there's something I'm missing out on, he comes to tell me. Not exactly the done thing; he could cause trouble for himself if somebody found out. I will make sure that doesn't happen.

'Are some of our colleagues still at the spot where the body was found?' he asked cautiously.

Ruge shook his head. 'Dr Czrisini maybe. Kienle had already packed his stuff away when I left them half an hour ago. There's a couple of uniforms to secure the area.'

'What about Dönnecke?'

'He's already gone. He thinks he already knows who did it.'

'Who?'

Ruge shrugged. 'He told a few of his colleagues, but not me. I was too far away. And ...' he hesitated, '... I didn't dare ask.'

'I understand,' Stave muttered. Chief Inspector Dönnecke had been in the CID since the Kaiser had been on the throne. He could be less than polite. 'Has he arrested the killer?'

'As far as I know, they're still looking for him.'

They passed by a wide expanse of ruins on the right-hand side. Stave glanced briefly at an old one-legged man who was piling up bricks in the shadow of a three-metre high wall. He's trying to build himself a shelter, he thought to himself. A novice. A police patrol will find him soon enough here on Ahrensburger Strasse. Or somebody will come along and steal all the building material he's collected. Probably just got back to Hamburg.

Then his thoughts turned to Wilhelm Meinke. Would the boy still be alive if he had arrested him that afternoon? Best not to think too long and hard about that one. Maybe the boy's body was already lying in some bush while he was spying on Ehrlich and Anna in the rose garden not far away. He felt uncomfortable, nagged by the idea that he was somehow responsible.

'Is the body still there?'

'Yes, unless Dr Czrisini has done his work faster than normal.'

Five minutes later they were there. 'Stave,' the pathologist said, though he didn't seem particularly surprised to see him. Ruge had parked the Mercedes on Tiergarten Strasse, between the train tracks and the wild shrubbery that grew at the edges of Planten un Blomen. The doctor and a few uniformed policemen were standing half-hidden behind some bushes.

The chief inspector glanced at the boy's undernourished body. Meinke had wanted to emigrate to America, he suddenly remembered. When he had first interviewed him back in the winter, the boy had mentioned that he had a relative in New York. He wondered if anybody would be bothered to try to inform him.

The hair on the back of the boy's head was smeared with blood, the dry earth around the spot where his head lay had turned dark.

'Trauma to the skull and brain,' Czrisini said. He had come up to where the chief inspector stood. 'From just looking at him, I would say two fractures of the skull, to the rear.'

'Two blows to the head?'

The pathologist nodded. 'Probably. The old rim of the hat rule: wounds caused by a fall are usually located where you would see them if the victim had been wearing a hat. Most caused by blows are located higher up on the skull.'

'Below the level of the brim of a hat, the victim would be more likely to see them coming.'

'Exactly, as is the case here. Did you know the boy?'

'Only slightly. I interviewed him twice. What's your opinion? Was he attacked here?'

'The patch of blood on the ground suggests so. Kienle didn't find blood anywhere else in the vicinity.'

'Meinke was standing among the bushes. Probably waiting for the next coal train to come along. His murderer creeps up behind him and delivers two blows to the skull.'

'With either a stick or a rock, I suspect. I may know more after the autopsy. I doubt that the boy would have seen his killer. But standing in the bushes he might well have heard him coming – rustling branches. With all those thorns not many people could get through without making a noise of some sort.'

'Or Meinke knew there was somebody standing behind him, just had no idea they were going to attack him. How long has he been dead?'

'From the temperature of the body, I would say since late afternoon. The murder was reported by a young couple around six o'clock. They had been intending to have a little fun together here in the bushes. The discovery took away their appetite.'

'Were there none of the other coal thieves around when the police showed up?'

'Vanished as fast as fans of the Führer did in 1945. They'll be looking for another spot to work from.'

'For the next few days, maybe. They'll soon be back.'

Stave looked around and waved to one of the uniformed police he'd known for years. If Dönnecke had said anything to anyone, then it was most likely to him. He walked over to his moustachioed colleague and said, 'I believe there's already a suspect?'

'We've already interviewed three kids,' he replied. 'They all did a runner but we caught up with a few of them. We're familiar enough with the coal thieves. We found them at home with their parents. They all told the same story. One of the wolf children had somehow or other crept up behind Meinke without him noticing when the fast train for Ostende was rattling past. He hit him twice on the head, possibly with an iron bar. Possibly with a police truncheon he'd got hold of somehow. There were differences on that point. Either way he ran off immediately after, before Meinke's pals could do anything.'

'Name?'

The policeman made a vague gesture, suggesting partly helplessness, partly lack of interest. 'A wolf kid. We have a description. No name. And obviously no address. We're gong to have to comb through hundreds of damn ruins. And even then there's no guarantee we'll find him.'

'Motive?'

'Probably an argument. These kids are always beating each other up. Sometimes worse. This is not the first murder we've had among the coal thieves. And it won't be the last. They need somebody looking after them.'

'Yes, I'm sure that's the problem,' Stave said wearily, and nodded to the policeman as he left.

Early Deaths

Grey light from the window. The sun was still below the horizon as Stave woke up with a start. It was his old nightmare, but different this time. He was tumbling through the ruins, his ankle still in good shape, feeling the heat of the blaze on his face. He'd almost reached his wife, when suddenly there in the middle of the flames stood Anna, her arm across her chest in that protective pose she adopted, turning away from him. Karl was sitting on the remnants of a wall singing a children's song. Stave knew the melody but couldn't make out the words. He still had it running through his head when he woke up. He glanced over at the balcony door which he had left open the previous night because of the heat. Had he screamed so loud he might have woken the neighbours? Maybe they could have heard him down on Ahrensburger Strasse? When he had been out on official business on the empty streets after curfew, he had sometimes heard groans or screams coming from the houses or Nissen huts around. It had simply never occurred to him up until now that he too might play his part in this nocturnal concert. He got to his feet, annoyed with himself, and closed the door, trying to stay as far from it as possible in the hope no one would see him.

He had done well to collect as much water as he could yesterday because there were only drips from the tap. He soaped himself and washed himself down with the water he had collected in the bath. Already it was covered with an oily film. Then he rubbed himself with a rough dry cloth until his skin hurt. Water from one of the jars to make coffee. He made a face. I must make sure I get home on time tonight, he told himself, so I can get to the nearest street pump before it gets dark.

He limped along Ahrensburger Strasse and onwards for at least an hour before he could banish all traces of his nightmare. Now it was Anna and Karl rather than Margarethe. It wasn't a good turn of events for his dreamland. I can cope with the dead more easily than with the living, he thought to himself, and wondered if that was why he was on the murder squad.

He pulled himself together. There was no proof he got on better with the dead. He still hadn't found Adolf Winkelmann's killer. If Wilhelm Meinke had been involved, it was too late to do anything about that. Had one of the wolf kids taken revenge for young Winkelmann? Was that motive enough? Or was Meinke silenced because he knew something? Because Winkelmann's killer would be safer with him out of the way? But if the second killing really was to do with one of the wolf children, then maybe it was the same one responsible for the crime committed down at Blohm & Voss? But what would the killer have been doing there? And why would one of the wolf children have killed him? Because the Hamburg kid with the good black market connections was trying to force his way into the ranks of the wolf children?

Stave tried to work out a way to get involved in the Meinke investigation. Cäsar Dönnecke was sixty years old, had lived through the days of the Kaiser, the Weimar Republic, the Nazis, the British occupation – he was part of the furniture. He had been careful enough or wise enough not to join the National Socialist German Workers' Party. Even so the British had gone through his file in detail in 1945 and even suspended him for a few weeks. But afterwards Cäsar Dönnecke had been resurrected from the fallen and reinstalled in his old job. He wasn't exactly somebody Stave could give orders to. Nor was he one of those likely to do a favour for Stave, who had never needed to be investigated by the British.

But one way or another there was a connection between Adolf Winkelmann and Wilhelm Meinke, one that he alone knew about:

Hildegard Hüllmann. I'm going to have to ask the young hooker a few more questions, he realised. She is part of the case.

Beneath her suntanned cheeks, Erna Berg was pale. Stave wondered how a pregnant woman managed to feed herself and her unborn child on the near starvation rations they were issued. I should have brought her something, he thought, feeling self-conscious.

'Do you know if Dönnecke is about?' he asked her.

'That old warhorse? He was with Cuddel Breuer this morning. Didn't look quite as happy when he came out as he did beforehand.' She gave a little laugh, then slapped her hand across her mouth, shocked by her own behaviour. 'Did you want to speak to him? About the dead boy? You knew him.'

One of these days one of the big wheelers and dealers on the black market was going to pay Erna Berg a salary. For the price of a couple of cartons of cigarettes – tiny slice of the profits, the chief inspector thought to himself – they would get wind of everything that went on up and down the corridors of the CID headquarters. The same cigarettes would allow his secretary to buy milk powder and a good lawyer for her divorce case. It was a good thing she was so incorruptible. 'I guess I'd better saddle up and find the old warhorse,' he said, nodding genially.

Two minutes later he was in Dönnecke's office, down at the other end of the corridor. He had family photos on his desk, certificates on the wall. It looked just as it always had done, except that there was no longer a photo of the Führer on the wall. Cäsar Dönnecke had a red face, with a ring of grey hair around the edges of his massive skull, like a laurel wreath. He had hands like coal shovels, a double chin, and a belly. There were a thousand rumours about how he must manage to fill it on a regular basis in these days of scanty supplies. But nobody really knew.

Dönnecke glanced up from his desk, where he had an open copy of *Die Welt*. He smelled like an old man. 'My morning read is a ritual and rituals are not meant to be disturbed, Stave, not without a very good reason.'

'My reason is Wilhelm Meinke.'

'That vagabond?' Dönnecke looked him up and down with his deep-set brown eyes. Clever eyes, Stave thought, alert. Dönnecke was one of those who let everyone know that even under the Third Reich, the police had only done their duty. For Dönnecke 'duty' had meant going down to the cellar with the Gestapo for their interrogations. What he had done while he was down there, nobody knew.

'Meinke was a witness in my case.'

'Bad luck, colleague. Now he belongs to me, at least what's left of him does.'

'The one thing might be connected to the other.'

'You want to take over my case?'

'I want information. I want leads to follow.'

'Forget it, Stave. Your kid was stabbed to death down at the ship-yard. Whoever did it is your problem. Mine was hit over the head by another vagabond like himself, as if he were a disobedient dog. I have witnesses and I have a description of the killer. We're after him and sooner or later we'll find him. I'll interrogate him and afterwards I'll hand him over in cuffs to the public prosecutor. Then – and only then – will you get a glimpse of my files.'

'What was the motive?'

Dönnecke raised his hands and let them fall with a heavy thump to his desk. 'A sack of coal? Three Lucky Strikes? A pallet to sleep on in an anti-aircraft bunker? An amenable widow? There's no law and order among these kids. They turn on one another like wild animals at the slightest provocation. The "wolf children" are the worst. *Nomen ist omen:* they are what they're called. The way things are going, they'll wipe themselves out. The boss gave me another case from the same background this morning. We don't have enough officers. If the British weren't so …'

'Who?' Stave interrupted. He realised his voice sounded cold.

Dönnecke gave a chilling laugh. 'An acquaintance of yours, I believe. She was picked up last night. Another of these wolf children. A little hooker down at the station.'

Stave stormed out of the office, strode angrily down the corridor. He went into his office and grabbed his hat from its hook. 'I'm with Dr Czrisini at the pathology lab,' he called out to Erna Berg.

Dönnecke had also left his office and was standing in the corridor, his legs astride, waving his newspaper like a fan. 'That's my case too, damn it!' he yelled after Stave.

A quarter of an hour later Stave was standing next to the autopsy table in the pathology lab. Daylight fell through the tall windows, reflecting on the white tiles, the stainless steel, the air filled with the heady stench of blood, urine, intestines and excrement. On one of the three dissection tables lay the body of Hildegard Hüllmann. Stave wouldn't have recognised the young prostitute, if Dr Czrisini hadn't dropped an organ that Stave didn't recognise into a steel bowl and then called him over, at which point he spotted the name card attached to one toe.

'This isn't your case,' he said.

'That's beginning to sound familiar,' Stave said, forcing himself to look at the body. Her skull lay open, the top neatly sawn off, her brain lying in a bowl next to her blood-covered head, her face thankfully unrecognisable. Her skinny chest had been cut open as had her abdomen.

'We'll sew her back up afterwards,' the pathologist assured him.

'I don't think there will be anybody turning up to say goodbye over the open coffin.'

'Except for yourself, maybe?'

The chief inspector thought back to the card he had given her with his telephone number on it and her cheeky answer that she would make her own inquiries. This girl's death is on my conscience, he thought grimly. I should have looked after her. 'She was a witness in my case concerning the murdered boy left on the bomb.'

'That fits,' Czrisini said.

Stave stared at him. 'What fits?'

'You're a bit late. You should have been here before I began work.'

'A stab wound, to the right side of her chest, an indication that the killer was left-handed.'

'Exactly. But in this case she was stabbed three times. Two of the blows seriously damaged her lungs; the blade must have been long enough to slice into both of them. The third blow shattered one of her ribs, so it didn't go quite so deep. The victim choked to death on her own blood, more than two litres of it in her chest cavity. From the temperature of the body, I estimate death to have occurred about twelve hours ago.'

'Middle of the night.'

'Either just before or just after curfew.' Stave stared at the girl's hands, which the pathologist hadn't touched. They were dirty, with a nasty rash on her left hand, but no sign of wounds. 'She would have fought back if she knew she was being attacked.'

'That doesn't mean she knew her attacker, or at least not that she knew him well.'

The chief inspector nodded. 'Indeed, could have been one of her customers.'

'Given the business she was in, she necessarily had to let her customers get close to her.'

'Any positive indications in that direction?'

'No sperm in the area of her vagina or rear. Or in her mouth. Nonetheless, Chief Inspector Dönnecke thinks it has to have been one of her clients.'

'Where and when was she found?'

'We heard in the early hours of the morning. I'd only just finished with another body.' Czrisini shrugged his shoulders resignedly. 'She was found by a barkeeper who'd finished for the evening and was on his way home. He reported it at the next police station where he had to be treated for shock. The blood that hadn't flooded her lungs was all over the street and the walls of a building nearby.' Czrisini shook his head, unmoved by any sentimentality. 'She was lying outside the door of a house shared by several families in Rostock Strasse, near the main station.'

'And even nearer to the Hansaplatz,' Stave muttered. 'Anything else?'

Czrisini turned away, bent over into a lengthy spell of coughing, then wiped his mouth with a paper tissue. There were beads of sweat on his head when he stood upright again. Stave noticed a few spots of blood on the tissue. The pathologist saw him looking and quickly crumpled up the tissue and threw it into a basket full of removed organs.

'I need a cigarette,' he coughed, and waved to a young man in a white coat filling out forms at a metal-topped table in the corner of the room. 'My assistant here can deal with the rest. Sewing the body up again, I mean.'

Outside, he sucked greedily on his Woodbine, smiling contentedly, until a thought occurred to him. 'There is something else, even if it's not obviously relevant to the case.'

'I'll decide that.'

'The kid was pregnant. Very early stages, scarcely more than a cluster of cells in her womb. Quite probably she herself had no idea.'

Stave suddenly felt sick, almost asked the pathologist for a cigarette.

'It might not have been the first time,' Czrisini added, without noticing that Stave had to hold on to the wall for support. 'There are indications of a possible abortion. Very primitively carried out, but that's hardly surprising. Risk of the job.'

'Risk of the job indeed, just like premature death caused by a brutal attack,' the chief inspector replied.

'She's not the first streetwalker to end up like that, and she won't be the last.'

Stave closed his eyes and thought for a moment. 'Did you also do the autopsy on Meinke?'

'Your other witness? This could be the link between them: they both knew you. You aren't the killer, by any chance?' He coughed again.

'Don't tell Cuddel Breuer.'

'Or Dönnecke. He's not exactly a fan of yours.'

'Officially, I'm not here.'

'I'm as silent as a tomb.'

Stave gave a weak smile, remembering the scene in the hallway back at CID headquarters. 'Dönnecke knows I'm here unofficially.'

'He could lodge a complaint against you with the Tommies,' Czrisini said, lighting up another cigarette from the stub of his Woodbine. 'I had Meinke in here a few hours earlier, on the very same table,' he went on. 'Took all night: trauma to the brain and skull, as suspected. Bone fractures, splinters in the brain, everything you could ask for. Bleeding in the brain. With injuries like that it's harder to draw conclusions than with stab wounds. But if I was forced to make a guess, I would say his attacker used the right hand rather than the left. And despite having a blunt instrument of some sort in his hand, he was smaller than his victim. That fits in with Dönnecke's suspicions and the testimony of the witnesses that the killer was a wolf child.'

'A right-handed child, whereas in the case of Winkelmann and Hildegard we're dealing with a left-hander.'

'And more likely an adult than a child. I couldn't swear to that in court, but it would fit: the height of the chest wounds, the force of the stabbing.'

'It couldn't be that simple,' Stave sighed.

'The answer is *no*.' Cuddel Breuer said the moment Stave entered his office.

'Two dead witnesses in the space of twelve hours, that's hardly a coincidence,' the chief inspector replied. He ignored his boss's suggestion that he take a seat.

Breuer stared at him. 'Of course it could be a coincidence,' he said at last. 'An unfortunate coincidence, but a coincidence nonetheless. It's not the first time two teenagers have been murdered in Hamburg in the course of a single day.'

'These two were children.'

'A street urchin and petty criminal who stole coal, and a hooker who worked down at the station. Their age doesn't come into it. What matters is their lifestyle. They weren't living the lives of children.' He raised his massive hands 'I wish these boys and girls lived in a different world too. But times are what they are. Just because two crimes were committed at roughly the same time, does not mean they are connected.'

'That's not what I was taught.'

'That was before the war, and all the mess we're in now. I think these two murders actually prove we're dealing with different issues.'

'In that case you must know more than I do.'

'No sarcasm, Stave. It doesn't suit you and doesn't do you any favours.' Breuer sat up straight in his seat and began to count on his hairy fingers: 'First of all: two victims, both of whom led what we can call "irregular" lives. Meinke was killed in the afternoon, Hüllmann that night. How could a single killer have found and killed both of them in such a short space of time? Secondly: the killer with Meinke's death on his conscience was seen – we have a description of the suspect. Vague, I grant you, but enough to suggest the murder has nothing to do with that of Winkelmann. In third place: if two killers with the same motive struck in two different places, that would indicate some form of larger organisation at work, and your investigation of the Winkelmann case has not given the slightest evidence of any such thing. And fourth: what is the hypothetical motive? Why these two children?'

'Because they knew something about Winkelmann that they weren't supposed to know.'

'You interviewed both of them. What might that be?'

Stave closed his eyes. 'I don't know,' he admitted. 'Give me the cases, boss. Dönnecke couldn't care less who killed these two children. He'll nail some wolf kid at random for Meinke, and bury the file on the girl because he doesn't think it's worth his while to go chasing some punter who kills hookers.'

'You may well be right,' Breuer replied with a smile, 'but you on the other hand risk messing up my whole department by going around treading on your colleagues' toes. They're sensitive enough, what with dealing with the Tommies. You won't work flat out to find the wolf kid who killed Meinke because that doesn't fit with the other two cases. And therefore in the end, after you've made a mess of the whole department, you'll have three unsolved cases on file.' Cuddel Breuer shook his head energetically. 'No. You deal with your case. I think one murder is enough to be going on with. Solve it. If – and only if – you come across leads that point directly to a connection with the murder of Meinke or the young prostitute, then I will let you work on that particular case. But only under those circumstances, and even then you'll have to work with Dönnecke.'

'Thanks, boss,' Stave said, and stormed out of the office.

'Glad to hear about your son,' Breuer called after him.

The chief inspector stopped in his tracks, turned around and closed the door again. 'You heard about Karl?'

'Sometimes even a CID boss finds out a thing or two,' Breuer replied with a smile. 'Congratulations, it must be a good feeling to be able to embrace a missing son again, particularly,' he hesitated, 'after the tragic loss of your wife.'

Confused and angry. Stave took himself off back to his office, wondering how Breuer had found out about Karl. Did it mean all his other colleagues knew? And was the boss's final remark maybe an oblique hint that word of his relationship with Anna had also got around? Stave wished it was already evening and everyone else had gone home, so he could get on with his investigation on his own.

He told Erna Berg about Karl's return. Just mentioning it casually to see what reaction he'd get. He had meant it just in passing, but when it came to it, he simply blurted it out. His secretary reacted with delight, congratulations, promising to be discreet. Stave cursed to himself: obviously she already knew, and was just play-acting. The whole corridor, probably the entire CID knew. They've all been wondering why I haven't said anything. He went into his office, said, 'I don't want to be disturbed,' realising as he said it, how impolite he sounded.

Concentrate on the case, he told himself, staring at the Winkelmann file. He would have loved to have the files on the other two cases to line up next to it, because sometimes that was how he spotted connections that otherwise weren't obvious. Meinke. Had he killed Winkelmann, perhaps in the course of an argument? And one of Winkelmann's friends, some half-crazy wolf kid, had smashed him over the head with an iron bar or truncheon in revenge? Why did somebody feel the need to kill Hildegard Hüllmann? Her murder resembled Winkelmann's. But if Meinke had killed Winkelmann, he couldn't have killed the young prostitute too, because he was already dead himself by then.

But if the first murder – Winkelmann's – and the third – Hildegard Hüllmann – were both committed by the same perpetrator, then what was the link with that of Meinke?

Stave could have hammered on his desk with anger. Three dead children. In peacetime, for God's sake! He felt consumed by impotent rage, against Cuddel Breuer, against Dönnecke, against the wolf children themselves. Don't be an idiot, he told himself. It's not one of them who's turning Hamburg into a hell. It's somebody else and it's your job to find him.

Start again. He would act as if the Meinke case didn't exist. Maybe Beruer and Dönnecke were right. It was a coincidence, carried out by one of the wolf children as the result of an everyday quarrel. If all he had to deal with was murder number one and murder number two, then there was an argument to be followed up: the girl had told Stave she was following her own leads. Where would she start? On the Hansaplatz or at the station, around the black marketeers and smugglers.

It was only a possibility. Nothing to take to Breuer. But enough for him to base his own investigation on.

He called Erna Berg. 'I'm going down to the station.'

'Where the dead girl used to hang out? What am I supposed to tell the boss if he comes looking for you?'

He gave her a conspiratorial smile, feeling in a better mood at last. 'Tell him I'm working on my case.'

On the way to the station he forced himself to walk slowly. To take deep breaths. Normally a walk in the fresh air cleared his head. But the sun was too hot for him to keep a cool head. He was thirsty. Don't start looking for revenge, he told himself, you have to keep a sober head. And he wanted to succeed in the case, to have something to show to his son, so that he could be proud of his father.

The air on the station platforms was suffocating: a mix of coal dust and the sweat of the passengers waiting for trains. Stave walked up and down the platforms holding his police ID under the nose of every adolescent girl not in the company of her parents. Scared looks, embarrassment, and a look of horror from girls who realised he was taking them for prostitutes. Stave couldn't care less.

Twice he was lucky, if that was the right expression under the circumstances. One young hooker had heard of Hildegard Hüllmann but said she hadn't seen her for several days. He couldn't get anything more out of her. The other one insisted she had never heard the name before. Lying, he reckoned, but if he arrested her, then Dönnecke would get wind of it and accuse him, correctly, of interfering with his case. He let her go.

He also kept an eye out for boys delivering suitcases to the trains or collecting them. But it was a waste of time. All the coaches were packed and there were hundreds of children toting luggage fighting their way through the crowds. Cuddel Breuer's right, he said to himself, I'm going to work myself to the bone and not solve either case.

Sweaty and tired, he eventually headed back, almost bumping into MacDonald by the entrance to the building.

'You look as if you've just been released from Rommel's Afrika Korps,' the young British officer called out to him, 'just after the battle of El Alamein!'

'Do you have something to say to me?' Stave croaked back at him.

'I'm actually here to meet Erna, but now that you mention it you and I could do with a little chat.' A shadow fell over his face.

'Let me guess. You're about to have your first meeting with the divorce judge. Things are getting serious.'

'So serious I've become the brunt of jokes down at the officers' club.'

'To your face.'

'Not yet. But behind my back.'

'Not all lost yet, then.'

'Churchill would have approved of your attitude. Shame you were on the wrong side.'

'I usually am,' the chief inspector replied.

'The divorce case begins a week on Thursday.'

'Eight days' time.' Stave could guess what was coming next.

They had wandered away from the CID headquarters across Karl Muck Platz as far as the music hall. On the steps in front of the concert hall was an ice cream seller's cart. A few boys were hanging about around it, although Stave noticed they didn't seem as desperate as usual.

'Let me buy you one,' MacDonald said, taking a leather wallet from his trouser pocket. He was astonished to find the ice cream seller waving him away, pointing to a handwritten sign on the side of his cart: 'Bring your own wrapper.'

'You have ice cream, but nothing to sell it in?' Stave asked the man, uncertain whether he found the situation amusing, shocking or just plain stupid.

The sullen old man nodded at the boys and said, 'Talk to them.'

Stave walked over to them, noticing that the grins on their faces grew wider with every step he took. 'Paper wrapper, please?' he demanded, with a grin of his own.

'We've heard that before,' the oldest of the group, maybe fourteen at most, quipped, holding up some green, grey and pink sheets of paper.

'Those are official forms!' he burst out.

'Official permission forms, regulation notices. You can roll them into a cone. Personally I find ice cream tastes best wrapped in a housing certificate.'

'Don't get cheeky with me. Where did you steal these from?'

'We didn't steal them,' the oldest boy said. 'We went down to the city hall this morning and bought them. They cost two *pfennigs* each.'

'I bet you're not going to sell them that cheaply to us,' MacDonald laughed.

'Just ten *pfennigs* apiece, and you get to choose your colour.'

'Nice business,' Stave mumbled. If this is the way things are heading then we're going to have problems.

MacDonald gave the kids a couple of coins, took two sheets of paper, rolled them and had the old man fill them with vanilla ice cream.

'Do you think those kids and that charming old man are in cahoots?' the lieutenant asked after they had walked on a few paces.

Stave shook his head. 'The old boy is just annoyed because he didn't think of it. He can't exactly chase them away or he'd ruin his own business. But they're not doing him any favours, because all his customers have to give them money before they can buy from him so they've less left to spend on ice cream. Clever lads.'

'Cleverer than I am,' MacDonald added. His brief high spirits had vanished again.

'You've got another eight days. I'm sure you'll think of something. After all, you do have connections.'

MacDonald shot him a brief glance, then shook his head. 'First rule with us is not to cause a fuss. A messy divorce is the last thing my superiors want. They'd be happier if I defected to the Russians.'

'Well, you're going to have to go through with it. Unless the divorce goes ahead, there's no way you'll be able to take Erna Berg back to England with you. And there'll be a doubt over the status of the child you're going to have.'

'Thank you for putting it so neatly. I know there's no way I can avoid the divorce case. I just want it to come to a satisfactory conclusion.'

'You mean you want to present your superior officers with a result impressive enough for them to overlook the whole business?'

'Yes. I can't stop the divorce being messy and unpleasant, but, ideally, I could ensure it doesn't affect my future with Erna. There's really only one way I'm going to be able to marry her without being posted elsewhere because of the scandal, and that's to solve the Blohm & Voss murder case. Then we'll all be happy.'

'You mean, providing we solve it within the next eight days.'

'If it takes, any longer, old boy,' MacDonald said with a wry smile, 'then your report will be my one-way ticket to Jerusalem.'

'Palestine?'

'The next war: Arabs against Jews. They hate each other and both of them hate the British even more. Not exactly much chance of me taking up with one of the natives out there. There's a much higher chance of taking a bullet or shrapnel from a bomb. Still at least that would simplify the divorce procedure.'

'Eight days is a long time, a lot can happen,' Stave replied. 'Thanks for the ice cream.'

That evening Stave couldn't stand sitting alone in his apartment for too long. He headed out for the allotments in Berne, just to see where Karl was living. It took him three quarters of an hour to get there. At times he took short cuts through seas of ruins that had once been apartment blocks, and occasionally found himself climbing over heaps of rubble, sending rats scurrying away from him. There were areas of long grass, bushes, a couple of birch tree saplings growing amid the rubble, sparrows, blackbirds. He came across a two-storey building where the façade had fallen away, the roof blown off and the windows shattered, leaving the upper floors still standing between the side walls, like some gigantic dolls' house. Inside, protected from rain and frost, but inaccessible to looters, stood a chest of drawers, with an oil painting hanging at an angle on the wall, and, almost obscene in its undamaged isolation, a gleaming white toilet.

Stave thought Anna might be interested in the painting, and wondered what she was up to. Maybe she was wandering around the ruins too, in the hours before curfew, checking out piles of bricks with her trained eye, looking out for wooden picture frames, for rooms hidden behind piles of stone and rubble. She had told him that those, if you could find them, were the best places to discover antiques and undamaged artworks. A family bible, a grandfather clock, a fine tea cup of Dresden china, which somehow had survived a bombing raid that had laid waste to an entire suburb of the city. He wondered if she would risk her life to get hold of that oil painting, climbing up into a building that could collapse at any minute to get her hands on a little treasure? He wondered how many times she had already risked her life for something similar.

He got to the little river that Karl had said led upstream to the allotment colony. It was reduced to barely a trickle. The cracked ground was mostly dry, baked hard by the sun. Stave was thirsty, but the stench from the water put him off. Then he came to a wooden door that had once been painted green, the entrance to a path, with a notice on it 'Allotment Club 1904'.

Behind it was a tall, thorny green hedge, gravel pathways, wire netting on fences made of planks, marking out a sort of chessboard pattern. Miniature fields planted in precise rows with potatoes, lettuce, cabbage, carrots, green beans growing up trestles, tobacco plants, all shaded by saplings of cherry, pear and apple trees. Each little square had a shed, in most cases about as big as a room, three of them had a brand new one, built with brick walls, proper little houses, with a door, windows, a gable and shingle roof, even properly plastered, but half the size of what people used to put up before the war. These however were the little castles of those who'd done relatively well out of the peace, who'd come into a small fortune. It used to be forbidden to erect dwellings you could live in all year round on the allotments, but today it didn't matter as long as the citizens of Hamburg had a roof over their heads. There were no more incorruptible city council officials coming round to scare people away.

Stave hoped Karl was in one of these proper little houses, but on knocking on a few doors, soon realised otherwise. A grumpy, suspicious man he'd woken up in the third house he'd tried, showed him the way to go. It was the very last allotment, bordered on the left by the stream, on the right by a neighbour's allotment and beyond by the scrubland that surrounded the entire colony. At the very edge of the allotment was a shed, though hardly worthy of the name: a little cube made of planks painted with white oil paint, a skewed door but no windows, and a roof made of dented corrugated iron with a rusty stovepipe protruding from it. In front on a terrace of sorts, made up of some sheets of metal salvaged from a ruin and laid out on the ground, was a wooden table and two chairs. All around were tobacco plants in full bloom, but no vegetables or fruit as far as Stave could see.

His son was on his knees weeding between two flourishing tobacco plants with leaves as long as his arm. His torso was reddened by the sun and covered in sweat. How thin he is, Stave thought to himself, holding up a hand in greeting.

'Heil Hitler!' Karl responded. Then, when he saw the expression on his father's face, added: 'It was only a joke.'

'A joke that can land you in jail these days!'

'Have you come to arrest me?'

Here we go again, thought Stave, and in what he hoped was a conciliatory tone added: 'I've only come to see how you're getting on.'

Karl got to his feet and, with a gesture Stave was surprised to recognise as proudly proprietorial, waved his arms to display his little parcel of land. 'May I introduce you to the original plantation of what will come to be known as the global brand "Karl Stave Classic", mild and smooth, and only half the price of John Player's.'

'You're really intending to make cigarettes?'

Karl laughed. 'We're in Germany. It isn't possible. The tax man has already been round.'

'Tax man?'

'You can lay waste to the entire country and annihilate the Wehrmacht, but the German Inland Revenue will always survive. An inspector has just left, you might have bumped into him. You should have arrested him. Made up any pretext you liked and tossed him into the cellar.'

Stave ignored the remark. 'What was a tax man from the revenue after here?'

'They're investigating every single allotment holder in the city. You're not allowed even to profit from your own allotment, in case they lose out on revenue from tobacco tax. You have to hand it all over and they give you two Reichsmarks for every kilo of tobacco leaves, and you get a ration card back for half of what you've handed over. Not bad business for the tax men, if you ask me, who take half of it without even having to crawl about on their knees between the damnably fragile plants.'

'So why don't you plant something else? Potatoes, for example?'

'Don't worry, I'll still have enough for myself.'

'But you can't eat tobacco.'

'These green leaves are banknotes growing out of the soil. And in any case it's not that easy to get anything to grow here.' Karl vanished behind the hut for a moment and came back with an old spade. 'Here, try digging with that.'

Stave took the spade, somewhat puzzled, found a clear patch of earth and rammed the spade into the ground. At first it was easy because the soil had been dried by the sun to the extent that it was powdery. Then, when he pushed the spade a little further he hit something solid. 'Feels like concrete,' he said, wondering if somehow the Nazis might have built a bunker underneath the allotment colony.

His son shook his head. 'Ice. The ground got so cold during the last winter that, despite the heat of the last few weeks, everything more than forty centimetres deep is still frozen solid. Try planting something that needs deep roots and the plant will just wither and die.'

'You're becoming an expert gardener.'

Karl nodded, taking him quite seriously.

'You wouldn't believe how much I enjoy it. Snuffling about between the leaves, even the heat and the mosquitos that bite me overnight. It's so quiet. Nobody shouting at me, nobody shooting. A bed that is hard, but at least clean. Neighbours who lean over the fence to say hello, but don't ask any questions.'

'Doesn't sound as if you want to come home with me for dinner.'

'This is my home now, Father.'

Black Market Practices

Stave left the house just before 8 in the morning to head out on the kilometre-long walk that took him towards the station, then down Danziger Strasse, and along Brenner Strasse to his destination, the Hansaplatz. The smugglers and black market dealers never turned up before ten or eleven and things only really got going around midday, at the moment when office and shop staff took their lunch break. But the chief inspector couldn't bear it in his apartment any longer. The rooms were too quiet, the space too small.

In the restaurant of the Würzburger Hof hotel in Brenner Strasse he had a cup of ersatz coffee with skimmed milk. 'We're out of sugar,' said a podgy waitress who looked as if she'd been working all night.

He had seven more days. No pressure. Pressure made for mistakes. But MacDonald was his friend, perhaps the only one he still had in this city. And for Erna Berg it was a potential disaster. She risked losing her lover and father of her unborn child, as well as custody of her first son. If Stave didn't come up with something better than he had so far within seven days, then he would also lose MacDonald and Erna Berg. He might already have lost Anna, and his son. From the following week on, he could find his life empty.

He only left the stuffy café late in the morning and strolled inconspicuously – or so he hoped – in the direction of the Hansaplatz. He hoped the revolver in its holster under his jacket didn't make too much of a bulge. At the end of Brenner Strasse, where it opened out on to the square, he spotted the people he was looking for. Two adolescents standing smoking in the doorway of a house occupied by several families. Lookouts. The uninteresting minor criminals of the Hansaplatz, the small fish who didn't even get picked up when the police carried out a raid. They were allowed to run away without anyone chasing them. No CID officer ever interviewed them; the worst that ever happened was that they'd end up before one of the British summary courts and get put away for a day or two.

He had nearly reached the doorway. If they decided to make a run for it now, he could probably reach out and grab at least one of them. But the pair just glanced at him indifferently. They clearly considered him just another citizen come to check out what was available on the black market.

He moved quickly, shoved them both backwards through the doorway into the stairwell. Stave followed, closing the door behind him.

'CID,' he hissed. He hoped neither of them had a knife; he had never had to fire on children before. His heart was pounding and he blinked fast to get his eyes used to the low light in the stairwell. The walls were painted green gloss, the closest apartment was up the steps towards the rear of the building. To one side was a closed door, which he assumed led down to the coal cellar.

The boys were about ten or twelve years old, and wore short lederhosen, open patched shirts; one of them had dark black hair, sandals that were too big for his dirty feet, the other was brown-haired, badly undernourished and barefoot. He turned towards the staircase.

'Forget it,' Stave called after him. 'I'm faster than you.' It was a bluff and he hoped neither of them had noticed his limp.

'We haven't done anything,' the brown-haired one insisted.

'Are you arresting us?' the black-haired one asked. 'My parents think I'm at school.'

'I don't care what your parents think. If you're smart they'll never even know about this conversation. If you aren't smart, they'll have to come and pick you up from the police station.'

'What do you want to know?'

'That's the way.' Stave took a deep breath and pulled out the photo of Adolf Winkelmann. 'Have either of you seen him before?'

The pair exchanged rapid glances, then the black-haired one shrugged his shoulders. 'If he's who you're looking for, you're a bit late. He's a goner.'

'You can see he's dead from the photo,' the other commented.

'You know who he is.'

'That's Adolf. He used to hate his name.'

'Surname?'

They shook their heads. 'He wasn't a friend of ours so we didn't ask.'

'But you know what he did?'

'It's a trap,' the brown-haired one blurted out. 'If we sing, you'll take us in.'

'On the contrary, if you don't sing I'm taking you in.'

'It hardly matters,' the black-haired one sighed. 'We stand lookout here every day. We know everybody who turns up here.'

Stave nodded understandingly.

'Yeah, so Adolf, he was like a courier. He picked stuff up at the station and brought it to the dealers here. Did the exchange either in the Würzburger Hof or the Lenz bar, in the back room.'

'What did he use to carry the things he was transporting?'

'Suitcases usually, unless it was something really small when he'd just put it in his jacket pocket. Once he used a shoe polish box to transport some stuff. But it was usually suitcases. We called him "the page boy" because he looked like the ones who carry stuff for rich people in hotels.'

'Not to his face though,' the brown-haired one added.

'Or he would have hit you?'

'Yeah, he could hit hard.'

'What was in the suitcases, usually?'

The two boys laughed. 'If we were that nosy, we wouldn't have a job as lookouts for very long.'

'But you must have wondered? Maybe got wind of something from one of the dealers? Maybe got a look inside when somebody opened one of them?'

They glanced at one another again, hesitated, then nodded. 'Adolf was dealing with pills, and ciggies, of course, and Dutch butter.'

'Pills?'

'Something that began with "P". Some people would go really wild to get hold of them.'

'Penicillin?'

'Yeah, that's it. No idea what it does. Some sort of Schnapps?'

'A bit more healthy than that,' Stave replied, thinking hard. Pity. Up until then he'd been reckoning it had been some sort of drug for athletes, like the cocaine or heroin they'd given a cyclist in the six-day race. Stuff like that would have been useful for boxers too. It would have been an excuse to interview Walter Kümmel again. But penicillin? Expensive stuff on the black market, but not exactly something that would interest a boxing promoter any more than anyone else.'

'Who was Adolf dealing with? Who picked up the suitcases from him?'

'No idea. The page boy would disappear into a back room with his suitcase and come out without it.'

The chief inspector thought the answer was a bit too quick. 'Well, that's a shame. I guess we'd better head on down to the police station.'

Within thirty seconds he had the names of three black market dealers, not that any of them meant a thing to him. He wrote them down. They might be of interest to his colleagues in Department S, if they didn't already know them.

By now the two boys were dripping sweat, and not just because it was so stiflingly hot in the stairwell. The longer the interview went on, the greater the chance someone would get wind of it. Nobody liked seeing the police around the Hansaplatz. And if a couple of the big dealers turned up, Stave too could find himself in a tricky situation. He took down the boys' names and let them think he was about to let them go. They both smiled with relief.

'One more thing,' he said, trying to sound as uninterested as possible. 'Adolf never had anything to do down by the port, did he?'

The brown-haired boy shook his head, but his friend nodded. 'A couple of weeks ago. Adolf didn't want to be just a courier. He was ambitious. I heard somebody mention it, somebody telling somebody, the page boy's down by the port.'

'Somebody who? When and where?'

'I really don't know. Not my business.'

Stave believed him. 'Do you know what he was smuggling from the port? Penicillin? Cigarettes?'

'No. He wasn't smuggling. At least not in this direction. Not according to what I heard. He never brought suitcases back from the port.'

The CID man thought for a moment he'd misheard. 'He never brought anything back from the port?'

'He didn't bring anything back, but he did take stuff there.'

'You mean he'd take stuff from the Hansaplatz down to the port? Stuff that was intended to go somewhere else?'

'What he did with it down at the port I have no idea. I can't imagine what anybody would want with that stuff.'

'You know, then, what it was that he was taking down there?'

'Recording tapes. Adolf was dealing in tapes. He was so proud he even boasted about it once, said he'd got a whole carton of Lucky Strikes. That was the last time I saw him.'

Stave strolled across the Hansaplatz. He'd given the boys a friendly nod and let them go. They'd slope off behind his back to warn the dealers who'd posted them as lookouts. But the chief inspector wasn't interested. He looked about. A well-dressed gentleman was talking to a haggard elderly man. Stave stopped a few paces from them, watching from the corner of his eye. The old man opened the long overcoat he was wearing despite the heat. From behind him three tough-looking characters ran up, jostling him, quickly, expertly frisking him inside the coat. There was a choked cry, sarcastic laughter, then the well-dressed gentleman threw the old boy a bundle of Reichsmarks.

The old boy was a dealer who needed to learn the ways of the world, Stave thought to himself. It was amazing people still fell for it. The trick was as old as could be, as old as the black market itself. The well-dressed type was a plant, who would look for an inexperienced, greedy or desperate dealer and pretend he was interested in doing a big bit of business. The dealer would show off his wares, and then the heavies would rob him at lightning speed. Then the plant would toss him a bunch of notes, so the victim could hardly complain he hadn't been paid. Not that he could exactly lodge a formal complaint anyway, given that what he was doing was illegal in the first place.

Stave wasn't interested. He had glanced across while the old boy was being searched just to see what he had: coffee. But it was tapes he was looking for. He spent two hours wandering around the Hansaplatz. Maybe he stood out too much, or maybe he was just unlucky, maybe he was looking for the wrong stuff in the wrong place. But he saw no sign of recording tapes.

The chief inspector was well aware that stuff from the black market found its way abroad: watches, jewellery, anything that was both small and valuable. There were big profits to be made: bring a couple of pounds of butter from Holland into the occupation zone and pick up a couple of diamonds in exchange. But recording tape? Who abroad was willing to pay for recording tape. You could buy it cheap enough in England or America. Why pay for it on the black market?

In the end he gave up, disappointed and uncertain what do next. Hildegard Hüllmann had said Adolf was dealing in recording tapes. The two boys had confirmed it. There had to be something in it, but what?

Stave walked down Ellmenreich Strasse towards the station. When he reached the corner where the Garrison Theatre was, he quickly pulled back into the shadows: Anna.

She was speaking to two men, a British captain and the plant conman he'd been watching just a couple of hours earlier. It looked as if they were all chatting like old friends, the two men smoking, Anna smiling and gesturing with her right hand. The scene wrenched at

Stave's heart. Eventually Anna reached into her handbag and pulled out something white, something painted, porcelain. Stave resisted the impulse to get closer. Two tiny cups, it looked like, and a tiny figurine, that of a woman maybe. It had to be Meissen porcelain, what the British called Dresden china, or something similar. For a moment Stave thought Anna was trying to get the conman and the British officer bidding against one another. But it seemed the deal had already been agreed in advance: the captain was interested in the figurine, the other man in the cups. The CID man was impressed by the sophistication of the trade. Because there was a British officer there, nobody was going to come up and arrest them. And Anna could be sure the black marketeer wasn't going to mug her. It had to have been her idea.

The pieces of porcelain, wrapped in old newspaper, disappeared into the pocket of a uniform shirt on one hand and the conman's brightly coloured jacket on the other. The thick bundles of Reichsmarks quickly, smoothly, changed ownership. Stave noticed how Anna swiftly put the English officer's money into her handbag, but took her time counting the notes the black marketeer had passed her. He realised that in that brief moment she had earned more money than he did in a month.

Anna said her goodbyes to the two men, who remained standing on the street corner. Maybe the black marketeer also had something to offer the British officer, Stave thought. He followed Anna discreetly, primarily to protect her now that he knew how much money she was carrying. Or at least that's what he told himself.

Without glancing right or left, she crossed the station, headed down Mönckeberg Strasse, without stopping at a bank. She passed the city hall and headed on down the Jungfernstieg. Stave's leg was hurting because he could hardly keep up with her. Anna turned left, along the Alster. Past the grandiose Four Seasons hotel, which still looked as if the war had taken place somewhere else. Anna disappeared into a shop next door to the hotel. The CID man edged closer: a jeweller's.

Stave stared at the exterior with its fresh plaster, its curved display windows, everything within them laid out against a black background: watches, earrings, necklaces. He was too far away to clearly see the prices written in an elegant hand on cards next to each item, but close enough to see that they were all at least in six figures. He squinted to try to make out anything inside the shop. He could just about see a petite, well-dressed woman behind the counter, and Anna leaning over a glass case. She's not just looking, Stave thought to himself, she knows exactly what she wants. Anna and the salesgirl moved towards the shop window in order to examine a piece in the daylight. The chief inspector quickly hid behind a builders' truck parked in front of the colonnade, and cautiously peeked out. Anna was holding up a ring, gold, without a stone.

Stave turned away, leaning back against the wooden side panel of the truck, blood pounding in his head. For a moment he couldn't shake off an image of Anna and Public Prosecutor Ehrlich standing together at the altar, with a golden ring glittering on her finger. Absurd. Maybe she was buying back an old wedding ring she had at some stage sold to the shop. But a wedding ring meant a husband. And if she was buying it back at some huge price, what did that mean?

I'm standing here like some fourteen-year-old kid watching the girl he fancies from the next class going to the cinema with another boy, he told himself. But he couldn't quite find it in him to laugh at himself.

He turned away from the jeweller's. He didn't wait to find out whether or not Anna actually did hand over the money in exchange for the ring. He hurried off, trying to meld in as inconspicuously as possible with the casual strollers along the colonnade and on the Jungfernstieg. He couldn't bear it if Anna saw him here.

Stave spent the rest of the day looking for recording tape. He walked up and down between Steindamm and Deichtorplatz, even going on one occasion as far as the steel girders of the Elbe bridges. Ruins on either side of him, broken here and there by the well-used short cuts that had sprung up. The air was a haze of heat. The chief inspector stopped to look at a wooden shelter built against a two-storey-high remnant of wall. A young woman had dropped a bucket on a string down into the river and was struggling to pull it back up. In the end she managed it and poured the water over the roof of her shelter. 'If I don't cool it down, the tar will melt,' she said, as if in explanation.

Stave was embarrassed to have been looking and hurried on. He took to the pathways between the bombed-out houses, feeling how the ground under the soles of his feet had been trampled by thousands of other passers-by until it was as hard as concrete. Adolf Winklemann could have taken any of these pathways, if he hadn't wanted to be spotted on the main roads. All of them eventually led close to the harbour.

The chief inspector looked around. He could make out dark openings of little caves amid the ruins, half-ruined entrances to cellars, broken water pipes, old heating stoves, as well as hollow spaces that had somehow remained intact when bits of concrete and stone balconies had crashed to the ground. A few of these spaces were as big as wardrobes, some so tiny that you could hardly put a hand in. Nearly all of them at least partly covered by grass or shrubbery. Every one of them an ideal place to hide something. Places that could be used to temporarily store stolen goods, more or less safe from the elements, easy to relocate, but for someone who wasn't looking for them, almost invisible. He wondered whether recording tape could be stored here without harm. Just on a whim he tried feeling around in a few of them, but apart from a few scratches on his hand from thorns, he found nothing. But then to search all of these little cavities just on the banks of the Elbe, it would take hundreds of men.

He wandered back to the little hut where the young woman was now sitting against the wall, resting next to her empty bucket.

'CID,' he said, pulling out his ID card.

'Better than the building control police,' she said.

The chief inspector couldn't help thinking how young she was. 'Have you been living here long?'

'Ever since the cold weather ended. Before that I was living in the flak bunker, and before that in Breslau.'

Stave nodded as if that was the most reasonable explanation in the world. He took out the photo of Adolf Winkelmann. 'Did you ever come across this boy in the ruins around here?' he asked.

'No,' she replied, closing her eyes wearily.

'Are you sure?' he asked again, holding the photo under her nose. She just shook her head.

'Thank you,' he replied.

'Poor thing,' she said, leaving the chief inspector to wonder if she meant the boy in the photo, or him.

Adolf Winkelmann could, of course, have avoided the ruins altogether, and gone along Mönckeberg Strasse, before taking one of the many routes that led down to the landing stages. Before, people would have noticed a boy out in the streets, because all children that age were meant to be in school. But now, with lessons being given in shifts, Adolf could have wandered around Hamburg's busiest streets from dawn to dusk without anyone finding it in any way unusual.

Stave thought it all through again in his head. The Hansaplatz: as a courier for smugglers, Adolf Winkelmann knew his way around. At one stage he turns up with recording tapes. Stuff he had got hold of on the black market maybe? Unlikely: nobody was peddling something so useless. So was he there because the Hansaplatz had become a sort of second home and he hung out there with his friends? Maybe it was just on the route from where he picked up the tapes on his way down to the port? Or did he have a hiding place there, in some hotel room or in the corner of some bar – like lots of other smugglers.

But what was the way from the Hansaplatz to the harbour? There were lots of possibilities, from Mönckeberg Strasse to the footpaths through the ruins, to short cuts that were hardly even visible to the naked eye. There was no way he could reconstruct Winkelmann's route.

The only thing left to do was to go back down to the harbour itself and take a look around there.

He woke up the next morning sweaty and still exhausted. It was Friday the thirteenth. There was still no water from the taps, and the supply he had collected was fast running out. Stave looked in his cracked mirror and saw a haggard, badly shaved face staring back at him. If things keep on like this, he told himself, I'm going to look like a POW returned from the gulags. He took the tram because he was too tired to walk. He'd lain awake half the night thinking about what he should do next.

The port was enormous: kilometre after kilometre of quays and docks, most of them badly bombed. Dozens of foreign freighters were laid up, along with fishing boats and ferries, hundreds of wrecks. And then there were the warehouses, the cranes, shacks, railway sidings covering areas the size of football fields. There was no chance he could ever search it all, and certainly not in the few days MacDonald had left. I need a tip-off, he told himself – and there was only one man who might be able to supply it: Tattoo-Willy.

Willy was the oldest and best-known master of his craft, who'd been in the business since 1902, when he was fourteen years old. He had also been a goldsmith in his time. During the hyper inflation of the 1920s he'd survived by painting postcards. But his real skill was painting pictures on human skin. It took him no more than five minutes to paint a sailing ship or a naked woman on to one of his customers, and fill in the colours. Then out came the electric needle. Stave had called him as a witness once in a murder trial. Back in 1938. Tattoo-Willy was well known to the CID, which was how Stave knew he had survived the war. If anyone knew what went on down at the port, it was Willy who in the course of nearly half a century had decorated virtually every seaman who ever wandered down the Reeperbahn. I hope he remembers me, Stave thought.

At 10 in the morning the Reeperbahn was a sorry sight: scraps of newspaper floating in the muggy air, vomit on the pavement next to bombed-out buildings, the stench of cigarette smoke, stale beer and urine, the cracked façades. No dealers, no hookers, no old tarts. The chief inspector turned right at Nobistor into Grosse Freiheit, a lane that ran past several three-, four- and five-storey buildings, famous for its role in a film by Hans Albers. A few of the buildings had been destroyed, the others were bars, table-dancing venues or night clubs. The walls were covered with painted pictures of naked girls and adverts for sparkling wine and schnapps. There were no lights on. Stave got out of the way of a British patrol. Grosse Freiheit was so narrow he was afraid the oncoming Jeep would run him over, and squeezed tight against a wall to avoid it.

Down towards the end was one building that looked most out of place: the Catholic Church of St Joseph. Grey stone columns and entrance, massive brickwork, and nothing behind it. The nave had taken a direct hit.

Opposite was what remained of No. 38, the left half of a four-storey building with a bar on the ground floor and above it three apartments. The façade facing on to Grosse Freiheit was only two windows wide, the plaster was a dirty yellow, the doors and window frames a brown-ochre colour, the wall where the other half of the building used to be was blank. Tattoo-Willy had his shop on the first floor.

Stave felt his way up the grubby stairwell. Outside Willy's apartment were two neatly written signs: 'Tattoos of all sorts in six colours, all guaranteed non-noxious. No side effects.' And heavily underlined: 'No black market deals.' That was new, Stave thought to himself, knocking on the door.

He had to wait a minute or two before an average-sized, elderly man opened the door, sparse hair combed over his bald head. He was wearing a huge pair of wire-framed glasses, his face wrinkled, but his body still obviously strong. Tattoos on both lower arms, up to his rolled shirtsleeves, which was as far as Stave could see, as well as on both hands. Stave wondered briefly if the old man had tattooed his own hands.

'Herr Kommissar,' Tattoo-Willy greeted him loudly.

'It's Chief Inspector now,' Stave replied automatically. It was one thing to draw a line under the Third Reich, but they might as well have kept the old system of ranks. 'You've lost weight,' he said.

The tattooist clapped a hand over his tight stomach. 'I weigh 108 pounds these days. Was 240 before the war. The Third Reich was hardly a great success in the culinary field. Fancy a tattoo, do you? Maybe a sheriff's star on your chest? Or a Soviet star, if you prefer? Very popular right now, especially among drunk English sailors. If their superior officers were to see ...' He tittered, and led the chief inspector down a narrow little hallway into the kitchen, where two wooden chairs stood next to a table. 'My workshop,' he announced. 'This is where they all sit: the Germans, the English, the Russians, the Dutch, the Americans. And now even a policeman.'

'Is this an inconvenient time?'

'Most of my customers roll in around eight in the evening, and then the trade is steady all night. I use the mornings for new drawings.'

'For work purposes?'

'Indirectly.' He laughed. 'I got out of painting postcards. What would I put on them? Bombed churches? Sunken ships in the harbour? Not the sort of thing people send to their nearest and dearest back home. I draw ships, fjords, islands, lighthouses. I travelled a lot in the old days: America, Holland, Scandinavia. So I remember the pretty things and turn them into tattoos for my customers. Most of them, of course, just want naked women on their backs or a heart with a monogram, in six colours. But some want the Statue of Liberty from New York, or a Dutch barge. What do you fancy? A squad car?'

'I'm just here for a chat.'

'I though that might be the case,' Tattoo-Willy said, disappointedly. 'I could have tattooed your new ranks on to your chest. That would have been a first for me.'

Stave gave a thin smile, and silently took the photo of the murdered Adolf Winkelmann out of his pocket and laid it on the table.

'This boy was found somewhere he had no business being – down at the port.'

'The boy from the shipyard? The one they found lying on an unexploded bomb down at Blohm & Voss?'

Stave's smile broadened. 'At least that saves me explaining it to you.'

The tattooist raised his hands. 'I didn't know the boy. Never came across him, he never came in here, nor did I see him on the Reeper-bahn. He came to mind because I thought it had to be the poor bugger a couple of shipyard workers told me about.'

'That's why I'm here. About the boy. And I'd like to know more about the shipyard workers. About sailors, casual workers, everybody who hangs about down around the port.'

Tattoo-Willy took another look at the photo. 'You think one of them might have done this?'

'The boy wasn't killed by a bit of roofing falling on his head.'

'Fire away.'

'Many of your customers mention the killing?'

'They did on the day it was in the papers. Not so much now. Just the normal stuff.'

'What's normal?'

He laughed. 'Boxing matches, football, jazz music, schnapps. And women, mostly women.'

'Nobody ever mentioned a possible suspect? Never let a name slip?'

'No. The Blohm & Voss workers weren't exactly thrilled to have the cops down at the shipyard. No offence meant. But you know a lot of them are communists. They're mad enough at the way the works are being dismantled. I wouldn't go down there on my own if I was British. But none of them had the faintest who might have killed the boy. Or what the kid might have been doing down there.'

'Given that we know the victim was involved in smuggling, where would you find smugglers down at the docks?'

'Everywhere.' The tattooist leaned back and took a long cold look at Stave, not quite so friendly as he had been. 'If you're going to start stirring in dirty water like that, you're going to disturb a lot of fish, and one or two sharks.'

'Nobody will ever need to know who named the sharks?'

'And you promise not to call me as a witness?'

'Not if I can avoid it. All I really want is to find who killed the boy. And a fourteen-year-old girl.'

'A girl too?' Tattoo-Willy nodded thoughtfully. 'OK, I'll give you a little introduction in the less than 100 per cent legal world of the port economy. Cigarettes are involved, but that's hardly a surprise. Particularly on the British and American freighters, but sometimes also on the Soviet ships. But those Russian Papirosi aren't quite so popular.'

Stave called up a vision of the giant freight ships tied up at the docks. 'Whenever a ship arrives with a new load, the price on the black market must tumble.'

The tattooist shook his head. 'They never bring a full load. It would be far too obvious. The British military police run checks. The smuggling is done privately by the sailors and sometimes the gentlemen officers too. They keep a supply in their cabins and bring a carton onshore stuffed up their jumper when they head out for the Reeperbahn.'

'What do they take back in exchange?'

'A half-hour of transient happiness, as a rule. Most of the ciggies are exchanged for schnapps and the services of the local girls.'

'What about tattoos?'

'That's not transient, that's for life. I don't bother to check if tax had been paid on the cigarettes. You're not going to rat on me, are you?'

Stave had no interest in causing Tattoo-Willy to stop talking. He waved his right hand in a dismissive gesture.

'The wiser ones do better business than they could here,' the old boy continued. 'They go down to the black market towards the end of the Reeperbahn. On the corner with Hamburger Berg.'

'What do they exchange them for?'

'Anything small enough for them to hide in their cabins and get past the customs men in New York or Liverpool. Rings, watches, hard currency. You wouldn't believe where you can find dollars or pound notes. Notes from back before the war. I thought the Nazis had banned all that.'

'What about recording tape?'

Tattoo-Willy stared at him in confusion. The chief inspector repeated the question. The old man shook his head, uncomprehendingly. 'What sort of crazy idea is that? Never heard of anything of the sort. Is that something you smuggle in or out? Can't imagine the British patrols paying much interest. Nor any customs officials on the other side of the big pond. And in any case tape recorders are big, at least bigger than a bundle of dollars. Why would anybody want to smuggle those?'

'Yeah, I've asked myself the same question.' Stave rubbed his forehead. The whole tape-recording thing just didn't make sense any which way round. The air in the kitchen was sticky and smelled of chemicals. Probably the dye or maybe disinfectant. He had an idea.

'What about medicine?'

'Yes, but not often. And the other way round when pills are involved. They don't make them in Germany any more. There aren't any to smuggle out of the country.'

'What else goes on down at the docks? The sailors bring stuff in and take it out. But what about the workers? What do they get out of it?'

'Sometimes the sailors and black market dealers need places to hide their stuff. And what could be more secure than the port or the shipyard? Your colleagues are always raiding the black market venues, and using grasses to rat on the dealers. But the harbour is British territory. Sometimes they carry out raids too, but the Tommies don't know their way around very well. And old maps aren't much use because so much was destroyed. There are thousands of places to hide a few cartons of cigarettes, or granny's old gold ring. A few of the workers got into the business straight away. There aren't any other Germans with such access to foreign ships. Or so soon after their arrival. Those boys, the clever ones, do the best business before anyone else. Right now, for example, the American "Liberty ship" *Leland Stanford* is in port, carrying 3,700 tonnes of sugar from Cuba.'

Stave recalled seeing the ship when he crossed the Elbe on a ferry after the initial investigations down by Blohm & Voss.

'The Tommies make sure nothing is stolen,' Tattoo-Willy went on. 'There are English military police all over the place. The opportunists can't even pinch a grain of sugar. Not that they want to. They nip down to the hold and drop off something more valuable, like jewellery or gold. Then they pull out a couple of bags in some dark corner of the hold where all of a sudden they come across cartons of Lucky Strikes. The Tommies are only looking out for people trying to steal the sugar, to make sure the white gold isn't being siphoned off. Meanwhile, right under their noses, the clever boys are taking thousands of ciggies. Then they're stored in some half-ruined warehouse or somewhere in the shipyard until the *Leland Stanford* has been properly unloaded and the Tommies are gone. That's when they take their treasure down to the black market.'

'Sounds as if these guys must be the richest men in Hamburg. So how come I've never been aware of this?'

'There's only ever two or three of them down there at a time. Most of the workers are real proletariat. They don't do stuff like that.'

'Why not? Some sort of working-class pride? Or communist ideology?'

'They're just no good with money. They get ripped off by the real pros. And they know it. Most of them would be quite capable of dumping grandma's jewellery somewhere in the darkness of the hold, and then get palmed off with a couple of cigarettes from some Yankee sailor. Try lodging a complaint! That's why they're happy enough to go through the dealers.'

'So who are they then, these pros who know which end of the hold they should leave stuff for which American sailor?'

'Lads with the right connections, international connections. Not the yobs hanging about the docks, but real businessmen in suits.'

Tattoo-Willy mentioned a few names that meant nothing to Stave. But he took note of them dutifully; they would be helpful to the boys from Department S. He was just about to close his notebook when he heard the last name: 'Walter Kümmel.'

'The boxing promoter?' Stave stammered, all of a sudden wide awake.

The old boy laughed. 'He's right in the thick of it. Very smart.'

'What do you mean "smart"?'

'Smart enough to get into the smuggling business in a big way without anybody knowing what he deals in.'

Stave suddenly recalled that the first time he had met Kümmel in Greta Boesel's apartment he had noticed a tube of pills in the boxing promoter's pocket. 'Penicillin?' he asked Tattoo-Willy.

The man shrugged his shoulders slowly. 'Pills are small, light, easy to hide and very profitable. Maybe, but I don't know for sure. Like I said, nobody talks about what he deals in. Kümmel is into big business, but just what sort of business, nobody knows.'

'That's about to change,' Stave said, shaking the old man's hand.

The chief inspector wandered back through the rubble, watching the red light of the setting sun appear to transform the remnants of bombed houses into ancient Greek ruins. A man who painted postcards could do something with that, he thought. Maybe these ruins would be around as long as those of the ancient temples. At least then you could charge people to come and see them.

He was bursting with energy, even if his mouth was so dry he could hardly speak and his stomach was aching with hunger. He had a lead. Walter Kümmel – I'll need to have a chat with him tomorrow. Stave had no idea who the boxing promoter was in league with or how he was making a profit, not had he any idea what his motive might have been in killing Winkelmann. What was the point? And did recording tape link him to the dead boy? Now all he needed for his mood to improve even further was the possibility that there might be somebody waiting for him back at his apartment. He forced himself not think about the empty rooms and the long lonely hours ahead of him.

Questions and Answers

Monday, 16 June 1947

A wasted weekend. Greta Boesel had told him her fiancé had taken a delivery for her down to the American zone and wouldn't be back in his office in the Chile House until Monday morning. She had mentioned a few towns and trading partners he was due to call on, but said she had no idea in what order he would visit them. Stave rang the firms she mentioned and also the CID in Munich, Wiesbaden, Frankfurt and Nuremberg, asking them to look out for a truck with the registration number the dead boy's aunt had given him. None of them called back. It was as if Walter Kümmel had been swallowed up by an earthquake. The chief inspector had spent hours sitting in his office next to a silent telephone. But then he reckoned that was better than sitting alone in his silent apartment, longing for the company of Anna or his son and slowly going out of his mind.

Then on Sunday evening MacDonald burst into his office and invited him to a jazz concert. Stave got the impression that Erna Berg somehow knew he would be spending the entire weekend in the office, rather than at home with his son. She had probably been worrying about him, and had asked her lover to take her boss with them. Stave wasn't very keen on jazz and didn't fancy playing gooseberry to the two of them, but he couldn't think of a polite way to turn down the invitation. In any case the lieutenant's good humour was just a front to cover up his nervousness. Just three more days. But he was too polite himself to ask Stave if he had made any progress.

So they set off in MacDonald's Jeep to a festival in Moorweide. The lieutenant for once was not in uniform. It was the first time

Stave had seen him in civilian dress, a light English summer suit with a hat to match. Better dressed than one of the black market dealers, Stave thought without a shred of envy.

It was hard to estimate how many people were packed into the festival tent. A thousand, maybe two? Mostly young and German, dressed in their best clothes. But there were also a few British officers and Americans who had possibly come from Bremen or Berlin, or maybe even had come up from the American occupation zone in the south for such a special occasion. The CID man found himself thinking of Walter Kümmel.

He was standing towards the edge of the smoky tent, hot and muggy beneath the canvas, the smell of sweat and black market perfume in the air. Gene Hammers and his trio were in full swing: screeching saxophones and trumpets, the thumping of drums and bass. Stave was staring at the musicians, sweating and dancing around in apparent ecstasy. Some of them were black. Apart from the odd occasion down at the docks and in some of the propaganda films in the old Nazi newsreels, Stave had never seen a black person before. Then a singer came on; she was wearing a white dress, her lips painted bright red, with black hair and a smoky, sensuous voice. She looked vaguely familiar and then he realised with astonishment that she was German, not American: Margot Hielscher. He'd seen her in films. Before 1945. Now she had become a passionate jazz singer. All the men were staring wide-eyed at her, and the Americans were shouting things that Stave thought it was just as well his poor English meant he didn't understand.

Stave wasn't going to dance; in fact, he would have crept out of the tent as inconspicuously as he could if it wouldn't have been impolite towards MacDonald and Erna Berg who were jigging about in the crowd, despite her baby bump. Jazz was loud, provocative, alien, very American to Stave who preferred classical music even if it did make his colleagues, who were all Zarah Leander fans, laugh at him. He felt left out in these new times.

However, the next morning heading down the Ahrensburger

Strasse he no longer felt alien: he was doing what he did best, following a lead. He hurried past the station, along Klosterwall, past Deichtorplatz, then turned right: the Chile House.

The spectacular, ten-storey office building stood like a great redbrick cliff, considered ultra-modern when it was built back in the 1920s. Now it looked like something from the future, brought back in a time machine to the rubble of 1947: triangular and totally undamaged, alone amid a sea of flame-scarred, windowless buildings with their upper storeys blown in. The Chile House was one of the most expensive office addresses in the city.

Stave passed the corner where 'Chilehaus A' was written in large metal letters over the entrance. He flicked through the notes he had made the last time he had visited Greta Boesel. The thin visiting card the boxing promoter had given him fell out. Walter Kümmel's office was in Building B, on the second floor. Stave went through the massive entrance into the inner courtyard. It was a vast space, but felt rather gloomy and depressing because of the high walls on each side that shut out the sunlight. On the other hand, for the same reason, it was a bit cooler. Stave gratefully wiped his sweat-soaked collar with his right hand. The courtyard was home to a café and a tobacco shop.

The door to Building B was open and dozens of men carrying briefcases were hurrying in with that Monday-morning expression of busy employees on their faces. Polished stone tablets on either side of the entrance displayed the names of the tenants, as if they were ancient inscriptions, designed to be there for thousands of years. The chief inspector took them in at a glance: 'Slomann. F.W & Co. Sales Office Chlorodont – 1' and above it: 'Hanseatic Boxing. W. Kümmel – 2.'

The internal stairwell had polished panels on the walls like smooth birch veneer; in a window niche on the landing were dark wooden chairs like those you might find in a confessional booth. From the landing upwards the stairwell was white tiles, as if one were going up into a swimming pool.

On the second floor Stave came to a reddish-brown wooden door with no bell. He knocked, but the door was so big he couldn't hear if there was any response on the other side. He tried the handle. The door was unlocked and he walked into an anteroom the size of a large wardrobe, with a tiny desk, a chair and an open, untidy filing cabinet. It didn't exactly look like it was a regular place of work. A summer jacket was hanging on rail, behind it a door with opaque glass, beyond which he could hear the voice of someone talking on a telephone. The voice of Walter Kümmel.

The chief inspector knocked on the door, then walked in without waiting for a reply. Kümmel was sitting on a huge desk of dark teak wood, a pen in one hand, the telephone receiver in the other, his feet up on an office chair. He was writing in a notebook as he spoke; Stave had the impression it was numbers, but he didn't have time to get a better look. Kümmel looked up in surprise, quickly ended his call, put the phone down and closed his notebook.

'You surprised me!' the boxing promoter said, standing up and holding out his hand.

'I thought your fiancée might have said I wanted to talk to you,' he said, shaking Kümmel's scarred hand.

'I thought you would call first.'

'Wouldn't have been much use, would it? I wouldn't have got through. Who were you talking to?'

'It was a business call,' Kümmel said, watching him carefully with his grey eyes. His Roman nose that had at some stage been broken was very tanned, the CID man noticed: Walter Kümmel had been outdoors a lot recently. You didn't get a tanned nose like that from sitting in a truck. On the wall behind the boxing promoter was a framed poster: 'Hein ten Hoff versus Walter Neusel, Summer 1946, Germany's First Professional Heavyweight Bout Since the War.' A lot of Stave's colleagues still talked about it. Stave could remember it too. It was what made ten Hoff famous. Next to the poster a pair of boxing gloves hanging from a nail, dark brown leather, worn and torn on the knuckles.

'Those are mine,' Kümmel said, having noticed the direction of Stave's glance.

'A sentimental streak?'

'My only one. What can I do for you?'

'How was your trip?'

Kümmel looked surprised for a moment, then nodded. 'You haven't come here to discuss the state of the roads in the different occupation zones.'

Stave decided on a full frontal attack. 'Did you know that Adolf Winkelmann was involved in smuggling?'

Kümmel laughed. 'So that's where the boy got his cigarettes? Sit down.' He himself sat down on the chair he had had his feet on. The chief inspector was more than a little disappointed to see how relaxed he seemed.

'The boy was acting as a courier for illegal goods between the port and the station. And at some stage in his last few weeks he began taking some very different merchandise down to the docks.'

'To the docks? That's quite a long way from our apartment.'

'Yes, it must have been worth his while.'

'So what was it he was smuggling?'

'That's what I'd like you to tell me.'

Kümmel shrugged. 'He wasn't hiding anything at our place, I can tell you that. Unless,' he was thinking to himself, 'it was something very small. So small that neither Greta nor I ever came across it. But you didn't find anything either, did you, when you searched his room?'

Stave suddenly cursed under his breath, remembering that they didn't search either the cellar or the other rooms in the apartment. If Kümmel had really been involved in the smuggling business then he would have long since got rid of anything he had been hiding there. Should he mention the tapes? Or the pills? He glanced around the office as casually as possible. He could see no tubes of pills. And certainly no tape recorder. If there'd been a tape recorder or any tapes lying around this little room they would have been very obvious. But pills? That was different. There could have been hundreds in

Kümmel's desk drawers. There could hardly be a better hiding place for illegal wares than Hamburg's most expensive business address, located exactly halfway between the station and the port. But the chief inspector didn't have a search warrant. He decided not to mention exactly what he thought was being smuggled. It wouldn't do any harm to keep Kümmel guessing as to what he knew.

'Could Adolf have diverted some of his aunt's deliveries to his own ends?'

'My fiancée's trucks carry sugar, lard, wood, wool – bulky, heavy goods but not so big and bulky that it would be more economic to transport them by train or canal boat. Hardly the sort of stuff I would try to smuggle.'

'What would you smuggle?'

A sharp glance from those grey eyes. 'It's not my line of business. From time to time I help out my fiancée. But all her business is completely above board. One of her drivers was ill on Friday. Measles! In a grown-up man! But, normally, dealing with my boxers keeps me busy.'

'But even a top promoter like you doesn't have a bout every week?'

Kümmel gave a broad laugh. 'I only need to stage one a year. At that first bout, ten Hoff versus Neusel, there were 30,000 in the audience. The return match is taking place on the seventeenth of October, at the HSV football stadium on Rothenbaum Chaussee. I've got 40,000 tickets. Sold out weeks ago.'

'Who's going to win?'

'Ten Hoff. He's young, 1.94 metres, 194 pounds. Walter Neusel is a brave old warhorse, but he's forty years old. The only way he can win is if he lands a lucky punch.'

'Would that be bad for your business?'

'They're both under contract to me.'

'So you win either way?'

'I always win.' Kümmel stretched out his arms. 'This is the house of winners. Whether you're selling car tyres or boxing matches, the only thing that matters is to get the product to the customer.'

'And that's how you end up in an office next to a toothpaste merchant.'

Once again Kümmel shot him a sharp, suspicious look. The sort of look one boxer gives another at the beginning of a round, Stave thought to himself.

'You never know. I might have different neighbours soon.'

'Is the toothpaste man moving out?'

'Make all the jokes you want. I'm the one who's moving out. To New York.'

'The Americans are giving you a visa?'

'They're going to carry me on high over the pond. I'm organising the sensation of the year: Max Schmeling's comeback.'

If I laugh, he's going to hit me, Stave thought. Better to stay polite. 'I thought Schmeling was older than Neusel?'

'Doesn't matter. He's famous. He still has a reputation in America. Remember those two fights against Joe Louis.'

'That was back before the war. If someone like Neusel at forty hasn't a chance against a newcomer like ten Hoff, how is Schmeling going to stand up against some American?'

'He won't,' Kümmel laughed, 'he's just my entry ticket. One bout over there and I'm in business in America. I have connections already: promoters in Boston and New York. Radio stations from the East Coast to California. A couple of American reporters were just here. A photographer from *Life*. Even a US Army general. He saw Schmeling in New York in 1938 and was desperate to get his autograph. I sorted it for him. Now I have a friend in the US headquarters.'

Stave wondered if the man had mentioned the general as a threat. 'When is the fight?'

'Spring or summer 1948. First of all Max Schmeling will fight here. We'll get about 10,000 spectators, half of all tickets reserved for British or American officers, to give them something to write home about. He'll fight Walter Neusel. Nothing can go wrong. He'll win easily and be on the next steamship to America.'

'I can see there's a lot to be made,' Stave said cautiously.

'Not as much as back in 1936 or 1938. The Americans will only give Schmeling and me half what they'll pocket for the fight. But half of a whole lot is still a whole lot, especially when it's all in dollars. I'm already a millionaire several times over, but in Reichsmarks.' He laughed. 'That's probably enough to buy a few packets of cigarettes. Apart from that, a nice house? Either bombed out or requisitioned by the English. A nice car? Nobody's making cars in Germany any more.'

'You could always invest your money, put it in the bank.'

'Yes, other people have thought of that in the past. Then you get a world war, crazy inflation, then another world war, then the black market and your money's down the toilet. Now there are still brave souls taking their money and putting it in the bank, while the Russians stand on the Elbe loading their rifles!' He shook his head, staring out of the window. But Stave had the idea he was laughing at him behind his back. 'No,' Kümmel said, 'there are winners and there are losers. That goes for countries too. Germany is a loser country. You just have to go outside and look up at the façades: nothing behind them but air and sky. America is a winner country. It's about time we recognised that and acted accordingly.'

'Maybe I can apply for a job as a sheriff,' Stave mumbled, getting to his feet. 'Thanks for your information and the tip!'

The chief inspector walked out into the open air, squinting at the bright sunlight reflected from a tilted window right into his eyes. The air in the internal courtyard of the Chile House was as fetid as in a coal mine. He headed slowly in the direction of Karl Muck Platz. Why would someone like Kümmel who was about to make the leap of a lifetime to America risk it all by getting involved in smuggling? And yet Tattoo-Willy had named him as one of the biggest godfathers in the whole smuggling scene down at the port. What was Kümmel dealing in? Medicine? But the promoter had just told him he couldn't care less about Reichsmarks or cigarettes. Was somebody paying him in dollars so he could afford the trip with Schmeling?

That would mean he was smuggling stuff out of Germany, not into Germany? But recording tape would only bring in a few dollars at most, if that. So what could it be?

Back in CID headquarters Stave was still struggling with the feeling he had missed something. He had seen something in the Chile House that had set off an alarm bell somewhere in his brain, but he couldn't think what it was. I'm too preoccupied with other things, he told himself, and it's becoming a problem. He closed his eyes and tried to go over again in his mind everything he had seen down at the Chile House. The board by the entrance with the boxing promoter's name. The tiny, empty anteroom. The door to the real office. Stave walking through it. Kümmel quickly ending his telephone call. Who had be been talking to? Was there a single word that Stave had overheard and was now running through his head? The telephone ...

'What an idiot!' he said aloud. The heat, it has to be this damned heat. Kümmel had been on the telephone when he burst into his office – with the telephone in his right hand. The pen, with which he had been making notes, had been in his left hand. Kümmel was left-handed.

Should he go straight to Ehrlich? Then, with the help of the public prosecutor, to a judge for an arrest warrant? Or at the very least a search warrant for the apartment in Fuhlsbüttel Strasse and the office in the Chile House. But what proof did he have? A statement from a tattoo artist on the Reeperbahn and the fact that Kümmel was left-handed. The prosecutor would laugh at him. Stave didn't even have a motive.

Once again he stormed into Cuddel Breuer's office. If only the boss would give him all three murder cases, then he could get a few more people working for him. If he had a few more officers, he could put one of them on to Kümmel, have him followed if necessary. MacDonald would get him permission for that. Then he could see what sort of business the boxing promoter was up to the rest of his time. And he might stumble across something that would explain the murder: a motive.

'Forget it, Stave,' Breuer said even after he had explained where his investigation had led him.

'Walter Kümmel is probably a smuggler.'

'That does not make him a murderer.'

'But …'

'No buts, keep your theories to yourself. I don't want to hear this getting around. Neither here in the office, nor among the British.'

'What have the British got to do with it?'

Breuer held up his hands. 'Occupation troops get bored, they always have done. The Tommies are there in this bombed-out city and don't know what to do, how to spend their time. Bored soldiers are dangerous soldiers, unhappy, unpredictable. Governor Berry does not want that and nor does Mayor Brauer. And nor do I.'

'And the British like their sport!' Stave added, resignedly.

'At last the penny drops. Good boxing matches are a good way of passing the time. Before I arrest the only man in Germany who puts on these matches for the Tommies I am going to need good evidence. More than just Tattoo-Willy. And more than just a man using his left hand to write. And even if you do manage to convince me and the British, at best that makes Kümmel a suspect for the murder of Adolf Winkelmann, but not that of Wilhelm Meinke or Hildegard Hüllmann.'

The CID chief dragged his bulky body over to the window and began to use a sheet of paper as a fan. 'This heat is making people crazy,' he snorted. 'And crazy people have stupid ideas.'

'Such as?' Stave asked, sceptically.

'Like strikes. Down at Blohm & Voss, for example.'

'That'll give the British something to think about besides sport.'

'No stupid jokes. It's already taking up the time of our friends down at Esplanade 6. The workers want increased rations. And of course they want to see an end to the continuing dismantling of the shipyard. There was a collective meeting this morning. Lots of red flags and a lot of speeches that could have come directly from Moscow.'

'If the English started dismantling our business, I'd consider becoming a communist myself.'

'The Tommies did dismantle our business, and then they put it back together again. Otherwise an old red like you would hardly be sitting in an office here on Karl Muck Platz.'

'Just along the corridor from you, boss.'

Breuer, who had been an old Social Democrat, nodded and smiled. 'At this moment a deputation from the workers is having talks with Messrs Rudolf and Walther Blohm and Governor Berry,' he continued. 'As far as I can make out, that will take a day or two and then we'll see what happens: either things will go back to normal or we'll have a strike on our hands. Up until then things down at the shipyard are, shall we say, tense?'

'As in just before the October Revolution?'

'That's what the British are afraid of. That's why there's been a change of policy. The British are no longer considering the murder down at the shipyard as a priority. The last thing Governor Berry wants is police snuffling about at Blohm & Voss, provoking the workforce: giving them some sort of excuse.'

'Am I to halt the investigation?' Stave blurted out, hardly able to believe his ears.

'No, I just don't want you going down to Blohm & Voss over the next couple of days. You're not to speak to any of the workers. Concentrate instead on the other aspects of the case. When the other matters have been resolved, then you can stick your nose back in down at Blohm & Voss.'

By then MacDonald was likely to be in Palestine, Erna Berg a divorcee and Walter Kümmel halfway across the Atlantic, the chief inspector reflected.

'OK, I'll concentrate on the other aspects of the investigation,' he said blandly, hoping Cuddel Breuer would believe his lie.

When Stave got back to his office he surprised MacDonald and Erna Berg in an intimate embrace. 'You're not trying to induce the baby early, are you?' he muttered.

The pair parted quickly. 'Sorry,' said MacDonald. 'Have to take a chance when you can,' and he patted down his uniform. 'Actually it was you I was coming to see.'

The chief inspector shot Erna Berg a warning look. 'What would you have done if it had been another of my colleagues bursting in here? Dönnecke, for example?'

'Dönnecke would never come to see you of his own accord,' his secretary replied, her face still red, but beaming. Her smile got to Stave. If I don't come up with something, this time next week you're out of here.

'As it is you've turned up at the right moment,' he said to Mac-Donald, nodding towards his office. 'We have a few things to talk about.'

'Business?'

'Things that we need to talk about just between the two of us.'

He led the lieutenant into his office and, with an apologetic smile, closed the door on Erna Berg.

'We are up to our necks in shit,' he said as soon as he heard the door click closed.

MacDonald raised his eyebrows. 'That wasn't an expression they taught me in German classes.'

'You know exactly what I mean.'

'I'm sure there's another way to put it in English. I'll think about it and tell you when it's the right moment.'

'This is the right moment,' Stave sighed, falling heavily on to his chair. Breuer was right. What they all needed was a thunderstorm. He looked out the window at a sky as grey as molten lead. The air above Karl Muck Platz was stagnant and there wasn't a cloud to be seen on the horizon. Stave told MacDonald about his interview with Walter Kümmel and about the threat of a strike at Blohm & Voss.

'Your boss doesn't want you to go down to the docks. My boss doesn't want me to either.' MacDonald ran a hand through the little beads of sweat glistening in his blond hair. He had gone quite pale.

'There's something rotten about the whole story,' the chief inspector declared. 'You could reach out and grab it, but I just can't manage to pull the loose ends together. Why would a successful boxing promoter risk his future for a bit of smuggling? And if he is involved in smuggling, what is it that is going out of Germany or coming in?'

'Even if we find out in the next couple of days, why would Kümmel have killed the boy?'

'There is only one place we are going to find the answers to all those questions.'

'Blohm & Voss.'

'It's just a pity it's the one place we're not allowed to ask questions.'

'I'm beginning to feel that shit around my neck,' MacDonald said. 'Who down there would ask to see our permit?'

'You still want to go down there, even though it's been expressly forbidden?'

'The trouble with you Germans is that you forbid so many things, and then pay attention to the fact that they're forbidden.'

'And you're a soldier telling me that?'

'I spend half my time ignoring orders and the other half trying to find a way around them.'

'That's the way to become a general.'

'A general who has no misconceptions about people obeying his orders.'

Stave nodded at his uniform and said, 'If you go down there dressed like that, you'll be lynched.'

'I can go in civvies, just like you.'

'You want us both to go, together?'

MacDonald laughed. 'Every morning hundreds of workers cross the Elbe on the ferries. And among them there are always a few men in suits with briefcases.'

'Engineers and accountants.'

'Soft types, like you and me. I'll get hold of a briefcase. Nobody will spot us.'

'Until you open your mouth. They'll hear your British accent.'

'Then you'll have to do the talking for us. You're the CID man, the pro.'

'OK, let's assume we get across the Elbe without anybody picking us out. Then what?'

Stave was thinking of the cranes and gantries that had been blown up, the shipwrecks along the quays. 'It's not exactly going to be easy to nose about over there, especially when we don't even know exactly what we're looking for.'

The lieutenant shrugged his shoulders. 'We'll play it by ear, see what we come up with.'

'And if we're found out?'

'In that case,' MacDonald said with a sardonic smile, 'there'll be nothing for it but to jump headlong into the Elbe.'

Docks

The temperature had reached 35 degrees. Stave would have preferred to go down to the landing stages in just a shirt and trousers but if he wanted to pass as an employee he'd have to put on a jacket and tie. The jacket at least concealed his holster and revolver. He had pulled the brim of his hat down over his eyes, in case one or another of the workers who'd been there on the day they found the body recognised him.

At first he didn't realise that the man who had came up to him in a dull suit somewhere between grey and blue was MacDonald. He, too, had pulled the brim of a hat down over his eyes, and in his right hand he really did have a briefcase.

'Automatic weapon in there, is there?' Stave whispered.

'Two sandwiches and a flask of tea. Hungry?'

'Just keep it closed. I feel about as inconspicuous as a man walking down Mönckeberg Strasse in his underwear.' The chief inspector looked around apprehensively.

A carriage on the overhead railway rattled up to the station. The doors opened and out poured welders, tallymen, stevedores in grey corduroy trousers and collarless, striped shirts, some of them with caps, most of them bareheaded.

Alcohol was officially banned down at the docks. They spoke, if at all, in short, rough sentences, a few curses in *Plattdeutsch* dialect, or even Polish. DPs, the CID man realised. Most said nothing as they headed down to the pier.

The ferries were lined up along the quayside, the puttering of their engines competing with the few rough words exchanged. Stave was pleased to note that at least a few other men in jackets and ties had turned up. Most of the workers looked tired, undernourished, unshaven, and stank of sweat, oil and beer. The chief inspector and MacDonald let themselves be carried along with the flow, on to the next ferry. Stave couldn't work out if there was supposed to be a system of some sort. We'll be across in a few minutes, he told himself, bolstering his courage. They sat crammed together on the wooden benches, the ferry swaying as ever more men piled on board. Then the engine sprang properly to life, sending up a dirty black cloud of smoke. Somebody barked an order and the last tether to the quay was dropped. They were out on the Elbe now, no turning back, Stave thought, looking at the men standing on board the deck. He was wondering if it really had been such a good idea to continue their investigations at the docks. MacDonald smiled at him. The young Brit looked as if he was off to a football match. But then maybe this was nothing to what the lieutenant had experienced in the war.

The ferries creaked as they crept slowly across the grey surface of the Elbe. The chief inspector tried to count how many of them there were, but the morning mist and the black smoke from their funnels made it impossible, not to mention a tugboat that passed in front of them blocking his view.

'On his way to fetch that tanker,' said an enormous man sitting on the bench near Stave. The chief inspector wanted to say something non-committal in return before he noticed that it wasn't him the man had been speaking to but his neighbour on the other side: all he could hear was a monologue in short, snappy sentences occasion-ally interrupted by a mumbled response from the other man who looked as if he could hardly keep his weary red eyes open. Stave tried to listen in, his head turned the other way – an old CID trick – so they wouldn't notice. It didn't take long for him to find out that the giant's name was Fietje Pehns. He was complaining about something called a 'stall'. It took the chief inspector a few minutes to realise that this was a sort of job allocation desk somewhere in the docks.

Pehns was one of thousands of unemployed workers or casual shift workers: they turned up at this 'stall' and were given a job for the day, if, for example, a ship had docked and there weren't enough full-time employed dockers to unload it and load it again. Pehns was complaining about Rahlstedt, where he lived ever since the English had bombed his home in St Pauli to nothing. He had to get up at 4.30 in the morning and earned just 7.60 Reichsmatks a day. He complained too about the trades unions, who only really cared about the full-time employees.

Stave learned that a few days ago the casual workers had organised a wildcat strike, despite the opposition of the trades unions. He listened to Pehns cursing and looked at his massive hands and wondered to himself what on earth he would do if somebody like him got really angry. That would be no fun at all. He would as soon have given up their whole plan, but then he saw MacDonald squeezed up against the hull opposite, looking out silently, no longer daring even to whisper. He had heard Pehns's tirade too. He followed MacDonald's gaze to a boat next to the quay from which the workers were already unloading coal. The Blohm & Voss shipyard lay just ahead, and behind them the main pool of the port where a freighter was already tied up. As they got closer he recognised the straight sides, wide stern and tall funnel, as well as the American flag and eventually the name: *Leland Stanford*.

'Bloody hell!' he exclaimed.

Pehns gave him a look of astonishment. He hadn't expected to hear an expression like that from a man in a suit. Then he smiled and clapped one of his giant paws on Stave's shoulder. 'Don't worry, mate,' he growled, 'these Liberty ships break down all the time. It's absolutely normal for them to stay around after they've been unloaded. But no sooner does something go wrong than our lads fix it for them. The boys at the shipyard will have it sorted and out of here on time.'

'That would be a relief,' Stave muttered. His heart was pounding. He felt as if he'd been uncovered. If only the damn ferry would get to the other side. It just had to be the *Leland Stanford*, the ship Tattoo-Willy had mentioned as being one of the main ships used by the smugglers, and now here it was laid up at Blohm & Voss. 'When is it supposed to set sail?' he mustered up the courage to ask. Maybe that would make him seem like an idiot, but he couldn't suppress his curiosity.

'First tide day after tomorrow,' Pehns said, scarcely paying attention. He turned back to his dozing colleague on the other side, to moan a bit more about the 'stall' and call for more strikes.

Tomorrow was their last day before the divorce hearing. If they still had nothing, then it was Palestine for MacDonald. Stave was sure he had heard the whole conversation. Then he felt an elbow nudge him. It was the lieutenant, who was once again nodding towards something going on over the side. It took the chief inspector a moment to understand what he was trying to tell him. They were passing Blohm & Voss. He could feel the blood in his temples throbbing. They had got on the wrong ferry. He could have kicked himself. He watched helplessly as they passed the shipyard and headed slowly onwards into the labyrinthine bowels of the vast port. On every side there were bombed-out warehouses. The ferry captain had to make a wide swing around the wreck of a steamship.

Now they were in Kuhwerder harbour, the next big basin beyond the shipyard: giant walls along the quayside, the grotesque sculpture of a bomb-hit crane, a large, relatively new freighter at one of the piers, a flag hanging limp from its stern. Stave noted the colours, blue, white and red, but he couldn't make out the pattern. It clearly wasn't a US ship or a British one. They were coming up to a little wooden quay. The workers were impatient, already on their feet even though the dock was still some ten metres away. MacDonald motioned to Stave that he should stay sitting. It wouldn't do them any harm to be the last off.

The chief inspector looked round as the gangway clunked down on to the wooden quay, and the boat bumped up against the wooden stays. They were going to have to walk the length of the harbour basin and then turn north for a few dozen metres until they reached the shipyard. The only question was whether or not two men in jackets would make it all the way across the quays, railway lines and bomb-damaged warehouses.

Eventually he stumbled down the gangplank, his legs still half asleep from sitting on the hard wooden bench. The ferry captain gave him a look that Stave thought was both scornful and suspicious at the same time. But it could just have been an instinctive mistrust of men in suits, or then again that he had never come across people dressed like that on this particular ferry. He avoided the man's gaze and pulled the brim of his hat further down over his eyes. Most of the workmen with whom they'd just crossed the river were standing on the quayside next to the freighter queued up at the 'stall'. 'Not sure it's usually the sort of work these "casuals" do,' Stave hissed between his teeth. They wandered on a bit until Stave could make out the name on the stern of the freighter: *Presidente Errazuriz*.

'I read about this ship in *Die Zeit*,' he said. 'That explains the number of people.' He didn't reveal that an internal message had been sent round police headquarters about it. 'The *Presidente Errazuriz* is a Chilean ship that docked last night with thirty-nine officer cadets on board, here for an official visit to Germany, which displeased Governor Berry, because officially Germany no longer exists. But there are 200 tonnes of food donated by "Friends of Germany" in Chile. I can imagine who those "friends" are: old Nazis who managed somehow or other to make their way to Chile after the end of the war.'

All of a sudden the crowd breathed in all at once. A crane, the only one still intact on this pier, was carefully lifting something from the hold of the ship. At first it looked to the chief inspector as if it were just a wooden case, but as it rose higher and higher he saw it was a sort of big cage with wooden flooring and latticework sides, with a bed of straw. MacDonald was staring at it in amazement.

'The Chileans have sent Hagenbeck Zoo some exotic birds,' he whispered. 'And,' he added, nodding with his chin at the floor of the cage where something could be seen moving, 'several extremely old giant turtles.'

'For turtle soup?'

'Hagenbeck is a Hamburg institution.'

'Hardly a priority in times like these. Just a few weeks ago there were people starving here and now you're importing giant turtles for the zoo?' He shrugged his shoulders. 'What do those things eat anyway?'

'Englishmen,' Stave hissed. He nodded towards a group of men who had got so close to the freighter that the sailors who had been standing guard were exchanging nervous glances. Suddenly a Jeep roared up with British military police on board.

'If they recognise me, we really will be – to use your colourful expression – up to our necks in shit. What are they doing here?'

'You need to read the German newspapers. It said in *Die Zeit* that the *Presidente Errazuriz* was going to take back some Germans who had family over there. And now half of Hamburg has discovered they have Chilean ancestors – or even Indians.'

And indeed they could now hear people in the crowd speaking Spanish. One man was waving papers in the clammy air. The sailors were shaking their heads, sweating and shouting out something nobody could understand.

'You really would have to be desperate to escape Hamburg to set sail with that lot,' the lieutenant whispered. The MPs were climbing out of the Jeep, which had come to a screeching halt. They had automatic weapons slung over their shoulders, their fingers on the safety. One or two of the workers were whistling, jeering and even cursing, and one of them burst into the 'Internationale'.

'This would be a good opportunity,' Stave said, 'for us to make ourselves scarce.'

They pushed their way forward to the ruins of a slipway of which only a part remained intact, its concrete beams rising above them. They would be less conspicuous in the shadow of the ruins. They moved slowly, talking to each other like two men on their way to work who knew exactly where they were going and what they were doing. At the end of the slipway was the skeleton of a giant crane, which they had to climb over carefully. They found themselves in an open area, baking hot with bushes as tall as a man growing between railway tracks that hadn't been used for years. They were at the end of the Kuhwerder basin. A slight turn to the left and the freighter now blocked any sight of them from the quay. MacDonald took a deep breath and ran a finger around his shirt collar.

'Do you think I dare take my jacket off?'

'Perhaps you ought to get used to the heat. I imagine it's pretty hot in Palestine.'

The lieutenant gave him a sidelong look. 'Maybe I should take you with me as my adviser?'

'A German policeman in the Holy Land? The Jews would just love that.'

'It's nice to be able to do one's friends a favour.'

MacDonald stopped suddenly. 'Bells,' he exclaimed.

Along the empty space next to the quay a row of bells gleamed in the morning sun, some as tall as a man, some as small as a beer bottle, some of them badly dented, others lying on their side as it they'd been casually tossed away like some giant's unwanted toy. Others sat there on wooden beams as if they'd come straight from the foundry. They had crosses, reliefs, coats of arms inscribed on them, as well as names of saints, and words in German, French, Polish, Danish.

'The bell cemetery,' the chief inspector said. 'We're going to have to fight our way through and it won't be easy.'

'Which churches do all these bells come from?'

The chief inspector waved an arm towards the horizon. 'From all over Europe. The Nazis took down the bells in every church, first of all those in Germany, then eventually in all the occupied countries. Important materiel for the war effort.'

MacDonald looked around him. 'It doesn't seem like they got round to melting many of them down.'

'That's where you're wrong. They collected them all here in

Hamburg, because most came by ship. There were supposed to have been 75,000 altogether.'

'There aren't 75,000 here.'

'These are just the ones that are left. About 8,000, people reckon. The rest are all either cartridge cases, artillery barrels or other weapons of war.'

'Rubbish, in other words.'

'These bells survived by chance. They had all been loaded on to a barge in 1945 to be transported elsewhere. Then your planes flew by again.'

'Let me guess: a direct hit.'

'Right here in Kuhwerder basin. A team of Hamburg salvage experts dredged them up again at the end of May 1945. Now they're waiting here until somebody takes them back to the churches they came from, provided, that is, they still exist, and if representatives of the churches from the countries they were taken from ever get around to collecting them.'

'Sounds like a money-making opportunity.'

'There will certainly be men who will make a small fortune out of it, probably the same people who took them down in the first place.'

'It's a skilled job.'

'Over there is the gateway to the shipyard,' Stave said, when they had finally made their way through the army of bells. 'That's the easy bit of our job over with.'

In front of them stood the gateway, with a barbed-wire fence and two bored-looking British military police. Out of bounds. If they had taken the right ferry they would have landed next to the shipyard itself. There were British guards there but in the mass of workers arriving in the morning it was unlikely they would have been individually checked. But here on the land side, there were only a few figures heading in the direction of Blohm & Voss, workers who lived on the south side of the Elbe or who preferred to walk through the long tunnel to the dockyard. Near the gate, on the right-hand side, was a little coffee shop, or rather a shack that sold old ersatz coffee and bread rolls with nothing much on them. A few workers were standing next to it with their Reichsmark notes already counted out, for the sake of speed.

The chief inspector was once again wondering how Adolf Winkelmann could have got into this prohibited area: by ferry he might have been able to sneak past the British, but wouldn't the workers have wondered what he was doing there, given that Blohm & Voss no longer employed adolescents? Nobody apparently had ever seen him, or at least nobody had admitted as much to Kienle, the police photographer, when he had gone round the shipyard showing the workers his photo. He must have come this way, from the land side, the CID man thought to himself, through the Elbe Tunnel, then made his way through the ruins to some point along the fence that was neglected by the guards and not noticed by the coffee shop customers, cut the wire and crawled through. He then wondered if he and MacDonald would have to do something similar.

The Briton had read his mind. He produced two pieces of paper from the pocket of his jacket and whispered, 'Just keep going as if everything were perfectly normal. Walk right up to the guards.'

'What are those?'

'Passes, in the name of Walter Holz and Werner Schmidt.'

'Forged?'

'Please! Genuine, I can assure you. My job gives me a few privileges.'

What sort of a secret service was this, Stave wondered, that could provide MacDonald with the papers he needed within a few hours, but would cut him loose because of a relationship with a married German? It had to be that British attitude to things. 'Do the guards know who we are?' Stave hissed.

'No, apart from a very few friends in the service, nobody knows. But if that sergeant had seen us sneaking around he would have shot us.'

'I'll try to keep you between him and me.'

'You know, you really should have been a soldier.'

By now they had reached the gate. The sergeant examined Mac-Donald's paperwork longer than he had that of the others wearily trudging past the guards. Stave hoped it was only because he had never seen them before.

'Move on,' the NCO said at last, handing back the passes and waving a hand impatiently.

'Where to now?' MacDonald whispered to Stave.

The chief inspector nodded towards a five-storey, dirty brown building in the centre of the yard. 'That must be the administration building,' he said, 'the only place where men in jackets and ties won't look out of place. We'll see where we go from there.' The warehouse in which Adolf Winkelmann had been found lying on the unexploded bomb was at the far end of the shipyard, hard to make out from where they were in the hazy air. None of the workmen headed in that direction; they were all off down towards the docks. It wouldn't be very clever of them to make straight for that building, Stave reckoned. And in any case, he couldn't imagine there'd be anything new to find.

At the entrance to the administration building they were nearly knocked down by a whole clutch of men in collars and ties, carrying briefcases, notebooks, clipboards, all apparently in something of a hurry. They were led by a man of about fifty, with an aristocratic appearance, wearing good linen and a pair of shoes of a quality Stave hadn't seen since the outbreak of the war.

The chief inspector nodded to MacDonald that they should follow the others. They got a couple of suspicious looks at first, but nobody said anything.

'That's Rudolf Blohm,' Stave hissed. 'The older of the two brothers who own the shipyard. I recognise him from pictures on the weekly newsreels.'

'The weekly newsreels from before 1945 or after?'

'From before 1945. He was a great friend to the Nazis. On the board of the German Museum in Munich, given all sorts of honorary positions, regularly a guest of the Führer.'

'Well, if the Nazis had paid me as much as they paid him to build the *Bismarck*, I might have shouted "Heil Hitler!" too.'

'You British sacked half of my colleagues, but you let this character still run around his shipyard.'

'A shipyard we are in the process of dismantling,' the lieutenant replied with a brief smile.

'Or so you think,' mumbled Stave but quietly enough to be sure the British officer wouldn't hear him. They were the last pair in the party hurrying along on the heels of Rudolf Blohm. Far enough back that any of the others who wanted to say something to them would have had to turn around, which none of them were prepared to do. But they were still close enough that the others assumed they were part of the group. They marched through the shipyard without anyone paying the slightest attention to them, until Stave suddenly realised where they were. 'That's where the boy's body was found,' he whispered.

Blohm stopped by the entrance, and immediately the youngest man in his entourage ran up and opened the wooden door. The shipyard owner marched in with the group following, Stave and MacDonald among them. The door slammed behind them, and Stave noticed that the young man who had opened it remained outside. Keeping watch, he thought to himself. Which was hardly surprising.

Because the building was no longer empty. All the machinery which on Stave's last visit had been lying outside had since been brought inside, supported on wooden beams or even packed in wooden cases, the metal gleaming and smelling of oil and grease, all polished up as if it had come straight from the factory. The hole in the roof through which the bomb had fallen had not, however, been repaired as yet. Stave thought he could still make out traces of blood on the ground, but told himself he was imagining it.

'Do we have all the documentation?' Blohm asked, without even turning round. A man with a briefcase dashed up to him and opened it. 'Soviet freight certificates, confirmation that everything was loaded on board the *Siberia*.'

'What was really loaded on board?'

'A few old bits of machinery that weren't usable, a pile of old iron, a lot of cigarettes and some cognac.'

Blohm nodded in satisfaction, pointed to the machinery in the hall and barked out orders. 'We need to build a solid wall in front of all this. Tall, solid, ideally made of iron, but wood if needs be. We need wooden cases. Get them from the freighters down at the docks, ones they're finished with and which are not needed any more. Fill them up with bits of machinery, engines primarily, from the cranes, or diesel engines – dismantle one of those old narrow gauge locomotives. Everything should be as old, rusty and dirty as possible. Pour some oil over it all and spill some on the ground too. We want our machinery to disappear behind a wall of junk covered in oil and grease. The Tommies don't like getting their uniforms dirty. If a British patrol should turn up, all they will find is rubbish and they'll soon clear off.'

'That's what you think,' MacDonald whispered.

'When will the trucks be ready?' Blohm asked.

'Next month,' the man with the briefcase answered.

'Good. As soon as they're ready, load all this on board and take them to the warehouses over in Harburg. It'll be safe there. But don't move all the rubbish. That would take too long. Knock a hole in the exterior wall and load the trucks from behind, but make sure it's somewhere that can't be seen by the British sentries. Have you got all that?'

A few of his hangers-on headed for the door and Stave indicated to his companion that they should follow them as they would be less conspicuous than if they stayed behind with Blohm and the core of his group.

'That man has no scruples,' MacDonald said.

'That's the way to get by no matter what happens,' Stave replied.

'What do we do now?' MacDonald whispered when they were out of the building.

'Head for the *Leland Stanford*. I'd like to know if it's really broken down. Sounds a bit of a coincidence.'

The men who had been part of Blohm's entourage were heading in all directions, so Stave thought it best if the two of them made their own way across the shipyard to the large quay where the Liberty ship was moored. It took them only a few minutes. The air round the ship's stern was so hot, you could have fried eggs on the deck. A few American sailors were standing bare-chested, smoking, next to the railings and glanced at them disinterestedly. A young officer standing on the bridge was reading the *Stars and Stripes* and blowing pink bubblegum. A couple of sweat-soaked workers were carrying a big, strangely shaped metal object in their oil-covered hands.

'Looks like a bit of damaged machinery,' MacDonald said. 'Maybe it was a coincidence after all.'

'Let's wait a bit,' Stave said. He nodded towards a crane lying on the cobbles as if it had been cut down by a scythe. 'Act as if we're following the boss's orders. He wants crane engines. There has to be one somewhere in that thing.'

'We're not supposed to be the sort of people who get their hands dirty.'

'We're just organising it, if anyone asks. Our real purpose here is to keep an eye on this American freighter to see if anyone takes something other than oily spare parts on board.'

They clambered over the wreck of the crane, pulling open a piece of metal plating here, tugging at a cable there. 'You do realise that if any of the shipyard workers is watching us, they'll realise we haven't a clue what we're doing?' MacDonald said, the sweat running down his brow.

'I do. It's the perfect cover. Workers always assume clerical staff to be idiots.'

'As long as they don't decide this is the moment to launch the revolution.'

'If they do, we jump on board the freighter. The Americans aren't keen on communists. We'll be safe on board the *Leland Stanford*.'

'Except that it has an engine problem,' MacDonald reminded

him. 'But in any case we might do better to delay our escape,' he prodded Stave. 'Look over there.'

Stave ducked behind the operator's cabin of the crane and looked up at the bridge of the ship where the bubblegum-chewing young officer had folded up his newspaper and was talking to one of the young shipyard workers, handing him a cigarette.

'No officer would normally allow a shipyard worker on to the bridge,' MacDonald said. 'And certainly not a German.'

'But there he is, even offering the guy a smoke,' Stave noted, nodding towards the ship. 'Look, the worker is holding something.'

'It looks like a jute sack, and obviously not very heavy.'

'Nor covered in oil. Clearly not a spare part.'

'Maybe it's something for the bridge? A compass or radio instrument?'

'There haven't been any precision instruments at Blohm & Voss for ages now.'

'Maybe. Remember what we just saw in that warehouse.'

'Yes, but Blohm isn't stupid enough to try installing something on an American ship that they themselves banned back in 1945. And in any case, precision instruments are transported in wooden or metal cases, not in cloth sacks.'

'A cloth sack that is just changing ownership.'

The shipyard worker handed over the sack to the young officer, lit up a second cigarette, gave an awkward wave in farewell and left the bridge.

'Right now what I'd like to do is storm that bridge and interrogate that officer,' Stave declared.

'I'm afraid you'd have to have won the war to do that,' MacDonald replied.

'In that case we will have to do with grabbing the worker as soon as he leaves the ship.'

'Now that sounds like a plan we can get away with.'

'As long as the other workers don't spot us, or we might start an October Revolution.'

'That wouldn't do me any favours.'

Stave would have given anything for a glass of water. His bottom lip was so dry it had split and hurt. Just to be sure he checked his revolver in its holster. At least he didn't have to worry about the weapon slipping out of his hand just when he needed it: he had sweated himself dry.

The shipyard worker appeared on the gangplank: he was stocky and muscular with hair a little longer than used to be common. He seemed relaxed, stopped in the gangplank linking the freighter to the quayside and lit yet another cigarette.

'Now?' MacDonald asked.

'The officer on the bridge will see us. Whatever the two of them were up to, we'd be warning him if we stopped the other guy right now.'

'But what if he rejoins his team? He obviously works somewhere here and will have workmates. If we grab him when he's back with them, then we really will start a revolution. And we can't spend all day here or somebody will eventually notice us.'

'Patience. Our friend doesn't exactly seem in a hurry to get back to work.'

For a moment the chief inspector forgot how hot it was, and how thirsty he was: the drama of the hunt had replaced both. The young worker strolled down the quayside, and along the narrow gauge railway tracks in the direction of one of the factory sheds that was little more than a ruin.

'There can't be anyone working in there,' MacDonald said.

'All the better. Come on, let's follow him.'

They clambered off the remnants of the crane. 'Don't look back at the ship,' the chief inspector advised MacDonald. 'We just walk along the quayside chatting, like any two ordinary clerical workers.'

The shipyard worker didn't look round. Then, by the remains of a brick wall, about a metre high and five or six across, he stopped.

'Maybe he's got something to hide?' the lieutenant wondered.

'Maybe it's himself he's hiding,' Stave suggested. 'I think he's having a little ciggie break where none of his colleagues can see him.'

And indeed, the worker disappeared behind the wall. Stave nodded to the British officer. 'Take your time,' he murmured. 'You never know if somebody on the freighter might be watching us. We walk along to the end of the wall, then turn around and come back on the other side.' Thirty metres to go, twenty, ten. The chief inspector pulled out his police ID card, and his gun. MacDonald had a gun in his hand too. Five metres to go. They turned the corner.

'Police, CID,' Stave called out, levelling his gun: 'Hands up!'

The shipyard worker choked on his cigarette smoke, began coughing and spluttering. 'You're as bad as the Führer's lot,' he spat out, but did as he was told and raised his arms.

'Name?' Stave shouted at him. He hated acting like one of the Gestapo.

'Herbert Gehrecke,' the man replied.

MacDonald was standing to one side, his weapon trained on the man's chest, a satisfied smile on his face. He looks as if he'd shoot this man without a second thought, Stave realised. Maybe he would.

'What were you doing on board the *Leland Stanford*?'

Gehrecke closed his eyes. 'You were watching me?'

Stave would have laughed at the naïvety of the question, if it wouldn't have been out of keeping with his tough guy act. 'What was in the bag you handed over to the American officer?' he barked at Gehrecke.

'It's really as if the Nazis are still in power. What do you want from me?'

'That depends on your answers. What was in the bag?'

'Two reels.'

'Reels?'

'Two tapes,' the shipyard worker replied irritably.

Stave's heart was pounding, but he tried not to let it show. His brain was working overtime. 'What sort of tapes?'

'How would I know? I don't have a tape recorder.'

'Were the tapes you handed over still in their original packaging? Or did they look as if they'd been used?'

'Used. They were in cardboard boxes that looked a bit battered.'

'From before the war?'

Gehrecke laughed. 'What else?'

'German?'

'There was a swastika on the box, and a stamp.'

'What sort of stamp?'

'No idea. Something official-looking.'

This guy was just an innocent go-between, the chief inspector told himself. 'Who told you to take the tapes to the American ship? How did you know which officer you were to give them to?'

Gehrecke licked his lips. Trying to think up a lie, Stave realised. He nodded to MacDonald. The lieutenant released the safety on his gun and aimed it a little higher, right at the man's head.

'Honestly, I know nothing,' Gehrecke protested, an uncontrollable tick causing the muscle of his left cheek to twitch. He looked as if he was about to cry. 'Who was it?' Stave pressed.

'I don't know. I didn't see. That's the basis of my business.'

'Your business?'

'I bring stuff to the Allies's ships when they're here being repaired at Blohm & Voss. I've been doing it for months now. People get to know. I get parcels left in my cubbyhole, with a note to say which ship it's for, who I should ask for, and what time I should turn up, and whether or not I'm supposed to collect something in return. The next day I find cigarettes in my cubbyhole, or maybe a pound of butter.'

'And what is it you deliver, usually?'

'Mostly I don't know. I never open the packets. I'm not interested. That's why I'm still alive.'

'If you're not interested, how did you know that the package you delivered today was recording tape?'

'Because it's all changed around here. I got a note a few weeks ago.'

'How long ago precisely?'

'Can't remember. It must have been just after the hunger winter, when the Elbe began to thaw and the first ships started coming in again. I got a note to say that in one particular warehouse there were dozens of jute bags with tapes in them. I was to take one of them and deliver it to an American ship. So that's what I did.'

'Didn't you ever stop to think about any of this? The unusual way of getting in touch with you? The unusual nature of the stuff you were delivering?'

A shrug. 'I suppose I was curious. A bit. But also relieved. Sort of. What would it matter if I was caught acting as a courier for recording tape? What could be illegal about that?'

'So what did you do?'

'What I was told. The next day I found a carton of Lucky Strikes in my cubbyhole. The American freighter was gone. The warehouse was empty.'

'But you didn't take all the rest to the freighter?'

'No. Odd, isn't it? Somebody must have come during the night and taken them all.'

'To the freighter?'

'I don't know. All I know is that they were gone. Then a few days later the same thing: a note in my cubbyhole, tapes in the warehouse, I take one jute sack to the ship, the next morning I get the cigarettes, the ship is gone and so are the tapes.'

'Was it an American ship that time too?'

'Yes.'

'The same one?'

'It's always the same one, the *Leland Stanford*. I'd love to know how they manage it, breaking down every time they come through Hamburg.'

Stave was now convinced there was nothing wrong with the ship. It was all a sham. Taking the ship to the yard, staying for longer than necessary. Somebody had to be making a fortune to go to all this effort. 'Which warehouse were the tapes left in?'

'The one with the unexploded bomb.'

The chief inspector wasn't surprised. 'The one where the murdered boy was found?'

'That's the one. Terrible thing to happen. I knew there was an unexploded bomb in there. I walked all round the shipyard after the end of the war and stumbled on it in there.'

'Didn't you report it?'

Gehrecke looked down at his feet. 'It was an ideal place to hide stuff. If anyone had looked in, they would have disappeared again fast. It was a great place for me to park stuff I had to deliver to the ships. That was my business plan: storage and delivery. It didn't make me much at first, because after 1945 there were hardly any ships coming into the port at all, never mind coming to the shipyard. But gradually it got better. I was surprised to find that place being used for the tapes. Seems somebody else must have had the same idea.'

Or somebody had been watching you, the chief inspector thought, though he said nothing. A warehouse full of recording tape. Somebody who had the ability to get the stuff there, either overnight or at the weekend. And could also get it on board a ship. But why would he employ a shipyard worker to take a couple of tapes to the ship in advance, in the middle of the day? It had to be somebody checking out the merchandise. Somebody on board had to be listening to the tapes. But what could be on them that was so interesting? Nazi secrets? Confessions? Who might be interested in stuff like that? Secret services. In this case the American secret service. Quite clearly MacDonald knew nothing about any of it. It would be interesting to see if he had come to the same conclusion. Perhaps now he really would try marching on to the *Leland Stanford* to interview a few people.

'Does the name Walter Kümmel mean anything to you?' he asked.

'Never heard it before.'

'Did you ever come across a stranger here in the shipyard?' Stave gave him a physical description of the boxing promoter.

'No, I'd have noticed somebody in a smart suit with a broken nose.'

It was said so matter-of-factly that the chief inspector didn't believe it was a lie. He was disappointed. 'Were you here the morning the murdered boy's body was found?'

'Not exactly. I saw a few colleagues looking around the parts of the shipyard that weren't being used. Old Blohm has a few ideas about what we can build up again and sent out a few teams. I reckoned they'd spot the unexploded bomb and that would be the end of my transport and storage business.'

'Did you know the boy?'

'Never seen him before. When I heard the alarm, my first thought was that the bomb had gone off. But the story soon got around. I took a quick look down by the warehouse while everybody else was waiting for the police and the fire brigade. Whoever the boy was he had nothing to do with the shipyard.'

'Was any of your special cargo there at the time?' MacDonald raised his weapon again.

'No! Honest!' Gehrecke exclaimed. By now he had been holding his hands up so long there were rivers of sweat running down his temples, his hair was glued to his head and there were dark patches appearing on the thin shirt he wore. Let him sweat, the chief inspector thought: he wasn't going to help.

'I had nothing in there. There were no ships in the yard.'

'Did anything you stored there ever go missing?'

The shipyard worker gave him a surprised look, then realised what he meant and straightened his face. 'You mean, did the boy ever steal anything of mine? No, not that I know of. I never noticed anything missing.'

'Not even tapes?'

He hesitated a moment. 'I never counted how many sacks there were. And I certainly didn't count how many tapes were in each sack. If somebody had taken one, I wouldn't have noticed. Would you mind if I lowered my hands?'

Stave acted as if he hadn't heard. 'After the murder, did you continue to use the same place?'

'Hardly. I'm not stupid. That would have been far too dangerous.'

'You found somewhere else?'

'I'm still looking,' he admitted. 'But it's getting more difficult all

the time. Old Blohm is turning everything topsy-turvy. I may have
to give up altogether,' he sighed dejectedly.

It sounded plausible enough, Stave reckoned. 'Where did you get
the tapes you just smuggled onboard the *Leland Stanford*?'

'I found them in my cubbyhole this morning. Along with a note
to tell me who to deliver them to.'

'Where is the note now?'

'I threw it into the water. It's safer like that.'

Stave suppressed a curse. 'Let's imagine it all goes as it did the first
couple of times: where will the rest of the tapes be kept?'

'I don't know,' Gehrecke spluttered. He's ours now, Stave told
himself, ready to collaborate. He gestured to the man that he could
lower his hands, but added, 'Keep them at wrist level.'

Assuming the man's story was true there was a stockpile of tapes
around here somewhere. And somebody was going to come here at
night to collect them. But I have no idea where the tapes might be.
And I have no idea who that somebody might be. But at least I do
know where they are to be taken and when. Because the freighter is
due to depart on the first tide the day after tomorrow.

'Come with us,' he told Gehrecke.

Stave and MacDonald put their weapons back in their holsters.
Gehrecke walked along in between them, showing no signs of resist-
ance. We just have to hope he keeps quiet and that the other workers
treat us normally, thought Stave.

They were lucky. It was lunchtime. The air was full of concrete
dust and the remnants of the destroyed cranes were too hot to touch.
There was nobody around. Stave reckoned the workforce were all
either in the makeshift coffee shop, or squatting somewhere in the
shade eating the sandwiches their wives or mothers had made. Stave
thought this could be a good moment to investigate the contents of
MacDonald's briefcase, but he thought there was every possibility
that Gehrecke would have less respect for a chief inspector munching
on a sandwich, and might do something stupid.

They walked up to one of the ferries, waking the dozing man at the wheel. He looked as if he was going to tell them where to go, but when he saw the look on their faces, he swallowed his annoyance and cast off.

Once they were back out on the Elbe, Stave took a deep breath. Gehrecke was sitting on his own at the stern. Stave sat next to him and took two photos out of his jacket pocket: photos of the dead bodies of Hildegard Hüllmann and Wilhelm Meinke.

Gehrecke went pale: 'You mean they're both dead too?'

'You know them?'

'Never seen either of them. Am I a suspect?'

The chief inspector was taken aback. He hadn't expected an answer like that. It wasn't impossible of course. He hadn't seen Gehrecke in that way because he was looking at the case from another angle. But don't get it wrong. He could well have been the killer. When he was leaving the *Leland Stanford*, though, he had used his right hand to light his cigarette. Stave handed him his notebook and said, 'Write down your name and address.'

The man was right-handed.

Stave looked at the clumsily formed letters, thought about the way the man had spoken, his behaviour, about his lack of interest in the whole business. Surely most people were fascinated with what was being smuggled in and out of the port? Surely anybody would look into a bag, would peel back the label on a package, if only out of curiosity. The opposite also made sense. Who would risk going backwards and forwards for months in the vicinity of an unexploded bomb just to store something or other when he didn't even know what it was? Who on earth would take a risk like that for a few ciggies and the occasional pound of butter? This guy next to me is a bit simple, he thought to himself, certainly far too simple to have been involved in a murder like this. But in answer to Gehrecke's question, he said only, 'I'm not excluding anything.'

Stave let the shipyard worker sit where he was at the stern. There's no way he's going to jump into the Elbe, he told himself as he sidled over to MacDonald. The British office was using his left hand to fan himself, even though he was sitting in the small area of shade cast by the boat's little bridge, but with his right hand still holding his revolver between his knees. 'Just in case our friend tries any tricks,' he said, in a quiet voice he clearly hoped the shipyard worker wouldn't hear.

'I'm going to arrest Gehrecke and interrogate him later. There's always the possibility we'll get more out of him. Also I need to persuade Breuer to carry out a raid the night after tomorrow so we can catch the smugglers.'

'Blohm & Voss is a no-go area, under British control,' the lieutenant reminded him, shaking his head. 'The German police have no access rights. And don't imagine the British are going to launch anything major. Not with the mood the way it has been of late. And certainly not over somebody smuggling tapes. And least of all when it involves one of our American ally's ships.'

Stave began to protest, but MacDonald held up a hand. 'I know that's where the boy was killed and you think the smugglers were responsible. Governor Berry wants the case solved, but not at any price. He doesn't want embarrassment and strikes down at the port, unrest in Hamburg and difficult conversations in London and Washington.'

'You mean in that case you wouldn't be on a ship to Palestine on your own? You'd have Berry with you.'

'What a good idea. At least then I'd have a friend in my new job.'

'So what do you suggest?'

'I'm going to take Gehrecke in my Jeep. He won't draw so much attention if he's in a British military cell. Down at your CID headquarters somebody might recognise him and tip off the smugglers.'

'Are you suggesting one of my men might be corrupt?'

'I'm saying they're badly paid. And one or two of them might not be too upset if we British have problems down at the shipyard. It might distract attention from a few things in their own past.'

'OK, fine. Gehrecke is yours. What do I do?'

'Is there anybody you trust 100 per cent?'

Stave thought of Ehrlich, but he was the last person he wanted to have to deal with at the moment. 'No,' he replied, realising as he said it how pathetic it sounded.

'In that case we're going to have to think up some way of handling this on our own, without any help.'

'You mean going down to the shipyard again?'

'The night after next, secretly.'

'There aren't even any ferries at night.'

'That's what I mean, we're going to have to think of something.'

They got out at the landing stages, the shipyard worker between them. It was only when they were standing on the road next to an English Jeep and MacDonald pulled out a pair of handcuffs and snapped them on the man's wrists that he understood: 'You're not cops at all!'

'It's too complicated to explain here and now,' Stave said. 'Nothing's going to happen to you.'

Gehrecke stared at him in disbelief and then at MacDonald: 'This was a set-up.'

'You will get a fair trial,' MacDonald said in a vain attempt to reassure him. It was the first time he had spoken to Gehrecke. 'If what you've told us is true, then you're just a tiny cog in the machine. The worst that can happen is a month or two in prison.'

'I have children at home,' the man protested.

'You should have thought of that before you got involved in business like this,' Stave growled. He didn't like Gehrecke and didn't like his nasty little game, but even so he felt guilty. 'You might get off with a warning,' he said, though he didn't really believe it.

The handcuffed shipyard worker got into the Jeep without making a fuss. MacDonald turned the key in the ignition. 'I'll call you on the phone,' he called over the roar of the engine, then set off down the road.

On his own long walk back home the chief inspector stopped at a little restaurant and ordered himself a potato salad with gherkins.

The gherkins were dried out and wrinkled, and the watery sauce that came with the salad was vinegary. But Stave hardly tasted it. He just chewed mechanically, threw a couple of coins on to the table and set off again.

Damn sun! He felt dizzy. How was he supposed to concentrate in this heat. I'm cursed, he thought to himself. It's as if I've got some invisible mark on my forehead, singling me out forever. The asphalt beneath his feet had gone soft in the heat and felt like some old carpet. Back in the bombing raids of 1943 the tarmac had caught fire. Women and children had run out of their houses to avoid the fire only to end up stuck in burning tar. They had pulled their feet out of shoes stuck in the road, only to find their feet in turn burned to bare bones up to their ankles. And then the fire caught up with them anyway. The following morning the local *Gauleiter* sent the police in to put up barricades to keep out ghouls, thieves, despairing relatives who still thought they could pull the remains of their loved ones out of the sea of burnt asphalt. Stave knew. He had been there, he knew how they felt. Just a few weeks previously he had tried to pull Margarethe's body out of the rubble of their bombed house, but she had been trapped between two concrete beams. He had pulled and pulled, until thankfully at last he felt a hand on his shoulder and someone took him aside.

Anna's right, he thought. I need to sort myself out. Otherwise I'm not going to feel a hand on my shoulder to pull me out of the ruins a second time.

Concentrate on the case, on the shipyard, on the smugglers, on the night after next. Then you can sort out your private life. MacDonald and he would manage it. They would conceal themselves somewhere near the *Leland Stanford* and wait. But what if it was not just one smuggler but a whole gang of them? They had two guns, and the element of surprise. But don't play hero, he told himself. Think about what you're doing. Don't start imagining yourself in some American gangster movie shootout, before you've even worked out how you're going to get across the Elbe at night.

But he felt as if there was hot lead running down his head. He couldn't think of anything that made sense. Later, he told himself, later it would be cooler. You can sit out on your balcony and work it out. There might even be water. A cold bath would be good.

When he finally reached the door of his apartment, he was so exhausted he at first didn't even notice the little note on the floor. He stumbled into the bathroom and turned the tap: water! A rust-red trickle, lukewarm. He ripped off his sweaty clothes and threw himself into the bath, letting the water cover him. He lay there for a good hour before he started to get goose pimples. A clean shirt. He was halfway to the balcony before he glanced down at the floor and saw a note in Karl's handwriting.

'Father, I'm coming round for supper tomorrow. I'll bring a lettuce I got in exchange for a couple of tobacco leaves, and I'll bring some tobacco too.'

Stave's heart was pounding, timings running through his head. Alternative strategies. No matter what time he left tomorrow and no matter how he managed to cross the river, it had to be dark by the time they lay in wait at Blohm & Voss. It was in any case going to be the shortest night of the year. What time would the sun set? Ten in the evening? Maybe even later. There was no way he would get back in time for supper. But he could hardly leave MacDonald in the lurch.

He would put a note on the door. He ripped a page from his notebook there and then, sat down at the kitchen table and wrote on it: 'Wait for me! I'm running late, something urgent that I can't put off. But I will be here.'

Stave read it through, crumpled it into a ball and threw it in the waste bin. Pathetic. He would write something else. A proper letter. He would think of something. He would be honest. He would save Karl. He would save Anna. He would save himself.

He would sort it all out when he got back from the shipyard. If he got back from the shipyard.

Under the Elbe

The next morning when Stave tried to take a breath he felt as if someone had placed a gag over this mouth and nose. His fingers were as swollen as if he'd been in a boxing match. If he had still worn his wedding ring it would have cut into his flesh. When he walked out on to the balcony and squinted into the bright sunlight it seemed as if the line of ruins had somehow grown overnight. A moment later he realised that on the horizon to the west a vast mountain of grey and black clouds were gathering low above the piles of rubble and half-destroyed houses. He licked his finger and held it up to test if there was a wind coming from the west. It would be a relief at last to have a storm hit Hamburg. Not a breath.

He searched his cupboards and desk drawers until he found an unused envelope and a clean sheet of paper. It had been ages since he'd last had any ink for his old fountain pen, even on the black market. A pencil would have to do. He sharpened it carefully with his penknife.

Then Chief Inspector Frank Stave sat down and wrote his son Karl the first ever long letter he had written him. He explained to him that he had never joined the Nazi Party because he had been put off by the endless atmosphere of aggression. That he had been saddened by the enthusiasm Karl had shown for the Hitler Youth. Admitted that he had never dared to persuade him otherwise, afraid that in the 'brown years' it would have cost him his career in the police, and in the hard times to come he would not have been able to feed his family. Then there was Margarethe's death. He described the terrible night of bombing in 1943 and how later, too late, he had found her body. He wondered if he ought to mention his crippled foot? Or tell Karl that after Margarethe's death he had spent the night standing on the banks of the Elbe? Later, he told himself, leave that for later. You're already asking him to cope with a lot. Karl volunteering for the army. Then the end of the war, the arrival of the English. The new beginning, how he had been promoted because he had a clean repu- tation. How he began looking for his son, spent days on the station platforms. The killer in the ruins he had spent much of the winter tracking down. Anna. He tried to be discreet, only hinted obliquely at love, and admitted he had no idea whether or not they had a future together. Let Karl work that one out for himself, he said to himself.

He took a new sheet, one that had gone yellow and was torn at one corner, but it was all he had left. The case he was now dealing with: the murdered orphans with no one to grieve for them. The smuggling down at the port. The big dealers who orchestrated it all. The curious business with recording tape. He told him about Erna Berg and MacDonald. The lieutenant's deadline. He admitted to his son, who had gone to fight in the war, that this officer who not long ago would have been an enemy, had become his friend. Stave told him that tonight he had no choice but to investigate down at Blohm & Voss, that he might have the chance to arrest a smuggler who had also murdered three children. He ended with a promise:

I will be back this evening no matter what happens. It will be late. But I will be here. Please wait for me, even if I am not back before dark. You have a key.

I love you,

Your father.

On the outside of the envelope he wrote in large letters: FOR KARL STAVE, PRIVATE AND PERSONAL. When he finally left the apartment, the chief inspector tacked the envelope to the outside of the door, at eye level. Everybody would see it, but what the hell?

As he left the house at Ahrensburger Strasse 93, it seemed as if the dark clouds on the far horizon had risen slightly. He felt more fit and confident than he had in days.

Down at headquarters Erna Berg was perched on the edge of her chair, drenched in sweat. She stared at her typewriter with the apathetic air of a badly bruised boxer who knew he still had to go back into the ring for the twelfth round.

'We'll have a thunderstorm by tomorrow at the latest, that'll make things easier,' he promised.

'Tomorrow James will be on the way out of here, unless something dramatic happens,' she whispered in return. 'To Palestine … do you think they'd let me go with him?'

We're more likely to be voting for a new Reichschancellor than the British are to send a German woman to the Jews and Arabs, Stave thought to himself. But all he said was 'Anything's possible' and smiled. She had no idea what MacDonald and he had planned for that evening. 'I'll do what I can,' he said.

'You?'

'Wait and see.' You never know, he thought, I might just manage to make you happy. Of course, it was also possible that by this time tomorrow not only her lover might be gone, but her boss too, because he had got himself thrown out of the police. Erna Berg could find herself working for somebody like Cäsar Dönnecke. That gave him an idea.

'I'm off to see the boss,' he told her.

'There is a very fine line between stubbornness and stupidity,' Cuddel Breuer was telling him five minutes later, 'and right now you're treading on it.'

'If you won't give me the case, then let me see copies of the files,' the chief inspector pleaded. What he wanted to find out was whether or not in the case of the murdered prostitute and coal thief, there had been any reference to tapes or the port. Anything that might give him a clue where they might be hiding them. That would be one more piece of evidence implicating Kümmel. Or an indicator as to whether or not the smuggler had accomplices.

'No.'

'Then at the very least tell me if my colleague, Herr Dönnecke, has arrested anybody yet?'

'As far as I know, there have been no arrests, no new leads and nobody new interviewed.'

No interest, thought Stave to himself, he just isn't interested.

'So what about you? Have you made any progress in your case?' Breuer's bright eyes studied him carefully. 'The English are getting more and more nervous about the growing unrest down at Blohm & Voss. Governor Berry has invited me over for tea tomorrow afternoon. I suspect we aren't going to talk about the weather.'

'You'll have something else to talk about,' the chief inspector said, getting to his feet. He wasn't going to make any progress here. He would have to ask somebody else for help. Someone he didn't even want to exchange two words with at present. It was time to go and pay a visit to Public Prosecutor Ehrlich.

I just hope I don't bump into Anna on the way, he said to himself as he headed towards the grand offices of the public prosecutor. That would be awkward. She would be convinced he was spying on her. And he would find it unbearable to find her close to Ehrlich again. Stave was lucky. The public prosecutor was alone in his office. His desk was covered with box files, letters, documents with official stamps – probably Wehrmacht orders, the chief inspector guessed. Ehrlich looked like the only person in the whole of Hamburg whose skin hadn't seen the sun. Only his eyes, behind his oversized spectacles, looked red. 'Not so long ago it was less of an administrative task to annihilate an entire race than it is now to bring one man to trial,' Ehrlich sighed.

'It's called progress, these days,' Stave said, 'and it will keep you in work for years.'

'That depends if anyone still cares about these cases in a few years' time.' Ehrlich waved a circling fly away with his hand and added, 'But I doubt you're here to listen to me complain.'

The chief inspector smiled: at the end of the day it was difficult not to like Ehrlich. 'Well yes,' he said, 'in fact, I'm about to break a few laws, and I'd like your help.'

Ehrlich raised his bushy eyebrows and said, 'Actually I'm well up to speed on broken laws.'

In the briefest of terms, Stave told him his suspicions about the smuggling going on down at Blohm & Voss, about the *Leland Stanford*, about Walter Kümmel, the boxing promoter, the British soldiers' friend, the big player on the smuggling scene, and the fact that he was left-handed. And he told him about his plan to go down to the docks that night.

'Alone?'

'With a …' Stave hesitated, 'British friend.'

'Whose superiors know as little about his plans as yours do about yours, I imagine.'

'That's why I'm here to clear it with you.'

'There's not a lot a German prosecutor can do in a case like this. If you're caught, you'll end up in a British court, not a German one. The case will never even come near my desk.'

'Apart from trouble with the British, I'm also likely to face a few problems with my own people,' Stave said.

'There might be something I could do about that,' Ehrlich said with a thin smile.

Stave leaned forward: 'It has to be done tonight,' he said with an urgency in his voice.

'Why the hurry?'

'Because the *Leland Stanford* weighs anchor in the morning. And because otherwise my British friend is going to be very unhappy, and so is a German girl.'

Ehrlich gave an ironic laugh. '*Cherchez la femme.* It's always the same romantic motive with some types of law breakers. With others,' he tapped a hand on the pile of documents in front of him, 'women aren't that important.'

Just how important are women to you? was the question Stave didn't dare ask. He hoped the public prosecutor wasn't thinking of Anna. But the public prosecutor was dealing with another circling fly. 'Very well,' he said. 'You and your English friend, whose name you aren't going to tell me, but I think I can easily imagine, are determined to risk both your careers tonight. And given that our smuggler friends tend to react rather quickly when they're disturbed, you are both risking your necks. There's nothing I can do about the latter, so you should be careful. But if you are caught I shall have a few words with my English friends. I have more of them than you do, and they're in higher positions. Positions of some power. I suspect that if you are caught, the worst that will happen is that you'll be put back in uniform on the streets for the rest of your career. But just about better than losing your job altogether.'

'My lucky day,' said Stave, and got up to go. But Ehrlich gestured for him to remain sitting.

'What do you think might be on these tapes they are so determined to smuggle out of the country?'

'I've no idea,' Stave replied cautiously, and not exactly dishonestly. 'At first I assumed they were empty. Why would anyone want used tapes?'

The public prosecutor followed Stave's eyes and nodded somewhat ironically. 'You obviously don't have a tape recorder, Chief Inspector, and that excuses your assumptions. But tape is just raw material – it's only when there's something recorded on them that they become interesting and potentially valuable. Something,' he paused for dramatic effect, 'like incriminating material from the Third Reich.'

'That had occurred to me,' Stave admitted. 'But what? Interrogations? I never heard anything about the Gestapo going to the effort of recording what they got up to in their cellars.'

'Speeches,' the public prosecutor told him. 'Back then politicians, police, officials, captains of the economy, said things which today they might find, shall we say, embarrassing?'

Stave thought back to Rudolf Blohm and the old weekly newsreels before 1945. 'Old speeches aren't necessarily damaging today.'

'Blackmail. They are being smuggled out of Germany to be used later to blackmail someone.'

'But why would the Americans pay for them? Why would a boxing promoter like Walter Kümmel get involved in something like that? I made inquiries. Kümmel was never in the Party, never caused any trouble. He was politically neutral. Now he's a business big shot. Why would he get involved in blackmail?'

'Questions I hope you'll be able to answer in a few hours' time. I've got my fingers crossed.'

Stave found himself staring at the Barlach lithograph of the two skeletons on the wall behind Ehrlich. Those could be MacDonald and me, he thought to himself. And then he found his thoughts wandering in another direction. 'Has Frau von Veckinhausen found any of your own missing art collection?' he asked, hoping that he sounded casual enough.

Once again Ehrlich gave him an ironic look. 'I'm afraid things don't work quite so easily. The stolen paintings aren't exactly hanging in some museum or other, but I'm hoping that Frau von Veckinhausen with her, shall we say,' he searched for a way of putting it, 'interesting connections to the art market as it is today, might eventually come across one or another piece which I used to be fond of.'

'Are you in regular contact with her?' Stave held his breath.

'No. All I've had from her so far are a couple of notes, testing the water, you might call it. But unfortunately I've seen nothing of her.' He stared out of the window.

The chief inspector had to work hard to suppress a sigh of relief. He just hoped Ehrlich hadn't noticed. 'Frau von Veckinhausen can be a bit taciturn at times,' he added, and this time he really did get up to go.

'Be careful,' the public prosecutor called after him as he grasped the handle of the door. 'I don't want to see a request for an autopsy on my desk tomorrow morning, with your name on it.'

'I'm not going to give Dr Czrisini the chance to cut me open.'

Stave had just got back to his office when the phone rang. MacDonald. 'I've worked out how we can get across the Elbe tonight.'

'We're going to fly?'

'No. We're going to sail.'

Stave slammed the door to the anteroom, sat down at his desk and used his left hand to wipe the sweat from his brow. 'The line's bad. I think I must have misheard you.'

The lieutenant laughed. He hadn't been in such good humour for days. 'Britannia rules the waves, even the little waves on the Elbe. We're taking a sailing boat.'

'I can't imagine anything likely to be more conspicuous than a sailing boat on the Elbe,' Stave said, horrified by the idea.

'There's always a light breeze across the river in the evenings. Nobody will hear us and nobody will see us. No engine noise, no lights.'

'No sailing boat, either. How do you intend to get hold of one?'

'Back in 1945 it wasn't just a few villas and a few theatres we requisitioned, old boy. There are one or two yachts available to His Majesty's officers.'

'What happened to the people they used to belong to?'

'A few wealthy Hamburg folk who by 1945 had disappeared. Their sailboats were officially confiscated. Now lying around in a few harbours on the Elbe. I'm thinking of a rather nice one that's there by one of the piers down on Baumwall, just waiting for an adventure. The *Albatross IV*. Up until 1938 it belonged to a rich banker who turned out to have the wrong religion for the Third Reich. It ended up in the hands of an SS-Obergruppenführer, who strangely seems to have disappeared from the face of the earth since March 1945. Currently it's being used by a colonel who has good connections with our Ministry of Defence. It's likely to be renamed HMS *Albatross IV*. Sleek, fast, thirteen metres. Perfect racer.'

'Sounds a bit beyond me!'

'What? You're not telling me you don't sail?'

'As a child I would chase the swans on the Alster in a dinghy. The swans usually won. That's the last time I sailed. I had a wife and child and a policeman's salary that was nowhere near enough to afford it.'

'Well that's enough to qualify you as ship's mate. All you'll have to do is help raise the sails, and pull a few ropes now and then. I'll do the rest. It's not far. From the Baumwall we only need to cross the river directly and we're at Blohm & Voss. Don't worry.'

'I'm not worrying. I'm just asking myself a few questions. For example, does your colonel know we're borrowing his yacht?'

'Of course not.'

'And aren't there British patrol boats on the Elbe at night?'

'Of course there are. We just have to be careful and start out late.'

'And what if one of them still stops us?'

'We show our ID cards and make up a story of some sort.'

'Such as?'

'I haven't thought of one yet. I'll start thinking about it seriously when their searchlights illuminate us.'

'I'm glad we're so well prepared. So even if we do get across the river without being stopped, what then?'

'Then we tie up the *Albatross IV* at one of the moorings in Kuhwerder basin, make our way unnoticed to the dockyard, get past the British sentries and hide somewhere near the *Leland Stanford*. When the smugglers turn up we take them on and then sail triumphantly back across the Elbe at dawn, the greatest maritime heroes since Sir Francis Drake. I'll get promoted and marry Erna. You'll get promoted too and will be able to marry whoever you want: all women love a hero.'

'Oh well, that all sounds just fine,' Stave said, closing his eyes.

'Have you got a better plan?'

'I don't even have a worse plan. When do we meet? And where?'

'Sellmer's Cellar Bar, near the fisherman's harbour in Altona: 7 p.m. We can eat and check the coast is clear down at the port, stroll leisurely down to the Baumwall, and then get our skates on.'

The chief inspector stared out of the window. The sky to the west was dark; he could see a sheet of paper dancing over Karl Muck Platz in the first real breath of wind there had been in days. 'We should meet up an hour earlier,' he said. 'It's going to get dark earlier than normal. There's a storm on the way.'

There was a brief silence on the other end of the line. 'At least that means we'll have enough wind. I'm a fair weather sailor though,' MacDonald said with a false air of nonchalance. 'Maybe I'll learn a thing or two tonight. See you at 6 then.' He hung up.

Stave told Erna Berg he was going out on an investigation somewhere in the city, left the building and hurried home. His letter to Karl was still on the door. Back in the apartment he changed his clothes, vague memories of his childhood drifting through his head: port, starboard, tacking manoeuvres. To turn the boat to the left, you had to turn the rudder to the right. Or was it the other way around? Not left, port. Stave had never really been out on the actual river in a boat. He hoped MacDonald knew what he was doing. He did, however, remember one thing from his childhood excursions on the Alster: you were likely to get wet. He remembered dinghies leaning to one side, water lapping over his feet, frothing, arms and legs wet: one of his friends had fallen over the side and nearly drowned.

He pulled on some old rough trousers he had last worn when he was doing up the apartment to try to impress Anna. He had neither sailing shoes nor any sort of sports shoes and this was hardly the moment to go looking for some on the black market. He would have to make do with his ordinary street shoes and hope he didn't ruin them, given that they were the only pair he had. And an old, dark blue shirt. A white one would show up at night. A battered old hat. He would take his rain cape too. The chief inspector rolled up the heavy waxed cape and squeezed it into an ancient leather rucksack, along with a pair of handcuffs. Finally he took his FN22 out of its holster, checked the magazine and put it in with the other things. He tried to tell himself that it was exciting, an adventure.

He got down to the Altona fishermen's harbour just before 6 p.m. The street alongside the Elbe was broad, lined with little narrow sheds made of brick, metal or wood. Next to them were warehouses for the fishermen's valuable catch, a few smokers' bars and a couple of restaurants. The very walls stank of rotten fish. Above the city the black clouds were rolling in. Gusts of wind alternated with calm. The chief inspector tried to time them: the gusts of wind were getting more frequent, and lasting longer. It was going to be an interesting crossing, he thought. People were dragging carts along the cobblestones, here and there trucks with coughing and spluttering engines crawled up to the warehouses. Out on the Elbe red buoys bobbed up and down. The ships from the North Sea would come in a bit later and the sailors would unload their cargo of fish over steel rollers directly into the warehouses. The steel rollers blocked the entire riverbanks so a few years back boats had been banned from landing their catches during the day, but even so the first customers were arriving. Restaurant owners, housewives, servants from the villas taken over by the British: workers whose job it would be to sort out the fish to be smoked, waiters with cigarettes in their mouths, British military police in thin green uniform shirts looking up apprehensively at the sky wondering if they would be off duty before the storm arrived. It was only a few minutes walk uphill from here to Röperstrasse, Stave realised. He could be with Anna in five minutes.

A steep narrow staircase led down to Sellmer's Cellar Bar. It was a big room with low ceilings and a view of the river on one side, some three dozen round tables, half of them already occupied. Stale cigarette smoke mingled with the scent of old fish and old cooking fat. Stave spotted MacDonald in the furthest corner of the room, at a table overlooking the river.

'You know there are two British military police outside?' Stave said.

'The food here is so bad that not even the British come in,' the lieutenant answered cautiously. He too was in dark, civilian clothing, with a rucksack on the chair next to him. On the other hand he was wearing light sailing shoes that no German could have afforded. Stave didn't mention them. As long as they sat here at the table, nobody would notice.

'What do you recommend?' the chief inspector asked.

'Well, the sole won't kill you.'

'Do you eat here often?'

'I like the captain,' MacDonald nodded towards the picture on the wall opposite of a weathered, white-bearded seaman in oilskins and a pipe in the corner of his mouth, staring earnestly into the distance.

'I've seen worse paintings,' Stave mumbled. 'Not many, though.'

The lieutenant laughed. 'This is where sailors come to talk about getting away from here, where restaurant owners and housewives come to talk about food. Spend one evening here and I find out more about the mood of the local populace than I would in a hundred interrogations. My superior officers are always amazed by the breadth and depth of my reports.'

'You'll go far.'

'As far as Palestine if things don't work out tonight.' MacDonald waved over an elderly, scrawny waiter who was clearing up at the next table, carefully pocketing a few scraps of tobacco for re-use. 'Two sole and two beers,' he ordered, dismissing the look of surprise on Stave's face. 'Don't worry. You're not officially on duty.'

'That's not what I'm worried about. I haven't drunk alcohol for months, if you exclude the bottle of brandy we polished off the other night. And that had pretty dreadful consequences the next day. I'm out of practice and likely to see everything double, then end up leaning over the side of the boat throwing up into the Elbe.'

'The beer has no more body to it than the sole.'

Half an hour later Stave had to acknowledge that MacDonald hadn't been exaggerating. The sole was at least a day old. The chef had tried to disguise it by leaving it so long in the fat that the scales had turned black, while the beer was served up without a head in greasy half-litre glasses.

'Just like it used to be in Scotland in the good old days before the war,' the lieutenant said, clinking his glass against Stave's.

The chief inspector, who hadn't had a full meal since 1945, didn't bother to make a sarcastic remark. He wolfed down the sole, scraping the last remnant from the bones, washing it all down with the weak brew, which did indeed taste somewhat bitter. But all the time Stave had the vague feeling MacDonald was watching him with astonishment and a degree of sympathy, and only finished his own fish so as not to embarrass his German colleague.

Stave felt guilty in respect of Karl who had said he was coming by for dinner, but by the time he got home – if he got home – he would be hungry and would have no trouble downing a second meal. 'I could get used to this,' he said, knocking back the last drops. 'I'm paying,' MacDonald said, nodding to the waiter. By now all the tables were full. So little light came through the dirty windows that the room was getting darker and darker. It was too early for dusk, though, Stave thought. That meant the storm clouds were approaching fast. He was about to make an observation to that effect when a loud bang resounded outside. Automatically MacDonald went for his gun.

'It's not a German panzer,' Stave reassured him, 'just thunder.'

'Do you hear the rain?' the lieutenant asked, as the skies opened above them.

A continuous stream of people poured down the steps towards the entrance, damp patches on their shoulders, wet hair, bright eyes. Even Stave felt relieved: no more brown, brackish water from the taps.

MacDonald prodded him: 'Time for us to go.'

'You really think this is the right moment to set off across the Elbe? Why not wait a bit? It's almost certainly just a heavy shower.'

'The point is that right now there's nobody out there. Come on!' Casually he threw a bundle of Reichsmarks on to the table, pulled out a waterproof and put it on. Stave didn't have exactly the same kit, but pulled on what waterproofs he had. Moments later they were outside on their own, the only figures to be seen far and wide on the banks of the Elbe. The cobbles were slippery, water running in dark rivulets between the ruins. The dimmed yellow lights of an approaching truck. No pedestrians. Stave pulled the brim of his hat down over his eyes and turned up his coat collar. They hurried past the bulky buildings of the landing stages. The entrance to the Elbe Tunnel ahead of them looked like a cube of light-coloured stone crowned with a dome from which a flood from the heavens ran like a waterfall. They could have crossed the river without getting their feet wet if they used the tunnel but the underpass, built way back in the Kaiser's day, was blocked with iron-railed gates. For a brief second, Stave flirted with the idea of trying to break through them. Then dismissed himself as an idiot. What tool did they have? And in any case two men trying to break through the gates were likely to draw attention.

Further along the Elbe, gusts of wind blew clouds dark and heavy with rain along the river. The chief inspector's feet were damp, his trouser bottoms wet and clinging to his shins.

'This is how I imagine summer in Scotland,' he japed at MacDonald.

'Oh no, we get a lot more rain than this,' the lieutenant replied, his mood getting better by the second.

They were at Baumwall, the wooden planking along the quayside wet and slippery. The chief inspector took a look around, but there was nobody in sight. The spire of St Michael's church jutted above the ruins of a chandler's shop, grey and forbidding and surrounded by dark clouds, like something from an old horror film.

'Hurry up,' MacDonald shouted over the noise of the torrential rain.

'It's a canoe!' Stave exclaimed.

On the river in front of them, between two mooring posts, lay a little wooden boat, long and narrow, like the fin of a whale, with a white-painted stern, a dark teak deck to the fore and aft of a tiny cabin, more of a cockpit really. To the chief inspector it looked no bigger than the seating space of a kayak. To the fore was a wooden mast with a boom almost the same length, along which the wind blew the reefed sail into the shape of a sausage. The *Albatross IV* might be thirteen metres long but the lieutenant had neglected to mention that it was little wider than a man. It looked more like a wooden torpedo.

'We'll never get over the Elbe in that thing. Not in this weather.'

'Swedish quality workmanship. It's a lot more stable than it looks,' MacDonald assured him. 'Just be careful getting on board. The teak is slippery.'

Stave stumbled into the little cockpit, banging his right knee against the long arm of the rudder. He sat there massaging it as the lieutenant cast off the lines to fore and aft and elegantly leapt aboard the *Albatross IV* as the little vessel drifted away from the quay. 'We can make do with the mainsail,' he said, nodding at the sail unfurled from the mast.

The chief inspector pulled at the rough rope until the yellow sail unfurled and landed on him. There's no way people aren't going to notice this, he thought to himself, and the sound it made flapping in the wind would be heard as far away as the tower of St Michael's. Yet nobody hailed them as they drifted out, the wind billowing the sail so far to the left that at one stage Stave thought they would tip over. But the little craft stabilised and shot out on to the river, into the choppy grey waves, white-tipped from the wind. The sky above them was a dark void with occasional streaks of lightning. Cold and damp soaked into the skin. While MacDonald worked at the helm for all the world like a fourteen-year-old boy in seventh heaven, Stave stared at the river, at the veils of rain drifting over it, but there was nothing to be seen, no dark shadows, no puff of smoke from a steamship, no bow waves from a fast-moving vessel.

'The coast is clear,' he called over the noise of the wind.

'We only need ten minutes,' MacDonald called back.

The chief inspector wished he still had the watch Margarethe had bought him for their fifth wedding anniversary, but when the black market started up he had sold it for a couple of pounds of coffee, which he had in turn traded down at the station for any news of his missing son from soldiers returning from the front or the gulags. He counted off the time in seconds, looking up and down the river and across it at the bulk of the dry dock, which grew ever larger, waves crashing against its concrete walls. The chief inspector tried to make out any sign of movement. But there was none. Another five minutes, he reckoned. The *Leland Stanford* lay on the sheltered other side of the dock, away from the Elbe. Would someone be there standing guard? If so, they would spot the *Albatross IV* at the very latest when they turned into the Kuhwerder harbour. Would an American seaman think they were some pleasure sailors turning into the harbour because they had been caught unawares by the storm? Or would he be suspicious?

The little yacht cut through the waves like a knife. Stave could feel himself physically relax: he was beginning to have faith in the elegant little craft, and to at last understand the basis for MacDonald's childlike enjoyment. Maybe I should try this some time, he told himself. He had no hobbies. Maybe he could take a dinghy out on the Alster? Maybe with Anna, and Karl? But when he thought about it, it all seemed so improbable that he forced himself to abandon the daydream.

They shot past the giant dry dock. The wind dropped, the grey water was calmer, their little vessel righted itself. The rain was still coming down in showers. The *Leland Stanford* lay next to them along the quayside. 'Ignore it,' MacDonald said quietly. 'There could be somebody on the bridge with a telescope.'

The chief inspector stared straight ahead. No matter how inconspicuous we try to make ourselves, he thought, they will still notice us and the appearance and colour of our waterproofs. And if they then spot us again on the docks a few minutes later, they will start asking questions.

'We'll tie her up at the ferry pier, jump off and head along the riverbank towards Harburg rather than Blohm & Voss,' he said. 'We want whoever is on board the freighter to think we are heading into the town to shelter from the rain. As soon as we get past the first shed we can make a wide turn and head back towards the dock.'

'Aye, aye, sir,' MacDonald called back.

Stave fumbled with wet fingers at the rope to lower the sail. The *Albatross IV* began to slow down like a tired swimmer as it drifted in towards the wooden dock. The Scotsman leapt ashore, pulled the stern of the vessel closer in to the dock and tied it up to a post. Stave struggled with his rope until eventually the lieutenant took it from his hands and said, 'Is that how you do your shoelaces?' But Stave had already turned away and was fetching their rucksacks from the little cockpit. He was afraid his gun might have got wet and would no longer work. 'Let's get into cover,' he said.

Right at that moment a shaft of lightning hit one of the cranes on the dock. For a moment Stave was blinded by the bright light, then deafened by the peel of thunder that followed it. A metallic stench of electricity filled the air.

'I think it might not be a good idea to hide in one of the cranes until the smugglers get here,' MacDonald commented.

They hurried along the pier until they found themselves behind a three-metre-high wall of a bombed-out construction shed. They ducked down and made a broad curve around the harbour wasteland. Stave was limping and, unlike MacDonald, the trained soldier who instinctively located and hid behind every possible cover, from heaps of rubble to bushes, had to keep stopping to look for his next hiding place. And even then it was hard work because his damn ankle kept hurting. About a hundred metres from Blohm & Voss they crossed the access road and hid behind the wreck of a boiler engine on the railway lines parallel to the road.

'Can you see anyone keeping watch?' the chief inspector spluttered.

'There always is. Probably inside the guard house. Having a smoke.' MacDonald nodded towards the red glow that appeared from time to time in the rain-soaked little shed. 'If he'd done that in the war, he'd have been dead long ago.'

Stave nodded towards a pile of old ship parts stacked like a wall a little bit to their right. 'That junk is almost as high as the fence. We could climb over it out of sight of the guard.'

'Just watch you don't cut yourself on the rusty iron.'

They tossed their rucksacks over the barrier, then the chief inspector grabbed hold of a chunk of metal and pulled hard on it. 'It seems stable enough,' he whispered, despite himself. He pulled himself higher, nearly slipping. His hands were covered in yellowish machine grease. He wiped them on his trousers. And then he was on top. He paused to catch his breath, lying flat on the wall of junk machinery. He could hear the British soldier cursing under his breath somewhere nearby. He hoped the guard wouldn't look in their direction. He put one foot lower until he could find a foothold in the wall of old iron strong enough to support his weight. Then he tried again to find one lower, but suddenly found himself stuck. He heard a sound like somebody tearing a sheet of paper, and realised it was his own waterproofs. He felt water on his shoulder. It will cost me a fortune on the black market to replace this, he thought. Then at last he was on *terra firma*, grass-covered cobbles.

'Look, over there!' MacDonald called to him breathlessly. They ran up to the fence where the lieutenant grabbed one corner and pulled it easily aside.

'We aren't the first to get in this way,' Stave noted.

'It's now illegal.'

They faced a narrow corridor between two almost undamaged sheds. Rain was pouring in mini-waterfalls from broken guttering and they had to keep jumping from left to right to avoid the worst downpours. The damp air still reeked with the sulphurous stench of cordite, the basis of the explosive the British had used to blow up the cranes. The chief inspector peered through a gap between two warehouses at the dark shape of the administration building. There were no lights to be seen. Just a hundred metres to go. They ducked behind a bush, both of them choking with sweat and rainwater. Ahead of them lay a giant grey shadow: the superstructure of the *Leland Stanford*. Light shone from one or two portholes and the bridge. There was no movement on deck. The flag at the stern fluttered in the gusting wind. The whole thing reminded Stave of a castle at twilight in some grim fairy tale; big, dark, threatening and inaccessible.

He glanced around. 'The passage between these two warehouses is the best way to get close to the docks,' he spluttered. 'Good cover. If I was a smuggler I would use this to get close and then make a run for it over the remaining few metres to the freighter.' He put his weight against a wooden door, only to find it closed with an ancient padlock. He cursed.

MacDonald smiled and brought a large screwdriver out of his rucksack. 'It did occur to me we might have to deal with a lock or two.' he said. 'Actually I was rather afraid the yacht might have been chained up. It wasn't but it was still a good idea that I brought this monster along.' He set to work and within thirty seconds the lock was lying in pieces on the rotten wooden floor. The wind immediately blew the door open with a bang against the wall. Stave found a lump of concrete rubble to prop it open. They slipped into the warehouse and then closed the door behind them again, using the concrete to keep it closed. They glanced around: machinery parts, the stink of grease.

'At least it's dry,' MacDonald noted. He glanced out through the crack in the door and said, 'So what do we do if and when our friend turns up?'

'We let him go past, then follow him and grab him before he gets to the end of the passage where he could be seen from the freighter. An ambush from the rear.'

'Sounds like you've done this before. But what if the smuggler doesn't come this way? What if he's so self-confident he just walks up to the *Leland Stanford* without trying to conceal himself?'

Stave nodded towards a boarded-up window on the far side of the shed. 'Can you see out of that?'

'Great lookout post,' said MacDonald who had hurried over to look. 'I have a clear view and nobody can see me.'

'Could you shoot from there if you had to?'

The British officer gave him a long, hard look. 'Of course. But shoot whom?'

'If our friend just walks along the quayside we'll never catch him if we run after him from here. We'll have to shoot him to stop him reaching the American freighter.'

'You really want to take him out?'

'I'm thinking about three dead children,' Stave replied grimly.

'And I'm thinking of Palestine and a pregnant woman,' MacDonald replied, pulling his heavy military revolver out of his rucksack. Stave reached for his FN22.

Stave watched from the crack in the door. Neither of them said a word. Every now and then he would glance over at MacDonald who would shake his head in return. Stave pulled his handcuffs out of his rucksack and put them in his trouser pocket. Outside the rain had turned the world monochrome: the buildings were grey and so were the bushes, the sky. The light itself was grey. Dusk had come and gone without a hint of a sunset, as if some mysterious hand had simply turned out one weak light after another. The rain drummed on the slate roof. Stave wondered if they would be able to make out anything at all in this weather in the middle of the night. He was shivering. He wondered if he would be able to shoot straight. That was if his gun would even work. Every clap of thunder made him jump. Every flash of lightning blinded him for several seconds – seconds in which he feared the figure they lay in wait for would flash by unnoticed.

After one uncomfortably close lightning bolt he forced himself to open his weary eyes wide; he held his breath and waved at MacDonald, who dashed over to him.

'There's somebody coming down the gangplank,' he whispered.

'Alone?'

'Yes'.

'Unlucky for him.'

It was a man, his face concealed by the dark. Walking briskly, above average height. Was he a hunchback? Then the CID man realised he was looking at a man with a waterproof cape and a hood, the hump on his back was almost certainly a rucksack. A big one.

He nodded to MacDonald. All he could see in the darkness of the shed was the British officer's two eyes. Three steps. Two steps. One.

The chief inspector threw open the door, leapt out into the passageway, raised his weapon and shouted, 'Police! Stop.'

Then the world exploded.

A bolt of lightning hit the radio mast of the *Leland Stanford*. Simultaneously a clap of thunder deafened them. Stave stood there frozen by the blinding light, MacDonald to his right in the doorway of the warehouse, in front of him the man in the waterproof cape. His heart began to beat again. He started to say something, but a fist hit his chin.

The lightning exploded again, only this time it was inside his head. Pain. Then more pain as he fell back and his head hit the cobbles. The walls of the warehouse spun around him. This guy's fast, Stave thought to himself as he tried to pull himself back to his feet. But his knees had turned to rubber. He still had his gun in his right hand, but it was shaking. He heard words, in English, then a shot.

'He's getting away!' It was MacDonald's voice.

Stave pulled himself up by leaning against the warehouse's rough brick wall, shook the cobwebs out of his head, dismissed the taste of blood in his mouth. After him! But which way? The quayside in front of the freighter was empty. All the lights on board the American freighter had gone out following the lightning strike. Stave could hear voices coming from the ship. He turned away, looked in the other direction. Two shapes, already far away. The villain was running back the way he had come, MacDonald running after him.

He hit me with his left fist, Stave realised. A left-hander.

He began running too.

Stave spat blood from his mouth as he chased them. He knew that with his crippled ankle he could hardly run very fast, but the training he had undergone to try to reduce as much as possible the impact of his injury had given him stamina. The British officer was sixty, maybe seventy metres ahead of him, Stave reckoned, and there was at least the same again to the man they were pursuing.

At one point he slipped on the wet cobbles, but stayed upright and ran on. The alleyway seemed endless, then they came out into the open. Heaps of rubble. A railway freight carriage lay on its side by the tracks. Bushes. The CID man stopped, looked around. Another flash of lightning. Two men picked out in the blinding light. He raised his gun, hesitated. Don't do anything stupid, he told himself. MacDonald was somewhere in between him and his unknown target. Keep going. The man in the cape was running over the rubble, MacDonald after him. Stave, further behind them, chose his route along paths with less hindrance. Second by second he was reducing their lead.

Then came the fence. With one fluid movement their unknown criminal bent down and passed through it as if the metal wire was only an illusion. It took MacDonald a few seconds to get through, losing him time. Stave bent down as he approached and found he could simply push his way through as if sweeping aside a heavy curtain.

The man was now running parallel to the Elbe on their left. They passed the ruins of some workers' houses, the only ones that had ever been built in this part of the harbour. Ahead of them lay that familiar cube of stone, the entrance to the Elbe Tunnel, a heap of history from the day of the Kaiser, all but undamaged.

Now I've got you, Stave told himself, doing his utmost to run faster. His heart was pounding, he was gasping for breath. But the tunnel was a trap: there was no way their unknown quarry could get through the iron grid that closed it off. He would run up to it, shake it, realise that it was locked and by then it would be too late. Just a hundred metres until he reached it. Fifty. Then he was there.

But he wasn't rattling the gate. He was reaching for something.

'The bastard has a key,' Stave shouted. How on earth could he have managed that? There was no better way of getting past the British guards on the dockyard. The smuggler could let himself into the Elbe Tunnel at night and simply stroll over to the docks while the patrol boats sailed back and forth above his head. 'Shoot!' he cried, with the last of his breath, 'Shoot, for God's sake!'

But MacDonald couldn't hear him. He ran faster and faster, gesticulating wildly. The gate was open now. The man ran into the tunnel. If he locks it from the other side, we've lost him, Stave realised. Coughing and spluttering, he came to a halt, raised his gun, his left arm supporting his right to steady his aim. And fired. The FN22 roared in his ears. MacDonald, the professional solider, threw himself to the ground. Stave fired again, and again. Their quarry ran off. But he had left the gate open.

The chief inspector caught up with the lieutenant who was pulling himself to his feet.

'I didn't hit you?' Stave coughed.

'You're a lousy shot,' the lieutenant, unharmed, replied.

In front of them was the great stone slab and the iron gate of the Elbe Tunnel.

Stale air. Yellow emergency lighting. The thing was a vast shaft of brown-tiled walls and pigeon droppings, the disturbed birds cooing and flapping in every direction. In the middle, among a forest of steel beams, was a lift big enough to take cars. The cabin itself was down in the depths. Stave listened out. On one side a staircase wound down the wall of the shaft in a giant double 'Z', a narrow steel structure with wooden steps. He could feel the reverberation of heavy footsteps: their quarry was running down it.

The chief inspector charged down after him, painfully aware that one false step and he would break his neck. Suddenly he stopped, thinking – where was MacDonald? The British officer had been left way behind. He looked back and could just make out a figure huddled against the tiles.

'What's the matter?' Stave asked, worried that he had, after all, hit his friend with one of his hasty shots.

'I get vertigo,' the lieutenant just about managed to say.

Stave would have burst out laughing had the situation not been so desperate. 'Close your eyes, and keep going down,' he said, turning back and resuming his descent.

Concrete. The bottom of the shaft. In front of him a passage barely wider than a single car. It was like a Christmas *Stollen* buried under thousands of tonnes of earth and above it the Elbe. Tiny white tiles on the curved walls, every so often with pale green depictions of fish, crabs and seashells. The glimmer of the emergency lighting seemed to bring the underwater world to life.

Far in the distance Stave could just make out a shape, and the sound of steps, running.

Even so he took the few seconds it required to take off his rain-coat. He could breathe more easily without it clinging to him. The man he was chasing was still wearing his rain cape, and at the other end he would have to climb up with it on. Stave set off in pursuit.

White tiles, green fish, white tiles. He took deep breaths, rhythmi-cally, kept his eyes in front. The gap was not getting any bigger but it was still too far for a handgun. He passed the mark on the wall that indicated the maximum depth of the tunnel. Onwards he ran, ever onwards. He could hear steps behind him too now. MacDonald, at last!

Their quarry disappeared into darkness at the far end of the tunnel where next to the wooden door of the lift the steps that led upwards began. The metal staircase resounded with the weight of the man's steps. Seconds later Stave reached the first step where he had to stop for breath, coughing and spluttering.

He stared upwards, into a giant cylinder that ended in the copy of the Roman Pantheon that stood near the landing stages. The thing had windows the size of those in a cathedral, so large that even now a tiny glimmer of grey light filtered through. The curved walls were decorated with brown relief portraits of the most important engineers who had worked on the vast project. Shaded images of severe-looking men in frock coats and high collars, looking down almost scornfully on all those who passed beneath them, their current visitors in particular. The steps climbed upwards in the familiar 'Z'. More than a hundred of them, many more.

The chief inspector took two steps at a time, his lungs burning, a veil falling over his eyes. It was not just his injured ankle that was hurting, but his calves and thighs. He was thirsty. His pulse was pounding so hard in his ears he could no longer hear. But he could still feel the reverberations from the steps above him.

Two steps, two more steps. Take a breath. The higher he got, the better he could see. The distance between them was less now. Should he try to shoot up the staircase, between the steps? Too dangerous. Ricochet. Keep going.

A curse from up above. Only a few steps to go. The entrance with the locked door was set back into the walls of the vast structure, leaving a short distance to cover between the top of the steps and the portal that led out into the open. The man ahead of him was pulling at the door, obviously exhausted, his hands shaking wildly. Then the door swung open.

Stave raised his FN22 and fired.

The boom of the shot sounded as if a great drum had been hit on both sides with the flat of a giant hand. A scream. The figure ahead of him dropped a bunch of keys, grabbed his right knee and fell to the ground.

The chief inspector was upon him, pulled out his handcuffs and clicked the metal closed on the man's wrists. There was blood on the ground, blood on the man's thigh just above the knee. Stave pulled back the hood on the man's rain cape.

'No more thoughts of America for you,' he coughed out.

Walter Kümmel. The boxing promoter lay at Stave's feet, his face ashen and soaked with sweat. 'What do you think this is, the Wild West?' he said with a brave but failed attempt at a smile despite his obvious pain. 'Giving me a taste before I set off?'

'You're not going anywhere, except to hell.' The chief inspector ripped a strip of Kümmel's trousers to make a temporary bandage for his wound. 'I'm arresting you on a charge of smuggling, and also for the murder of Adolf Winkelmann, Hildegard Hüllmann and Wilhelm Meinke.'

Kümmel shook his head. 'I'm not going to let you get away with that. You have no proof.'

At that moment MacDonald stumbled up the final few steps, his face pale but his revolver in his hand. 'Pity about those upcoming boxing bouts.' The lieutenant glanced down at the wounded leg. 'The bullet's still in there. He won't die. But he's never going to forget it either.'

Stave's heart was pounding. He felt dizzy. Concentrate, he told himself. Kümmel is every bit as exhausted as you are, and he's in pain, bleeding and in shock from the arrested. If you're going to pull one over on him, now's the time. Bluff him. 'Capital crime means an English court,' he coughed out. 'Murder attracts the death penalty. Your only chance of saving your neck is to confess.'

It was a lie, and against all the regulations. All the evidence Stave had put together wouldn't even amount to enough to bring charges, let alone get a 'guilty' verdict. For the merest moment, the lieutenant shot him a questioning look, then he got the message. 'Ten years,' he said, still breathing hard. 'Then, according to English law, you can appeal for parole. You've made a lot of influential friends with your boxing bouts. Maybe someone will put in a good word for you? But if you're destined for the scaffold, there'll be nobody standing up for you.'

Kümmel closed his eyes. Stave was afraid he was about to lose consciousness. But then he opened his eyelids and gave a resigned nod. 'Sounds like a deal I can't refuse,' he said.

'You did murder Adolf Winkelmann?' the chief inspector continued.

'Yes. Let's just call it a bit of necessary business. The boy left me no alternative.'

Stave took a deep breath, but tried not to show his relief. 'He was damaging your smuggling business?'

'The boy was an incorrigible thief. He stole tickets to my boxing matches and palmed them off on the black market. He stole cigarettes around the house. And some time during the spring he began to sell recording tapes off his own bat. He was crazy about jazz. He wanted to record the concerts out at Moorweide and the music played in the British officers' clubs.

'I caught him in the shed at Blohm & Voss. He was sitting on an unexploded bomb rummaging around in a sack full of tapes I had hidden there. Tough as nails, these war kids.'

'Not quite tough enough.'

Kümmel laughed then immediately followed it with a groan of pain. 'What was I to do? There was Adolf sitting on the bomb grinning when I came in and offering to go fifty-fifty with me. He wanted half of the tapes in exchange for not betraying me to the British. "Fine," I told him, as if I was impressed by his cool nerve. I walked over to him, and the pathologist can tell you the rest.'

'You stabbed the boy in cold blood.'

'A blackmailer crazy enough to sit there on top of an unexploded five-hundred-pound bomb doesn't exactly leave you many options. Either you give in or,' he hesitated, 'you do what you have to. I took the tapes and left. I was afraid the bomb could go off at any moment. I should have risked it and tossed the boy into the Elbe.'

'But why take the risk at all? Why kill him? They're just tapes,' Stave asked, taking the rucksack from Kümmel's shoulders and glancing into it: tapes in cardboard boxes with the Nazi eagle and swastika and the letters 'RRG'. 'What's on them?'

'Music.'

'This isn't exactly the best time to be making jokes.'

'Classical music. The Berlin Philharmonic. Furtwängler. Playing Beethoven, Wagner, Mozart. All the greats.'

'I thought the only "greats" you recognised were boxers?'

'You just don't understand,' Kümmel closed his eyes, exhaustion overwhelming him. He pulled himself out of it with a look of extreme pain. 'Have you got a cigarette?'

'You do smoke, after all?'

'Only on special occasions.'

The chief inspector searched his pockets and produced a soggy packet of Senior Service with a sailing ship on the front. Apt for the occasion. 'I doubt I'm going to be able to light one for you.'

'Just put the thing between my lips. It'll help me breathe.'

'We'll play your tapes from beginning to end back at CID headquarters.'

'That will be good for your education. The Berlin Philharmonic are rather better than the fiddlers hawking around the ruins here in Hamburg. "RRG" stands for *Reichs-Rundfunk-Gesellschaft*. Recordings made before 1945. By the best of the best, nothing less for Herr Goebbels.'

'How did you get hold of them?'

'Pure chance. One of my fiancée's drivers drove a truck full of tapes out of Berlin at the end of 1946, just before the great famine winter. Greta was furious because he insisted on using them as payment and what use were old tapes here then? She had hundreds of the things piled up in her living room when I came across them.'

'And you realised there was business to be done?'

'That's what makes the difference between winners and losers.'

'Why would the Americans buy them? They all listen to jazz.'

'They listen to classical music too. And they are mad keen on Europe's geniuses. They're buying up old masters' paintings, taking our best professors from our universities, getting German architects to design their skyscrapers. And you can't beat the combination of Furtwängler and Beethoven.'

'So the boxing promoter became a music promoter?'

'Not at all. I would really have to have been crazy to sacrifice my career for the sake of a few smuggled tape recordings. I was using them as promotional material.' Kümmel closed his eyes again and shook his head. Stave felt like a slow-learning child sitting in front of an impatient teacher. His right hand was twitching with rage. He put the safety on his weapon; the last thing he needed to do was execute the man.

'I want to get my fighters to America. Big business needs big promotion. Reporters, camera teams, the weekly news. The best way to get people interested in America is the radio: live reporters at the ringside, hysterically commenting on every blow landed. Millions of listeners. There are hundreds of radio stations in America. In Texas, Colorado, Iowa, places you've never even heard of. Totally different from Herr Goebbels's *Reichsfunk* or even the few stations the British let us have here. Private little radio stations run like local newspapers. Run by businessmen, for profit. And they need more than boxing matches for their broadcasts. They need to fill up the airtime, with the best stuff they can get hold of, at the lowest price.'

'German music,' Stave's hand had stopped twitching.

'Classical music is harmless. Of course lots of stations aren't interested in Beethoven. They play only jazz. But a minority are, and over there a few is still a lot. There are dozens of stations that play classical music.'

'I hide the tapes around the harbour. Then I get them on board ships bound for New York. A partner of mine over there copies them on to long-playing records and sells them on cheap to the radio stations.'

'Good business for you and your partner.'

'Just for my partner. Not for me. At least not straight away. I sell the tapes for next to nothing, a few dollars each, pocket money. A joke compared to the effort involved. But,' and despite the pain he was in Kümmel finally managed a smile, 'in return radio stations all over America, from the east coast to the west, from Alaska to the Mexican border, owe me a favour. They know me over there, and they remember my name.'

'And if and when you and your boxers ever cross the Big Pond, then they'll broadcast your boxing matches. In exchange for Furtwängler, they broadcast Max Schmeling live. But what I don't understand is all this secrecy. Surely you could just have got a licence? Tapes aren't exactly illegal material that you have to smuggle out. Nobody would have been interested.'

Kümmel gave him a long hard stare with those luminous eyes of his. 'Because the American side of the business is a grey area,' he explained. 'Is it legal to make copies from German tapes and broadcast them? No American wants to get involved in a court case. That's why they prefer to keep a low profile.

'The *Leland Stanford* brings over a small load every time. Not all at once. That could cause trouble with customs in New York. And in any case sending them all at once would defeat the purpose. By the time I got to New York, people would have forgotten my name. The deliveries were meant to keep going on a regular basis until I got there – then Adolf came along. The boy would have messed up the system. This was my ticket to America and the boy just didn't understand. If he hadn't been sitting on an unexploded bomb smiling so glibly at me, I might have been able to explain it to him.'

'What about the girl?' Stave asked, a harshness back in his voice. 'Why did Hildegard Hüllmann have to die?'

'Was that her name? The little whore turned up a few days afterwards, knocked on the door of our apartment, said she just happened to be passing by. Cheeky brat.'

The chief inspector cast his mind back to the girls' home, but said nothing.

'She claimed to have been Adolf's girlfriend, bombarded me with accusations.'

'How did your fiancée react?'

'I'm glad to say Greta was out with one of her deliveries. I'd never seen the girl before, never heard of her. She used language a sailor could have learned a few lessons from. Accused Greta and me of having Adolf's death on our consciences. I was taken aback and tried to find out exactly what she knew. I never did, but just the fact that she had turned up on our doorstep was shock enough.'

'So you murdered her?'

'No. I faced her down, told her other people had had it in for Adolf. No names, no details, but I told her I could prove it to her. She wasn't interested, said she was going to the police. An unusual approach in her line of business. I promised I'd get proof and meet up with her again.'

'On the Hansaplatz?'

'That was her suggestion. And that we meet at night. She made it all a bit easy for me.'

Stave tried to keep his anger down. 'And what about Wilhelm Meinke?' he asked as calmly as possible. 'Why did the little coal stealer have to die?'

Kümmel leaned back. Stave realised he was relaxing, no longer on his guard.

'Never heard of any Meinke. No idea who that is. You can't accuse me of anything there, because I haven't had a hand in that.'

'Hand,' Stave thought to himself. Meinke's murderer had been right-handed. Perhaps the unbearable Dönnecke had been right on that. One of the wolf children might have done for Meinke. He felt all of a sudden as if someone had turned off the electricity that had kept him running for the past few hours. He glanced over at MacDonald.

'I'll fetch the military police.'

'If you go back through the tunnel and report to the guard there, it'll cause a fuss.'

'I'd rather swim across the Elbe than deal with those stairs again. I'll hail a patrol car.'

The lieutenant stumbled out of the door. The storm was over, the rain merely a shower now. The chief inspector had no idea what the time was. There was nobody about on the landing stages. It must be after curfew time, he reckoned. Every German would be at home and just British Jeeps trundling around the empty streets. As a pedestrian in civilian clothing, MacDonald would be noticed straight away. He would be back before long.

A few minutes later he heard the growl of an engine and MacDonald arrived with two military policemen. 'Everything in order?' he asked.

'Get this thug out of my sight,' Stave said. Then he realised he was still gripping his gun. The two military policemen were watching him nervously. He forced a smile and put his weapon away.

The two men in uniform lifted the handcuffed Kümmel under the arms and dragged him, ignoring his groans, to the first of two Jeeps, piled him on to the rear seat and secured him to the vehicle with another set of handcuffs.

'He'll be a hard nut to crack in court,' Stave whispered, closing his eyes and thinking of the huge pile of papers on Ehrlich's desk and the slim file on his own.

MacDonald was in a better mood. 'We have a confession in front of two witnesses, and who could be better witnesses than a German police inspector and an officer of His Majesty. We have a suspect for the Blohm & Voss murder; we've arrested the killer of a young girl; we've put an end to a smuggling racket that had gone unnoticed for months. And we've been so discreet that not one American citizen has got wind of the entire business. Obviously we will simply let the *Leland Stanford* weigh anchor in a few hours' time. No bad blood in Washington. Everybody in London happy. At least one less problem at the dockyard. The governor will be a happy man.'

'And Palestine will seem further away than ever.'

'I would like you to be a witness at our wedding when all this messy business is over. Do you fancy sailing the *Albatross IV* back across the Elbe with me? A patrol car will take us over. The rain's stopped. It'll be a pleasure cruise.'

'Britannia rules the waves,' Stave said with a friendly but dismissive wave, 'but the German CID rule the pavement. I'd prefer to walk home.'

Stave waved goodbye to the British officer and promised to turn up next morning at Governor Berry's residence with a full official report. Then he set off. It would take him one and a half hours, he reckoned, maybe two. He would be exhausted. But at least after the rain the air was clean and cool. The cobbles steamed and shone below the ruins that reared above them like ghostly castles. His footsteps sounded loud amid the rubble.

Just a few streets away Anna would be asleep in her basement apartment. Every step took him further away from her. I would love to put my arms around her right now, he thought, lie down next to her, inhale the scent of her skin, her long hair, fall into a deep and dreamless sleep. He had so much to tell her.

He thought of Adolf Winkelmann, the smuggler, the dealer who had lost his life, all for the sake of a few music tapes. Hildegard Hüllmann, the wolf child who had to die because she wanted to know who had killed the boy who had given her the only flicker of hope in a life of violence and degradation. Wilhelm Meinke, the coal thief, maybe murdered by another wolf child in a crime that Stave had failed to solve, while the officer in charge had almost certainly already forgotten the case. Lost children, lost families. We, their elders, did this to them. We turned them into orphans, destroyed the world around them, and now we push them around, throw shit at them. We might at least punish those who murder them.

And then at last his thoughts turned to Karl. Would he have read the letter he had left pinned to his door? Would he be waiting for him when he got home? He hoped so.

Afterword

The children named in this book are fictitious but their stories are real. By May 1947 the two main churches in Hamburg occupied with refugees had counted some 40,000 orphans. Children who either through the bombing or other violence caused by war had lost both parents. Volunteers were unable to find a single living relative for some 21,000 girls and boys. Over a thousand of these children were living not in homes but roamed the devastated city streets alone or in small groups. They built themselves shelters or slept in the Nissen huts or flak bunkers. They survived by dealing on the black market or stealing coal. Or prostituting themselves.

'Wolf children' was the name given in East Prussia and other eastern areas of the former Reich to those that had lost or become separated from their parents as they fled west. The youngest were barely six years old but they wandered for months, even years, through forests and the ruins of devastated villages until a few at least reached the western occupation zones.

A few of these 'wolf children' wrote of their experiences later, notably Ruth Kibelka in her book *Wolfskinder. On the Borders of the Memel River*. Yet popular memory in Germany today has all but forgotten them, and their fate.

A few peripheral characters in the book are real, notably Hamburg Mayor Max Brauer and British Governor Vaughan H. Berry. The singer Margot Hielscher appeared with an American jazz band at Moorweide. Tattoo-Willy really did have his studio on Grosse Frei-heit, although the description of the property is based on what is standing there today. The trial that led to the shooting of British prisoners-of-war took place with those named in the account here, although obviously not with the involvement of the fictitious Public Prosecutor Ehrlich. Journalists at *Die Zeit* will recognise that Ludwig Kleensch represents a former colleague with a different name and whose career took a different path. There was also a widowed transport business operator, as well as a post-war boxing promoter who had the boxers Max Schmeling and Hein ten Hoff as well as many others under contract and had his offices in the Chilehaus. The historical characters on which the promoter and transport businesswoman are based had different names and most certainly had nothing to do with smuggling or murder. That is pure fiction.

I have also taken several other dramatic liberties such as changing by several months the date of the performance of Wolfgang Borchert's *Draussen vor der Tür.* Theatregoers will, I hope, forgive me.

A few of the places mentioned have remained largely unchanged, even if they are used quite differently today: including both well-known ones such as the Chilehaus or the Elbe Tunnel, and less well-known such as the police headquarters or the girls' home. Some other venues have gone forever, such as the institute in which my fictive pathologist Dr Alfred Czrisini dissected his corpses. In its place today stands the Sophie Barat Roman Catholic School.

The American freighter *Leland Stanford* did visit Hamburg, but there is nothing to suggest it was used for smuggling.

Recordings made by the former *Reichs-Rundfunk-Gesellschaft* were indeed smuggled out of Germany, and the classical music recordings made before 1945 were issued as records in the USA and distributed to radio stations. This early example of music piracy did not, however, come to the attention of the authorities in 1947 but only six years later.